The Other MR.DARCY

Monica Fairview

SOURCEBOOKS LANDMARK™
AN IMPRINT OF SOURCEBOOKS, INC.®
NAPERVILLE, ILLINOIS

Published by Sourcebooks Landmark, an imprint of Sourcebooks, Inc.
P.O. Box 4410, Naperville, Illinois 60567–4410
(630) 961–3900
FAX: (630) 961–2168
www.sourcebooks.com

Library of Congress Cataloging-in-Publication Data

Fairview, Monica.
  The other Mr. Darcy / Monica Fairview.
    p. cm.
  Originally published: London : Robert Hale, 2009.
  1. Courtship--Fiction. I. Title.
  PR6106.A38O84 2009
  823'.92--dc22
                            2009021800

Printed and bound in the United States of America
VP 10 9 8 7 6 5 4 3 2 1

In loving memory of my mother
Sophie
You would have laughed

CAROLINE BINGLEY SANK TO THE FLOOR, HER SILK CREPE DRESS crumpling up beneath her. Tears spurted from her eyes and poured down her face and, to her absolute dismay, a snorting, choking kind of sound issued from her mouth.

"This is most improper," she tried to mutter, but the sobs—since that was what they were—the *sobs* refused to stay down her throat where they were supposed to be.

She had never sobbed in her life, so she could not possibly be sobbing now.

But the horrible sounds kept coming from her throat. And water—*tears*—persisted in squeezing past her eyes and down her face.

Then with a wrench, something tore in her bosom—her chest—and she finally understood the expression that everyone used but that she had always considered distinctly vulgar. *Her heart was breaking.* And it was true because what else could account for that feeling, inside her, just in the centre there, of sharp, stabbing pain?

And what could account for the fact that her arms and her lower limbs were so incredibly heavy that she could not stand up?

She was heartbroken. Her Mr Darcy had married that very morning. In church, in front of everyone, and she had been unable to prevent it.

He had preferred Elizabeth Bennet. He had actually married her, in spite of her inferior connections, and even though he had alienated his aunt, Lady Catherine de Bourgh, whose brother was an earl. Caroline simply could not comprehend it.

She had that tearing feeling again and she looked down, just to make sure that it was not her bodice that was being ripped apart. But the bodice, revealing exactly enough of her bosom as was appropriate for a lady, remained steadfastly solid. So the tearing must have come from somewhere inside her. It squeezed at her with pain hard enough to stop her breathing, and to force those appalling sobs out even when she tried her best to swallow them down.

She rested her face in her hands and surrendered to them. She had no choice in the matter. They were like child's sobs, loud and noisy. More like bawling, in fact. Her mouth was stretched and wide open. And the noise kept coming out, on and on.

On the floor, in the midst of merriment and laughter, on the day of William Fitzwilliam Darcy's wedding, with strains of music accompanying her, Miss Caroline Bingley sobbed for her lost love.

A long time later, someone tried to open the door. She came to awareness suddenly, realizing where she was. The person on the other side tried again, but she resisted, terrified that someone would come in and catch sight of her tear-stained face. No one, *no one*, she resolved, would ever know that she had cried because of Mr Darcy.

Whoever was on the other side gave the doorknob a last puzzled rattle, then walked slowly back down the corridor.

She rose, straightening out her dress, smoothing down her hair with hands that were steady only because she forced them to be.

She needed to repair the ravages her pathetic bawling had caused. At any moment, someone else could come in and discover her. She moved to look into a mirror that hung above the mantelpiece.

And recoiled in shock.

For the second time that day, she lost control completely. Her hand flew to her mouth and she squeaked—for that was the best word one could honour it with—squeaked in absolute horror.

For there he was, reflected in the mirror, sitting with his legs stretched before him, watching her gravely. He was a complete stranger. He had sat there, all that time, silent witness to the one moment in her adult life when she had broken down in such an utterly demeaning fashion.

Like the snap of a riding-crop, her surprise jolted her into motion. The heavy sensation scattered. She spun round to face him.

"How dare you sit there and watch me, sir, without the courtesy of letting me know of your presence!"

The stranger stirred and came to his feet. His face, which had been in the shadows, entered the light as he shifted, and she drew in her breath. In her befuddlement, she thought for a moment it was Darcy himself. Then she knew it was not, merely someone who resembled him, somewhat, someone with a clear family relationship.

"You are entirely correct," said the stranger. "I have been very remiss. I realized my error after the first minute. But by then it was too late. I could not interrupt such an outpour, and I felt it would be ill advised of me to try."

"If you were a gentleman," she remarked, with as much haughtiness as her anger would allow her, "you would have left the room."

He waved his half-empty glass towards the door. "Unless I left through one of the windows, I really had no option but to stay." His hand indicated the rest of the room as if to prove to her the truth of his words. Because she was still befuddled, her eyes followed it, noting that the room had no French doors, and that the windows were quite narrow.

"Well," she persisted, but her anger had abandoned her, to be replaced by exhaustion, "you ought to have thought of something."

"I did try," said the stranger. "Believe me, I tried. It was not a spectacle I relished."

The spark of anger rekindled, along with the sharp sting of shame. "And you have the gall to refer to me as a spectacle?" Those deplorable sobs were threatening to burst out again. They made her voice uneven and appallingly unfamiliar to her ears.

His eyes remained grave, though the corner of his mouth moved, just marginally. "I was not referring to you. I was simply remarking that I would have rather been anywhere else than a witness to your grief."

His statement mollified her. Indeed, she could think of no response. She rearranged the wrinkled skirt of her dress around her, gathering together the shreds of her dignity. What did it matter, after all, what this stranger thought of her? She would most likely never see him again.

Then it crossed her mind that he had complete power over her, that he was in fact free to disgrace her completely if he revealed her outburst to the assembled guests.

"I would be grateful to you, sir, if you would be good enough to keep this episode to yourself," she said, her gaze lowered to the ground, abject in her fear.

He came forward and with a touch of a gloved finger, raised her chin so that she looked up into his eyes. There was sympathy in them.

"You may consider this episode forgotten," he said. "But if at any time you wished to speak about it, I would be honoured if you would confide in me."

She did not want pity. Nor would she let him take advantage of her weakness. She stepped back out of his reach, stood up straight, and answered, her voice quite distant.

"That would be highly unlikely, sir. We have not even been introduced."

With that she swirled round and, her footsteps deliberate, she walked to the door, opened it, and closed it firmly between them.

Chapter 1

A DARK FORM GLIDED OUT OF THE FOG, GROWING STEADILY LARGER, then resolving itself into the shape of a carriage. It drew up to the house, claiming every right to stop there.

"We are not expecting visitors, are we, Charles?" said Caroline Bingley, turning to her brother Charles, and his wife, Jane, formerly Jane Bennet of Longbourn.

"Certainly not," said Charles, tossing aside the book he was reading and rising eagerly. "Did you recognize the carriage?"

"I cannot see clearly through the fog," replied Caroline.

"It is hard to imagine anyone wanting to drive in such weather," said Jane. "But I would welcome the company."

After being cooped up in the house for two days with only her brother, his wife, and her widowed sister Mrs Louisa Hurst, Caroline was badly in need of diversion. Briefly, curiosity propelled her towards the window. Then dignity won and she came to sit on the sofa, picking up the book her brother had put down.

By and by the sound of footsteps outside the room rewarded her patience. The door of the parlour opened and the footman announced their visitor.

"Mr Darcy."

Caroline jumped and dropped the book. To cover her confusion, she busied herself fumbling with the book on the ground. When she looked up, however, it was not Darcy's familiar face that she saw.

The eyes that regarded her were not brown like Mr Darcy's. They were deep blue, and framed with long black eyelashes. Their gaze pierced hers with inappropriate directness. They suggested an intimacy that brought the blood racing to her face. Another jolt went through her and she almost dropped the book again. "I believe we have not been introduced," said the stranger.

"This is my sister, Miss Caroline Bingley," said her brother. "Mr Robert Darcy, Fitzwilliam Darcy's cousin. Mr Darcy made a brief appearance at his cousin's wedding, but was called back home suddenly. He has recently returned to England from the Colonies."

"From the United States of America," Mr Darcy corrected. "That is the current term, I believe. From Boston."

He put out his hand to take hers. Caroline shifted the book from her right to her left hand and in a kind of waking nightmare placed it in his. He bowed over it.

"Delighted to make your acquaintance, Miss Bingley," said the voice she remembered only too well.

He was waiting. What was he waiting for? She realized everyone was looking at her expectantly. "A pleasure," she said stiffly, because she did not trust herself to say more. Fortunately, nobody seemed to expect more of her because Mr Darcy greeted Louisa and took a seat close to Jane.

"What a pleasant surprise you have given us," said Jane, in that calm voice of hers. "I have not seen you since we were last in Derbyshire in May. I hope you mean to stay with us for some time."

"Yes, yes," said Charles, beaming. "You must stay as long as you wish."

But Mr Darcy—the other Mr Darcy—looked grim.

"I would be very pleased, under any other circumstances," he said. "Unfortunately, I have come to convey unwelcome news." He looked gravely at Jane. "I am here to take you to your sister's side. Darcy sent me with the carriage to convey you to Pemberley."

Jane's face drained of colour. She leaned quickly forward and clutched Mr Darcy's hand. "Oh—pray tell me! What has happened?"

Mr Darcy shook his head. "I will tell you everything, but first you must make arrangements to leave."

Jane looked around her in agitation. "I must send a message to my family."

"Mrs Darcy expressly said not to mention anything to your family," said Mr Darcy, "She does not wish to alarm her parents unnecessarily."

"Then it cannot be so very alarming," said Charles, looking relieved. He walked to the back of the sofa where Jane was sitting and placed his hands on his wife's shoulder.

"Yes, you are probably right," said Jane, but she continued to stare at Mr Darcy in distress.

"Shall I inform the maids to start packing?" asked Caroline, standing up. Jane was not one to make quick decisions at the best of times, and she was clearly distraught now.

"Yes, thank you, Caroline," said Jane, giving her sister-in-law a weak smile. "You are so good at taking care of things."

When Caroline returned, Jane was still sitting on the sofa, engaged in a hushed conversation with Charles. Mr Darcy was standing by the fire, warming his hands.

"Mr Darcy," said Caroline, "I am sure you must be very cold and tired after your journey. I have had a fire lit in one of the guest chambers, and I will have a bath drawn up for you. The housekeeper will show you to your chamber."

"Thank you. You are very kind," he said. With a slight bow, he left the parlour.

Having assured herself that he had gone, Caroline walked across the room to Louisa and drew her chair next to her sister's. "Have you discovered the nature of Elizabeth Darcy's illness?" she asked Louisa in a half-whisper.

Louisa nodded. "I believe she is ill as a result of her confinement. She lost the child, and she is very weak after losing blood. It seems she is quite dejected, and will only be cheered by her sister's presence."

Caroline was glad Mr Darcy had left the room. She wondered that such a delicate topic had been discussed openly by a gentleman. But after all, Caroline had been the only unmarried lady in the room, and he did not speak in front of her.

Still, revealing Eliza's condition to everybody showed a certain lack of restraint, and perhaps a tendency to gossip. Caroline fervently hoped that he had not gossiped about her.

"I think it is only an excuse to have a member of her family by her side in Pemberley," murmured Louisa. "I am certain Mr Darcy has forbidden them from visiting, which is quite the right thing to do. Such common persons should not be tolerated at a grand estate like Pemberley."

Caroline squirmed. Her sister could be quite extreme when she did not like somebody. "Hush," she said. "That is absurd, and you know it. She would not send for her sister so urgently, if that were the case. Besides, the Bennets have visited Pemberley at least twice since the wedding. You must not say such things. You do not wish to offend Charles, do you? They are *his* connections too."

"I would not offend my dear brother for anything. He has been so kind to me after my dear Mr Hurst's sudden death. And Jane is all a sister-in-law should be. But it would be too much for me to pretend I like the rest of the Bennets."

The whispered conversation of Charles and Jane had stopped. Afraid they had overheard Louisa's comment, Caroline held her breath and prepared herself to say something to repair the damage. Instead, Charles came to his feet and pulled Jane up, giving no indication of noticing anything wrong. Caroline breathed a sigh of relief.

"I think it would be best if Jane and I set out in Darcy's carriage. If we leave tonight, we will need to spend an extra night on the road," said Charles, "but we will reach Derbyshire sooner. I do not wish to delay a moment longer than I must. Jane is really most anxious to reach Elizabeth." He turned to his sisters. "Caroline, neither you nor Louisa are required in Pemberley."

"Oh!" cried Jane. "But Caroline must accompany us. I have never dealt with a household as large as Pemberley. She will know what to do." She looked appealingly at Caroline. "You will come with us, will you not?"

"The housekeeper, Mrs Reynolds, is very capable," said Caroline, smiling faintly, "you do not need me."

"But what will you do here, then, with us away?" said Jane. "Charles, you must convince her to come."

"Yes," said Charles, impatient to set out. "You may as well come to Pemberley, if we are to remove there. You, too, Louisa. There is little to amuse you here when we're gone. You need not hurry. I am sure Robert Darcy is tired after such a long journey, and would prefer to rest a day or two. Upon his return, however, he can escort you there. Meanwhile, you could oversee the packing."

He went to the window and peered out. "You will probably be more fortunate with the weather, too. I admit I do not like travelling in the fog." Lines of worry etched his face.

"Pooh! It will not be foggy all the way to Pemberley!" said Louisa. "But what are we to tell the Bennets if they call? They will descend upon us as soon as the weather clears, you may depend upon it, and we will have to explain your absence."

"I will send a note informing them that Eliza is taken slightly ill, and that I am going to attend her," said Jane. "If they call and shower you with questions, you must say we disclosed nothing more than that."

"Knowing Mrs Bennet, that will surely arouse her determination to discover all the details," said Caroline.

"I am sure you are more than capable of keeping my mother at bay," said Jane, with an affectionate smile.

"I am, indeed," said Caroline, and embraced her quickly. "Now go, get yourself ready. Your sister is expecting you."

"You'll take charge of the arrangements, then?" asked Charles. "I would be most grateful."

"Of course," she said.

But when they left the room, Louisa remarked, "What would they do without your management, I wonder, Sister? They rely far too much on you." She sighed, drawing her black dress about her. She was growing restless of wearing widow's weeds, and had already had several dresses in grey, black and white, and lavender made, anticipating the end of her one-year mourning period. "You are always so busy you scarcely have any time for amusement. I do wish my dear Mr Hurst were here. Then we could at least play cards together."

Caroline said nothing. Her memory of Mr Hurst differed too

strongly from her sister's. Louisa had lost him quite suddenly after Christmas almost nine months ago, when he did not awake after a long night of cards and drinking. With the passage of time, his character had gradually improved in her eyes, until he was in danger of becoming a saint.

"I like taking care of the household," said Caroline. "It gives me something to think about."

She rose as she heard the sound of a door opening. She had to make the travel arrangements, but she also had something else to deal with. She had to contrive to rid herself of Mr Robert Darcy. For she remembered him all too well. More than ten months had passed since that brief encounter at the wedding, but she had not forgotten a moment of it. It had been the biggest humiliation of her life.

It was with that in mind that she waylaid her brother as he emerged from his chamber, pulling on the first of his gloves.

"I know, Charles, that you are eager to leave, but I would like a minute of your time," she said.

Charles, always willing to please, paused in the doorway. "Yes, of course, Caroline. Is there something wrong?"

"I cannot help but feel the situation rather awkward. We are to travel with a single gentleman who is a stranger to us. You and Jane are well acquainted with him, since he was there when you stayed in Pemberley. And, of course, he is Mr Darcy's cousin. But he is a bachelor alone with two unmarried ladies, and we will have to put up at more than one inn on the way. There are issues of propriety to consider. Mama would not have approved, I am certain."

Charles looked rather surprised by her assessment of the situation. "By God, I think you're right. I had not thought about it quite that way. I have heard nothing unfavourable about him, and I found him a capital fellow."

"I cannot rely on you to recommend him, Charles," said Caroline. "You are generally inclined to like everyone."

"True enough," said Charles. "I suppose it is rather awkward. But what's to be done, in the circumstances?"

"This is far from an ideal situation, but as Louisa is a married lady and could be considered a chaperon, perhaps you could pen a quick note to Darcy's cousin Colonel Fitzwilliam? I believe he is currently in London. If you could invite him to join us, I am sure that would make the situation more acceptable. Two gentlemen must be preferable to one, particularly since Colonel Fitzwilliam is a friend of the family, and is known to be perfectly respectable. And it has an added advantage. If we are to make a house party in Pemberley, it would even out the numbers with the ladies."

"Well, yes, I believe you are correct," said Charles, relieved that a solution had been found. "Except our trip to Pemberley is not exactly a house party. We must not forget that Mrs Darcy is unwell."

"I am sure that once she sees you and Jane, she will recover quickly from the doldrums. There could not be two sweeter people than you in the world. And besides, what could be more pleasant than a party of house guests? It will cheer her up considerably. Pemberley is so far from everybody. Surely she would be happy to have company?"

"You are probably right, Caroline. In any case, since it is the best answer at such short notice, I will send post-haste for Colonel Fitzwilliam, and request his assistance, if he can spare the time."

"Thank you, Charles," said Caroline, planting a quick peck on her brother's cheek. "You are the best kind of brother one could hope for."

Caroline did not waste her breath trying to convince Charles and Jane to wait until the next day to set out. Charles often gave in to impulse, and was ready to move at the drop of a hat, as he always said. So she saw them off with a sense of relief that she, at least, did not have to leave right away. She knew her brother too well. He would order the horses driven too hard, or try to put off changing them until the last possible minute, then discover it had become too dark for them to continue further, or that the horses were too tired, so they would be forced to put up at some shabby inn.

"I cannot help but wonder at Mr Darcy," said Louisa. "What could have impelled him to send us that foreign cousin of his? I do not see why we should be forced to endure his company."

"I imagine he meant him to travel back with Charles and Jane, but since Charles is in such a rush to leave, that cannot be expected." Caroline sighed. "Well, I for one do not desire to be thought discourteous to Mr Darcy's cousin, but I wish he had not come. In any case, my brother has written to Colonel Fitzwilliam requesting him to join us, so we will have congenial company," said Caroline.

Louisa, startled, cast her a knowing look, which Caroline ignored. "And you have no choice but to endure his company, unless you would really prefer to stay behind in Meryton. Then you would spend all your time with the Bennets instead of the Darcys."

Louisa shuddered. "I would journey through ice and snow rather than stay in Meryton if none of you is here."

Caroline smiled. "That was what I would have guessed. Though some of the Bennets do improve upon acquaintance, I must admit

I am looking forward to going to Pemberley. I have not been there for some time. I am curious to see what changes Eliza Bennet has made to the house."

"Whatever they are, they cannot be good," said Louisa. "We must be prepared to find Pemberley ruined beyond repair, unless Mr Darcy has been firm with her, and forbidden her to change anything. That is what *I* would have done."

"Ah, but then *you* would not have married Eliza Bennet."

Louisa snickered. "Very true! But you must remember to call her Eliza Darcy. She has been married several months now. And you have no excuse for forgetting, since we saw them in London in April. Mr Darcy will take offence."

"You need not fear," replied Caroline. "I will not call her Eliza Bennet in Mr Darcy's presence. When have you known me to be discourteous to Mr Darcy?"

"*That* was because you planned to marry him," remarked Louisa, pointedly. "And he *would* have done it, if it were not for meeting the Bennets. I still scarcely believe that both Mr Darcy and our brother succumbed to the charms of the Bennet girls."

"I cannot regret our brother marrying Jane," said Caroline, "for a sweeter girl you could never find." She rose. "We have to hope that the Bennets do not call on us before we set out. I will not know how to explain to Mrs Bennet the reason for our departure."

"You may depend upon it, she will find out. People like Mrs Bennet always seem to know everything," replied Louisa.

Caroline was too well bred to avoid taking dinner with Mr Robert Darcy. In fact, she did everything she could to ensure that Cook served up an excellent meal, even at such short notice. But the situation proved quite uncomfortable, for at the last moment, just when Caroline was preparing to go downstairs, Louisa excused herself, saying she was unwell and would take a light supper in her room. Caroline knew very well her sister wished to avoid the American's company, but she had created a problem. Caroline was now a single lady dining alone with a single gentleman.

It was not improper, of course, since he was a family guest. The presence of the footmen, moreover, made everything respectable. But it left Caroline with the undesirable task of entertaining someone who was a complete stranger, and maintaining a conversation through several dinner courses without assistance.

As they went in, however, Caroline consoled herself by thinking that things surely could not turn out badly. She knew herself quite skilled in conversation, and more than capable of dealing with someone who might not understand the conventions of English behaviour, but who, however, was not completely without manners.

She kept up a stream of inane chatter until dinner was announced and they settled to eat. Caroline paused in her conversation while the footmen served from the dishes. It was clear that Mr Darcy was waiting for such a pause, for he broke in quite abruptly.

"You must not think yourself compelled to entertain me all through dinner, Miss Bingley. I am quite content to eat without talking."

Caroline was taken aback, and did not know how to respond. Such a statement was unprecedented in her experience.

"Do you not think it would be quite uncomfortable, Mr Darcy, to be sitting here in silence, with nothing but the sound of chewing echoing through the room?" She had not meant to challenge him, but as soon as the words were uttered, they filled the room with her resentment. She had been trying her utmost to be polite, and this was her reward!

"Oh," said Mr Darcy. "I never listen to the sound of chewing. I consider it quite improper to do so."

Caroline peered at him, trying to determine if he was serious. His manner was grave and composed, and gave nothing away.

"In that case, Mr Darcy," she said crushingly, "let us remain mute."

If she had hoped to discomfit him, she was sadly disappointed. He ate his dinner in perfect contentment, giving no sign of noticing that anything was lacking. She seethed inwardly. She had determined to say nothing until he did. But, as the quiet lengthened, she shifted in her chair, growing more unnerved by the minute. It became harder and harder for her not to speak.

"Miss Bingley," said Mr Darcy, "I can see you are quite vexed with our agreement. I would not for anything cause you distress, particularly since I can see you have been at pains to have a very enjoyable dinner prepared. May I compliment you on your choice of dishes? And on the skill of your brother's cook? I do not wish to ruin such a pleasant meal. I shall certainly exert myself to converse, if it will make you feel better."

Caroline immediately grasped the opportunity to take control of the situation once again. "I am very relieved to hear it," she said. "I do not know what you are accustomed to in Boston, but here it is simply not done to sit silently over dinner."

"In company, perhaps. But surely in private many family members may prefer not to talk, especially if they do not get along very well."

"That may be true in *some* families. I assure you it is not the case in mine. And dining with you can hardly be called dining in *private*. So you see, Mr Darcy, your argument does not hold."

"Why would you not consider our dining *private*? Apart from the footman, who is wishing himself invisible, and must be tired of standing there so motionless, it seems to me we are completely private."

"You are a guest here, Mr Darcy. And a single gentleman. I need not remind you that any attempt to suggest that our meeting is private indicates an undesirable situation of intimacy."

Mr Darcy smiled. "Ah. Of course," he said, "that is what you fear. Intimacy."

"Mr Darcy!" said Caroline. "I do not wish to continue this conversation."

"But Miss Bingley, it was you, and not I, who wished to exchange social niceties. I am quite content to be silent."

Caroline clamped her mouth down on the retort she would have liked to make, focusing her attention on her food. She applied herself to the venison in front of her, attacking it vengefully with her knife. A spurt of sauce flew from her dish and spattered the table. The footman reacted immediately and dabbed at the tablecloth with a napkin.

She sat back in her chair, aware of Mr Darcy's eyes on her. His expression was perfectly bland.

"Thank you," he said to the footman, as the latter withdrew to stand against the wall.

She picked up her fork once more and began to toy with her food. Mr Darcy took up a mouthful of venison and chewed it with evident enjoyment.

This would not do. If he did not know how to conduct a dinner conversation, it was up to her to set an example. "We are expecting a friend of ours, a gentleman, to arrive from London the day after tomorrow, to accompany us to Pemberley. Colonel Fitzwilliam.

Perhaps you have met him? He is a cousin of Mr Darcy's, but unrelated to you, I believe."

"Yes, he is related to Darcy on his mother's side," said Mr Robert Darcy. "I have met him. He is a very engaging gentleman. He will be a welcome addition to our party."

"We are thinking of departing three days from today, if that is acceptable to you. I would not wish to hold you up here, if you have business elsewhere."

"I have no pressing business at present," he said. "When I attended Darcy's wedding, I was in England because a business venture of my father's necessitated my presence. But I was recalled to Boston when my father fell suddenly ill." He looked down into his plate. "I returned to England only to tie up matters here to do with inheritance. My late father's venture did not have a chance to succeed, unfortunately."

"I am sorry to hear of your loss," murmured Caroline.

"You did not know him," replied Mr Darcy. "It was certainly a loss for me." He stared into the distance, engulfed briefly in his memories. When he looked at her again, he smiled ruefully. "But I hardly think you would be interested in that. In any case, after I wrapped up his affairs here, I have had nothing to do but kick my heels first in London, then in Derbyshire, waiting for the chance to sail back to Boston."

"I would have thought it would be impossible to return, with the blockade still in place," remarked Caroline. "Surely you must wait until the war is over?"

"The New England coast is not part of the blockade. Though after the débâcle in Boston Harbour last June, the blockade has tightened, and the risk has become too high. Especially with Bermudan and American privateers attacking British merchant ships. Why, the

USS Argus was operating in British waters when they captured it just three weeks ago. Can you imagine their audacity?"

His eyes twinkled with amusement. She did not share the joke, of course.

He waited while the footman had removed the tablecloth and brought in the pudding, then resumed. "Even if I were willing to risk it, it has become close to impossible to find a ship that will take passengers."

"It was your country that declared war on Britain," remarked Caroline. "I have never quite understood the reasons for it."

"If a desire for independence and non-interference is incomprehensible to you," said Mr Darcy, his eyes sharp, "then I am afraid explaining the situation will serve no useful purpose."

A dark tension filled the room, thick like molasses. Caroline realized she had taken a misstep, and endeavoured immediately to repair it.

"I did not wish to mock your country's demands," she said. "I meant only to question them. This is hardly the time to engage Britain in another war, when Napoleon himself is at our shores, threatening to destroy our very way of life."

Mr Darcy raised an eyebrow. "I was not aware that you had an interest in politics, Miss Bingley."

"I am not as empty minded as you choose to believe," retorted Caroline. She busied herself with slicing a carrot on her plate, not wishing to see his reaction to her statement.

"I have not yet had time to form an opinion about you, Miss Bingley," remarked Mr Darcy. "As you pointed out quite rightly earlier, we have just today been introduced. I would not be so quick to judge you. I hope you will return the favour by not presuming you already know how I think." He spoke coldly.

Puzzled by his sudden coldness, she turned to examine him closely, but his face was tilted away from her, unlit by the candles, and she could not determine anything.

"Since you seem determined to speak your mind, I hope you do not mind if I speak mine," said Caroline. "We began our acquaintance under rather unfortunate conditions." She paused to allow him to register that she referred to their first encounter. "However, since it appears we will be spending some time together, though not in private, I should add, I think it best we should begin anew."

"Ah, but you would not deprive me of this opportunity to get to know you better, Miss Bingley, surely? It is only because we are in private that we can have this conversation at all." He smiled charmingly, and though his words ruffled her, she took them to indicate agreement. She smiled tightly in return, and ignored his attempt to provoke her.

"I am glad we understand each other, Mr Darcy, for now I can rest easy. Perhaps you could humour my singular need for conversation by telling me more about your life in Boston? I am very curious to form a picture of it."

No man, thought Caroline, could resist the chance to talk about himself, and Mr Darcy was no exception. He seized the opportunity to launch into a series of tales and anecdotes. To her surprise, he was quite entertaining, even managing to make her laugh at one or two of his stories.

She was glad, however, when it was time for her to withdraw to allow him to drink his port. She excused herself and went upstairs.

Her evening with him had proved exhausting. If she could not trust him to follow the basic dictates of etiquette, how could she trust him in anything else?

For she could not forget for a moment how much she depended on his goodwill not to reveal her secret.

Chapter 2

CAROLINE WAS INTENSELY RELIEVED THE NEXT DAY WHEN HER maid informed her, as she served the usual morning chocolate in bed, that the fog had disappeared. Caroline's spirits lifted. The weather being fine, Colonel Fitzwilliam might even reach them before nightfall, for it was barely twenty-four miles from London to Meryton.

She had her breakfast brought to her in chamber, which was not her habit. She could little afford it this particular morning, in fact, when there was so much to do. There was Colonel Fitzwilliam's visit to prepare for, preparations to undertake for the trip, and instructions to give to the servants for the time they would be away. But she wanted to avoid the breakfast room, for she did not wish to encounter Mr Darcy alone, and she knew Louisa would not be down before noon.

Her precautions proved to be pointless. When she enquired about his whereabouts, she was told that Mr Darcy had gone out riding early and planned to take a light luncheon at the inn in Meryton. When he still had not come back by late afternoon, she concluded hopefully that he was just as anxious to avoid *her* as she to avoid *him*.

She was in the parlour with Louisa when he returned. Louisa was embroidering, while Caroline sat at the writing table, trying to make sense of the ledger, and sifting through a bewildering collection of Charles's bills. Mr Darcy bowed politely and informed them that he had been gathering information for their journey, since on the way to Netherfield, it was his cousin's coachman who had guided him.

"You need not worry yourself about it, Mr Darcy," said Louisa. "After all, as a stranger in our country, you cannot be expected to know these things. When Colonel Fitzwilliam arrives he will be more than capable of arranging the journey for us."

"I prefer to know as much as possible when I travel, Mrs Hurst," said Mr Darcy. "I am possessed of a strange independence of spirit, and a curiosity that drives me to learn what I can about any project in which I am engaged. And I am eager to discover what I can about England. Besides, it is by no means certain that Colonel Fitzwilliam will be spared from his duties. Have you received word?"

"He may ride over without sending a message," said Miss Bingley. "Especially if he sets out today from London."

"I can only hope he is able to come," said Mr Darcy. "For I feel you will be disappointed if he does not."

Caroline smiled civilly. "I do indeed hope he will come."

"In any case," he said, "you need not worry if he doesn't. I have consulted Paterson's and feel quite comfortable selecting our route. I have decided to take the Great North Road."

"The Great North Road?" said Louisa, frowning a little. "It is not our usual route to Pemberley. Are you sure it is the best way?"

"It is the post-road to Edinburgh," said Robert Darcy. "And it is the way Darcy suggested on the way down."

Louisa shrugged. "If Mr Darcy suggested it, we cannot go wrong," she conceded. "We always travel on that road to Scarborough. We stop at the George in Stamford, and we purchase cheese at the Bell Inn in Stilton."

"Stilton?" said Robert Darcy, wrinkling his nose. "It has an odour, and a rather strange colour. And it tastes—well, the less said, the better."

"Stilton is an acquired taste," said Louisa, stiffly, "I would not expect it to please just *anyone*. It is not a *common* cheese." She gave a disdainful laugh.

"If we do go by the Great North," said Caroline, "we will stop for the cheese. However, Old North Road might be preferable."

"We can consult the strip maps together, if you wish," said Mr Darcy. "I have no objection to taking another route."

Caroline had more urgent things to do than pore over maps in Mr Robert Darcy's company. She shook her head. "When Colonel Fitzwilliam comes," said Caroline, "I am sure he will give you the benefit of his experience, since he has travelled these roads numerous times."

"I bow then to his superior knowledge, in that case," said Darcy, quite cheerfully. "*If* he appears on the scene."

"Then it is settled," she said.

Mr Darcy rose. "If you will excuse me, I will withdraw to the library. I have seen one or two books here that interest me, and would like to take the opportunity to explore them. Your brother keeps an excellent library."

Caroline accepted the compliment with a condescending nod of the head.

As soon as the door closed behind him, Louisa came quickly to sit by her sister. "How little he knows! Such ignorance! He has no breeding at all. As if anyone with taste could not like Stilton!" She mulled over this incomprehensible idea for some time. "And did you notice how helplessly windblown his hair was?" she added, as though that clinched the matter.

"He does not seem very concerned with his appearance," responded Caroline, mildly.

"And what impertinence on his part to plan the journey for us!" continued Louisa.

Much as she objected to Robert Darcy's presence, Caroline found herself coming to his defence. "In all fairness, Louisa," she said, "it is nothing more than I would expect. Surely you do not want to take care of the travel arrangements as well as the household tasks? And in the event that Colonel Fitzwilliam is unable to escort us, I would be very glad to know that he was well enough informed about the roads and would not lead us astray."

"Phew!" said Louisa. "The coachman can deal with all that."

Though Caroline agreed that his conduct lacked a certain polish, she could not help feeling that Louisa was in danger of going too far. Her remarks to him were designed to give offence, and that would not do.

"As long as he is our guest, Louisa, we are obliged to be civil at least."

Louisa took up the cushion she was embroidering and focused her attention on her stitches. "Sometimes, Caroline," she said, "you are too concerned with the niceties. I do not think we have any obligation towards him."

Mr Darcy chose that moment to return. It was clear he had overheard Louisa's remark.

"I hope you are not speaking of me," he said, cheerfully, "for I must say I agree with your sister, Miss Bingley. You must not feel yourself obliged to me in any way. I dislike above all else to be thought an obligation."

"There are social rules, Mr Darcy, and I prefer to follow them, even if you are little inclined to do so," replied Caroline. "Shall I ring for some tea?"

Mr Darcy settled himself on one of the upright white and gold striped armchairs. "Yes, that would be delightful," he replied.

With tea requested, Caroline went back to her ledger, only to be interrupted by Mr Darcy.

"I have found something that I have wished to read for some time," he said, tapping his book with the satisfaction of a ginger cat that has caught a bird. "Edward Gibbon's *Decline and Fall of the Roman Empire*," he said. "It is in several volumes. I hope you have no objection to my borrowing the first of them? I will, of course, return it to you in Pemberley."

"You may borrow the whole library if you wish," said Louisa with a dismissive wave of her hand. "Charles never reads, and I find its contents quite tedious. I wish he would replace all those dull old books with newer ones. My father bought the collection from an earl whose fortunes were in disarray, and I believe the earl bought a race horse with the money. *He* had the better end of the bargain."

"Did the horse win any races?" asked Robert Darcy, all innocence.

"Not that I know of," said Louisa, with a quick laugh.

Caroline poured Darcy the tea, suppressing an urge to giggle. He took it from her, leaned back in his seat, and threw her a mocking glance. "No sign of Colonel Fitzwilliam yet, I see," he remarked.

Caroline's back stiffened. "Perhaps he will be here tomorrow," she said lightly, determined not to allow him to rattle her, though why she should be rattled by the mention of Colonel Fitzwilliam she could not imagine.

He grinned in response. "I am eagerly awaiting his arrival," he said. "I cannot wait to benefit from his superior experience."

Caroline did not dignify the jibe with a response. But it occurred to her that it was by no means certain that Colonel Fitzwilliam would be able to take time off from his military duties, and it was quite possible that they would be travelling to Pemberley with only Mr Robert Darcy as company.

As nightfall approached, in fact, she began to doubt that the colonel would join them. He had sent no word. Very likely he had been posted somewhere with his regiment, and had not even received her brother's letter. She resigned herself to the idea that their journey would be uncomfortable. Despite Mr Darcy's confidence, there was more to travelling than which road to take. Some of the inns along the way had inferior horses, or provided inferior service or were very slow. Their journey in such situations could be considerably lengthened. Still, as long as they were able to stop at the George in Stamford, they were at least guaranteed one night of comfort.

But just when she had accepted the inevitable, a commotion in the courtyard suggested the colonel's arrival. Caroline did not wait for him to be announced and hurried immediately to the doorway. She welcomed him warmly as he dismounted, taking him by the arm and drawing him into the house in a manner that seemed to please him. It took only Louisa's remark that he had come to save them to make him feel that his fast gallop from London was well worth his while, and he was soon comfortably installed in their presence, with Mr Darcy quite sadly neglected. Though one would hardly suppose he noticed, as he was so engrossed in the book he had found.

For the first time in weeks Louisa suddenly came to life at the dinner table. Caroline realized, watching her, how much her sister suffered from her forced retirement to Netherfield, with only the village of Meryton close by. Louisa did not fare well in the country. She was too engrossed in London society to be happy away from it. She seized on Colonel Fitzwilliam's presence to deluge him with questions about friends and acquaintances she had not seen since they left.

Caroline and her sister had spent part of the season in town. But Louisa's mourning confined them to a small circle of friends. And though Caroline herself was not in mourning, she was constrained by her sister's circumstances. She could not hold dinner parties or evenings in the Bingley town house, and eventually felt embarrassed accepting other people's invitations when she could not issue any of her own. Moreover, it became more and more difficult to be merry when her sister was so plainly discontented. So they had left town at the end of June, just after the height of the season, and resolved to settle in Meryton until Louisa was in half-mourning. It had now been three months since they had been in Town.

The colonel replied to Louisa's questions with good humour. But when it seemed that they would never come to an end, Caroline was forced to intervene.

"Oh, do give Colonel Fitzwilliam a chance to take a breath, Louisa. You have plied him with queries the past half hour at least. You are depriving him of his food."

She smiled sympathetically at Colonel Fitzwilliam, who smiled back warmly. "Oh, I do not mind at all," he said, handsomely.

"I am sorry, Caroline, to have seized the conversation," said Louisa, slyly. "I am sure you have enquiries of your *own* to make."

Caroline flushed. She could not correct her sister in public, but she did not know how to put an end to her lack of discretion. She did not wish Mr Darcy to know anything more about her private concerns.

It was time to change direction. For in the midst of Louisa's thirst for gossip, Mr Darcy had been completely neglected. No one had addressed a single word to him since the beginning of dinner.

"My enquiries can wait for another time," said Caroline, smoothly. "I was rather more interested in knowing the latest news of Napoleon."

Colonel Fitzwilliam nodded approvingly. Mr Darcy, who looked like he was ready to slide under the table, sat up straighter in his chair and paid immediate attention. "Ah, yes," he said, "I am very eager to hear the latest news, for I have been unable to obtain a newspaper in Meryton."

"There is nothing new, in fact. Napoleon is licking his wounds after the defeat in Berlin, and is struggling to retain control of his supply lines by withdrawing to Leipzig. He has sustained heavy losses, and his army has dwindled. The next few weeks should be decisive. Who knows, perhaps the war will be over sooner than we think."

Louisa shrugged. "I find this talk of war too dismal," she said, peevishly. "Napoleon is much too far away to attack England, so his movements are of no concern to us, surely?"

"I am afraid they are of vast concern to me," said Colonel Fitzwilliam, "for if the war does not end soon, it is likely my regiment will be sent to fight. But you are right. Military matters hardly constitute suitable conversation for ladies' ears."

Caroline, who would have liked to learn more about the latest events of the war, would have protested, but by the time she began to speak, Colonel Fitzwilliam was entertaining them with the latest news about London theatre.

"The talk of the town is Delpini's *Don Juan*, though it is but a pantomime, and plays at the Lyceum. I have not seen it, but those who have are showering it with praise. Otherwise there is little of interest at the moment."

"Oh," said Louisa, her eyes shining, "you cannot mean that. The theatre is one of the things I miss most in London. Why, it was just a year ago that the new Drury Lane Theatre opened its doors, with Robert Elliston performing *Hamlet*. I am sure no one spoke of anything else for days. Do you recall the occasion, Colonel Fitzwilliam?"

"Of course," replied Colonel Fitzwilliam readily. "Elliston was all he should be. He cannot hold a candle to Kemble, for he lacks the necessary decorum. But he plays a tolerable Hamlet."

Caroline turned to Mr Darcy graciously, noting that he had not contributed a word. "Are you fond of *Hamlet*, Mr Darcy?" said Caroline, in her role as hostess.

"I suppose it is a good kind of play," said Mr Darcy, "if you like graveyards and skeletons."

Louisa gave a gasp of outrage. "How could you, Mr Darcy? When it is the work of the great Mr Shakespeare!"

Colonel Fitzwilliam turned to her. "Perhaps in the colonies they do not venerate Mr Shakespeare as we do, Mrs Hurst."

But Caroline had noted the gleam in Mr Darcy's eyes. "I do believe he is teasing us," she said. "For I have read that, in the *United States of America*," she paused to emphasize the words, "there is a lively tradition of theatrical performances, and that Shakespeare is very much in vogue."

Mr Darcy gave her an appreciative glance. "Very true, Miss Bingley. I am afraid you have quite caught me out. How could I avoid admiring Shakespeare, when the masters at my Latin School, that venerable institution, instilled it in me? How could I set aside those oh so famous words when they were drilled into my head?

'Alas, poor Yorick!—I knew him... and now, how abhorred in my imagination it is! My gorge rises at it. Here hung those lips that I have kiss'd I know not how oft..." He raised his glass in salute. "No, it is not something one is likely to forget."

Since Caroline could not decide whether he was mocking himself, his school, or Shakespeare, she thought it wiser not to respond. There was more to him, perhaps, than met the eye. However, she had no intention of coming to understand him better. Their worlds were far apart, and she appreciated her position in society too much to find interest in anyone who so clearly was not a part of it.

Across the dinner table, Caroline eyed Colonel Fitzwilliam with approval. It was good to be with a gentleman who understood his place in the world. One knew precisely what to say to him and how to behave with him. And he was a handsome man. His chestnut hair fell over his light brown eyes in just the right way, and his shoulders filled his coat nicely. He was impeccably dressed.

Her scrutiny returned to Mr Darcy. His dark hair—quite like his cousin's—was arranged in fashionable waves, but the waves were irregular enough to appear wild. His clothing was elegant and well cut, but was just a little too loose on his frame, as though comfort was more important than correct fitting. As for his high standing collar, it did not reach quite as high as it ought in a gentleman who wished to be thought proud.

But then he turned, and his gaze met hers, and she noticed that he had very fine eyes. So fine, in fact, that she found it impossible to look away. They were intensely blue. They caught the moving light from the candles and shimmered, rippling between shadow and light. For a minuscule moment, she was riveted, fascinated by the flickering shades within them. Then reason asserted itself and she wrenched her head aside.

Flustered, she turned to request more wine from the footman.

The following day Caroline saw little of either gentleman. She was busy with the type of household arrangements that preceded a long absence—ensuring that all the packing needs for their journey were in hand, seeing that the covers were placed on the furniture, and organizing the tasks of those servants who would follow after them. And she was spared the trouble of planning dinner, for the two gentlemen sent word that they would take their evening meal at the inn in Meryton, where Colonel Fitzwilliam was to meet some of his acquaintances.

Caroline was surprised, therefore, when Mr Darcy was announced just after dinner. She had just settled down to some sewing and was looking forward to a relaxed evening before they set out on their journey. Louisa remarked, quite without civility, that she had not expected to see him tonight.

Mr Darcy was unperturbed by this less than cordial welcome. "Oh, I have never mastered the ability to spend the night before a journey carousing. I find myself quite unable to wake up early enough, and it puts me quite out of sorts the whole day."

He sat down at Caroline's invitation.

"If you cannot hold your cups well," remarked Louisa, "I suppose that *would* be the case. Mr Hurst, I recall, was quite capable of drinking several bottles of port, playing cards until the early hours, then rising after two hours of sleep and setting out on a long journey." She sighed. "But I understand not everyone could be his equal."

Mr Darcy inclined his head, his face impassive. "You are perfectly correct," he said. "*I* for one would not be able to undertake such a thing."

Caroline could not help but admire Robert Darcy's restraint. She herself was quite tempted to say that perhaps if he had not indulged himself so badly, Mr Hurst might still have been with them. But one did not say such things, of course. She could, however, make amends for her sister's rudeness.

"You are perfectly correct, Mr Darcy, for you will make a poor companion if you were nursing a headache the whole day. It would be rather uncomfortable to be confined in a carriage for hours with someone who is determined to do nothing but growl."

"I would never be so bad mannered as to growl at you, Miss Bingley, no matter what the circumstances," said Robert Darcy, irrepressibly. "In fact, now that I think about it, I do not believe I have ever been guilty of doing such a thing."

Caroline sighed. Her attempts to put him at ease seemed quite wasted. Certainly he did not appreciate them. And she had no idea if he was flirting with her or not, since his words could be understood in any number of ways. But she had no intention of encouraging him, if that was his intention.

She reached for the bell pull. "I will have Cook bring you something light to eat," she said. "I know the inn at Meryton serves supper very early, for they keep country hours, and you are undoubtedly hungry by now."

"You are really very kind," said Robert Darcy.

"I hope Colonel Fitzwilliam will not be sleepy tomorrow," said Louisa, her mind still dwelling on their earlier exchange. "For I *had* hoped to question him more about our friends in London. I am so out of touch with everyone!"

"I am sure you will have the opportunity to talk to him," said Caroline. "But I hope you will not exhaust him with your questions."

"Oh, I need not stand on ceremony with him. He has been our brother's friend forever. And you must not hold back, either, Caroline," she said, throwing her sister a knowing look. "For I know you are anxious to enquire after a *particular* gentleman."

Under Mr Darcy's scrutiny, Caroline felt the blood rise to her face. "There is no one in particular I wish to discuss," she replied, stung by this betrayal of confidence. And to someone they scarcely knew! "You will agree, Louisa, that I am acquainted with several very presentable young gentlemen in London."

"All at the same time, Miss Bingley?" said Mr Darcy. "I must admit I am quite impressed."

Caroline pressed her lips together tightly. Louisa had started this, but Mr Darcy was only too happy to find a reason to roast her.

"Come, come, Mr Darcy," said Louisa archly. "You must admit that is a possibility. Caroline has many admirers. She is accounted a beauty in Town."

Mr Darcy exclaimed in surprise. "Well, I never!" he said, peering at Caroline closely, as if he had never seen her before. "Now that you mention it, I see there is some truth in that judgement. I am grateful to you for drawing my attention to it, Mrs Hurst. I apologize, Miss Bingley, for not having realized it earlier."

Miss Bingley did not know whether to blush or to be angry at his brazenness. Since she could not decide on one or the other, she contented herself with chastising her sister. "You should not to speak about me like this in front of strangers, Louisa."

"But Mr Darcy is hardly a stranger, Caroline."

Caroline could not believe her ears.

Robert Darcy raised an eyebrow. "She has a point there," he said. "I imagine I know quite a number of things about you that are not generally known."

She turned away quickly, pretending to busy herself with rearranging some ornaments on the table, and bit down on her lip to prevent herself from retorting. Insufferable man! To taunt her about that single moment of weakness! Never before had she regretted anything as much as that moment of emotional display at Mr Fitzwilliam Darcy's wedding. The memory agitated her so much that before she knew it she had broken her resolve to stay silent.

"A *gentleman* would refrain from such references." She realized too late that she had aroused her sister's suspicions.

"What references, Caroline? What are you talking about? Did you have a prior acquaintance with Mr Darcy?"

Caroline was thrown into an agony of confusion. How could she answer her sister in a way that would satisfy her without lying outright?

"We were only introduced two days ago," interceded Mr Darcy, smoothly. "Which was a great loss to me, had I but known it. Especially now that you have alerted me to Miss Bingley's reputation as a beauty. However, I intend to remedy the situation very quickly."

He smiled at Louisa, and to Caroline's surprise, her sister tittered. "Mr Darcy!" said Louisa, coyly. "What nonsense is this?"

Caroline remained steadfastly unsmiling. She had allowed him a hold on her by giving in once to her feelings in a moment of weakness. But if he thought she could be influenced by a few meaningless words of flattery, he would find he was very much mistaken. She was not such an easy nut to crack, and she would make sure he knew it.

Chapter 3

DESPITE MISGIVINGS ON CAROLINE'S PART, COLONEL FITZWILLIAM rode over from the inn before seven o'clock the next morning, their planned departure time. She might not have noticed had they not discussed it the night before, but the colonel suffered from the effects of his late night. All attempts on Louisa's part to engage him in questions about London failed, for he was reluctant to speak in more than single syllables, and spent much of the morning with his head against the window, snoring softly.

Robert Darcy, on the other hand, was perfectly alert. This gave neither of the ladies any pleasure, particularly since he cast several cynical looks at the colonel's sleeping countenance, and seemed generally to regard the situation with amusement. To make matters worse, since Colonel Fitzwilliam declined to take any interest in the journey, it fell upon Mr Darcy to determine when to stop, which he did by consulting his borrowed copy of Paterson's.

They stopped for their cheese at the Bell Inn at Stilton, despite the protests of Mr Darcy who objected to the smell that filled the carriage. It was quite useless to point out that they could not possibly smell the cheese inside when it had been placed outside, on the box. He insisted that the odour was quite overpowering.

By the time they reached Wansford, Caroline began to reflect quite cheerfully that if they continued at the same rate, they would make Stamford by late afternoon. Then on the morrow, if they started early enough, they would reach Pemberley. She cheered up, indulging in the hope that the journey would prove much easier than she had anticipated.

Her optimism was soon dealt a blow, however. A loud cacophony reached them, and the carriage began to slow down. Strident cries and shouts rang out, accompanied by a strange unfamiliar din that sounded as if a whole orchestra of ill-matched horns were playing at the same time.

"What could that be?" said Robert Darcy.

"If it is what I think it is," said Colonel Fitzwilliam, undoing the fastening on the window, "I doubt we will be able to reach Stamford for some time." He put his head out, then slumped back with a resigned look. "Unfortunately, it *is* what I thought. A large flock of geese is blocking our way, and the cries you hear are the drovers shouting their warnings to the farmers to keep their own stock out of the way."

"Oh, not geese!" Louisa groaned. "They are such smelly, nasty creatures! Now we shall be delayed for hours."

The carriage slowed to a crawl, then came to a standstill.

"Surely it cannot be as bad as all that?" said Caroline. She leaned out of the window to survey their situation. An enormous gaggle of geese occupied the road. It stretched on and on, the birds waddling along in an orderly fashion, kept in alignment by a long line of drivers with birch rods walking alongside the roadway. Caroline was struck by the strangeness of the geese's feet. Their webbing was dark, thick, and uneven. They all seemed to have some sort of disfiguring disease, which left their feet blackened and rough looking, with specks on them like sand.

Far ahead, the drovers rode on horseback, distant outlines visible upon the horizon, though their strange cries reached the carriage clearly.

The coachman blew on the yard of tin he used to call the tollgate keepers, trying to make the geese move aside and let him pass. They honked and hissed aggressively in return.

"Oh, this is ridiculous," said Louisa. "We are on a post road, not a drover's road. They cannot let their geese run wild on a public way. There must be some ordinance against it."

Since the geese were evidently on the public road, no one had anything to say.

"I wonder what's wrong with their feet," said Caroline, unable to keep her eyes off the strange blackened forms.

The geese, however, did not seem to be in any kind of pain. They plodded along quite cheerfully, indifferent to the coachman's attempt to drive them off the road. They were undaunted by the horses, and even when the coachman raised his whip and slashed it through the air, they scuttled away only briefly, cackled at the noise, then resumed their lumbering walk. One or two of them fluttered their wings to fly, but landed inelegantly with a plop, causing a burst of angry invective from the geese around them.

"I think we should resign ourselves to a very long journey," said Colonel Fitzwilliam. "I do not see any way through."

"We cannot give up so easily," said Robert Darcy. "Surely we can do something." He opened the door and descended. Uttering a loud, high-pitched shout, "Yee-haa!" he swept his hat forwards and backwards like an oar.

The geese moved aside, squawking in indignant protest.

"Come and join me, Fitzwilliam," said Darcy. "Perhaps we can scatter them."

Colonel Fitzwilliam leapt from the carriage with a laugh.

"I can't promise to reproduce that same blood curdling sound," he said, "but I will do my best." He let out a high pitched yell, "Yoo-hoo!" It did not remotely resemble Mr Darcy's, but it proved equally effective in moving the birds. Soon the carriage was surrounded by clonking geese and it jerked forward, moving at a snail's pace.

Louisa covered her ears. "I wish they would stop that infernal noise," she said, "I can feel a megrim coming on."

But the cries of the two gentlemen had added to the mêlée. Along with the high pitched cries of the drovers and the protesting squawks of the geese, the volume rose considerably. The noise invading the carriage from all sides was indeed overwhelming. Louisa, quite beyond dignity, covered her ears with her hands, her face crumpled with distaste.

Caroline, who had at first been quite rattled, now found that the discordant sounds brought out in her a strange urge to laugh. With her head out of the window, she watched the undignified antics of the gentlemen and the strident response of the geese in amazement, then leaned back into her seat and began to laugh, softly at first, then louder and louder.

Louisa stared at her. "Do control yourself, Caroline," she said, scowling. "As if we do not have enough noise without that dreadful laughter."

Louisa's contorted face only served to boost her merriment. It was really quite out of her control. She could not recall laughing so loudly since she was a child.

Louisa, seeing nothing in the situation to laugh about, threatened to throw her out if she did not stop.

"In that case, Louisa," she answered, still chuckling, "I will relieve you of my presence."

She opened the door of the carriage. She had no clear idea what she planned to do, but she did not want to wait in the carriage. She felt a strong need for action.

Robert Darcy, who was the closest to them, came immediately to help her descend. "Coming to join in the revelry, Miss Bingley?" he asked, quizzingly.

"I would like to make myself useful," she said, with an attempt at severity. But since her face was bright with laughter, Robert Darcy grinned in response.

"You would not like to join us, Mrs Hurst?" he asked, poking his head into the carriage.

Louisa shrank back in her seat and shook her head. "I think you are all being quite giddy," she said. "It is this country air, no doubt."

"We have little choice in the matter," remarked Mr Darcy, "How does the saying go? *What is sauce for the goose is sauce for the gander?*"

"What nonsense!" she snapped. "What does the saying have to do with anything?"

"I am afraid I am not known for my good sense, ma'am," responded Mr Darcy, turning back to his task.

Caroline took out the pins of her bonnet, one by one, and peeled it off her head. Copying the gentlemen, she swung her bonnet from side to side. Still, she did not go so far as to start shouting in that ridiculous manner.

"You should do it right, Miss Bingley," said Mr Darcy, regarding her appreciatively. "Why not let your hair down?"

She ignored him. Geese surrounded her from every side, and she had a moment of fear when a few of the brave ones rushed towards her as if to attack. But a swing of her bonnet drove them away, and she laughed. The geese retreated to the sides of the road, out of the way of the swaying object. Meanwhile one of the drovers ahead of them stopped, leaned on his long stick, and, chewing on a blade of grass, watched their efforts with astonishment.

Robert Darcy spotted the drover. He was a boy of about sixteen with an intelligent look in his eyes. "Is there no way to get the geese off the road?" he asked.

The drover shook his head. "They'll be stopping every minute to eat the grass if we did that. It's only by sticking to the road that we can keep 'em moving."

Colonel Fitzwilliam, who had been a little ahead, came back to join them. "We have accomplished very little," he remarked. "We will just have to hope they leave the road soon." He turned to the drover, who was still chewing at the same blade of grass. "Are you taking them far?"

The lad took the grass from his mouth. "Nottingham," he said, briefly.

Colonel Fitzwilliam guffawed. "Surely you do not mean Nottingham!" he said. "That is thirty miles away!"

The drover nodded, and replied that of course he meant Nottingham. Where else would they be going, when it was time for the great fair? The gentleman had surely heard of it.

Colonel Fitzwilliam clearly had not. "It's the biggest fair in England!" said another of the drovers, who had come to see what the uproar at the back was about. "Some of the drovers have come from as far as Norfolk."

Caroline, by now overcome with curiosity, enquired about the disease that had blackened the geese's feet.

The two lads roared with laughter at her question and slapped each other on the shoulders, amazed at her ignorance. Finally, one of them, realizing that she was waiting for a reply, explained to her,

THE OTHER MR. DARCY

very patiently, as if she was slow-witted, that the feet of the geese had been covered in tar so they could walk the distance. Realising she was still confused, he added kindly that it was like putting shoes on them, as it helped protect their feet.

Mr Darcy eyed the long trail of waddling geese that stretched as far forward as the eye could see. "How many geese do you suppose there are?"

The lad with the grass blade shrugged. "One of the drovers can tell you exactly—Mr Stacey, or Mr Manton, since they're the ones who do the reckoning, but I heard Mr Manton say there were upwards of ten thousand."

Louisa, who was in the carriage behind them, was calling for Caroline.

"For heaven's sake, come back in, Caroline. I don't know what you think you're doing, but that is no place for a lady," she said.

"Your sister has the right of it, Miss Bingley," said Mr Darcy. "We can't clear away ten thousand geese with our hats."

"There is nothing we can do," said the colonel to Louisa as he entered the carriage. "But one of the lads has told me they plan to stop at a drover's inn a few miles ahead, to feed the geese and have a drink, so the geese will be off the road and penned in. I am afraid, however, we will have to change our plans. We cannot possibly take the road through Nottingham. We will have to continue on the Great North Road and travel to Matlock on one of the crossroads."

"As long as I can stay the night at Stamford," said Louisa, "I do not greatly care what road we take tomorrow."

This was easier said than done. When they reached Stamford, they found it bustling with activity, with carts, wagons, and carriages everywhere, as well as cattle and sheep. At the George they were met with the news that there was no accommodation to be had anywhere within ten miles, with the situation growing worse the closer they drew to Nottingham. Colonel Fitzwilliam and Mr Darcy looked quite grim at the news.

"It seems the whole world is heading to Nottingham," said Mr Darcy. "And to top it all, there is to be a cockfight at the inn, so a crowd of gentlemen who are not going to the market are here today."

"We could drive further north," said Colonel Fitzwilliam. "But it is by no means certain that we will find a place to spend the night if we do."

Louisa, who disliked crowds excessively, was becoming quite flustered. She remarked crossly that she could not very well be expected to spend the night in the carriage.

"There is another possibility," said Colonel Fitzwilliam, hesitantly, "but I cannot be certain it will work either. Some friends of mine have a small estate not too far from here. The Loughs. You may have heard of them. I shall hire a horse and ride over to request their hospitality. I will go alone, since it is faster, especially if the road is crowded. If you are willing to wait here, I will make enquiries."

Caroline expressed her earnest thanks. "You will quite tire yourself out, riding there and back, especially after we have travelled for so long."

"It will be worth it if we find ourselves with a roof above our heads, and you and Mrs Hurst are saved from sleeping in the carriage," he replied, with a smile. "Besides, they do not live very far away."

Louisa, too, thanked him prettily, but when he left, she expressed her doubt that he would find the Loughs at home. "For it would be a happy chance indeed if they were," she said. "Our luck does not seem to be holding."

Caroline thought it best not to answer.

"I hope he returns soon," added Louisa, peevishly, "for if the Loughs are not prepared to receive us, we will be forced to drive on until we find a place to lodge. It will be quite dark by then, and I am heartily tired of sharing the road with cattle, geese, and all the vagrants and troublemakers in Lincolnshire."

Louisa eyed a gaudily dressed young woman who had stopped a well dressed gentleman. Caroline, following her sister's glance, leaned forward to see what had caught her interest. "This is a very unsavoury place to wait," said Louisa, drawing the curtain quickly. "We ought to have gone with Colonel Fitzwilliam. We are losing precious time here."

"Come, Louisa," said Caroline. "You are not improving the situation by complaining, for we can do nothing now but wait. I for one," said Caroline, "am grateful to Colonel Fitzwilliam for exerting so much effort on our behalf. I am sure he will return as soon as he can. But I must admit that my throat feels rather parched, and a light nuncheon, if it could be found, would do very well."

"Your wish is my command, Miss Bingley," said Mr Darcy, overhearing her. He was standing outside, leaning on the carriage door, and surveying the scene around him with interest. "It will not be possible to command a private parlour in the inn, I suspect, but I am sure *something* can be arranged."

He disappeared into the crowd. Louisa immediately began to vent her spleen, blaming Mr Darcy for everything. "This is entirely his fault," she declared. "If he had not insisted on taking the Great North Road, we would not have been in this situation. We should never have agreed to be guided by a foreigner. Anyone else would have known about the Nottingham Goose Fair."

Caroline forbore from pointing out that none of them, including Colonel Fitzwilliam, had known anything about it, although they should have anticipated there would be a fair somewhere along the road, since October was traditionally the month for fairs. Eventually Louisa, having uttered her opinion of Mr Darcy in no uncertain terms, fell into silence. But since she did not receive the satisfaction of anyone to agree with her views, she remained sullen.

Robert Darcy was absent for so long, however, that Louisa bestirred herself to peep carefully out of the window from behind the curtain. "I wonder what has become of Mr Darcy," she remarked. "No doubt the revelry has proved too tempting for him, and he has joined in, forgetting all about us. It is only to be expected, for I am sure I do not know many gentlemen who could resist a cockfight. Poor Mr Hurst would not have missed a cockfight for the world, for he was very fond of them." She sat back. "Oh, I am quite out of patience! I wish we had not come."

Caroline controlled the urge to snap at her sister, for it would only have made their position more uncomfortable.

"This is what comes of relying for our comfort on an upstart," continued Louisa. "One cannot expect him to do things right."

"Enough, Louisa," said Caroline, finally losing all patience. "You are going too far. Mr Darcy is trying his best to help." She rose and pushed back the curtain. "I prefer to have some light," she said, firmly. "We cannot cower here in the dark."

Louisa peered out of the window. "They ought to ban such things," she said. "They are a great inconvenience to everybody."

"Well, they are certainly an inconvenience to us," said Caroline. "But I would think they are very useful for the farmers who have geese to sell."

Louisa threw her a sceptical glance.

Just then a large wagon with mawkish colours rumbled past them. The bright colours were clearly designed to attract the eye. The flap of the wagon was up, and a woman with enormous girth stood before them, staring out onto the crowded road. Her arms were as large as tree trunks, and her shoulders almost spanned the width of the wagon. Caroline had never been to a fair, but she had heard accounts of it, and she was delighted to realize that the large person before her was what they called a Fat Lady.

The Fat Lady caught her watching and winked. Caroline, not sure how to respond, turned away, but her eye was drawn again to that large form, and she found the Fat Lady smiling broadly, revealing an uneven row of black teeth with several gaps where the teeth were missing.

"Come visit me at the fair," cried the Fat Lady, waving at Caroline.

"It might be interesting to visit a fair," said Caroline, wistfully, as the wagon rolled on by.

Louisa snorted. "I have never liked fairs."

"You have never been to a fair," said Caroline, remembering her own childhood when she had longed to go to a village fair but had been chastised. Her mother had made it clear that fairs were set up for the enjoyment of coarse minded people who only needed an excuse for revelry and thieving.

"Yes, and I am glad to say it, for they are nothing but excuses for revelry and thieving."

Caroline examined her sister to see if she was joking, but her lips were pursed and she radiated disapproval.

Caroline could not help being amused. "Do you know, Louisa, Mama used to say exactly that."

Louisa frowned. "I am not surprised, for anyone with any claim to gentility would say the same."

Caroline's reply was interrupted as Mr Darcy emerged from the inn, striding purposefully towards them. Behind him were two footmen, carrying with them trays filled with a variety of cold meats and pies.

"Oh, Mr Darcy!" exclaimed Louisa, as he opened the door. "You are so clever!"

"Nuncheon is served," he said, bowing.

Caroline's mouth watered at the sight of food. "I am very thankful, I must say. I had not thought you would return so soon." she said. "Though I admit I have never eaten in a carriage before. I have taken lemonade, of course, but this will be my first experience with food."

"But that cannot be," said Mr Darcy. "Surely you have been to Gunter's?"

Louisa twittered. "That is not quite the same," she said, "since Gunter's only serves ices and confections."

"We can start a new tradition," said Mr Darcy.

Mr Darcy himself ate outside, as was also the custom at Gunter's. Caroline thought of the quiet elegance of Berkeley Square and, comparing it with their present surroundings, smiled. "Well, it is rather strange to be doing this here," said Caroline. "But I cannot say I dislike the idea."

Louisa grimaced, licking gravy awkwardly from her chin as it trickled down from a piece of pie. "I cannot say I like it. But I am learning not to expect the conventional from Mr Darcy, so I must be resigned." She bit into the pie again, however, with every appearance of enjoyment.

The dishes and the trays having been removed, Caroline realized she was growing cramped in the enclosed carriage. She envied Robert Darcy, who had finished eating and drifted away.

"I would like to take a turn around," she said. "I need some air."

"Surely not, Caroline! You cannot!" protested Louisa.

Caroline opened the carriage door and stepped out, calling out to Mr Darcy, who came towards her.

"Is it not vastly entertaining?" he said.

"I would not go quite that far, Mr Darcy," said Caroline, "but I think a short walk would do me good."

"What do you think, Mrs Hurst? Would you too like a walk? I would be happy to accompany you."

Louisa replied that nothing would induce her to walk among such an unruly mass of people. And she remarked, in an ominous undertone to Caroline, that she did not think *Sir Cecil* would approve of her behaviour at all.

Caroline, flushing deeply, threw a quick glance to see Robert Darcy's reaction to her sister's remark. But he was moving away and had not heard.

The cockfight was the biggest attraction of the day, and it was there that most of the crowd congregated, but an assortment of people heading to the fair were passing through town on their way, which gave Caroline the opportunity to experience some of the excitement of the fair without the great inconvenience of the crowds.

A hawker descended from his cart and opened a gigantic bag, displaying ribbons, laces, frills, and combs. Caroline had no interest in what he had to sell, but his vivacious character, and the way women flocked around him, diverted her, so that she stood watching. When Robert Darcy offered to buy her some ribbons, she did not object, and laughed at the hawker's clever attempts to sell her more.

Then there was a fortune teller, who had set up a bender tent in the square.

"Shall we have our fortunes told?" said Mr Darcy.

Caroline hesitated. The idea frightened her, and the sight of the fortune teller herself, who came to the entrance and beckoned her, did nothing to allay her fear. The fortune teller was a tall, buxom woman, with enormous blue eyes and long tresses of thick black hair, but there was something about her commanding presence and piercing eyes that made Caroline uncomfortable. However, before she could protest, Robert Darcy had guided her to the tent. Caroline entered, passing through a curtain of strung beads, and sat on a small carpeted stool opposite the woman before her. The light was dim, and there was a haze of perfumed smoke in the tent, but Caroline could see the fortune teller clearly. The black-haired woman grasped her hand and inspected the palm, tracing the lines with her fingers.

"You must lose yourself to find yourself," said the gypsy woman, in a matter-of-fact tone. "Only then will you find happiness."

Caroline waited for more, but the woman rose and pulled aside the bead curtain. The fortune telling was at an end. Completely dissatisfied, Caroline emerged from the tent, thinking that even the smallest coin in payment was wasted.

"So, did she promise you marriage and a dozen children?" asked Mr Darcy, his eyes twinkling.

"No, she did not," retorted Caroline, wondering why she should care about the fortune teller's words. "She promised me nothing. Her fortune telling was nothing but a hoax."

Robert Darcy laughed. "On the contrary! If she had wished to hoax you, she would have promised you the world, and then you would have been well satisfied."

But Caroline remained discontented, and lost interest in the bustle around them. "We ought to return to my sister," said Caroline. "She will be worrying."

⁂

When they returned to the carriage they discovered that Colonel Fitzwilliam had preceded them.

"Where have you been, Caroline?" said Louisa. "Colonel Fitzwilliam has been waiting for an age. It was ill considered of you to disappear like that."

"It was entirely my fault," said Mr Darcy, chivalrously taking the blame. "It was I who induced Miss Bingley to have her fortune told. But we have returned now, safe and sound."

Louisa sniffed but did not comment further. Colonel Fitzwilliam looked grave. "I hope you have not exposed Miss Bingley to some of the more unpleasant sights to be found at a fairground," he remarked.

"No indeed," said Caroline, her voice sharper than she would have wished. "I have spent an agreeable time, and that is all there is to it."

Her sharp tone did not escape Colonel Fitzwilliam, who must have realized that his remark had not found favour in her eyes. "My apologies, Miss Bingley. I had not meant to suggest anything improper in your behaviour. I admit I view country fairs with disfavour, and I would prefer them be far less frivolous. But enough of that. I have good news. The Loughs are quite delighted to receive us all, and have extended an invitation for us to stay as long as we wish. As it turned out, our arrival is fortunately timed. They are having a house party, and have a dance arranged for tonight, and several other entertainments for the next few days, so we can be sure of enjoying a pleasant stay."

"Which is just as well," said Louisa. "Since Colonel Fitzwilliam has informed me that the fair will last around eight days. So we have little choice but to remain."

"I think the roads will be more passable in three or four days, when everyone is at the fair. We should leave then," said Colonel Fitzwilliam. "If we wait until the fair is over, we will encounter the crowds returning home."

Caroline could not feel comfortable with the idea of imposing on people they did not know, especially when they were holding a house party and had many other guests to entertain. But Colonel Fitzwilliam assured her that they were very kind, and felt no hardship at all in including their party among the house guests, though he warned her she might be obliged to share a room with Mrs Hurst.

"That would be no problem at all," she hastened to say. "I hope nobody will have to be moved for our sake."

"Mr Darcy and I, perhaps, will be sent to sleep in the stables," he said, with a smile. "But that will be no inconvenience to anyone, I am sure."

"*You* may sleep in the stables, Fitzwilliam," replied Mr Darcy. "But I will sleep in the great outdoors, with the stars above me and the ground beneath."

"Now *that* is romantic fustian," said Caroline. "I would think it would be vastly uncomfortable."

"As a soldier who has seen some campaigning," said Colonel Fitzwilliam, "I can assure you it is more than uncomfortable. I would not do it willingly if I had any other choice."

Mr Darcy sighed. "Very well, Fitzwilliam, I will sleep with you and the horses for company."

They set out in good spirits, and in no time at all, they came to a halt outside Emelton Hall, the Lough country residence. Louisa, in particular, was excited at the prospect of a dance, though she could not participate because of her mourning. Caroline seemed to be alone in feeling a churning of unease as they descended to meet their hosts. She did not take easily to strangers, for there was always an element of uncertainty in meeting someone new. One never knew quite where one stood.

She could not like the scheme. But she was glad for the shelter, and, with that in mind, she cast aside her misgivings, and prepared herself to make the best of a situation she had not chosen.

Chapter 4

THE LOUGHS GAVE EVERY APPEARANCE OF WELCOMING THEM. Mr Lough was a tall, slender man in his late twenties. His wife, by contrast, was quite short and inclined towards plumpness. She was very animated and playful, and with small blue twinkling eyes.

"I very much fear we must be *de trop*," said Caroline, "especially when you have so many guests to entertain already."

"Oh, no," replied Mrs Lough. "The more the merrier. I love nothing more than entertaining, and I am very fortunate in my husband, for he is much inclined to indulge me."

The clear affection between the couple put her immediately at ease, and as she went upstairs to the small room she was assigned— thankfully not with Louisa—she focused her attention on the dance that evening. Her first problem was simple: how to appear to best advantage when the case she had brought on the carriage did not contain a ball gown. Fortunately, she brought with her a formal evening dress, though it was by no means splendid. With that resolved, she found herself facing a larger problem. They had arrived too late to attend dinner, and she had no idea of the type of people she was to encounter in the ballroom, or if, in fact, she knew any of them. ·

Thus she was filled with nervous anticipation when she left her room to descend the stairs with as much composure as she could muster.

The moment Caroline stepped into the ballroom, however, her confidence returned. She knew so many faces there, she need not fear any unpleasant surprises. Her status was well established and she did not have to be on her guard.

Louisa had arrived ahead of her, and was engaged in conversation with a married lady distantly related to Mr Hurst. Caroline noted with some amusement that her sister was wearing one of her half-mourning lavender gowns.

She felt particularly at an advantage when she spotted Robert Darcy standing alone in a corner, speaking to nobody. She would introduce him, of course. She was not obliged to do so, but she was prepared to be courteous, since she knew so many people who were present. But she would do so carefully, without suggesting in any way that, simply because he had arrived with them, he was perfectly acceptable in their circle.

With that purpose in mind, she weaved her way through the ballroom to where he stood. He grinned when he saw her.

"I am quite flattered, Miss Bingley. I see you cannot stay away from me. You have crossed the whole ballroom to stand next to me," he said, arrogantly playful. He was elegantly dressed, his black coat beautifully tailored, and his cravat tied in a graceful though unfamiliar knot.

"Not at all, Mr Darcy," she replied. "I came in this direction with a specific purpose in mind, which is to introduce you. I am well acquainted with many people in the room, and you will find that they move in the best circles."

He bowed. "I admit that I was deceived in you, Miss Bingley. I would have thought you would have been quite content to leave me to wilt away in a corner, completely bereft of company."

Really, he was quite ridiculous. She bestowed a cool smile on him, and, placing her arm delicately on his offered elbow, she steered him in the direction of a large, red-faced gentleman in old-fashioned breeches.

"Mr Olmstead. May I present—"

"Mr Robert Darcy! We have met. How are you, my boy? Miss Bingley, delighted to see you again."

"You are acquainted with Mr Darcy?" said Caroline, taken aback, for she could not imagine how they could have met.

"Of course. We have hunted together. Capital shot, you know. I suppose that comes of having a military man for a father, don't you think?" Slapping Robert Darcy on the shoulder, he opened his snuff box and offered him some snuff.

"No thank you," said Robert Darcy. "I am not accustomed to taking snuff."

Mr Olmstead's nostrils flared as he breathed in the snuff, first into one nostril, then the other. "Your loss, my boy. This is a particularly good mix. First class, I tell you. Especially now that, thanks to the Laurencekirk hinge, I'm able to keep the snuff dry even in the dampest weather. Best way to keep snuff, I can assure you. Had the box sent down to me from Scotland, you know."

"I am glad to hear it, sir," said Robert Darcy.

"Is Mrs Olmstead here?" enquired Caroline.

"Yes, yes. She's here somewhere." He waved a large hand vaguely round the room. "She'll be delighted to see you."

Caroline tugged discreetly at the corner of Robert Darcy's sleeve. He excused himself politely and moved away.

"Why do I feel so much like a pet poodle that you are showing around?"

She continued to move forward without turning to him. "You are certainly very far from being a pet poodle," she said, calmly. "Pet poodles are very carefully groomed, Mr Darcy."

"Do you wish to undertake my grooming, then, Miss Bingley?"

Caroline wished she could hiss, but it was unladylike. On occasions like this, she disliked the rules of etiquette imposed on her.

"Ah, there we are. I can see Mrs Olmstead over there by the window," she said, instead.

But they never reached Mrs Olmstead. A gentleman she did not know approached them. Robert Darcy introduced him as Mr Forthe.

"Delighted to meet you, Miss Bingley. May I have the honour of next dance?"

"Er…" She paused, since she knew nothing about the gentleman. She waited for a signal from Robert Darcy, who knew him better. But a glance at Mr Darcy proved completely unhelpful.

"Thank you," she said, allowing herself to be led away by someone she knew nothing about.

She was to be equally embarrassed at the end of the dance when Mr Forthe, leading her back quite properly to Robert Darcy, was puzzled to find he had disappeared.

"No doubt he has gone to fetch me a drink," said Miss Bingley, though she thought it very unlikely. Most probably he had forgotten all about her and had gone to the card room. She hoped he would lose a great deal of money. "I will wait for him here."

"Then I leave you in good hands, Miss Bingley," said Mr Forthe, bowing and moving away.

She stood for a moment where he left her, as if she really did, in fact, expect Robert Darcy to suddenly appear. Just as she was about to move off, satisfied that she had done what she could to keep up appearances, however, she discovered him coming in her direction. He was carrying two glasses, and accompanied by a gentleman who looked vaguely familiar.

"I thought you might like some sherry, Miss Bingley," he said.

"How kind of you, Mr Darcy," she said, with exquisite politeness. "Thank you. I normally drink ratafia, but I do not dislike sherry."

"I'm afraid you have me to blame, Miss Bingley," said his companion. "Darcy was sure you would like ratafia, but I prevailed upon him to bring you sherry."

She wanted to reply, but she could not recall the gentleman's name. She glanced enquiringly at Mr Darcy. This time he came to the rescue. "I believe you are acquainted with Mr Richard Pole. He is a good friend of mine," he said. "We live on adjoining properties in Derbyshire."

Mr Pole had an engaging personality, and he soon had Caroline laughing as he recounted the behaviour of a cousin of his who aspired to be a Corinthian.

"…and the worst of it," he said, "was that he was boasting to Darcy, who is already well known to be a Corinthian of the very best order."

"Darcy?" she asked, puzzled, for she had not conceived of him as a sporting gentleman.

"He means me," said Robert Darcy. "Although, of course, he exaggerates."

"Of course I meant you," said Pole, looking puzzled in turn. "Who else? And I do not exaggerate. He is a regular out and outer and a top-sawyer, and has the best science of any man in my acquaintance."

Robert Darcy laughed. "I do not think Miss Bingley understood a word of that cant of yours," he said. "And I do believe she thought you meant my cousin, Fitzwilliam Darcy."

"I see," said Pole. "Yes, Fitzwilliam Darcy is an exemplary gentleman. One of the best," he said, "but I would not call him a Corinthian." He excused himself suddenly. "Sorry, I have to make my escape. My mother's coming this way, intending no doubt to introduce me to some chit barely out of the schoolroom." He slid deftly into the thickest part of the crowd, his mother chasing after him.

Robert Darcy laughed. "Amazing things, mothers. Especially when they are determined to marry you off."

"Well, your mother is too far away now to pursue you."

"Precisely. Why do you think I am in England and not in Boston?"

"Come, Mr Darcy, do not tell me you have come all the way to England to escape your mother."

"No, I cannot pretend that, though she was certainly trotting out the heiresses for me. At least here I do not have to endure all that." His face darkened. "Though if I had known it would be so difficult to go back, I would have gladly endured it a little longer."

He caught sight of her sombre expression, and lifted his eyebrows. "One should never talk seriously in a ballroom," he said, lightly. "Is that not somewhere in the etiquette books? Ballrooms are for dancing. Yet here I am, with a young lady who is accounted a beauty in Town—or so I have heard—and all I have done is prattle. May I engage you for the next set, Miss Bingley? After you have finished your sherry, of course."

Caroline resented his reference to her sister's foolish remark. She was about to refuse, but if she did, she would be forced to sit out the set. Then again, part of her was curious to see how well Mr Darcy could dance. She put down the sherry, her glass still half full.

"I would be delighted," she said.

The next moment, however, she regretted her acceptance. Her number was called to lead the set. She wished ardently she did not have to dance with Mr Darcy, for she did not know his style at all, did not even know whether he was a tolerable dancer.

"You hesitate, Miss Bingley," he said. "If you would rather not lead the set, or if you find dancing too tiring, we could perhaps withdraw and sit it out."

"That *would* be against the rules of etiquette, Mr Darcy," she said, rising immediately to the challenge. Prompted by the spirit of mischief, and perhaps wishing to show him the superiority of her dancing—and the excellence of her dancing masters—she chose a figure that was complicated and demanding. She ignored the slight ripple that went down the line once she announced the steps, and applied herself grimly to the reel.

But it was one thing to dance this figure in the safety of a small room, where only the dancing master and her chaperon watched, and where she could sit down when she grew tired, and something completely different here, with everyone watching expectantly. And if she had thought to catch out Robert Darcy, she quickly discovered her mistake. He not only executed the steps perfectly, but he danced with a vigour she was required to complement, as his partner.

Every eye was upon them, since they were setting the pace, and her pride drove her to match her skill to his, as if it was not a dance at all, but an act of defiance. She rarely danced so energetically, and with anyone else, she would have chosen a much simpler form. Exhilaration seized her. He was light and nimble. She was light and nimble, too, countering his steps with hers, positively flying off the ground. Her heart began to beat fast, and her breathing grew laboured. Robert Darcy, however, remained at ease, as relaxed as if they were dancing a minuet.

By the time they reached the bottom of the line and were able to stop, her side had started to ache.

"You are a very skilled dancer," said Mr Darcy to her, now that they had some moments to stand still and catch their breath. "I admit, you did not strike me as the type to enjoy a reel."

"I enjoy dancing generally," said Caroline, as briefly as she could. He was right, of course. She did not particularly enjoy a reel. Then she realized it was *not* true. For in some strange way, she was enjoying this one.

"I am glad, then, that I was able to partner you when you were leading the set. If someone else had been leading, and they had chosen an insipid dance, I would never have discovered this hidden talent of yours."

There was that gleam in his eye again, and she could not tell if he was mocking her or complimenting her. The best method of defence, she thought, was surprise. "And I would never have discovered how sure-footed you were, Mr Darcy," she said.

He had not expected a compliment. He examined her, suspicious of her meaning. She turned away slightly, to hide the small smile that hovered on her lips. But before either of them could say anything more it was time for them to lead again.

Once again, she threw herself into a whirl of movement. Beads of perspiration gathered on her brow, and under her dress her skin grew damp. She had known young ladies who dampened their petticoats to make the thin material cling to their forms. She would not have to do so. The idea made her smile. Opposite her, Robert Darcy grinned, as though he knew what she was thinking, and she flushed at the unruly direction of her thoughts.

When the music finally stopped she was left grasping for breath. But there was one more dance to go. She would have liked to slow the pace a little and introduce something simpler, but it would have seemed odd. So once again, she chose a complicated form and, once again, she struggled to hold her own against Mr Darcy, who danced like a demented dancing master, but remained cool as a cucumber, completely indifferent to the looks that were being sent his way.

The moment the second dance ended, she fled to take refuge in the ladies' retiring room. She hesitated before looking into the mirror, dreading what she would see there. If anything, she looked worse than she had imagined. She stared at the tendrils of hair that had tumbled from beneath her turban, at the sheen that covered her face and at blotches of colour that tainted her cheeks. It was as if they belonged to someone else. She looked like a hoyden, not at all like Miss Caroline Bingley.

This would not do at all. She must put a stop to this folly. She had spent years at Mrs Drakehill's Seminary for Young Ladies learning how to become a lady. What would Mrs Drakehill say of her now?

It was her fault entirely. She *knew* that he was to be avoided. She *knew* his conduct was not quite what it should be. Yet she had allowed him to provoke her into dancing just a little too fast, skirting the edge of propriety, and leading the other couples in the dance to do the same.

A twitch of conscience intervened. Her own behaviour had hardly been ideal. She had abandoned him straight after the dance, without even excusing herself, leaving him stranded. That was hardly acceptable behaviour. He was, after all, a stranger to their society. And he was, in some way, her responsibility. It was her duty to guide him through the complex rules that governed polite conduct.

But when she emerged from the ladies' retiring room, her hair once more tucked in where it belonged, her face cooled to a delicate paleness, her dress smoothed down into stylish folds that no longer clung to her, he was nowhere to be found.

Her eyes searched the ballroom for several minutes before she perceived him. A very pretty lady in her early twenties was draped over his arm. She was talking to him excitedly, her ringlets swaying as she laughed. He seemed to know her well, and it was clear he enjoyed her company, for he patted her hand from time to time as he drew her to the dance area. They settled into the dance with familiar grace. It was a country dance, and every time they met they would chatter, then break apart.

"Excuse me, Miss Bingley." Caroline jumped as a voice to her side broke into her thoughts. It was Colonel Fitzwilliam. She hoped he had not noticed her observing Robert Darcy.

"This is a welcome break from riding in the carriage, is it not?"

She was very glad to return to polished conversation after that decidedly unsettling experience. She was so delighted to find herself on familiar ground, that she turned to Colonel Fitzwilliam with far more friendliness than she was accustomed to display.

"Indeed!" she said, smiling cordially. "Although I must confess I am a little tired."

"It is only to be expected. But I am glad that we have had this chance to stop on the way. It has added to my enjoyment of the journey. I am very fond of dancing."

"As am I. I am sure we will contrive to organize a dance in Pemberley, once we are there."

"Ah, if only I could be sure of that," he replied, with regret. "I do not think I will stay long enough. I may be forced to return to London."

"Surely not? You do not have any pressing engagements? You must stay for a few days at least. I am certain you will be more than welcome at Pemberley. Your cousin is very attached to you."

Colonel Fitzwilliam seemed pleased at her insistence. "Oh, my cousin likes me well enough," he said. "But I cannot forget the reason for our voyage. Mrs Darcy must be too unwell to receive visitors."

The familiar pang Caroline always felt when she heard that name threatened her composure for a moment. She did not imagine she could ever bring herself to like Elizabeth Bennet. "Perhaps," she said, trying to appear cheerful. "But after you have crossed such a distance to reach them, I hardly think you will be turned away!"

"Well, I am glad you think so, Miss Bingley. I am sure you would not permit it," he replied.

"Oh, I do not flatter myself that I have any influence with the Darcys," she said.

"I am sure you could not help being an influence," said Colonel Fitzwilliam, gallantly.

Caroline danced with the colonel then went in to supper with him. As the evening passed, the unfortunate reel receded into the background. But she could not help noticing that Robert Darcy danced with several young ladies, and seemed generally sought after.

She could not make up her mind if she was exasperated or relieved that she need not exert herself to introduce him.

Colonel Fitzwilliam proved to be a charming companion over supper. He went out of his way to amuse her, and paid her a number of compliments which were neither too extravagant nor too convoluted. As they returned to the ballroom and the orchestra prepared to begin playing again, they encountered Robert Darcy, who laughingly requested Caroline to save a dance for him, if possible.

"I am afraid they are all taken," said Caroline. She was not quite ready for another dance with him.

"In that case I will leave you to enjoy your evening," he replied, and, bowing, excused himself.

Colonel Fitzwilliam watched him go, then turned to her with an expression she could only describe as stern. "I would like to speak to you, if I may, Miss Bingley. I know it is hardly proper, but I wonder if you will accompany me into the garden. I have something in particular to speak about."

Caroline's brother Charles had known the colonel for years. She did not suspect for a moment that his conduct would be other than that of a gentleman, so she did not hesitate to agree to go into the darkened garden with him. And after the crowd and crush of the ballroom, the cool air outside would be very welcome.

No doubt he wished to warn her about Robert Darcy. She did not need the warning, of course, but she was curious as to what the colonel had to say about him. Perhaps he could tell her something specific. In any case, the colonel's opinion was more reliable than her brother's.

As soon as she stepped out, however, the cold hit her like a slap in the face. She had expected the day to cool off, but not so quickly. The breeze was light, but it had a sharp and bitter edge. The moon was hidden behind a cloud, but there were patches in the sky where the stars shone like tiny slithers of shattered glass. No one else was in the garden. It was madness to come out on such a frosty night. Such weather was a strong deterrent to outdoor trysts.

"Forgive me, Miss Bingley, for speaking plainly. I hope what I have to say will not cause any offence. If it does, I apologize in advance."

She inclined her head gracefully. "I beg you, Colonel Fitzwilliam, there is no need for apology. I know that your concern for me prompts you."

He seized her hand. "Yes. You have guessed it exactly, Miss Bingley—Caroline."

His behaviour seemed excessive, and Caroline was not sure she liked his use of her first name. She hoped he did not take her permission to advise her as an invitation to familiarity. She pulled her hand away stiffly.

"I have a very high regard for you, as you know," he said, looking embarrassed at his lapse. "Otherwise I would not have approached you as I am doing now."

His insistence on telling her this seemed very long winded. She gazed longingly at the ballroom. The bitter cold seemed to be seeping into her very bones.

He searched for the right words. What could be so offensive that he hesitated so much? Caroline wished fervently he would come to the point. Perhaps he thought her an innocent schoolgirl who would be shocked by what he had to say about Mr Darcy. She braced herself for something quite scandalous.

Meanwhile, her fingers were growing numb. She could see her own breath, outlined in grey against the dark night sky.

"The fact is, I have long admired you, and thought you a model of propriety," he said.

He really was taking an interminably long time. She wished she had thought to bring a shawl, or a spencer. Or a blanket. A blanket was just what she needed.

Her hands were turning numb as well.

"I have always endeavoured to act in a proper manner," she responded.

Her teeth were beginning to chatter.

"There has long been friendship between your brother and I, and I have met you on so many occasions even when you were still in the schoolroom. So I feel as though I have known you for years."

By now she was shivering in earnest. She tried to close her mouth so that the loud hammering of her teeth did not interrupt Colonel

Fitzwilliam. She did not want to appear ungrateful, for he was, after all, trying to warn her. She had never thought of him as inclined to beat about the bush. He had always seemed direct and articulate. This laboured prelude was quite disappointing. Why did he not come out directly and warn her about Mr Robert Darcy? It showed an unexpected weakness of character. She was not happy to discover it out here in the cold, in short sleeves, in a thin muslin dress that offered no protection.

But apart from taking his arm and pulling him in the direction of the ballroom, she could not think of a way to interrupt his earnest discourse without appearing quite ill-mannered.

The numbness was moving up to her elbow. Idly, she wondered what happened to people's arms if they froze.

"Yes, it does seem so, does it not?" she said, trying to prod him on, since he had now fallen into silence. "I believe, in fact, that we have known each other at least for five years now."

With his foot, he pushed away some pebbles that lined the pathway. He was looking so intently at the ground that Caroline wondered if he had discovered something of interest there. She waited.

Finally, he looked up. "The fact is…" Again he paused.

She was going to die. She was going to turn into a block of ice and fall flat on the ground, straight in front of him. There would be a scandal. Everyone would know she had accompanied him into the garden alone.

"The fact is," he said, a note of resolve entering his voice. He stepped towards her and looked her in the eye. Here it was, finally. She no longer cared what he had to say about Mr Darcy. She just wanted to return to the ballroom.

"I was wondering if you would do me the honour of granting me your hand in marriage."

Caroline stared at him, stunned. For a brief moment she forgot about the numbness in her arms. Of all the things in the world, she had not expected this. Colonel Fitzwilliam? Asking if she would marry him?

She tried to think straight. But her knees were shaking with cold and she could no longer feel her feet at all in their thin silk slippers. There he was, however, awaiting her answer expectantly.

Thankfully, her tongue was not frozen, so surely she could say something? Caroline tried, but her lips were so stiff she was afraid they would crack. "Urrgh…" she began.

It would not do. He had done her a singular honour. She must somehow make her lips move.

To her relief, they responded to her effort.

"I thank you, sir, for the honour you have done me." The words were a little slurred. She hoped he would not take offence, for it was not intentional. "I have always had a very high opinion of you, Colonel Fitzwilliam."

He was waiting for something else. She struggled in a half-frozen fog to find clarity. "This is all rather unexpected." She had never known how difficult it was to speak with teeth clattering against each other. "I hope you will grant me some time before I give you an answer."

He was disappointed, she could tell, but bowed with all the good grace she would have expected of him. "Certainly, Miss Bingley. There is no hurry, of course. I would not presume to press you for an answer."

"Thank you," she said. At last, they were returning. She took his offered arm and walked with him, holding in check the impulse to rush headlong into the welcome warmth.

They had almost reached the doors when Colonel Fitzwilliam stopped abruptly and turned towards her. "When I received the letter from your brother inviting me to join your party on its journey to Pemberley, I assumed you were behind the invitation. I took it as a form of encouragement, since I showed you a marked interest when I last saw you in London. Was I mistaken?"

Caroline blinked. Such a thing had simply not occurred to her. She had never thought for a moment that he nourished a tendre for her. She cast her mind back to her time in London, and could barely remember his presence.

"I am sorry," she said, ruefully. "I was unaware—" Then, realizing how that would sound, she rephrased her sentence. "I had thought you merely chivalrous, as you generally are. I did not think your attention was aimed particularly at me."

He took up her arm again, considering her words. They walked. The warmth of the ballroom drew closer, now within reach, and she stared at the candlelight as if that alone would be enough to sustain her.

Colonel Fitzwilliam stopped again. "But in that case, why extend the invitation to me in particular? Why not to anyone else you are acquainted with? Sir Cecil Rynes, for example. He is a good friend of yours and your brother's, is he not?"

His mention of Sir Cecil was too close to the mark to be pure coincidence.

"It would be more appropriate to ask my brother that question, since it was he who penned the letter," she replied, skirting the truth just a little. "Perhaps he thought you would enjoy the chance to see your cousin."

She started to walk again, because she could no longer stand still. He followed after her.

"You will give my proposal serious consideration?" he said.

It was her turn to stop. "Yes, of course. Why would you think I would not?"

He shrugged. "I had thought that you felt some partiality to me when I made it, but now it appears I am mistaken."

She linked her arm in his and drew him towards the vitality of the ballroom. "I will give very serious consideration to your proposal," she said, able now that they reached the French doors to throw a smile at him. Even at the risk of cracking her lips.

They stepped in.

The warmth flowed towards her and enveloped her.

"Oh, there you are!" cried Louisa, emerging from the crush of people. She had clearly been watching the doors, although Caroline had scarcely spoken to her all evening. "I was worried about you. I saw you disappear into the garden some time ago. I was about to send Robert Darcy after you." She threw an accusing glance at Colonel Fitzwilliam.

"I assure you," said Colonel Fitzwilliam, "she was perfectly safe with me."

"Of course," said Louisa. "I did not mean to imply otherwise."

Colonel Fitzwilliam gave a deep bow and excused himself. "Now that I have delivered you safely to your sister, I hope you will excuse me."

Louisa restrained herself until he was out of earshot. "What were you thinking?" she hissed. "How could you go out into the garden for so long alone with a gentleman?"

"Well, well," said an all too familiar voice. "Who would have thought it? Miss Bingley alone in the dark with a gentleman. Tut tut." Robert Darcy shook his head disapprovingly.

Caroline threw him a murderous glance. The effect was destroyed, however, by the fact that her teeth, for some odd reason, were still chattering, even though she was inside. Robert Darcy's expression switched to one of concern.

"You are blue with cold," he said. "You did not go out without a shawl, surely? There is frost on the ground." Despite his words, there was no condemnation in his tone. "Mrs Hurst, your sister has taken a chill. Would you be so kind as to bring down a shawl from her room to wrap around her? I will take her to the library, to warm her by the fire."

The sense of urgency in his voice forestalled any protest and sent Louisa hastily from the ballroom. Robert Darcy took Caroline's arm firmly and led her through the mass of bodies into the calm of the corridor, then to the library. At the doorway, she drew back.

"I should not be alone with you here."

"Nonsense," he said. "You need a warm fire."

"Nevertheless, Mr Darcy, I have no desire to be caught in an inappropriate situation."

"Surely," he said, "you do not suspect me of planning to take advantage of you?"

"No," she said, trying to sound haughty. "However, we are surrounded by people who know me, who will love the tiniest whiff of scandal. They will not care that you were warming me because I am cold. They will only see that we are alone."

"You would rather catch your death of a cold, I take it!" His voice was heavy with impatience.

But when she would not budge, he blew out a resigned breath.

"Very well," he said. "Stand here in the doorway. That should be safe enough. I will ring for a servant." He pulled the bell, and within a few minutes a footman had appeared.

"What is your name?" said Darcy.

"Daniel, sir."

"Well, then, Daniel. You are needed to provide respectability for Miss Bingley. She has taken a chill and needs to stay by the fire."

"Very well, sir."

Caroline still delayed. "I am not so very sure that the problem is resolved."

But the fire beckoned and lured her. Robert Darcy pulled an armchair for her very close to it and she sat down, extending her legs to allow the welcome heat to seep in.

She sat up in alarm as pain shot through her.

"Something is wrong," she gasped. "My hands and feet…"

"It is nothing to worry about," said Robert Darcy. "It will pass. It is only the sensation returning to you as you begin to unthaw."

"It cannot be…"

"It is like the ice breaking and melting on the surface of a pond," he said, soothingly. "It will pass."

The pain claimed her attention, and she did not wonder at his words. Slowly the pain subsided, and with it came warmth. It was heavenly, after the torment of the cold, and as the heat from the fire soaked into her body she allowed a sleepy drowsiness to overtake her. She leaned back her head and closed her eyes.

Her sister's voice woke her. Louisa was holding out the shawl. Robert Darcy took the shawl and arranged it carefully around her. For a moment the image of her mother tucking her into her bed came to her. Mama used to draw the sheets around her just the same way he had. She smiled drowsily and snuggled more comfortably under the cover.

"You do not think she will fall sick, do you?" she heard Louisa ask anxiously. "Our cousin Maria was carried away by the muslin disease a few years ago from venturing out in the cold without a spencer."

She wanted to tell Louisa that she was perfectly fine, but a heavy lethargy prevented her. Robert Darcy's voice came from a great distance. "It is possible, if she stays warm and takes enough rest tonight, that she may be perfectly well tomorrow. But we must take all possible precautions. Would you be so good as to order some hot broth to be taken up to her room?"

Her last thought was that she ought to warn Louisa not to leave them alone.

Chapter 5

THE NEXT MORNING CAROLINE AWOKE WHEN A SUNBEAM, escaping from a gap in the heavy curtains surrounding her, found its way onto her face and slipped between her eyelids. She was surprised to find that she was in her own bed. Someone must have carried her upstairs last night while she was asleep. Vague memories floated back to her: the resolute voice of her sister, then that of Mr Darcy requesting the footman to carry her. Her vision fell on her shawl, draped now over the side of the chair.

Propping herself up against a cushion, she checked for any signs of a chill. Everything felt perfectly ordinary. Nothing indicated that anything untoward had occurred the night before, not even a sniffle. She had suffered no ill effects from her foolish interval in the cold, after all.

Thanks, of course, to Robert Darcy. She was under an obligation to him. His quick thinking had saved her from certain illness.

She could not forget, of course, that she was in his debt in that other matter as well. But she did not wish to return to *that* painful memory. Even now it was still raw.

Caroline turned her thoughts instead to Colonel Fitzwilliam. He had certainly picked an unfortunate time and place to ask for her hand in marriage. His timing could not have been worse. That alone would have been enough to prejudice her against accepting his proposal.

She strove to consider the situation rationally. She should not refuse him, simply because he had chosen a bitingly cold night to speak to her. It was October, after all, and one did not expect frost in October. Besides, she liked Colonel Fitzwilliam well enough. He would make a good-natured husband without being too demanding. He was the younger son of an earl, which was undoubtedly in his favour. He was a friend of the family, and cousin to Mr Darcy. All these were strong points in his favour. He was penniless, and made no secret of it, which was not in his favour, though, as an officer in the army, if he were to fight against Napoleon, it could mean substantial prize money and chances for promotion. Besides, with a portion of £20,000, she did not need to marry for money.

All in all, it was a proposal she would do well to consider seriously, and she wished now she had been more encouraging last night. If it had not been for that pestering cold!

However, truth be told, what seemed an advantage could often be a disadvantage. He was an officer, yes. But there was no end to the war in sight. He could be sent to the Peninsula at any moment. She might marry him, and then spend years on end waiting for him to come home on leave, or worrying that he would not return at all. He might even die in battle, and she would become a widow without having experienced any of the advantages of marriage.

And then, of course, there was Sir Cecil Rynes, who had not yet asked for her hand, even though he had paid her marked attention when she was last in London three months ago. She would have no hesitation accepting Sir Cecil. But what if she had been mistaken in his intentions?

Her mind in a whirl, she floundered. She could not decide. Colonel Fitzwilliam would have to wait for his answer.

Meanwhile, her gaze landed on the shawl draped over the side of the chair, and she could not help but think of its warmth when Robert Darcy set the shawl around her shoulders.

When she made her way downstairs to the breakfast room, she discovered from one of the other guests, Mrs Germain, that a large party had already set out to ride to hounds.

"If you had come down just half an hour ago, you would have been able to go with them," remarked Mrs Germain. "Though I admit I have no great love of the hunt myself."

"As for me," said Caroline, "I would as soon miss it as not."

"Miss what?" asked Robert Darcy from the doorway.

"I was just explaining to Miss Bingley that the hunting party has already left," said Mrs Germain.

Caroline seized the chance to pay him back in his own coin.

"I would have thought a Corinthian like you would be the first to join in the hunt."

"It depends, naturally, on what that Corinthian was doing the night before. Perhaps, for example, he was *nursing* a headache, and was unable to rise early enough," he replied, leaning on the doorframe.

Caroline wished now she had not tried to taunt him. It was a poor way to repay his kindness. But she could not retreat now.

"Then you will have to suffer the consequences. You have no choice but to spend the day with the ladies," she said.

"No gentleman could possibly object to spending his time with the ladies," said Mrs Germain. "Provided they are stimulating company, of course. Which means young and pretty, like Miss Bingley here, and not ladies of a certain age, like me."

"Oh, but they must be witty and entertaining as well," he replied immediately. "Though why you malign yourself, Mrs Germain," he continued, "I do not know. You are well aware that you are stimulating company. Why, you are the best chess player of my acquaintance, and I am always eager to match my wits to yours."

Mrs Germain laughed. Her laugh was a loud rumble, and filled her whole body, so that it shook from top to bottom, from her rouged cheeks to the tips of her buckled shoes.

"You flatter me, Mr Darcy, indeed you flatter me. You are a sharp player, there's no doubt of that. But I would certainly love to match my wits to yours, if you will spare the time. However, I would not like you to neglect the younger ladies to humour an old one like me."

"You need not worry, Mrs Germain," he said. "Do you think me incapable of enjoying both? You seriously underestimate me."

Mrs Germain's body shook again. "Oh, I would never do that, Mr Darcy. I am sure you are more than capable." She came nimbly to her feet. "I will hold you to it, Mr Darcy. You must prove your worth. I will be waiting for a chess game."

He moved away from the doorway and bowed as she passed him. Once Mrs Germain had left, he drew out a chair and sat close to Caroline.

"I am glad to see you are in full bloom today," he said, searching her face closely. "There are no consequences from yesterday's chill?"

"No, none at all," she replied. She swallowed her pride and ploughed on. "I would like to thank you—"

"Oh, do not, please, Miss Bingley. I did nothing except make sure you were kept warm. You must remember I was raised in a much harsher climate than England. The winters can be ruthless in Boston, and I have seen the consequences of exposure to the cold once or twice. It is not something I would care to repeat."

"Nevertheless, you rescued me from my own foolishness. Not only did I go out into the garden alone with a gentleman, which was cause enough for reproach, but I did not even think to dress appropriately. You may laugh, but I should have known better. I lost a young cousin of mine to muslin disease a few years ago. She was foolish enough to think herself indestructible, and went about in the thinnest muslin no matter what the weather. Like many young ladies at that time, since it was the fashion, she was taken seriously ill. If only I had fetched the shawl—"

"I can afford to laugh now, because the danger has passed. Believe me, last night was no laughing matter. I am aware how quickly a chill may turn dangerous. But we need not care about that now. All's well that ends well," said Mr Darcy. "You have suffered no ill effects, so you need not lash yourself unnecessarily."

She stiffened. "I am not lashing myself, Mr Darcy. I am trying to thank you."

"By blaming yourself," he said. "Should I allow you to wallow in it, I wonder? Should you dress yourself in sackcloth and ashes and strike yourself as the monks did in times gone by? How should you be punished for your sins?"

She rose, hardly able to keep her annoyance in check. "I am sorry, Mr Darcy, that my attempt at politeness amuses you. Perhaps I should leave you to sit here and chuckle over my words—alone."

He restrained her by lightly encircling her wrist with his fingers.

"I am sorry if I offended," he said, sounding contrite. "I have this habit of exaggeration. It often gives offence. Pray do not leave. You have not finished your breakfast. I promise I will talk only of harmless subjects, like the weather or some such thing like that."

She took a seat again, carefully withdrawing her wrist from his grip.

Silence reigned for a moment. As her fork clinked loudly against her plate, she resolved that she would not repeat the experience of their dinner at Netherfield. She would keep up a monologue if necessary until she finished her breakfast.

"Were you raised entirely in Boston, Mr Darcy?" she asked. It occurred to her that in his speech at least, he was very like an English gentleman, even when he clearly was not.

As if reading her mind, he smiled. "Yes, entirely. I have been told that there is little in my way of speech or my manners to distinguish me from an English gentleman. Though not everyone would agree about my manners," he added, in a self-disparaging tone. As if waiting for a reply, he paused. "An English gentleman can be created as well in Boston as here. My mother was eager to raise me as an Englishman. She is related to the Welds, one of the Boston First Families. They are very influential. And she is very proud of the Darcy name." When he received no reaction, he continued, "After marrying my father, a naval officer, she became obsessed with his country of birth, and sent for governesses and tutors from here to raise her children. I can claim that I know more of the history of England than that of the country of my birth."

"That is because you have no history," said Caroline.

"We may not have a list of the names of kings and queens to recite, but you may be certain that we have a past." He smiled, but his tone was prickly. "But that is another matter entirely. Perhaps," he said, steering the topic in another direction, "you might care to tell me your idea of the ideal English gentleman."

Caroline smiled, on comfortable ground here. There could be no doubt what constituted an English gentleman. "An English gentleman is a gentleman by birth," she said, with absolute certainty.

Robert Darcy's eyes danced. "So I have heard. But tell me what you consider the qualities that define him."

She looked at him with pity. Anyone who was a gentleman would know the answer to such a question. But she decided to humour him.

"An English gentleman must be cultured, well educated, and must observe the proprieties under all circumstances," she asserted. "He must dance elegantly and play the pianoforte tolerably well. He must be meticulously dressed in the latest fashion. He must be proficient in riding, hunting and fishing, sword fighting and perhaps boxing, though some might consider boxing too rough and common. He must command respect at every turn, and must carry himself confidently and proudly."

The corner of his mouth twitched. "Good God! And do you know any such gentleman?"

"Of course," she replied, nodding confidently and sending him a satisfied smile.

"What a paragon he must be!" he said. "But please continue with your definition, for it is most instructive. Has a gentleman no responsibilities? How does he spend his days? Does he do nothing?"

"If you mean work," replied Caroline readily, "Then naturally that is to be avoided. However, a gentleman will busy himself with matters of his estate and the management of his properties."

"But has he no obligations towards others?" insisted Robert Darcy.

"Well, it goes without saying that he must care for his tenants, and be concerned for the welfare of those who are dependent on him. That is an unspoken law."

"Then all gentlemen deal well with those in their care?" said Robert Darcy.

"Those who are worthy of the name," she replied.

He went to the side table, helped himself to some pickled herring, and returned.

"But what of those who neglect their properties and gamble away their inheritance while the tenant homes fall into disrepair? What of the father who is indifferent to the well-being of his children? Or the brother who casts out his younger sisters to depend on the charity of others? Are these then to be considered gentlemen? Merely because of their birth?" He spoke in an impassioned manner that embarrassed her.

"I know none who is guilty of such conduct," she replied. But she could think of many such cases in Society. Still, it did not mean there were no gentlemen who were upright and respectable.

She struck back at him. "Are you perhaps a republican, Mr Darcy? Do you subscribe to such ideals as those of the French Revolution? Are you one of those who, like Napoleon, would deprive the rightful owners of their property and divide their estates among the rabble?"

Robert Darcy put his hands behind his head, and, leaning back, he inspected her with lazy amusement. "I believe I have angered you, Miss Bingley."

"Not at all," she replied, tartly. "There will always be those who have more money, and those who are less fortunate. That is the way of the world. And meanwhile, we have a gentlemanly code to ensure that gentlemen will behave as they ought, and not give in to lawlessness and their baser instincts. After all, without laws and standards, disorder will reign, as it did in the Revolution."

Robert Darcy shook his head. With a broad smile, he came to his feet. "This is far too serious a conversation to have over breakfast," he remarked. "Not when the sun shines so brilliantly outside. I am afraid neither of us has adhered to the agreement we made at the beginning."

"What agreement?" she asked.

He gave a gasp of exaggerated outrage. "You cannot have forgotten so quickly, Miss Bingley! We agreed only to discuss bland subjects, like the weather, for example. What do you think, will the sunshine last, or should we make the best of it and go for a stroll outside?"

"I doubt very much it will last. But that does not require great powers of prediction. Only a basic experience of English weather," she replied. Then she realized she had not answered the rest of his question. "I think a short stroll would be quite the thing," she said, "but on one condition."

"Already setting conditions?" he said. "Can a gentleman never have peace? Oh, but I forgot. I cannot possibly qualify as a gentleman," he sighed. "Very well. What is your condition?"

"You need to give me time to fetch my pelisse."

He stared at her, then guffawed. "Why, Miss Bingley," he said. "I do believe that was a joke!" His face twisted in comic surprise, and she was forced to smile. "Certainly. By all means fetch your pelisse. I have no desire to be trapped in the library with you yet again."

Naturally, he had to spoil it.

She returned downstairs to find him engaged in conversation with Colonel Fitzwilliam.

"Good morning, Miss Bingley," said Colonel Fitzwilliam, gazing at her intensely. He took her hand and, to her embarrassment, brought it to his lips. Caroline was very aware of the watchful eyes of Darcy.

"A beautiful morning, is it not?" said Colonel Fitzwilliam.

"It certainly is," she said.

"We are planning to discover the grounds," said Robert Darcy. "Perhaps you would care to join us?"

The invitation displeased Caroline, since she had not yet determined how to behave towards the colonel. She braced herself.

"Much as I am tempted," he replied, addressing her, "I fear I must decline. I have not yet breakfasted, and I am in need of strong coffee."

Robert Darcy laughed. "That will teach you to down so much port at one sitting."

"I barely touched the port. I was particularly careful not to," protested Colonel Fitzwilliam.

Robert Darcy prodded him in the direction of the breakfast-room. "I do not wish to pick a quarrel with a man who has not yet eaten. Have your coffee, then come and find me. I will be more than happy to oblige at that point, if you still desire it."

Colonel Fitzwilliam smiled ruefully and withdrew.

"Did you stay up until the early hours with Colonel Fitzwilliam then, Mr Darcy?" said Caroline conversationally, as they stepped out into the bright sunshine. It was a crisp, autumn day, with a bite to the air that promised frost again at night. For now, however, the sun was warm on her skin, and she relished it. Though she probably ought to have brought her parasol.

"Yes. And he had some significant news to impart," said Robert Darcy.

"News?" she asked.

"You need not feign innocence, Miss Bingley," he said. "He has already informed me that he asked for your hand in marriage."

Caroline tightened her lips. She had not wanted Robert Darcy to know what had transpired. It frustrated her no end that he was so well informed about her private concerns. Could not the colonel have kept the information to himself?

Well it was not Darcy's fault that the colonel had chosen to confide in him.

"Yes, indeed," she replied, briefly. If he was hoping to learn more, he would be disappointed

"Little wonder, then, that you were so absorbed that you did not notice the cold," he remarked. "You puzzled me yesterday. But now that I know the facts, I would say *that* accounts for it."

"It does not account for any such thing. I was well aware of the cold, but I could not find a way to leave without causing offence."

"Come, come, Miss Bingley. Let us have the truth. You mean to hide your romantic inclinations from me. But the truth of the matter is that few ladies can resist having a gentleman fall to his knees before them and propose marriage."

The reality of the situation was so far from his depiction that Caroline could not help exclaiming, "But I assure you, Colonel Fitzwilliam did no such thing!"

"What? And now you will tell me he did not express his undying devotion, either."

Caroline tried to recollect what Colonel Fitzwilliam had said. Her thoughts had been so taken up by the cold, and his proposal had so taken her by surprise, that she had paid little attention to his words. But now that Robert Darcy mentioned it, she realized that Colonel Fitzwilliam had not in fact expressed sentiment of any kind.

"Gentlemen of my class, Mr Darcy, do not generally advocate such sentimental notions. Our marriages are a matter of convenience and rational choice."

"So he did not express his undying devotion? No wonder you were so cold, in that case."

"You are quite absurd, Mr Darcy. I was cold because the weather was cold. It is quite simple."

He shrugged. "But did you not wish for it, just a little?"

"No," she replied categorically. "I did not even notice that it was missing, until you pointed it out."

"I confess myself quite baffled," he replied. "I cannot think of marriage in such indifferent terms," he said. "I admit to having quite romantic notions about it."

She threw him a disapproving look. "I am sure you do, Mr Darcy."

"And you despise me for it, do you not?" He was smiling.

Caroline did not think her opinion mattered one bit to him. He was simply baiting her for his own amusement.

"I can neither praise you nor despise you. It is not for me to judge your conduct."

"Oh, Miss Bingley," he said, lightly. "But I think you already have."

She was not sure of her footing in this strange banter of theirs, so she took refuge in silence.

They continued to stroll along the garden path for a few moments more.

"I wonder if we could resume one of our previous conversations, Miss Bingley," he said. "You have told me you know a perfect gentleman. Is that the gentleman in London? Is he the one your sister mentioned? Sir Cecil?"

She should not be surprised. Nothing escaped his notice, it seemed. She wanted to groan out loud, and to ask him to go away.

"You will have it out of me, whether I wish it or not. So I will save time and inform you of his identity. His name is Sir Cecil Rynes."

"I am not acquainted with him," said Robert Darcy.

"As I said before, I do not think we move in exactly the same circles."

"I hope I do not move in circles at all," said Robert Darcy.

She must not encourage him by laughing. But her mouth twitched of its own accord, betraying her.

"Let us return to this gentleman of yours. Is he really such a paragon as you described? The perfect gentleman?" he asked.

"Yes, Sir Cecil is the embodiment of such an ideal," she replied firmly, refusing to allow him to sow any doubt in her mind.

"Why then," he asked, "is he not here? Surely he would have been willing to escort you to Pemberley? Instead, here you are, forced to endure my company, and to receive proposals from Colonel Fitzwilliam while shivering in the cold."

"I fail to see in what way this should concern you."

"Oh, it does not concern me at all. But I am plagued by a tendency to be curious, and I have never quite succeeded in controlling it."

"I have no intention, in this situation, of satisfying this tendency of yours. Perhaps, if you deny it often enough, it will shrivel up and die. And then you will be very well rid of it."

"Ah," he said, smiling. "But that would be such a terrible loss."

Were it not for the fact that his goal was to extract gossip about her own life, she might have laughed. But she had no intention of revealing any more of her own affairs to him. He already knew far too much, far more even than her own brother.

"Not for those who are harmed by such gossip," she said, severely.

"Now you malign me. I have no interest in rumour-mongering. In fact, you will rarely meet a person who is less inclined to pass on information. I just like to be possessed of the facts. I find that it prevents misunderstandings."

"What misunderstanding are you referring to, in this case?"

"The possibility that you may be encouraging Colonel Fitzwilliam while you are already committed to another." He spoke seriously now. His gaze, as it met hers, glittered with an emotion she could not identify.

"How dare you suggest such a thing, sir?" she said. Her voice was slightly raised, but at this moment she did not care. "What have I done to encourage Colonel Fitzwilliam?"

"Why did you not invite Sir Cecil to accompany us?" he asked, still completely earnest. "Why did you invite the colonel instead?"

Colonel Fitzwilliam had asked the same question yesterday. And now Robert Darcy was seizing upon it as if it proved her guilt. What was she guilty of? Of what were they accusing her, exactly?

"I think I told you before, Mr Darcy, that I am not obliged to explain my conduct to you."

"I am trying to protect a friend of mine."

"Since when was Colonel Fitzwilliam your friend?" she cried. "I have certainly never heard of it."

Robert Darcy bowed. "Perhaps you are right. I am allowing my concern for him to override my sense. Come, let us not quarrel. I find myself confused by the turn of events, that is all. I apologize if I have overstepped any boundaries."

But Caroline was not to be so easily pacified. Stung by this repeated suggestion that there was something improper about her conduct, she spoke with more emphasis perhaps than was necessary. "You asked me about my relationship with Sir Cecil. Well, I will tell you. I have reason to expect a proposal from him, and if I receive it, I will accept."

She waited as two young ladies whispering and laughing rounded a corner, then continued, more quietly, "But there has been no proposal yet, and until that happens, I am free to consider anyone else who *does* request my hand. I fail to see what is improper about that."

A few minutes passed before he spoke.

"I wish to apologize yet again," said Robert Darcy. "You have been open with me, and I will return the favour by being open with you. I should point out to you, perhaps, that my concern with Colonel Fitzwilliam's situation stems from having encountered a similar situation in my own life." He gestured her to a stone bench in a corner between two hedges.

"I was once very much in love with a young lady. She was considered the perfect match for me in every way, so my family strongly encouraged the connection, as did her family. The date of our wedding was set, and everything appeared to be going perfectly."

He paused. He leaned back on his hands, his eyes fixed on the hedge above them. "Then the night before the wedding she came to visit me. She informed me that she had, in fact, been secretly engaged to someone else for years, and that they had been waiting for her to come of age to get married. I had appeared on the scene and offered for her, thus complicating things considerably. She had married her husband in secret that very day, a day after her birthday. In the circumstances, naturally, she needed to cancel our wedding."

He sat up and dusted some gravel from his hands. The hard bench had made red imprints on his palms. He ceased talking as if to inspect the blemishes.

"The only mercy was she had told me before the ceremony. I had just enough time to inform the clergyman who was to marry us, and to leave a notice on the church door saying the wedding would not take place."

He made a dismissive gesture then ran his fingers through his hair. "It hurt, shall we say. It hurt a great deal. But the worst of it was—there was no need for any of it. Had she confided in me at the beginning, I would have been spared the humiliation of having gone so far, as well as the embarrassment of cancelling the wedding at the last minute. At least my pride would not have suffered."

His eyes bore into hers. "That is why, Miss Bingley, I have become tenacious about this issue. I have come to believe that directness and openness are vitally important if one is to avoid painful and sudden revelations. In your case, I wished to spare Colonel Fitzwilliam. It is none of my concern, I know. But if you are engaged to someone else, I hope you will be kind enough to inform him of the fact rather than giving him false hope."

Caroline was not sure how to react to his confession. She had never been the recipient of a gentleman's confidence before, except for Charles, of course, and did not know what was expected. Part of her wanted to comfort him, the other part said that surely he would not welcome pity, and that a grown man did not need to be comforted.

And the biggest part of her wanted to thump him on the head with her reticule, and tell him not to interfere in her affairs.

So she sat there, twisting a braid from her pelisse around her finger, and said nothing at all.

Robert Darcy rose and held out his hand to her. "I think we have had quite enough candour to last us for some time. Let us return to a more commonplace topic."

She stood up, relieved to be able to return to small talk, even if it did not feel entirely comfortable any more. "We seem to be incapable of doing so," she said, with a controlled smile.

"I am sure if we exerted ourselves, we would succeed. I will nudge you in the right direction. What do you think of the weather, Miss Bingley?"

"I believe, Mr Darcy, that rain clouds are moving in," said Caroline, looking up at the perfectly blue sky.

"Do you?" said Robert Darcy, throwing back his head and examining the sky as though he had never seen it before. "I seem to be struck by some kind of colour blindness—temporary, I hope— for when I look up I see only blue."

"Alas, Mr Darcy, I have to say you are right. About the colour blindness, at any rate. I can see unmistakable signs of rain. It will rain by this afternoon, you may count on it."

"May I, by Jove? Then so be it," he said, his good humour restored. Glad that he had thrown off his sombre manner, her spirits lifted.

"Now that you mention it, I believe I do see a hint of a cloud, just over there." He pointed to the west, though there was nothing there to be seen at all.

They were so busy looking up at the sky that they did not pay attention to the small pond set in the ground in front of them. Caroline noticed it at last moment, but it was already too late.

"Mr Darcy!" she cried, but instead of looking down he looked at her. His foot struck one of the rocks scattered around the pond and before she knew it, he was tumbling forward into the water.

She clutched at his coat, but it was not enough to steady him. He hurtled forward with a loud splash. He could not drown, of course, for the pond was small, and the water shallow, but she imagined that the water was very cold.

"Hold on to me," she said, as he struggled to bring himself up.

Completely drenched, he cursed under his breath. Miss Bingley tried her best to ignore his rather shocking invectives.

"Please remember, Mr Darcy," she said, as she helped pull him to an upright position, "that you are in the presence of a lady."

He was so outlandish, standing there in the sun. Water poured from his flattened hair, out of his ears, from his flopping cravat and his wilting collar, from inside his sleeves, from the bottom of his coat, and water sloshed in his boots as he took a step forward. He resembled a crazed water spirit brought to earth by some trick of the gods.

Caroline took one look at him and dissolved into helpless laughter. She laughed so hard she had to sit down abruptly on the rock and almost fell in herself. She laughed as she had not laughed since she had gone to Mrs Drakehill's Seminary for Young Ladies. And with that laughter, some of the ice inside her began to crack.

Louisa found them just a short time later. She eyed Caroline dubiously, no doubt wondering if her sister had caught a fever from the night before.

Louisa's arrival was like a splash of cold water. Caroline sobered up immediately under her sister's searching look.

"Mr Darcy—" she said, trying hard not to look at him. She did not want to start laughing again. "—Mr Darcy fell in the pond."

"Yes, I can see that, Caroline," said her sister. "But it is certainly no laughing matter."

"No, of course it is not," snapped Caroline. "It was just that—"

"—it was so unexpected," completed Robert Darcy. "And I was not harmed, so the matter was not so very serious, you see, Mrs Hurst. But you must excuse me, ladies. I need to change before anyone else sees me and falls into a paroxysm of laughter. I have a horror of being laughed at, you see."

He set out on his way, waddling in such a droll manner that she could not stop the croak that escaped her. He turned and shot her a wounded look, then continued on his way.

"You do not seem quite well, Caroline," said Louisa, breaking into her thoughts.

"I am perfectly well, Louisa," replied Caroline. "You may put your mind at ease. I have recovered fully from yesterday's chill."

"That is certainly a relief," said Louisa. "Though your behaviour both last night and today leaves much to be desired."

"But you have not heard my news!" said Caroline, dangling this morsel in front of her sister to distract her from the lengthy sermon that was brewing.

Louisa's expression immediately changed from condemnation to eager attention. "What news is that? Pray tell me immediately, Caroline."

"Colonel Fitzwilliam has asked me to marry him."

"What a cunning creature you are, Caroline! No wonder you sent for him to accompany us to Pemberley. I would never have thought you would be so clever about it. You have done very well."

Caroline blew out a frustrated breath. Everyone was determined to think she had schemed and plotted to make him offer for her. "I did not do it in the hope that he would ask for my hand," she said. "I am not even sure I will accept."

"You cannot convince me that you had no hand in it. You may be holding out for Sir Cecil," continued Louisa, "but it would do you no harm to have someone in reserve, just in case Sir Cecil fails to come up to scratch."

Caroline rose, impatient to end the conversation, but Louisa was not so easily discouraged.

"There is nothing shameful in wanting to be married. You waited far too long for Mr Darcy to propose, and look what came of it. You are no longer young, Caroline. You run the risk of becoming an old maid, and remaining our brother's dependant for life. Surely you would not want that?" chided Louisa. "Imagine how Mrs Bennet will gloat!"

"Since when should I care for the opinion of the Bennets, of all people?" said Caroline, staring at her sister in amazement. "You have always had nothing but contempt for them."

"My dear Caroline," returned Louisa, "I am only saying that if you do not marry soon, you will have that detestable Mrs Bennet giving you advice on how to find a husband, and preening herself on her success with her daughters."

"Louisa!" protested Caroline. "I think you have said quite enough."

"I am merely trying to help."

"I have had enough of well-intentioned people today, thank you," said Caroline. "I will go inside and join Mrs Germain in a game of chess."

"Mrs Germain?" said Louisa, stunned. "The corpulent lady with giant feathers on her turban? Surely not, Caroline! She is not even remotely fashionable."

"I do not have the slightest idea if she is fashionable or not. But I have heard she plays a remarkable game of chess."

With that, she walked away in the direction of the manor, leaving her sister to follow behind her.

Chapter 6

CAROLINE RUBBED HER FINGERS TOGETHER, TRYING TO CONTROL her exhilaration. She had not played chess for several years, not since Mrs Drakehill had caught her and her friend Sarah playing secretly in the school library, using stolen candle ends to light the chessboard.

The chessboard she had played with at school, however, had been very simple, a plain Regence set that she and Sarah had acquired stealthily on a shopping expedition. This board, however, clearly reflected Mrs Germain's passion for chess. It was an old bone Dieppe creation, intricately carved, with real figures painted in colours, the bishops in bi-corn hats, the knights as sea-horses, and the king and queen in court dress with powdered wigs.

The moment Caroline saw it she had exclaimed that she had never seen a more beautiful set. Her father's had been a rosewood from Calvert, stamped underneath with the address that she had memorized like a prayer when she was a child, "189 Fleet Street." She had been fond of the elongated chess pieces, though they were not well balanced. She had learned to place them carefully on the board so they did not tip over. Her father had never acquired that ability. He invariably knocked them down, then cursed and said he would order another set, but he had never done so in his lifetime.

These chess pieces sat firm and solid on the board. And she had a worthy opponent. Mrs Germain was a cunning player.

For a moment, Caroline's excitement dimmed as she thought how her father would have loved to play with such an expert opponent.

She brushed the feeling off. Father rarely had time for his daughters, but he enjoyed a game of chess. He had taught Caroline to play when she was very young, about seven perhaps. "To keep me company," he had explained to her mother, who had mocked the idea and urged him to teach his son, Charles.

"Charles does not have the mind for it," said Father. "Caroline has. She is as sharp as a needle, that one."

She had hoarded the compliment because Father rarely praised her, and because of that, concentrated all her efforts into learning the skill, eager to please him, and later, she had relished the times they spent together, leaning over the chessboard, engaged in battle. She remembered well his astonishment and pleasure the first time she had defeated him.

"Your move," said Mrs Germain. "You will do better if you concentrate."

A quick look at the board revealed that Caroline's queen was in peril. She changed strategies, hoping to catch Mrs Germain off guard.

But Mrs Germain recognized the strategy immediately.

"A good plan," she said, as Caroline made her move. "But too little, too late," she said, as she moved into position, already setting up for a checkmate.

It took only a few moments' reflection for Caroline to acknowledge that she was defeated. She threw up her hands in surrender.

"You play well," remarked Mrs Germain.

Caroline, to her own surprise, felt a flush rise to her face. "Nothing compared to you. I understand now why Mr Darcy was eager to play with you yesterday."

"Ah, yes. Mr Darcy is very kind to find time for me."

"It was kind of *you* to play with me this morning. I fear I am not quite at your level."

"You simply need more practice. But tell me, who taught you to play, Miss Bingley?"

"My father, Mr Edmund Bingley."

"Ah," said Mrs Germain. "Yes, of course. That would account for it. I played against your father many times." Mrs Germain watched Caroline closely, clearly trying to gauge her reaction.

"Did you indeed?" said Caroline, eagerly. "I did not know you were acquainted." She knew few people who knew her father. Caroline's mother had discouraged contact with his former friends or business associates after they married, claiming that such connections would destroy her daughters' chances of contracting suitable marriages.

"I knew your father when he was young, before he married, and before he moved to London." She looked coy, and Caroline tried to imagine her as a young lady, and her father as a young man.

She wanted to ask Mrs Germain about him, but what could she ask?

Mrs Germain smiled kindly. "Your father and I considered marriage at one time," she said, wistfully. "We were quite in love. But nothing came of it. My father did not approve. We were landed gentry, and Edmund Bingley was in trade, you know, and not quite good enough for us. He was not yet so very rich at the time. Not what he became just a few years later. A very clever man, your father, with a shrewd eye for business."

She paused, lost in her own thoughts. "So I married Mr Germain instead. My family thought it advantageous. He was from an old family and was older than I. The only good thing to be said about him was that he did not live long." Her body rumbled and her eyes sparkled with laughter. "I will give you some advice, though in my experience no one ever heeds it. If you are going to marry for connections, find a shrivelled old man who will die quickly. But if you marry a young one, make sure it's for love, or it won't do at all." Her body quivered with laughter, continuing until she began to wheeze. Caroline rose and went to her side in alarm, but Mrs Germain waved her away.

"Don't worry about me," she said. "It will go away by itself. Go and find your Mr Darcy."

"He is hardly *my* Mr Darcy!" exclaimed Caroline.

"Go, go!" said Mrs Germain. "Just ring for my maid before you do."

Caroline left the small parlour for the larger drawing room, having made sure Mrs Germain was taken care of. Her mind was still reeling with the knowledge that at some time, her gruff and distant father had been in love. She could not imagine it. But then, she knew nothing about him at all. He had told her nothing about his past. It was as if it was a blank.

Rain slashed against the windows as she passed through the hallway. The rain that she had predicted the day before had arrived. Games were organized in the drawing room in the event of it being wet, when everyone would be confined indoors. She did not particularly care for the kind of games one played at house parties, especially charades, but it gave everyone something to do when it was impossible to venture out.

A distinct drone rose up in the drawing room as she entered, resembling a swarm of flies circling over some discarded sweetmeat. All eyes turned towards her. She looked down at her clothing, wondering if she had forgotten to put something on, or if there was a large blot on her dress.

"Allow me," boomed Mr Olmstead, "to be among the first to congratulate you." His voice carried loudly in the room. "I hear you are engaged to be married."

Caroline felt the announcement as a physical blow. She jerked backward in shock. "I am sorry, sir. I'm afraid I do not understand."

"You're a sly puss," he said playfully. "But if you don't wish to speak of it, I won't push you. I wish you very happy, my dear." Caroline realized that those around her were listening to the exchange with interest. She did not know what error had led to this mistaken belief, but she had to refute it immediately before it spread any farther.

"Indeed, sir, you have been misinformed. I am *not* engaged to Colonel Fitzwilliam."

It was Mr Olmstead's turn to be puzzled. "Colonel Fitzwilliam?" he said. "No indeed! No one has said anything about Colonel Fitzwilliam," he remarked jovially. He drew closer, and whispered in her ear, "I am speaking of Sir Cecil Rynes."

Caroline's hand flew to her mouth. "But how—"

"Aha!" said Mr Olmstead. "You are well and caught. Confess, child."

"But—"

"Everyone is speaking of it. *That* cat is quite out of the bag. It is no use trying to keep it a secret any longer."

Caroline shook her head vigorously. "No, but you must not, Mr Olmstead!" she cried.

Mr Olmstead frowned. "Must not what? I'm afraid you have quite lost me."

"There is no such engagement. Oh, if Sir Cecil were to hear of such a thing…" She wrung her hands, gazing around her desperately. Oh, what kind of nightmare was this?

Mr Olmstead, beginning to realize Caroline was in earnest, took her aside. "Hold your horses, Miss Bingley. If that is the case, the less said about it the better. We must squash the rumour immediately," said Mr Olmstead, his eyes searching immediately for his wife. He drew Caroline to a corner, as far out of hearing as possible in a crowded room.

"I understand such a match would be desirable to you?" he queried.

Caroline nodded numbly.

"I can see then why you would not wish such a rumour to circulate. Sir Cecil might take it very badly indeed. It really won't do at all." He patted her on the back of her hand. "Don't you worry, my dear. I shall enlist the help of Mrs Olmstead. *She* will know what to do."

"But how…?" She had meant to enquire how he had come to know of it. He had glimpsed Mrs Olmstead, however, and was striding towards her, with Caroline in tow.

Her thoughts in shambles, she tried to imagine who could have started such a rumour. She was acquainted with many people here, but she could think of no one who might have instigated the rumours. She had been very careful in her dealings with Sir Cecil, after her bitter experience with Mr Darcy, and her interaction with him had been quite guarded. Yes, there had been a few whispers here and there that had vaguely linked the two of them, but nothing that suggested a full-fledged relationship. The rumour could only have been started by someone who knew of her interest in Sir Cecil.

The blood drained from her face. There were only two people who knew. Her sister was one, and Louisa was too canny to have spread such a rumour. The other was Mr Darcy.

As if conjured up by the thought, he appeared in the doorway.

"Mr Olmstead," she said, interrupting his single-minded charge across the room. "I believe I know the source of the problem." She pointed her chin significantly towards Robert Darcy.

"Mr Darcy?" said Mr Olmstead, bewildered. "Surely not?"

But to Caroline, at that moment, only one person existed. She could not understand how he could look so normal, so perfectly calm, as though nothing at all had happened. He could not be so entirely cold-blooded as that! She burned with his betrayal. How could he? After all his fine talk about openness and honesty? She had known, right from the start, that he was not to be trusted.

It was her fault entirely. She should not have confided in him. When he had mocked the very concept of a gentleman, and had never even tried to claim that honour for himself. He had as much as acknowledged that he was not. She should have known he would not be bound by the gentlemanly code.

She had to confront him and make him see the damage he had caused her.

"Miss Bingley?" said Mr Darcy as she approached him. "Have I unwittingly offended? You look quite prepared to guillotine me."

"A guillotine would be too good a fate for you," she replied.

Mystified, he scrutinized her. She made sure he could read nothing in her face.

"I need to speak to you. In the library. Now." Her imperious tone left no room for him to refuse her.

"In the library?" he said, raising a brow, attempting to diffuse the tension.

She had never had the impulse to strike anyone before. At this moment she would have liked nothing better than to wipe that self-satisfied look from his face with a hard slap. But if *he* was no gentleman, *she* would at least remember that she was a lady.

Besides, she had never struck anyone in her life.

She preceded him into the library, leaving him to follow. He deliberately left the door open.

Hah! Now all of a sudden he was concerned about her reputation.

She stamped back and slammed it shut with her foot. The sharp crash gave her some satisfaction. That, and the dismayed expression on his face.

"How can you!" she began. "How *dare* you betray me in this manner?"

He really was a good actor. She could almost believe the baffled incomprehension on his face. "Betray you?"

"Let us put aside pretences. I know, and you know, that you are the source of the rumour that is now circulating among the guests about Sir Cecil's betrothal to me. Do not even try to pretend otherwise." Her anger was like the crushing weight of a rock pressing down onto her lungs. She had to stop. She could scarcely breathe.

"*You* may not think of it as a betrayal," she continued, by and by. "Since you seem to be devoid of even the most basic concept of proper conduct. I doubt very much you would be scrupulous enough to think of it as a betrayal."

The face that had been bewildered a moment ago had frozen into a tight, controlled mask. All feelings were wiped from it. The mask frightened her, but she would not let him intimidate her.

"I'll have you know that you have ruined *everything* for me!"

He made no answer.

"Can you stand there and deny it?"

"Will denials make a difference?" he asked, his voice casual, a striking contrast to that vacant mask. "It is quite clear that you have made up your mind about my character. I wonder what motives you have attributed to me for spreading such a rumour. What nefarious purposes do you think I have? I would be interested to know if you have discovered the depths of my villainy or not."

His mocking tone set her teeth on edge. "You mean to diminish the impact of what you have done by making me ridiculous, I know. You will not," she retorted. "As for your purpose in disclosing what I told you in confidence, you do not have to have one. It may simply be a partiality to gossip. Or it could be malice, and the pleasure of seeing lives ruined by a few well placed words of yours."

"This, then, is your opinion of me! This is how you regard me!" The blank mask slipped for a moment, then was restored. "It would be of no avail, then, to deny anything. I have been tried and judged already. I told you earlier that I did not like gossip, and I explained to you exactly why I was asking so many questions, but my words clearly made no impression upon you. You are determined to think ill of me, no matter what, simply because I am different from what you are accustomed to."

Now he had taken refuge in injured pride. She had heard somewhere that even the darkest villains thought their actions perfectly justified.

She turned her back and went to the window to avoid answering. There was no point in argument. Confronting him had accomplished nothing in any case. It would not repair the situation. Nothing could. The damage was done.

Word would undoubtedly reach Sir Cecil. She could not deceive herself into thinking he would now step forward and ask her to marry him. He was proud, and quite accustomed to being sought out by young ladies eager to better themselves. Sir Cecil was too much a man about town to accept that such a rumour was circulated purely by chance. He would think her stupidly conniving, and he would deny the gossip. He would not let his hand be forced.

She leaned her head against the glass. It was hard and cold against her brow.

She would be the laughing-stock of Town.

The window looked out onto the stable, a wide, squat, brick building. The bricks blurred, merging into a long indistinct wall that blocked her vision. She realized she was crying.

And of course Mr Darcy, yet again, was a witness.

She waved her hand towards him in dismissal. "Please leave me alone," she said, her voice choked.

When there was no sound behind her, she turned to look. She was alone.

Chapter 7

THERE YOU ARE, MISS BINGLEY!" SAID MRS OLMSTEAD, ENTERING with Mr Olmstead behind her. "We've been searching for you everywhere."

Mrs Olmstead advanced quickly across the room and grasped Caroline's hands in hers. "Oh, you poor thing! I cannot tell you how sorry I am about this unfortunate rumour," she said, examining her face earnestly. "But have no fear," she said, unknowingly echoing her husband, "we will set everything right at once."

"No use hiding in the library, child," said Mr Olmstead. "Got to face them, or they'll be like hounds on the chase." He took out a pinch of snuff and inhaled deeply. "Above all, you must keep your head."

She had only one desire now, and that was for this day to be over. There was no making things right. The last thing she wanted was to face the rumour down. What she *did* want was to go to her chamber and hide and then to take the first post back to Netherfield. And she planned to stay in Netherfield and bury herself in the country until nobody remembered her existence.

"I am very sorry," she said, shaking her head. "I know you mean well, but I cannot face anyone until I have determined what to say. I really need some time by myself to think things through."

"Very well," said Mrs Olmstead, with a sympathetic smile. "But there is nothing like a cup of tea to make one feel better when things go horribly wrong. I will ring for a tray to be brought up."

"No!" said Caroline, then, at Mrs Olmstead's startled expression, she corrected herself. "Thank you Mrs Olmstead, but I do not believe I could drink a single drop."

Mrs Olmstead was not one to take offence easily. She nodded her head and began to push Mr Olmstead towards the door.

"In that case, we shall leave you to work out a strategy, Miss Bingley. But you must send for us the moment you think of something. Meanwhile, I am sure we will find a solution. Don't you worry. Three heads are better than one."

Much as they might desire to help her, she did not think they could do anything, for there really *was* nothing to be done.

Her thoughts drifted to Robert Darcy, the man who had brought this upon her. She had trusted him. Just for a moment, out in the garden, in the sunshine, she had stepped beyond the limits of social interaction and she had revealed something to him she had hidden from others. Duped by his laughter and his unconventional behaviour, she had allowed herself an unguarded moment.

The world had no place for unguarded moments, not for a woman. It was merciless. One word could change everything. A woman's world could collapse because of a word.

Yet she had entrusted a stranger, an *outsider*, with her hopes and plans.

Let it be a lesson to her. It was a lesson she ought to have known, since it had been drilled into her for many years. But she had not fully understood it. She should not have thought to step outside the rigid barriers of convention. They were set up to protect her, yet she had put them aside the very first time she had met someone who did not fit inside them. Well, now she knew better. Though, like a child, she had to be burned to fully understand the danger.

Quick footsteps approached, and she wondered if Mr Darcy had returned, perhaps to apologize. But it was Louisa.

"I would never have believed this of you, Caroline!" said her sister, shutting the door behind her. "Do you have maggots in your head? How could you?"

"How could I?" asked Caroline. She had had quite enough. "How could I what? Do you think I deliberately set out to circulate this rumour?"

Her voice was loud and shrill in her ears. But she was not so lost to propriety to risk having anyone overhear her. She clamped down on her jaw and waited until she was calm enough to continue.

"Do you think I started the rumour to force Sir Cecil to marry me? Is that what you think? Do you think me so utterly devoid of intelligence as to do such a thing? I know very well that if even a whiff of this rumour reaches Sir Cecil's ears, my chances are completely destroyed with him."

Louisa considered her words with a sceptical frown. "No, I suppose not. It would be beyond foolish. Though I did wonder if you were gambling on the hope that he would make you an offer to save you from scandal."

Caroline laughed bitterly. "I have no such illusions about Sir Cecil. His affections are not engaged. Our connection was based on mutual convenience alone."

Louisa perched on the edge of a sofa.

"Then who spread the rumour?"

"Mr Darcy is the only one who knows about Sir Cecil."

Louisa sat up even straighter. "Mr Darcy? Oh, no, Caroline! You did not tell him, surely! Did I not tell you he was not to be trusted?"

She stood up and began to pace the room. "All this is entirely my brother's fault. It was Charles who got us into this tangle. He should have refused to put up Mr Darcy as a guest. After all, what do we know about him? He is not one of us. But Charles is only too willing to like people. It is a fault that will come to haunt us."

Caroline sat down, and gestured to her sister to sit next to her. "None of this is any good to me," she said. "What I need is someone who can help me decide what to do."

But Louisa had not finished. The more she spoke, the more perturbed she grew. "You would think a brother's first concern should be to see his sisters well married. Yet he places us in the hands of chance acquaintances at every turn, and leaves us very much to our own devices. We may as well have no brother, for all the protection he affords us."

"You cannot blame Charles for this situation, Louisa. I am the only one to blame, for I ought not to have told Mr Darcy about Sir Cecil."

"Yes," said Louisa. "Yes, that is quite true." She took a seat on a tall chair opposite Caroline. "I really cannot imagine what you were thinking. To confide your most intimate secrets to an outsider! What in heaven's name came over you?"

Perversely, now that Louisa agreed with her, she felt obliged to defend herself. "Sir Cecil is hardly my most intimate secret. And it was you who mentioned him to Mr Darcy in the first case."

"Caroline, you cannot mean to reproach *me*. I never spoke of him to anyone, let alone Mr Darcy."

"I am not blaming you. But you *did* mention Sir Cecil within his hearing, when we were in Stamford. You cannot deny it."

"I recall no such thing," said Louisa.

"Well, I do," said Caroline, despairingly.

"I will not stay here to be insulted and accused of all manner of unjust things!" said Louisa, jumping up. "Oh, if only Mr Hurst were here. *He* would not have allowed you to hurl accusations at me like this!" And with those words, she hurried through the door, leaving Caroline to her own devices.

An hour later, Caroline had reached the only possible conclusion. She knew she could not afford to delay a moment longer. It would take only a single letter sent to a friend in Town for the news to spread like wildfire. In one thing Mr Olmstead was right. She had to confront the situation, not cower in here, staring at the walls. She would face everyone over luncheon, and make a public announcement that it was all just an unfortunate misunderstanding.

She dreaded the very idea. Just imagining it made her head pound and her fingers tremble. It was unlikely, moreover, that her announcement would substantially change the outcome. She was no green girl to believe that denying a rumour would scotch it. Nevertheless, she had to denounce the whispers publicly, if only to prove that she did not start them herself. That, at least, should count for something. She hauled herself up and moved with leaden feet through the doorway.

She arrived to find luncheon already informally laid out. The sight of the food unsettled her stomach, and she feared that she would disgrace herself by being sick. A large number of people were milling around, waiting for the signal to storm the table.

This was certainly the best moment for an announcement. She took hold of a glass and a spoon to draw everyone's attention.

As if to echo her, Mr Olmstead clanged on a glass with a spoon.

She groaned inwardly. She could not conceive what Mr Olmstead intended to say, but she had the feeling it would only make matters worse, particularly since he had not even consulted her. She began to wish for a natural catastrophe—a whirlwind, a flood, an earthquake—anything to draw attention away from what was about to happen.

"Mrs Olmstead and I wish to be the first to make this announcement," he said. "The happy couple planned to keep this a secret, but we have routed them out and they can no longer conceal the truth from us." He paused dramatically. Enjoying the silent anticipation in the room, he opened his snuff box, took a pinch, and sniffed. The snap of the box as it closed resounded through the room, jangling Caroline's nerves.

"We would like to announce the engagement of…"

Caroline's eyes opened wide. What were they doing? She had thought Mr and Mrs Olmstead were on her side. Her heart hammered like a woodpecker's beak. She waited for the axe to fall.

"… the engagement of Miss Caroline Bingley to Mr Robert Darcy."

Caroline's audible gasp filled the room. Dozens of eyes swivelled towards her and pinned her with their gazes.

Mr Darcy, looking in command and perfectly at ease, came to take her hand.

"Show your teeth," he murmured. "You are good at that. Everyone is watching."

She grinned like a puppet, a gaping, empty grin that was frozen on her face. This was beyond everything. She did not think matters could become worse. An acrid taste rose up in her throat and she felt as if she would choke.

"A toast to the happy couple!" said Mr Olmstead, and, from nowhere, footmen appeared with flutes of champagne to toast Caroline's disgrace.

The toast broke the silence, and animated chatter clamoured all around her. Then people began to press towards her to wish her well. Mr Darcy stood by her side, aloof and formal, smiling.

"Thank you," she said.

"Thank you," she said again, and wondered why she was thanking everyone.

"Thank you," she repeated, until she no longer knew what the words meant, for they sounded like words from some nonsensical rhyme that children recited.

Colonel Fitzwilliam appeared in front of her. He bowed with practised correctness, but his eyes glinted with suppressed fury.

"You could have spared me," he said to her between stretched lips. "If you had told me before, I would not have gone through what I now realize was a mortifying display two nights ago. And to think that you promised to give my proposal serious consideration, when there was no reason at all for me to hope!"

"I am sorry," she said, for what else could she say?

He shot a daggered glance at Mr Darcy. "And you! Could you not have told me the truth when I unburdened myself to you? I should have known better than to trust you."

He did not wait for an answer. He turned on his heels, in military style, and marched out of the room.

It was too much to consider that she had lost two chances of marriage in one blow. For now she must go through this pretence of being engaged to Mr Darcy, who had not the slightest intention of honouring the engagement, she was certain. Nor had she, for that matter.

She could never reclaim her relationship with Colonel Fitzwilliam. For how could she explain the situation to him? To do so, she would have to admit that she had hoped to marry Sir Cecil, which simply compounded her guilt. Then she would be forced to account for the desperate measures taken by the Olmsteads to help her out. Few men's pride could be appeased by such a convoluted justification.

The crowd around them thinned as people embarked on the elegant spread of food their hosts had provided. Soon, she hoped, she could escape to her room where she would remain closeted until it was time for them to leave.

"Caroline!" said Louisa, smiling. "You have salvaged the situation after all!" She turned to Mr Darcy. "You have done very well for yourself, Mr Darcy. My sister would never have agreed to such a match if she had not been in desperate straits. You must consider yourself very lucky."

Caroline's face, she was sure, was the colour of her ruby earrings and pendant. She was at a complete loss for something to say, though her mouth tried to open and utter some words. Her sister's rudeness dismayed her. Louisa should at least acknowledge that he had done the right thing by stepping forward and coming to her assistance.

Caroline need not have worried, however. Mr Darcy was perfectly able to deal with Louisa himself.

"I *do* consider myself lucky," said Mr Darcy, smoothly. "Though I consider *you* luckier, since you will now be connected to the Darcy family through your sister. It is considered quite an honour, I have heard." He did not smile, and Louisa, who did not know what to make of that remark, tittered uneasily.

Mr Darcy, driven beyond patience, abandoned his place next to Caroline and stalked away.

"I do not see why he is so offended. I was only speaking the truth. I wish you were not engaged to *him*," said Louisa, in a whisper. "But needs must, I suppose, and you have done a creditable job of redeeming yourself."

"It is all Mr Darcy's doing, and you must remember that," said Caroline. "He has at least made amends for his misdeed."

She took advantage of a short lull in her unwanted popularity to approach the table. Picking up a plate, she proceeded absently to fill it. Without paying attention, she placed a morsel in her mouth, then grimaced as she realized what it was. Glancing down, she found she had placed three lobster patties on it.

It was the last straw. She detested lobster patties. Tears threatened and she held them back through sheer will. She handed the plate to a passing footman and abandoned the notion of food altogether.

A lady came up to her and introduced herself as Miss Tims.

"So, Miss Bingley," she asked, eying Caroline suspiciously. "Where did you first meet Mr Darcy? You must tell us all about it." Two young ladies flanked her, looking eager to scrounge whatever information they could. Caroline remembered Miss Tims as the lady who had been leaning on Mr Darcy's arm in the ballroom two nights ago. Even now she was casting furtive glances at him where he stood across the room.

"We had not thought Mr Darcy's feelings were engaged when he was in Town in the summer," remarked one of her companions.

"It has all been rather sudden," she replied, trying to sound dreamy rather than evasive. "You perhaps know my brother Charles. He is a close friend of Mr Fitzwilliam Darcy, who is Mr Darcy's cousin."

"Oh, yes, of course. No doubt you met Mr Darcy often in Pemberley."

Caroline smiled and turned to respond to someone else who had come to gorge on the gossip.

"Does Mr Darcy intend to settle in England?" asked Mrs Palmer, a lady in a grey dress and a white cap that covered every inch of her hair.

"You will have to ask Mr Darcy about his plans, ma'am," replied Caroline, though surely as his fiancée she would be expected to know. After all, she would need to agree if he planned to take her with him to Boston.

She received one or two doubtful glances, but overall she managed to deflect the questions well enough.

"Dear Miss Bingley! What excellent news!" said Mr Olmstead, approaching her. He beamed from ear to ear. Leaning towards her, he whispered, "Are you satisfied with our solution? A good one, eh?"

She had no choice but to smile. Mr Olmstead was so very well intentioned, he did not realize that his blundering had brought on a whole other set of problems. Of the two evils, she supposed, her present entanglement was by far the lesser one. In view of the harm the first rumour would have caused for her socially, she *ought* to be grateful, but she had not yet regained her balance enough to do so.

"You and Mrs Olmstead have been more than kind. I owe you a great deal," she said.

"Oh, don't thank me," said Mr Olmstead. "It was Mr Darcy's idea, after all."

For the second time that day, Caroline felt the blood drain from her head. She put a hand out to support herself, reaching for Mr Olmstead's arm, afraid for a moment that she would fall to the floor. This was one revelation too many on a day such as this.

"Are you quite well, my dear?" asked Mr Olmstead.

"Things have been moving too fast for me," said Caroline. "I am not accustomed to such sudden reversals of fortune."

Mr Olmstead beamed benevolently and took out his snuff box.

"It is too bad females don't generally partake of snuff nowadays," said Mr Olmstead. "I think a sniff of this would make you right as rain." He winked. "Had mine laced with whisky, you know."

"That sounds too strong for me, Mr Olmstead. Tobacco and whisky all at once! Though I must admit I would not mind something rather strong right now," she added wryly, wishing that life were that simple.

"A stiff glass of whisky?" he whispered. "That should take the edge off the shock."

Caroline struggled not to reveal her horror at the suggestion. All it needed was for her to reek of spirits.

"I fear I must forgo that pleasure as well, Mr Olmstead."

"Of course," he said. "You have to keep your wits about you. But I'm glad to see the colour's coming back to your face," he said. He hovered for a few more minutes, then set off. "If you no longer need me, I shall see if I can find Mrs Olmstead before dinner. I had something particular to speak to her about."

Her next well-wisher was Mrs Germain. The large woman congratulated her warmly at first. As those perceptive eyes studied Caroline, however, she made no attempt to conceal her scepticism.

"For a young lady who is soon to become a bride, I find you lacking that special glow I would have expected." she said. "'*Something is rotten in the state of Denmark.*' In other words, I smell a fish. Particularly since you mentioned nothing at all earlier when we discussed Mr Darcy."

"It was uh—very sudden."

"It must have been," she said brusquely. "Because I heard something before the announcement that led me to believe your thoughts lay in a completely different direction."

Caroline wished Mrs Germain would not persist in airing her views so loudly. "I cannot explain matters just now, Mrs Germain. I beg you not to speak of it," she replied, lowering her voice, and hoping the older lady would not take offence.

"I understand," replied Mrs Germain. "But if you ever find yourself in a spot, or you just need a quiet talk, I'd be more than happy if you would come and find me," she said. "I have good large shoulders for people to cry on." Then, with a quick rumbling laugh, she was away, light as a feather despite her size.

Caroline watched as Mrs Germain hastened over to Mr Darcy. She said something to him, playfully hitting him with her fan, and for the first time since their talk in the library, a genuine smile crossed his face. But when Mrs Germain made another remark, they both glanced in her direction. Caroline turned away quickly, but to her dismay she found herself looking into the eyes of Colonel Fitzwilliam, who was just returning.

He bowed to her and took himself as far from her as possible. Caroline wished again she could tell him exactly what had happened, but she could not. The schism between them could not be crossed.

"You've forgotten to smile," remarked Mr Darcy, appearing at her side unexpectedly. He continued to stand there, exchanging pleasantries and joking with whoever approached them. Caroline resented his hovering presence bitterly, for she had not forgiven him what he had done, even if he had taken measures to undo it. His willingness to salvage her reputation redeemed him a little in her eyes. It showed, at least, that he possessed a conscience. But she could not forget so easily.

Besides, she knew little enough about him or his financial standing. His apparent gallantry could mask a devious motive. It was just possible that he was a fortune hunter, and that the whole thing had been an elaborate ploy to force her to marry him.

Perhaps he had not spread the gossip maliciously. Perhaps he had dropped the reference by accident. Perhaps, as an outsider, he had not known the impact it would make.

But she doubted it.

The time came when, in the stream of questions and congratulations, she reached a point when she felt that if she did not disappear somewhere by herself soon, her painted smile was in danger of becoming a sneer. Mumbling an excuse to nobody in particular, she slipped out to visit the retiring room. The door opened as she reached it, and two young ladies emerged. Their heads close together, they giggled and whispered, then, when they saw her, fell silent, and passed by her awkwardly.

As if from a distant dream, their faces flashed through her mind as she had last seen them. She had been standing in the garden, talking to Mr Darcy.

She had noted their presence fleetingly at the time, and hoped they had not overheard her. What was it she had been saying? She had been angry that Mr Darcy had questioned her relationship with Sir Cecil. She had mentioned that she was anticipating an offer from him, and that she would accept.

And they had wandered past her at that exact moment.

She leaned against the wall, and took in a deep breath, shivering as the truth struck her.

She had wronged him. It had not been Mr Darcy who had betrayed her after all.

Chapter 8

THERE WAS NO OPPORTUNITY TO SPEAK TO HIM PRIVATELY THAT night, and the next morning they set out again for Pemberley, hoping to circumvent the eight day Nottingham Goose Fair, which was by now in full swing. They could not delay, for to do so would be to risk being caught in the crowds leaving the fair on their way home.

Nobody expected to enjoy the journey. A cloud of unspoken conflict hovered above them. Nevertheless, when Colonel Fitzwilliam announced that he would not continue with them to Pemberley, but return to London instead, a wave of protest rose up, and a chorus of voices urged him not to break his journey.

Robert Darcy tried to make light of whole thing. "Come, Fitzwilliam. Surely you will not abandon us at this stage of the journey? We are almost in Pemberley. Complete the journey with us, then you may return. You and I will hire horses and ride. It looks like we will be spared rain today."

The clenching of Colonel Fitzwilliam's jaw was the only indication that riding with Robert Darcy was hardly more appealing than spending time in the carriage with Caroline. She made a polite effort to convince him to continue on to Pemberley, though she knew very well that his feelings ran too high for any chance of reconciliation at present.

She was not afraid she had caused Colonel Fitzwilliam lasting pain, since she did not think him particularly attached to her. As a second son to an earl, he needed a financially advantageous match. Still, it would be some time before his pride would allow him to think of her with anything but anger, and nothing she said now would change that. She wished that she had answered him at once when he had asked for her hand. But she had not known her own mind at the time, and could not have predicted the events that followed. What was done was done.

She watched him leave with regret, and with a fervent hope that one day they would again be friends, for she genuinely liked him.

Their carriage was just starting down the drive when Caroline heard her name being called. She signalled for the coachman to stop immediately.

Mrs Germain was running from the house, carrying a box tucked under her arm.

"I am very glad that I was able to catch you before you left," she said breathlessly. "I have something I particularly wanted you to have."

She held out the Dieppe chess set Caroline had praised so highly the day before.

Caroline gasped in protest. "Oh, no, Mrs Germain! You cannot! I cannot accept it. It is far too valuable for you to part with."

"I want you to keep it. It holds many memories for me, but I think it belongs to you. I will be glad to know you are playing with it. I know you will use it well."

Caroline, touched deeply by Mrs Germain's kindness, stepped down and kissed her warmly on the cheek.

"Thank you," she said, struggling to hold back her tears. "You cannot know what this means to me."

"Oh, but I do. Otherwise I could not have parted with it for the world. Perhaps we will have the opportunity to play together again soon. I want you to know you will be very welcome to visit me in Town."

Caroline nodded, words failing her.

Mrs Germain gestured towards Mr Darcy, who sat above them on the box. "If you will take advice from an old woman like me," she said, in an undertone, "I would hold onto a young man such as that. They do not come one's way very often."

Caroline smiled and shook her head. Mrs Germain did not understand her situation. "Thank you for your advice," she said, politely.

"I see I have wasted my breath," said Mrs Germain, with a chuckle. "Nobody ever takes my advice." She waved warmly to Mr Darcy. "Take care of her, will you, Mr Darcy? She's the daughter of a special friend of mine."

Mr Darcy bowed. "You may put your mind at rest, Mrs Germain."

Caroline was worried that a day spent inside the carriage with Louisa would prove too much for her raw sensibilities. But Louisa had played loo and casino late into the night, and had nothing to say beyond remarking that she was glad Robert Darcy was out of their way, for she was hoping to catch up on some sleep.

From worrying that she would be forced to talk to three other people, Caroline found instead that she had nobody to talk to at all. Left alone with her thoughts, she sank into dejection, trying in vain to comprehend how she had managed to bring herself into such a tangle so very quickly.

When they had set out from Netherfield, their biggest problem had been which road to take. How simple her life had been. Now, in just a few days, her life had turned topsy-turvy, and she was at a loss how to restore it to its equilibrium.

The most pressing problem was to speak to Mr Darcy. She had been terribly wrong, and her behaviour was unpardonable. She winced as she remembered what she had said to him. The words burned into her like a hot iron. How could she ever make amends? A lifetime of apologies would not suffice to make up for what she had said. Yet he had repaid her detestable behaviour with generosity. Which did not mean that he had forgotten her insults. One glance at him when they stopped to change horses was enough to convince her that he remembered them all too well. He was polite, but he kept her at a very long arm's length.

She had to find a way to revoke her words and to convince him that they were spoken only in the heat of the moment. But how was she to do it? The labours of Hercules seemed easier. She stared out of the window, watching the green countryside roll by, finding nothing in it to distract her.

"I cannot quite accustom myself to the fact that you are engaged to Robert Darcy," said Louisa, waking up quite suddenly. "You should have seen how many people approached me yesterday to ask me where you had met. I replied as I thought I ought, given the circumstances. I told everyone that Mr Darcy was a friend of the family, which is perfectly true. You would not believe what a stir your engagement has caused. I was quite amazed! I gather you have disappointed more than one young lady who wished him for herself." Louisa pondered over this. "I cannot for my life see why that should be the case. Yet it seems your Mr Darcy is generally liked. Still, the sudden announcement has given rise to speculation."

"It is not unknown for a couple to meet and become engaged in a short time," said Caroline.

"No, but there are bound to be wagging tongues, and calculations about when the child will be due."

Heat flooded into Caroline's face.

"Oh, for heaven's sake, Caroline," said Louisa, "You need not be missish. You know people always gossip when a hasty engagement is announced."

"Well, you cannot expect me to relish the prospect," said Caroline.

Louisa shrugged. "It hardly matters. You will marry and they will be proved wrong. Oh, but what an evening! What a pity you missed it. I do not know what came over you, shutting yourself up in your room. I would have thought you would have enjoyed the attention. I was excessively diverted."

Louisa continued in that vein for some time. At several points Caroline almost interrupted, tempted to bring her sister into her confidence, and to reveal that the engagement was nothing but a sham. But Louisa's tongue could be loose at times, particularly if there was an advantage to revealing information, and Caroline could not be sure of her silence. She was glad, therefore, when Louisa lost interest in the topic and moved on to recount the latest gossip she had heard from London, and to describe her interactions with some of the guests she had met at Emelton Hall.

As the end of the day approached, Caroline grew more and more restless. She *must* talk to Darcy tonight. Tomorrow they would be in Pemberley, and she could not be sure when they would have a chance to be alone. She bitterly regretted the behaviour that made such an encounter necessary.

They crossed the Trent, and, passing by the ruins of an old castle, reached their destination, the Clinton Arms in Newark-on-Trent, just as night fell. Despite a lavish dinner put before them by the landlord, Caroline was too agitated to eat. The cool formality of Robert Darcy was so unaccustomed, it filled her with dread.

The moment they finished dinner, she pulled back her chair. "May we take a walk, Mr Darcy?" she asked. "If I promise to wear my woollen pelisse?" she added, attempting a weak joke in the hope that it would ease her tension. "I have something particular to speak to you about."

After a moment's hesitation he nodded curtly and allowed her to precede him outside into the village square.

She had to quicken her steps to keep up with him. He moved with a coiled watchfulness that belied his apparent ease. "I owe you an apology, Mr Darcy," she said.

Nothing in his stance changed. He continued onwards, his movement fluid, graceful, and alert. Well, what had she expected? That he would melt at her apology?

She licked her lips, which had gone dry. "I was upset and overwhelmed by the turn of events. It was a bolt out of the blue. I had hopes, or at least plans that were important to me, and they suddenly fell into ruin." Even as she spoke she knew her words were wrong. Trying to find excuses for herself was not her purpose here. "But that does not justify anything. I accused you of something I should have known you would never do." She paused.

"I know I have caused offence." The words were so inadequate she could almost laugh.

"You need not fear you have offended me, Miss Bingley. At least, not you in particular. Not more than anyone else, except that perhaps you were more honest. You remember the wagons in Stamford, carrying performers to display at the fair? I often feel like one of the shows featuring a Freak. Since I have come here, people in society peer at me as though I am a strange specimen, and make remarks to me they would never make to each other, thinking that I lack the wit to understand them. I have grown quite accustomed to it. So yes, Miss Bingley, you offended me, but I do not rate it particularly high in my list of concerns." There was anger in his statement, yet he spoke without rancour, with a heavy acceptance as though he had already resigned himself to it.

Caroline knew she ought to grasp his meaning, but she felt befuddled instead. His talk of Freaks confused her. How could he say that, when he was so clearly popular? "I am sorry," she said. "I do not understand. I wish I could."

"I cannot help you, Miss Bingley," he said, his lips curling.

"Is it because you are not one of us?" she asked, uncertainly.

"Yes, ma'am," he said, touching the edge of his hat. "Now you have hit the nail on the head."

She shook her head to clear it. They spoke the same language, but they were worlds apart.

Light from the windows around the square lit up the cobbled ground in small patches. The sound of hoarse singing and drunken revelry reached her from one of nearby inns. It was incongruous, but it grounded her in reality. She returned doggedly to her purpose.

"I cannot be responsible for what others have done. Only for myself, and I must make amends. I should not have reached the conclusion I reached. And I had no right to accuse you, having suspected such a thing, unless I had clear evidence. My wretched tongue!"

He halted abruptly. In the semi-darkness, his voice came from the shadows, his face invisible.

"No," he said, and for a moment she thought he was saying he could not forgive her no matter what she said. "*That* at least you must not regret. You spoke your mind. If you had not, how would I have known what conclusion you had reached? It would never have occurred to me that you might think I was the source of the rumour."

"But I should not have said what I said. I should not have accused you of being without scruples. You were right." She paused, hesitating to say it. "I *did* distrust you from the very beginning." Then, because she could not help it, she added, "You must admit our first encounter did not go very well, so I have *some* justification."

"I concede that I should have acknowledged my presence to you that day. It was a misjudgement on my part. It did not seem important at the time." He raised his hands in a gesture of surrender.

"It was important to me."

"I know that now," he said.

"Still, it does not excuse my behaviour," she continued. "Even if you were at fault—which I know now you are not—there was no call for me to say the things I did. My behaviour was abysmal. It was quite, quite unpardonable."

"You are once again indulging in a fit of self-accusation," said Robert Darcy, "and it serves no purpose at all. If it makes you feel better, I accept your apology." His shoulders had lost that coiled tension that they had held earlier, though his voice remained distant. "We have many matters to discuss, and I will take this opportunity to do so."

He had accepted her apology, but she felt no better. And words could not be unsaid, after all. They inhabited the space between them.

"Very well, Mr Darcy. Let us discuss other matters."

"Regarding our engagement," he said in a practical tone. "When the Olmsteads approached me, I knew there was no other remedy for the situation but to announce our engagement. I knew also that it was hardly an ideal solution. Something had to be done quickly, and nothing else came to mind. I am sorry there was no chance to warn you. But we did what we could, and now must deal with the results."

She nodded. "I am grateful to you—"

"I am not saying this because I expect gratitude," he interrupted, "but because we have a few problems ahead of us which must be resolved."

"I imagine there is a whole mountain of them," said Caroline.

"You are prone to exaggeration, Miss Bingley," he replied, with a hint of a smile. "Let us reduce them to a few. First and foremost," he continued, "do we tell the Darcys and your family? Do we convince them that the engagement is real, or do we reveal the truth?"

"Do you think we ought to reveal the truth?" she asked, knowing she would hate to expose herself and her hopes to be dissected, for there was no other way to tell the truth. But she would abide by whatever he decided.

"I think it is a better alternative than having them think the engagement is real. But I realize that you are reluctant, especially since it means revealing the truth to my cousin Darcy, so I will leave the decision to you. It is, after all, a private matter. Which brings me to the next concern I wish to raise. I am sure you have already reached this conclusion, but I prefer to be explicit. I have always believed in speaking openly to prevent misunderstandings."

She thought of their conversation in the garden two days before. Was it really only two days? It seemed as if weeks had passed.

Mr Darcy hesitated. When he spoke, he sounded quite remote. "You will not like what I have to say, perhaps, but it is the truth. I want you to have no illusions about our engagement. It is not real, and never will be. I am a stranger here in England, biding my time until the war between us is over so that I can return. I do not wish to complicate my life by becoming involved with an English lady." He stopped and passed his hand through his tousled curls. "Even though I was brought up as an Englishman, I find it difficult to accept some of society's rules here. Odd though it may seem to you, I am not comfortable being idle. I like to work. I am afraid *some* New England Puritan values have rubbed off on me, despite my mother's efforts." There was a hint of laughter in his voice, but it quickly disappeared. "I inherited a successful business in Boston, and I intend to make sure it continues that way."

A long pause followed. She sensed that he was grappling with words, trying to choose the right ones. "What I say now is not intended to disparage you or hurt you in any way, so I hope you will not take it as an insult. I wish only to make things perfectly clear. If I were, by any chance, to cast my lot with someone here, it would not be with someone like you."

She told herself he did not mean it as an insult, but it wounded nevertheless, to hear it spoken so plainly.

"I do not know how to say this without causing offence," he continued, and she braced herself for another onslaught. "You and I have nothing in common. We would not deal well together. You are rigid in your opinions and have very specific notions of right and wrong. Propriety is the goal of your existence, and for you the rules of society are paramount. You have a position to maintain, and that is what dominates your life."

Caroline shut her eyes. She deserved all this. Even though he did not say these things with malice, there was no mistaking his undertone of disapproval. She deserved it.

"I, on the other hand, care little for the approval of society. This has been a bone of contention between me and my mother for many years. I take after my father in that, and I am unlikely to change. But that is another matter entirely." He shrugged. "So you see, we would not match." The note of finality lingered in the empty square around them.

Her first impulse was to defend herself. But it would not do. It would be tantamount to arguing that they *would* match. And in that he was absolutely right. Of course they would not.

He stopped and turned to face her. "You are a striking and elegant young lady, and clever to boot. I enjoy your company. But it cannot go any further. I would not say this if we were not engaged. But under the circumstances, I must be sure there are no false expectations. You must agree to this. It is my condition for continuing the engagement."

"Of course," she said, haughtily, her pride stung. "You have my word that I will not beg you to continue."

She started to walk quickly back in the direction of the inn, the darkness around them a shield against him.

"I am sorry, Miss Bingley," he said. "I have been harsh, but it is for the best." He caught up with her easily. "I hope you do not plan to return to the inn. We still have matters to discuss."

"Very well," she replied, slowing down. "The night is cold, however, and I do not wish to be out too long."

"I would not keep you out if we did not need to sort matters out before we reach Pemberley," he said, in a tone that held a hint of apology. "*If* you decide you wish to maintain the pretence a little while longer, I am quite prepared to do it. When a suitable interval has passed, you can announce your desire to be released from the engagement. We can use the excuse that you hoped to persuade me not to return to the United States, and that when it came to it, you could not bear the idea of leaving England. I think people would understand your reasoning, even if they did not fully approve of you breaking the engagement."

She must have made some sound, because he paused and looked at her.

"You disagree?" he said.

"No."

"Good. In the meantime, we will not announce the engagement in the newspapers. The less said about it, the better. The quieter we keep it, the less gossip there will be later. But I would suggest staying away from London for a few months to avoid being in the public eye."

She thought of Sir Cecil. There would be no chance at all of resuming that relationship.

"I am afraid you cannot attach too many hopes to Sir Cecil," he said, as if reading her thoughts. Were her emotions so apparent? "I am sorry for that, but the situation could not be salvaged, one way or the other. At least this way you have escaped with your pride intact."

He had thought about it. He had concerned himself about her, even though he did not like her. She felt humbled by his concern.

"I am very much indebted to you, Mr Darcy. I do not know how I can ever repay you for your kindness."

"I am glad to be of service," he said. His voice was still reserved, but some of the hardness had worn off. "Is there anything more you wished to discuss?"

She took a deep breath and, bringing her thoughts into focus, considered. "No. Only that I *would* prefer, at least initially, for no one to know that the engagement is a deception. The alternative is too uncomfortable, at least for now."

"I can understand that," he said.

"So, difficult as it may be," she said, surprised to find herself suddenly quite light-hearted, "we must put aside our differences for the time being and pretend to like each other, if we are to present ourselves as a betrothed couple."

Silence reigned. For a moment she wondered if he would refuse. "It will not be so very difficult to pretend," he said, "since I *do* enjoy your company. But only if you promise not to hurl accusations at me."

She was glad to see his bantering manner had returned.

"I can only promise to try my best," she said, with a playfulness that was only slightly forced.

"Then we will call a truce. At least for a little while." He held out his gloved hand. She took it, not quite sure what to do with it.

"One generally shakes hands, when offered a truce," he said.

"Oh." She shook his hand, feeling gauche.

"I can see you would rather I kissed your hand, as a gentleman should do with a lady. A handshake is perhaps too masculine for your sense of propriety."

He brought her hand to his lips and kissed the tips of her fingers. His behaviour was perfectly correct, but he conveyed the impression of doing something risqué. She could feel the heat of his lips through the cloth and it flustered her.

She stood around uncertainly after he had released her hand.

"Shall we return to the inn now?" he said. "Even though we are engaged, I do not wish to prolong our absence. We need to be careful not to give rise to gossip, since we are to part later on."

She flushed. He was right to remind her, of course.

They returned silently to the inn and separated for the night. Caroline went up to the bedchamber she shared with her sister, leaving Robert Darcy behind to linger in the tap-room. She was relieved to find that Louisa was asleep. Casting her pelisse onto the back of the armchair, she sank down onto her bed, wondering where things had begun to go wrong.

She had always thought herself very competent. She had been confident of her goals and her ability to accomplish them. Then, one by one, the threads she had woven had begun to unravel, and now she was left with nothing but a tangle.

A scene from her schoolroom days rose up in her mind. She was in the parlour at home, engaged in some needlework. She even remembered the pattern she was embroidering, a small robin sitting on a branch and surrounded by snow. It was just a few weeks before her mother's death when she was fourteen. She had asked her mother how she and her father had met. Her mother had not answered. Instead, she had advised Caroline about her future.

"Never let yourself be swayed by emotions," her mother had said. "Emotions are fleeting. They come and go. But reality stays with you forever."

The words had seemed so wise. So that when her mother had continued with her words of advice, Caroline had committed them to memory, following them as she would a Biblical commandment.

"Reality can be hard, but a lady is not without recourse. If she can manage the man she marries, she can manage her life. The most important thing to a gentleman is flattery," said her mother, and the young Caroline listened intently. "If you can appeal to his vanity, he will stick to you like a burr. Gentlemen, above all, desire to feel indulged and pampered. It is their greatest weakness. And any intelligent woman will learn how to use that weakness to her advantage."

Caroline had always believed explicitly in her mother's capacity to achieve what she wanted, for she had managed the family with an iron fist concealed by a fashionable, feminine glove. Had she not, after all, forged Father from a rough youth into a proper gentleman, received in society and welcomed in the very best circles? Caroline had heard the story so often, and seen the results so clearly that she never doubted it.

Following her mother's dictum, Caroline had entered society determined to allow nothing to sway her from her objectives. When still quite young, Charles had introduced her to Mr Fitzwilliam Darcy, and she had decided almost immediately that he was the gentleman she wished to marry. She had exerted every possible effort to win him. She had flattered him and indulged his every whim. She had praised him on every occasion. She had admired his conduct, his clothes, his penmanship, his letters, his sister, his home. And it had not been far from the truth, for she had fallen quite in love with him. But despite every effort she had made, it had not worked. Providence, in the name of Eliza Bennet, had conspired against her.

And now, yet again, in spite of every effort on her part to fix her interest with Sir Cecil, Providence had intervened and taken him from her. Fortunately, she had not grown attached to him as she had done with Mr Darcy.

Her mother had not spoken to her about Providence. Nobody had told her that Providence had a way of disrupting all the best placed plans.

Certainly her mother could not have anticipated her meeting Mr Robert Darcy. Nor could she have imagined her daughter engaged to him. Nor imagined the scorn he displayed towards her daughter. For even if he had not meant it unkindly, Mr Robert Darcy had made it clear that he did not think her worthy of his interest.

Well, one man's meat was another man's poison. What did it matter after all if he liked her or not? In a few weeks—perhaps sooner—their engagement would end, and she need never encounter him again if she wished.

Meanwhile, as always, she would make the best she could of a very unpleasant situation.

Chapter 9

I~T DRIZZLED THE NEXT MORNING, AND DARCY ABANDONED HIS~ box seat to join them inside. Caroline was relieved to see that he was prepared to make himself agreeable. She did her best to reciprocate, but she was gripped by an unaccustomed sense of gloom, and despite all Mrs Drakehill's lessons, was unable to recover her poise. Her social ineptness was so noticeable that even Louisa observed it.

"I hope you mean to leave that long face behind when we arrive in Pemberley," said Louisa, "for you must remember the purpose of our visit is to cheer up Elizabeth, not cast her into despair."

Caroline would have resented her sister's words, except that they reminded her that she ought not to allow her feelings to be so apparent. She made a concerted effort to appear cheerful, and by the end of the journey had recovered enough that she was able to laugh at some particularly absurd comment made by Robert Darcy.

They approached Pemberley just as the rain cleared and the sun emerged, casting an orange hue on the world around them. Caroline could not help drawing in her breath at the sight of the large, elegant building. She had hoped to be mistress of it once. Now she arrived as a guest, but her eye still appreciated its beauty. Her spirits began to lift, for it was an old familiar place and she was glad to be there.

Mr Darcy emerged from the house to greet them. Her heart stopped beating for a moment. He was as she remembered him. His dear brown eyes, the hair he carefully arranged over his brow, the knot of his cravat—all was unchanged. But in other ways he had changed. His expression was less haughty, his carriage looser, his expression softer than she remembered, and he smiled more readily.

She realized the moment she saw him how strongly he resembled his cousin.

Her heartbeat returned to a normal, steady rhythm. All would be well. There would be no unexpected emotional displays. Her humiliating infatuation was gone. The sense of relief was so strong her knees weakened and she stumbled. Mr Darcy caught her and steadied her.

"Welcome to Pemberley, Miss Bingley," he said.

Then everything sprang into motion, and she turned her attention away from him. There was Jane waiting eagerly for them. And Charles, who beamed when Louisa, then Caroline, threw their arms around him affectionately.

"Anyone would have thought I had been away for years!" he said, in his usual way. "What a fuss!"

But he loved it, and Caroline was truly glad to see him.

Jane stepped forward and embraced her. "I am very glad you have come, Caroline," she murmured, close to her ear, "for I find Pemberley too large and overwhelming. I am quite terrified. I am sure you will manage the household far better than I. Everything seems quite a muddle."

"Then we will all just have to muddle through together," said Caroline, squeezing Jane's hand reassuringly.

They were propelled inside, and there was Miss Eliza Bennet—no, Mrs Darcy—lying on the sofa in the drawing room looking pale and gaunt and quite unlike herself, her face drained of its customary vigour. Eliza's illness had never seemed real to Caroline until now. Shocked by the sight, Caroline went quickly to Eliza's side.

"You do not look well at all, Mrs Darcy!" she cried. "Oh, I do hope our presence will not fatigue you. Maybe we should not have come."

A twinkle came into Eliza's eyes, and with it a touch of colour to her cheeks. "Come, Caroline! What is this *Mrs Darcy* business? You have always addressed me by my first name. As for fatiguing me, on the contrary, I am so sick of lying in bed looking up at the ceiling. Believe me, I know every blemish on the walls, every chip in the paint, every speck of dust on the furniture. I am ready to throw out everything in my bedchamber and refurnish the room from scratch."

"It is lucky, in that case, Eliza," said Louisa, "that you have a wealthy husband."

Caroline shot Louisa a dark look. The visit was doomed to disaster if Louisa could not control her tongue.

"I would not advise it, Eliza," said Caroline brightly, trying to make light of the tasteless remark. "You look too tired to undertake such a thing now. You may choose colours that appeal to you at the moment, just to be contrary, only to find you dislike them intensely later on."

"Oh," said Eliza, "You need not worry that I will be doing anything so foolhardy. I was not serious. I was simply giving vent to my frustration. I dislike being idle, you see," she said.

"Yes, I recall very well that you think nothing of walking three miles in inclement weather," said Louisa.

"Exactly," said Eliza, smiling. "You know me well."

Her smile broadened as Robert Darcy approached. She held out her hand to him. "Robert," she said, "I am very glad to see you again. I felt very bad that we sent you such a long way to fetch Jane for me. You did not have to go yourself, you know. We could have sent a messenger."

He took her hand in his. "If I have helped you feel better, Cousin Elizabeth, then I am content. I can see already that your sister's presence has been beneficial."

"It is good to have you back in any case. I hope you do not plan to rush off to London very soon," she said.

"I am at your beck and call, cousin. Your wish is my command," he replied, raising her hand to his lips.

Georgiana Darcy entered at that moment, and all attention centred on her. Caroline found her much improved since she last saw her. She had been lanky and awkward but had now developed into a very pleasing young lady.

"Why, Georgiana!" said Louisa. "I would hardly have recognized you. You have changed so much!"

"For the better, I hope," said Georgiana, pertly.

"You must not fish for compliments," said Darcy. "It is not polite."

"Allow me to disagree," said Robert Darcy. "She knows she is pretty and wants us to acknowledge it. What is wrong with that?"

"Thank you, cousin," said Georgiana. "I am very pleased you have returned, for now I shall receive all the compliments I could possibly hope for. Pray say you are planning to stay, and do not intend to ride back to your home any time soon."

"Oh, I would not miss such a gathering for anything," said Robert Darcy.

Georgiana clapped her hands. "Good," she said. "Things will be far merrier now." She threw a sweeping look around which encompassed everybody. "I am happy to see you all," she said, graciously. "You are all most welcome." She abandoned her hostess role as suddenly as she had taken it up. "You will be giving a dance, will you not, Fitz?"

Louisa looked outraged. "*Fitz?*" She cast Darcy a questioning glance. "Since when have you called your brother Fitz?"

Georgiana giggled. "Since Cousin Robert taught me to do it. I will admit that I was terrified the first time. But Fitz just looked at me and threatened to call me Georgie back. I don't do it all the time," she admitted shyly, "just when I want to get his attention. So, Brother Fitz, will we have a party?"

Darcy threw a glance at Eliza. "I very much doubt it, *Georgie*. Eliza is too fatigued for such an undertaking."

"But she would not have to do a thing," cried Georgiana. "I will arrange it all. And I will enlist the help of everybody. You *must* let me take charge, brother."

Darcy sighed. "What do you think, Eliza?"

"I think it would be something to look forward to," she said. "Though I cannot contribute as much as I would wish."

"You will not contribute at all," said Darcy sternly, brooking no argument.

For a moment, he was like the Mr Darcy Caroline had known. Then he looked at Eliza and she knew he had changed irretrievably.

When it was time to go down to dinner, Caroline found herself feeling more tired than she would have expected from such an uneventful journey. Her throat felt as though someone had scrubbed it with a brush, and she was beginning to sound hoarse. It was barely noticeable, but Robert Darcy, who was seated between

Georgiana and Louisa, glanced at her sharply as she fell into a fit of coughing.

"Remind me," he said, speaking across the table to her. "I have a very potent medicine for chest congestion at my house, something I brought with me from Boston. I will ride over in the morning and bring you some. It is very effective in fighting infection. The recipe is an indigenous one that a friend of mine learned from the Sachem of an Indian tribe."

"Oh, how thrilling! Have you encountered any Indians yourself?" said Louisa. "You must tell us all about them."

"I am sorry to disappoint you, but I have not," he replied. "There are very few native tribes in the area around Boston, though I believe there are a small number of villages remaining on Nantucket Island and some other far-lying areas. But my friend at Harvard College made a study of their languages, and he is forever braving the wilderness to find them and to learn more about them. I have been fortunate to receive the recipe for this remedy through him. It has saved me and my sisters from illness on countless occasions."

"But what are they like? The Indians, I mean," persisted Louisa.

"I cannot tell you," said Mr Robert, smiling. "Perhaps one day you will meet my friend and you can question him all about them."

"It would be most unlikely," said Louisa, "unless you brought him here to visit."

"Until the hostilities between us and the Americans are over, no one, not even Robert will be able to travel to Boston," said Darcy. Eliza was not at the table with them, finding it too tiring to sit up for the whole meal, and Darcy's manner seemed more withdrawn without her. There was a query in his voice, which his cousin immediately detected.

"Since I have no way of anticipating when the hostilities will end, I cannot predict my behaviour. But for the moment, I mean to make some improvements on my property, and I do not imagine I will be leaving any time soon."

Darcy seemed satisfied by the answer, and the conversation took another direction.

By and by Charles raised the subject which she had hoped to avoid, for the time being at least. "You have not told me anything about your journey, apart from mentioning your visit to the Loughs. I am all ears. I want to hear everything."

A lull in the conversation made everyone look at Caroline, awaiting her answer with interest, with the exception of Robert Darcy, who looked suddenly very interested in his food.

"There is so much to tell. We stopped at Emelton Hall in Lincolnshire to stay with the Loughs. They are friends of Colonel Fitzwilliam. It was very agreeable," she replied. "There were many of our acquaintances there, and—"

Louisa broke in. "I do not know how you can sit there so calmly when I am practically bursting to tell them the news."

"What news?" said Jane, looking at Caroline curiously.

Caroline cast a look of entreaty at Robert Darcy. For a moment, it seemed he would not respond. Then he stood up slowly and, lifting his glass solemnly, he requested everyone to prepare for a toast.

"I hope you will be happy to share in our news," he said, his voice filling the room. The silence of anticipation as they listened for his next words stretched Caroline's nerves to breaking point. "Miss Bingley and I have agreed to become engaged."

Pandemonium broke out. The glasses that were poised for a toast were abandoned as everyone tried to question the newly engaged couple at once. Georgiana rushed round the table to embrace Robert

Darcy and to plant a kiss on Caroline's cheek, all the time exclaiming that she could not believe it. Charles scraped back his chair and strode over to Robert Darcy. He slapped him on the shoulder and said that he could not have wished for a better brother-in-law. "Though you could have waited to ask my permission to address her first," he added.

A string of protests rose up as the ladies present pointed out that Caroline was of age and did not need his permission to marry, and he raised his hands up in good-natured surrender.

Jane gave Caroline an affectionate embrace and wished them both as much happiness as she enjoyed with Charles.

Only one person remained in his seat. Darcy had said nothing since the announcement. His expression was grave, and he observed the two of them with a thoughtful expression.

The chaos came to an end when Eliza appeared in the doorway, a large woollen shawl wrapped round her shoulders.

"I heard the noise from my parlour and came to see what was happening," she said. "Something out of the usual must have occurred to evoke such a reaction."

Darcy threw down his napkin and strode quickly to his wife. He led her to a chair, supporting her carefully, and making sure she was comfortable before returning to his seat.

"Eliza, you will never guess it. Cousin Robert and Caroline are engaged!" cried Georgiana, her eyes sparkling.

"Is that so?" said Eliza, raising one of her brows. "Well, that is news indeed! I would never have thought it."

"Nor would I," said her husband.

Something more should be said. Caroline did not think either Mr or Mrs Darcy had received the news with any degree of pleasure. "You have not yet drunk to our health," she said, seizing upon the first thing that came to her mind.

The toast that ensued was loud and full of good wishes.

But to Caroline everything rang hollow. She was plagued by guilt as the implications of what was happening struck her. She should have listened to Robert Darcy. No good would come out of announcing their engagement to their families. There could be nothing but trouble in maintaining the deception.

More and more she felt herself sinking into a bog, slowly going down and unable to extricate herself, for every move she made seemed only to make matters worse.

Chapter 10

S HE WOULD HAVE CONTINUED IN THIS VEIN, HAD NOT SALVATION
come from a completely unexpected source.

It was late afternoon the next day. The gentlemen had recently
returned from grouse shooting, and Caroline was walking idly in the
garden when Robert Darcy appeared next to her. A day of activity
suited him well, for he seemed quite cheerful, though there was still
a watchfulness about him she could not like.

"I have brought you the medicine I promised," he said. "Though I
can see now that you do not need it, for you have not coughed yet."

"You do not mean to say you rode to your home to fetch it!"
exclaimed Caroline. "Oh, you are very obliging."

"I promised you I would bring it, and it would not do at all to
neglect my betrothed," he replied, a twinkle in his eye.

"Oh, do not speak of that, please! I am truly exhausted trying to
find the best way to extract myself from this coil."

"Then let matters rest for the moment. I am sure an answer
will come, once you cease to worry over it so much. Have you not
noticed it is always so? No sooner do you put a problem aside than
a solution occurs to you. For now, let us simply enjoy this crisp
autumn day. I love nothing more than the yellows and browns of

the leaves. Though I admit I miss the bright red of the maples at home. Autumn is the best season of the year in Boston. The colours are unmatched anywhere else, I believe."

Caroline surveyed the trees. She was too much a town person to pay much attention to nature, but as she examined the leaves the sun began to sink towards the horizon, and she suddenly saw the scene with eyes of an artist. The landscape was awash with colour. The sky was tinted with purple and red, the trees shimmered with yellow, and the green grass was dotted with leaves of orange and brown. She was a proficient painter, and it occurred to her that she would like to capture such a moment on canvas.

"It is quite perfect," she said. "Mr Darcy has arranged his gardens very well, has he not? I admit that William Kent's style of gardening has something to be said for it. Was it not he who said "Nature abhors a straight line"?"

"I could not say, Miss Bingley. I bow to your superior knowledge."

"Still, I cannot help feeling that if Mr Darcy's father had placed the lake a little more to the right, more in line with the house, the effect would have been more pleasing. But then, I follow rather old-fashioned ideals of landscaping. I have always favoured symmetrical French gardens. I find the structure and order more satisfying than the effects of wilderness that are currently in mode."

"You are joking, are you not? About the lake, I mean."

"Joking?" For a moment her mind was a blank. Then she concluded he was mocking her taste. "I told you I was behind the times," she said, defensively. "My father had a French designer brought in from Paris to set up the gardens at our home. That was when I was still a child. But I remember it very clearly. I loved the way everything was laid out—the sculpted hedges, the intersecting lines, the fountain dancing in the centre. I could not imagine anything more perfect."

"I was not questioning your taste, Miss Bingley. You were in earnest, then, about the lake."

Something was evading her, she was sure. If only she could determine what it was.

Robert Darcy turned to her, his eyes glittering with mirth. "I am sorry, Miss Bingley, but I fear I must explain. You will hardly credit it, I know, but what you are looking at is a natural lake."

"A natural lake? On Mr Darcy's grounds?"

"I am afraid it is true."

She contemplated the idea. "How extraordinary! I would not have thought it."

"Our Darcy, it appears, has hidden aspects to his character."

"Well," she said, blinking, as though expecting the offending lake to disappear from view. It did not. "No wonder it is lopsided."

Mr Robert threw back his head and laughed, very loudly.

His laughter was infectious enough that she laughed with him, without really knowing why.

At that moment a carriage came tearing up the driveway. Its alarming speed did not bode well, and without a backward glance, Caroline hurried towards the house. The instant the carriage stopped, the door flew open and to her complete surprise Lydia Wickham jumped out. She paused briefly when she saw Caroline. "Oh, where is my sister? Where is Lizzy?" she cried. And with that she hurried into the house.

Caroline, seeing the astonishment in Robert Darcy's eyes, enlightened him. "That is Lydia, Eliza's sister. She did not attend Mr Darcy's wedding, so you must not have met her."

"I did not stay long enough at the wedding to meet anyone. I was called away too suddenly. But I thank you for enlightening me."

They hastened after her, wondering what could have brought her there in such a desperate state. No sooner had Lydia reached the parlour when she ran in and threw herself into Jane's arms.

"Oh, Jane! Where is Lizzy?" she sobbed, loudly, "I am *so* unhappy!"

Caroline, feeling like an intruder, entered the parlour, followed by Robert Darcy. She sat next to Georgiana on the sofa and struggled to make sense of the incoherent explanation Lydia poured into her sister's ears.

Jane patted her sister on the back and handed her a handkerchief. "I cannot understand a word you are saying," she said, soothingly. "Come now. Calm down a little and then you can tell us everything. And if you wait I will send for Eliza, so you need not tell the same story twice."

She was interrupted by a discreet cough from the butler, who announced in the manner of one giving a rebuke: "Mrs Eleanor Miles. Captain George Trewson."

Lydia, whose sobbing had obscured the butler's proclamation, was instantly forgotten the moment her companions entered the room.

Caroline almost gaped at the vision in front of her. Mrs Miles was by far one of the most beautiful young ladies she had ever seen. She floated forward with an elegance that every woman must envy. She was a tall vision of loveliness in a pale green dress, beautifully cut and at the height of fashion, bordered with layers of intricate lace. Behind her, Captain Trewson, in his red regimentals, was no less a striking figure. No statue of Adonis that she had seen matched the perfection of his features. The neatness of his attire and the shine of his boots would have put Beau Brummel to shame.

"Forgive us," said Mrs Miles, in a musical voice. "We had not meant to intrude on you like this. My brother and I planned to stay the night at an inn, and send a message to announce our arrival, but

Mrs Wickham would not hear of it. And truth be told, we preferred to see that she was settled in safely before going on our way."

There was an immediate chorus of objection, which came as much from the gentlemen as from the ladies. Louisa was eying Captain Trewson as if he was a confection she planned to eat. Georgiana was gaping up at him with a young girl's love-struck expression, and even Jane seemed not to be able to tear her eyes away.

Meanwhile, Charles, who had been writing a letter, rose to fetch Mrs Miles a cushion, and Robert Darcy hovered behind her seat.

"You must not think of staying at an inn," said Darcy, entering with Eliza. "None of the inns hereabouts is of a very high standard. They are all either draughty or prone to infestation."

"Yes, you must indeed stay," said Eliza. "If you are friends of Lydia's, we would hardly turn you away from our doorstep." She smiled as Captain Trewson bowed exquisitely to her.

"Mrs Darcy is most kind," said Captain Trewson, in a voice with rich melodious tones that had a soothing effect on Caroline's nerves. "We would be happy to take advantage of your hospitality. We will be leaving tomorrow, however. My sister and I would not dream of trespassing on such a cosy family gathering."

Lydia, realizing that nobody was paying her the least attention, pulled herself up from Jane's arms and threw herself onto an armchair, gazing from one person to the other with big tragic eyes.

"You cannot imagine what has happened," she announced loudly, then bent her head to examine her fingernails.

"Do tell us, Lydia," said Jane, who was always kind. Lydia needed little more encouragement than that.

"Oh, pray tell, Lydia," said Eliza, sitting close to Jane on the sofa.

"It's that horrid, horrid Wickham!" said Lydia. "Oh, I don't know how I will endure it." She hid her face in her hands. "If it had not been for the kindness of Captain Trewson and Mrs Miles, I am sure I would have drowned myself in the river. For it is not to be borne. He has run off with a young lady from Newcastle, a Mrs Greene. Have you ever heard such a stupid name? I'm sure I haven't. And he left me a note saying I should not expect him back. Oh, Lizzy, what shall I *do*?"

Caroline flinched in shock, though she should not have been surprised at Wickham's behaviour. She had warned Eliza Bennet about him on several occasions before Lydia married him, though Eliza had paid no heed to her at the time. Wickham was insolent and infamous, and had done Darcy a very bad turn, though Caroline was not privy to the details. Then Lydia had eloped with him, quite scandalously, and now she was suffering the consequences.

Robert Darcy was the first to respond. He was the most inclined to pity her, for he knew nothing about Wickham, nor of the circumstances of Lydia's marriage. "What a terrible blow, Mrs Wickham!" he said. "But I am sure it is all a misunderstanding and will be sorted out. In any case, it is indeed very fortunate that you were discovered by the captain and Mrs Miles, and that they brought you here to be with your sisters." He smiled at Mrs Miles.

Lydia, feeling slighted, and recognizing that further tears would have no effect, rose restlessly to look out of the window, though it had grown quite dark outside. Jane went and took her by the hand, and they left the room together with Eliza, presumably to talk in the privacy of the bedchamber.

Lydia's problem soon receded to the background. Refreshments were brought in, and the Trewsons became the centre of all attention. They answered the multitude of questions aimed at them with unaffected cordiality, and it was discovered that Captain Trewson, in addition to his striking good looks, had at his command a multitude of entertaining tales and anecdotes. Mrs Miles was good-natured, and possessed pleasing manners. She commanded attention, but she did not put herself forward, which did much to redeem her from the ruffled sensibilities of the ladies who were eclipsed by her. The brother and sister retired early, pleading tiredness after a long journey.

All in all everyone was in agreement that the two arrivals were a delightful addition to the company.

The next morning Caroline woke up to a commotion at the front of the house. There was much ado, with shouting and clanging and a great deal of coming and going. She wondered if Mrs Miles and her brother were leaving. She had not said good-bye, so, donning a shawl quickly, she opened the window and leaned out.

The scene that met her eyes was one of utter chaos. Baggage and boxes were strewn across the driveway, and footmen hurried backwards and forwards to the shrill orders of a voice she was soon able to recognize. She drew back from the window and resolved to spend the day in bed.

But the door to her room opened, and Louisa came in, catching her just as she dived under the covers.

"You *must* come down," said Louisa in a harassed voice. "You *cannot* leave me to deal with Mrs Bennet. She has not been here longer than ten minutes, and already the house is in disarray."

"Leave me alone," said Caroline. "I wish to sleep."

"I hope you do not intend to tell her of your engagement. She will spread the news before you know it, and by the time the announcement appears in the newspaper, the information will be quite stale. "

Caroline sat up suddenly as reality crashed back down on her. "Louisa, I do not wish a *soul* to know about the engagement. You must not write to anyone. Mr Robert Darcy has not yet informed his family of it, and it would be too bad if we announced it without at least informing his mother."

"I wish you had told me that before, as I have already written to several of my friends," said Louisa. "I had Mr Darcy frank the letters and send them out. I'm afraid the news is already circulating. I do not know how you meant to keep it a secret when you proclaimed it to all and sundry at the house party."

Caroline groaned. "I wish you had not done that, Louisa. You have been too hasty. I am not even entirely certain Robert Darcy and I will suit."

Louisa dismissed her words with a wave of her hand. "You cannot be undecided when the deed is already done." Louisa eyed her shrewdly. "If you do not intend to continue with this engagement—and I cannot say I blame you for it—you should terminate it immediately. Within a few days. It will cause a great deal of speculation, but it will blow over quickly. After all, there has been nothing official. No marriage settlement has been made and nothing has appeared in the papers. Caroline, you can do far better. If you set your mind to it, I am sure you can capture someone much more appropriate for our station in life. I have been thinking about it, and I am certain Mr Robert Darcy will not do at all. Perhaps you can convince Colonel Fitzwilliam to propose again. You are clever, Caroline, you will think of a way."

For once her sister's words found fertile ground. As if sensing it, Louisa left the room, allowing the seeds she had sown to grow.

Caroline sank back in her bed and stared upwards. The imperfections on the ceiling's surface brought to mind the words of Eliza

Bennet—Mrs Darcy. She waited for the familiar rancour to rise up to her throat, but no emotion surfaced. She thought of Eliza calmly, without resentment. In fact, she could almost see herself coming to like her.

Her maid Molly, who, despite leaving Netherfield a day later, had arrived a day earlier than Caroline since she had taken the other road, entered with some hot chocolate. Caroline sipped it slowly, amused at the furore accompanying Mrs Bennet's arrival.

The door burst suddenly open and Lydia rushed in. Caroline gasped at her impertinence.

"You might have asked if you could come in," she said, coldly.

But Lydia was immune to disapproval. "La!" she said. "Not when I have come with news. You will never guess who is here. My whole family! Is it not the most fantastical thing? Now we are all gathered here. And Mrs Darcy—I like the sound of that name, don't you?—has promised us all a house party. And she will be inviting some gentlemen from London. I am so glad Wickham ran away, otherwise I would not have been here, and I would have missed the fun."

Caroline wondered if there was any way to get rid of her, short of telling her in no uncertain terms to leave. She finished her chocolate, rose from her bed, picked which garments to wear, and dressed, while Lydia continued to prattle, ruminating on the names of officers who should be invited.

"I hope you will not think me rude," said Lydia, suddenly, "but I have remembered someone who really ought to be invited. I must tell Eliza to include him." With that, she bounced out of the room, leaving a blessed silence behind.

"What a relief!" said Caroline, as Molly put the finishing touches to her hair. "She never stopped talking once! And yet here I was, a prisoner in my own room, unable to escape, since I was not yet fully dressed!"

"That young lady can talk the hoofs off a horse," remarked Molly.

Caroline laughed. "She certainly talked my ears off."

"There's no harm in her. She's just a child," said the maid.

"I cannot agree with you. She is thoughtless and selfish."

Molly shrugged. "My sister was like her, all giddy and full of fancies. Once she was married and the babes began to come, though, she changed her tune."

Caroline smiled. "Then perhaps there is hope," she said and left it at that.

As soon as she was dressed, Caroline descended to the drawing room to greet the Bennets. The Bennet girls, Kitty and Mary, were busy studying fashion plates with Georgiana. Mr Bennet was already settled in a corner with a newspaper. He got up and bowed when she entered, stating that it was quite a change to see her in Pemberley instead of Netherfield, then returned to his reading.

"My dear Miss Bingley," said Mrs Bennet, taking Caroline's hands in both her own. "We came as quickly as we could when we heard the news. It was very naughty of Jane to leave Meryton without telling us!"

Caroline struggled to find an excuse for her sister-in-law, for they had left rather abruptly, but Mrs Bennet had already moved on. "What do you think of Pemberley? Is it not grand? I believe it is grander even than Lady de Bourgh's house, though I have not seen it, but so they tell me, and *that* is something." She patted the sofa next to her. "Was it not clever of me to marry off Lizzy to Mr Darcy? Indeed, others have said the same. 'Sister,' said Mrs Philips to me the other day. 'Sister, you should become a matchmaker, for once you have set your mind to securing a marriage, nothing will stop you.' I cannot claim all the credit for marrying my daughters off, of course. They are all very pretty girls, so it took very little on my part. They have their looks from me, you know, for I was quite pretty myself once. I turned quite a few gentlemen's heads, did I not Mr Bennet?"

At the mention of his name, Mr Bennet sat up enquiringly.

"I was saying to Miss Bingley that I was quite pretty myself, once," said Mrs Bennet. "Would you not agree, Mr Bennet?"

"I must agree, for there could have been no other reason for me to marry you, otherwise," he said, and returned to his reading.

Mrs Bennet appeared quite satisfied with his reply. "Oh, Mr Bennet! You must not tease so! People will think you serious. There, you see," she continued, turning back to Caroline, "as I was telling you, they have their looks from me. But you cannot trust everything to looks, you know. Careful planning is often necessary, and I flatter myself I am successful at it."

"You were not successful in Lydia's case, Mama," said Kitty, with the tactlessness of the young. "For her marriage has proved a disaster. He has run off with a married woman and is never coming back."

Mrs Bennet's eyes rounded, and her mouth turned into a perfect O. She cast a nervous look at Caroline. "What silly nonsense you are talking, Kitty! I do not know how you think of such things," she admonished.

"It is not silly nonsense," said Kitty, sullenly. "Lydia told me so herself."

Mrs Bennet stood up in a hurry and excused herself. "I must speak to Lydia immediately. Oh, if that is true, I do not know what will happen to me. I can already feel a spasm coming on! It cannot be true!" She hurried from the room, clutching a handkerchief to her mouth.

Caroline, considering that she had greeted the Bennets as politeness dictated, made her excuses and headed for the breakfast room. Mrs Miles and Mr Trewson were there, partaking of light refreshments.

"I am glad to see you still here," said Caroline, pleasantly surprised. "I had thought you gone by now."

"We have been prevailed upon to stay a few days," said Captain Trewson. "And though we have business in Town, I for one could not quite resist such agreeable company."

The room was bright and sunny, and Caroline could think of no pleasure greater than to watch two such graceful creatures. They sat at one end of the table, and she chose a seat next to them. However, they got up just then to serve themselves at the side table, and when they sat down again they chose the other end.

Robert Darcy came in and made to sit next to Mrs Miles, but she gave him her seat.

"We were just leaving, Mr Robert," she said.

Caroline thought it odd that they were leaving just moments after they had filled their plates. But Robert Darcy, who had sat on the far end of the table, merely wished them an enjoyable morning, and moved his plate next to hers.

"No point in shouting across the table," he said in a friendly manner.

"I can see that I am only second choice, however. Had Mrs Miles not left, you would not have been so concerned about shouting across the table."

He chuckled. "You are entirely too sharp, Miss Bingley. But surely you cannot blame me for my interest. Is she not exquisite?"

"She is very beautiful," said Caroline.

"I now see the evils of being engaged. How am I to attract her attention when I am already promised to someone else?"

"If you wish me to release you, just say the word," she said, thinking of her sister's advice. "Perhaps the sooner, the better."

"Oh, you need not worry. I have no serious designs on Mrs Miles. If matters develop, we will contrive something." He rose, wiping his mouth on a napkin. "I am sorry to leave you so soon, but I promised to take Mrs Wickham off Cousin Eliza's hands. Georgiana and Jane are trying to organize the party with Eliza, but Mrs Wickham will not give them a moment to think. I will take her riding."

"Poor Mr Robert," said Caroline.

"Oh, I shall do well enough. She is just young and spirited." He bowed. "So are we in agreement?"

She could only think he meant the engagement. "Yes," she said.

It was now Mr Darcy's turn to come to the breakfast room. He passed Mr Robert in the doorway and went to the sideboard to inspect the food.

"I hope everything is to your satisfaction, Miss Bingley."

"Yes, thank you," said Caroline.

Instead of helping himself to the food, Mr Darcy took a turn around the room. He appeared to be in some discomfort. He paused to look out of the window. Then he took another turn around the room. Finally, just as Caroline was ready to leave, he strode purposefully towards her.

"Forgive me, Miss Bingley," he said, "but I require your attention. I have something of a very private nature to discuss with you."

And he closed the door.

Chapter 11

Mr Darcy's footsteps resonated loudly on the marble floor as he came towards her.

"I have given the matter considerable thought," he said abruptly, "and I have reached the conclusion that an engagement between you and my cousin would be a mistake."

Caroline, who for years had pursued Mr Darcy, could not help but wonder at this sudden statement. For a wild moment, she wondered if he was about to make some kind of declaration, to say his marriage to Elizabeth was a mistake. If he was, she could only think that it had come much too late.

"I believe," she said, mildly, quite at a loss, "that it is your cousin who must make that decision."

"My interference is well intentioned, I assure you," said Mr Darcy, still in that abrupt way of his. "I have my cousin's interest at heart."

The idea of a declaration died a quick and final death. She mocked herself for imagining it even for an instant.

"I do not quite comprehend your meaning, Mr Darcy," said Caroline, proudly.

"My cousin is from a different country. He is not accustomed to English ways, and he does not know you. You are forgetting,

Miss Bingley, that I know you very well." He strode to the window, his boots striking the floor vigorously. "It occurs to me that your interest in my cousin is very sudden. You are seeking an advantageous marriage, which is quite understandable in your situation. However, I would not wish my cousin to be hurt in the process. I know you can be quite tenacious when you desire something."

She stiffened. Surely she had heard wrong? After all the time he had known her, was that all he could say of her? That she was *tenacious*? When she had spent so many nights of her life dreaming about him? When she had struggled so hard not to reveal to him the truth about her feelings?

Anger rose up in her, sharp and bitter. But she controlled it. She was determined not to let him provoke her into saying something unwise. She had learned her lesson well.

"I have not had time to be *tenacious*, Mr Darcy," she said calmly. "Things have happened much too quickly for that. I appreciate your concern for your cousin, but I do not think it entitles you to address me in this manner. Nor does it give you the right to interfere."

"As the head of the Darcy family, it is incumbent on me to understand the nature of this engagement. I have every right to question your plans for my cousin's future. I do not know how you contrived to bring him to this point, but I am entitled to know."

She stared at him in outrage. How could he possibly suggest that she had bullied Mr Robert into marrying her? As if Robert Darcy could be so easily manipulated! As if he suspected his cousin of being a weakling! She was not sure if she was more indignant on her own behalf or on that of Robert Darcy.

"If you wish to find out, I suggest that you talk to your cousin," she said, trying her best to be civil. "If you are worried that the marriage will be a disadvantage to him, may I remind you that I have a large sum of money at my disposal?"

"Do you consider twenty thousand pounds an advantage? When you must surely be aware of how much he is worth? There is not a matron in London who would not wish him for her daughter. He could make an excellent match. And I intend that he will."

It was ridiculous for her to be so angry when the engagement was not even real, but it was growing more and more impossible for her to remain silent.

"Allow me to express my doubts about this matter. You are forgetting that his fortune, such as it is, comes entirely from trade."

"Miss Bingley, I believe you forget yourself!" He strode back down the room to where she sat and stared down at her haughtily. "You can hardly be unaware that he is a Darcy," he said. "I do not wish to speak ill of your family, but you have put me in an impossible situation. You can hardly claim the same social standing. *You* do not come from an old and revered family."

He waited for his words to sink in, then continued remorselessly. "You are very much mistaken when you say I have no right to interfere. I have every right to interfere. The man you are seeking to marry is my cousin. And furthermore, until such a happy event as the birth of a son, Robert is my heir. Pemberley and everything else that I possess will pass over to him, in the event of my death. Even if he did not inherit my property, his own estate is respectable enough to tempt the most fastidious of the London matrons."

He resumed his pacing. His face had gone pale, and he struggled for the appearance of composure. He came towards her again and halted before her.

"It is my duty to interfere if I think that he is entering into a marriage that is unsuitable, to someone who does not care for him and, moreover, is not his social equal."

His disclosure dazed her. She had not known Robert to be Mr Darcy's heir. But her astonishment was nothing to the anger his words provoked. This, then, was how he viewed her? Yet she had pursued him for all that time, secure in the belief that she was his social equal, and that a match between them was possible. Fool that she was!

"Your cousin has already chosen to marry me," she said, unyielding. "We are engaged, and have announced our engagement to the world."

Mr Darcy's lips tightened. "An engagement can be broken," he said. "It *should* be broken. Robert is new to this country. He needs to look higher if he is to be accepted by his peers. *Your* family, and your connections, such as they are, will only hinder him."

Caroline's control snapped. It was one thing to talk of the engagement as generally unsuitable, and another to attack her family. "I do not see how you can talk in this manner when you selected as your own wife someone who has even fewer family connections."

"I will thank you, Miss Bingley, *not* to speak of my wife in this manner." His voice was ice cold. "Eliza is the daughter of a *gentleman*. Can you say the same of your father?"

She was breathing quite heavily now. "You interfered before in my brother's affairs, and almost destroyed his happiness. I will not allow you to meddle in mine." She stood, determined to put an end to this exchange. "I will not end this engagement simply because you have determined that I am unworthy."

"That remains to be seen," said Mr Darcy. He bowed stonily and left the room.

Caroline collapsed into her chair, breathing in ragged breaths and trying to regain some semblance of calm. She could scarcely believe what had transpired. How dare he think her below his cousin's notice? How dare he try to break off their engagement? She had not known him to be so puffed-up with his own consequence. And she had actually been foolish enough to wish to marry him! She had clearly been blinded by her feelings. He was nothing more than an arrogant despot. She pitied Eliza Bennet.

It was not to be wondered at that Eliza's health had declined so quickly, and that in a few months she had become so desolate.

Her first goal was to speak to Robert, before his cousin had a chance to waylay him. She requested one of the grooms to send Mr Robert Darcy to her the moment he returned from his ride, and, arming herself with her pelisse, waited impatiently for him in the garden. Mr Darcy's words echoed through her mind, over and over. The interlude between them seemed almost unreal, like a fragment from a nightmare.

Finally, Robert Darcy's familiar figure appeared, and she almost ran to him. She stifled an impulse to throw herself into his arms and cry.

"Miss Bingley! Has something happened?"

"No, no—at least, nothing of a serious nature."

"Thank heavens for that!" he said, clearly relieved. He led her to a bench and sat down beside her. "You must tell me immediately what happened."

She gave a little laugh, embarrassed now that she had to put the whole thing into words. "I am afraid I have quarrelled with your cousin. I cannot tell you how unpleasant it was!"

"If I had known that would happen," he said, "I would not have left you alone with him in the breakfast-room."

"I wish you had not," she said, turning over her hands and examining her kid gloves. "He seemed quite certain that I have entrapped you into marriage, and that I am not worthy of you, and—a host of other things." She could not tell him that Mr Darcy thought her Robert Darcy's social inferior.

Mr Robert peered intently into her face. "No wonder you're distressed! Darcy, of all people!" He took her right hand and held it between his. "You must be terribly pained. I know you must have been anxious about meeting him again after—after the wedding."

He surprised her yet again with his astuteness. Caroline withdrew her hand gently from his, though it had warmed her inside, and made her feel safe. But it was too intimate.

Besides, his sympathy was based on a mistaken assumption. "No, it is not that at all. I no longer harbour any feelings for him. I have scarcely given him a thought since I arrived." She rose, agitated, and studied a climbing rose bush, running her finger carefully across the sharp tip of a thorn. "I do not understand how he could say such things. I had always supposed he regarded me as an equal. Yet I have never been subjected to a harsher snub. And to be told I should break off the engagement because you should marry higher!"

"Did he say that, by God? I do not know what has come over him. Why should he care about whom I marry? Just a little more than a year ago, he scarcely knew of my existence."

"That is what I wondered. Then he said that he has every right to interfere, since you are his heir."

"That is all very well, but—" He stopped, clearly struck by something. "Ah."

His sudden reserve unnerved her.

"What is it? What have you discovered?"

"There may be more to it than meets the eye, Miss Bingley," he said gently. "I must ask you to make allowances for my cousin. There is something else that I am not at liberty to speak of. I believe it accounts for his behaviour. You must trust me when I ask you not to take to heart what he said to you."

She stood very still. "You are asking a lot of me."

"I know," he said. "But I believe you can find it in yourself to try and forget what he said."

Somehow, he had managed to soothe her. Though she was still angry, the nervous agitation she had experienced earlier had disappeared.

"I will try," she said. "I am afraid things have become more difficult now, however."

"What do you mean?" he asked.

She bowed her head, not wanting him to see the flush that stained her cheeks.

"It is silly of me, but I feel I *cannot* end the engagement now. It would be too humiliating. He will think it is because of what he said and will be encouraged to become all the more tyrannical in his behaviour."

Mr Robert regarded her gravely. "It was very wrong of him to speak to you this way, and he has raised your hackles, and done far more damage than he could know. Yet I cannot perceive Darcy as so very tyrannical. At times, perhaps, his sense of responsibility can drive him too far, and he is inclined to organize other people's lives as he pleases. Do you wish me to speak to him and explain the situation?"

It was the simplest solution, yet her pride would not permit her to take it. "I have been too insulted to set aside my pride so easily," said Caroline, honestly. "It seems mortifying to think I owe him an explanation when I do not."

Mr Robert nodded. "Then I will say nothing. Although I will be hard put when he approaches me to warn me against you," he added, with a teasing smile.

Warmed by the smile, she found herself smiling back. "I hope you will at least defend me against his charges."

"Perhaps," he said. "However, not being a gentleman..." For a moment he seemed serious, and she was afraid he meant to throw her remarks back at her. Then he grinned, and she could not resist hitting him playfully with her reticule.

"My word!" said a voice. "Young people nowadays seem lost to all sense of propriety."

They turned around to see a gentleman in vicar's clothing standing watching them. Caroline, feeling guilty at being caught, placed her hands behind her back and blushed. Mr Robert bowed.

"Mr Bass. I hope you are well. May I introduce you to my fiancée, Miss Caroline Bingley. Reverend George Bass."

"How do you do, Miss Bingley? I feel it incumbent on me to warn you, as a man of the cloth," he said, in a voice heavy with gravity, "that even if you are engaged to be married, you must never allow a man to take too many liberties. It will not do at all."

Miss Bingley, about to retort angrily, caught Mr Robert's glance. The suppressed laughter in his face dissolved her resentment, so she was able to answer, with every show of meekness, "Thank you, Mr Bass. I will keep your advice in mind."

He regarded her thoughtfully. "A lady must never be too careful. One small slip, and she is a fallen woman."

"I daresay she is," said Mr Robert. "Especially if she falls to the ground."

Mr Bass stared at him suspiciously. "I do not follow your meaning, sir. Perhaps you would care to explain?"

"I simply meant that the lady would be extremely fallen." A small snort escaped Caroline, who was really trying her utmost to be solemn.

Mr Bass's watery blue eyes peered at her closely. They were large and bulging, and put her in mind of a frog. "I do not see what could possibly be amusing," said he, pushing his lips forward in irritation. "I can assure you, it is a fate worse than death."

"Too few women take it seriously enough, in my opinion," said Mary Bennet, approaching from behind them with her sister Kitty. "That is why the world is full of unfortunates who live a sordid life of squalor and misery."

The watery eyes revolved and came to rest on the new arrival. "My sentiment exactly," said Mr Bass.

"I do not know if you have been introduced. Miss Katherine Bennet," said Mr Robert, "and Miss Mary Bennet."

Mr Bass's gaze passed over Kitty, but he appeared struck by Mary, who regarded him earnestly.

"There is no need for introductions. We met on a previous occasion, when you were in Pemberley earlier in the year."

Mary nodded gravely. "You are perfectly correct, sir."

"I see you are taking a stroll," said Mr Bass. "I feel it my duty to escort these young ladies around the garden. One cannot be too careful, after all."

"Yes," said Mr Robert. "One cannot know what dangers lurk in the corners, awaiting such delicate blossoms."

"Precisely," said Mr Bass, offering his arm to Mary.

"*I'm* not a delicate blossom," said Kitty, loudly. But Mary pulled her by the arm, and she had no choice but to join the vicar in his stroll.

The moment they were out of hearing, Caroline let out the laughter she had been holding back and was joined immediately by Robert. "How can you say such outrageous things?" she said.

"Very easily," said Mr Robert. "I cannot help it, in fact. It is one of my most grievous faults. My father often warned me against it."

They had no chance of pursuing their conversation, however, since Lydia came running out of the house. "You *must* hide me!" she yelped. "I'm trying to rid myself of Mama. She follows me everywhere. She means to ask me about Wickham. What does she think I can tell her? I don't know where he is, and I hope never to see him again. But there she comes. I can hear her behind that hedge. If she asks, tell her you have not seen me." She dashed round a corner just in time to escape Mrs Bennet, who came hurriedly in their direction.

"Have you seen my poor darling Lydia? She is quite inconsolable," said Mrs Bennet. "I cannot bear to think how much she is suffering. And all because of that wicked, wicked Wickham."

Robert obligingly pointed her in the direction in which Lydia had disappeared.

"Oh! How can you be so unfeeling?" said Caroline.

"If Mrs Bennet does not find Lydia she will enlist our help. *I* do not wish to spend the rest of my day chasing after her. I have done my duty by taking Lydia for a ride, and that is enough. But perhaps you would like to do so? She will lead you on a merry chase."

"I do not wish to spend the day chasing Lydia, either. However, I should join Jane, Eliza, and Georgiana. I am sure they require help writing invitations. And I promised I would help with the planning."

"I would offer to help, but it sounds as if four heads are more than enough. If I am not needed, perhaps I will go in search of Mrs Miles. With your permission, of course, my betrothed."

Caroline laughed. "You have my permission."

She could give her permission. It did not mean, however, that she approved.

Chapter 12

ONCE SHE ENTERED THE HOUSE, HOWEVER, SHE COULD NOT banish from her mind the picture of Mr Darcy as he had spoken to her that morning. Instead of joining Eliza and her sister, she went to her bedchamber and lay on her bed. Never in her life had she imagined that Mr Darcy regarded her as he did. But no matter how much she congratulated herself on not being tied to such a man, it did not make her humiliation any less palatable.

She had never taken her position for granted, but she moved in the best circles, and she had come to accept it as her right. It was her mother who had established them in society. She had sent Caroline and her sister to a distinguished private seminary to turn them into young ladies.

But accomplishments, good manners, and the considerable connections they had made with other young ladies from excellent families did not change the fundamental facts. Their fortune had been made through trade, and her father, with all the riches in the world, had not been born a gentleman. His family was well respected, and he had acquired an estate that rivalled Pemberley in size, though it had been sold after his death, but the fact remained that he had made the money himself, through his own effort and persistence.

It would have been far better if her mother had not tried to make them more than they were. She had suffered all those years at Mrs Drakehill's Seminary and emerged with nothing.

She stared at the ceiling and thought of Eliza, who also stared at the ceiling.

She sat up in her bed suddenly. Mr Darcy had married Eliza. And Eliza's relations were dubious though her father was a gentleman. She had one uncle in trade, the other an attorney. Yet love had made Mr Darcy blind to Eliza's position in life. He had married her, in spite of his objections.

She would not languish in her chamber, bemoaning her fate.

A new sense of purpose drove her out of bed. She *would* find someone. She had always counted on her position in society and her fortune to bolster that position. She had counted on Mrs Drakehill's schooling, and her mother's instruction.

But she had never counted on herself.

She peered at herself critically in the mirror. Her hair was askew, her complexion blotchy. There were dark circles under her eyes. But she was handsome enough. Certainly, as handsome as Eliza. She was accomplished. And she was clever. Time, then, to rely on something else entirely.

❦

She drew on that resolve when she went down to the drawing room before dinner, for she needed to face Mr Darcy with some degree of composure. She steeled herself against Mr Darcy's cold greeting. She made no attempt to claim Mr Robert, whose attention was taken by someone else entirely. She would not allow anyone to affect the giddy sense of excitement she had experienced that morning. Something of her new determination must have shown in her face, for she intercepted several questioning glances cast in her direction.

Jane came to her immediately and sat beside her. "You are looking far better this evening than you have looked for a while," she said, quietly. "I have been worried that you were unhappy, living with us in Netherfield, away from London and society. Tell me it is not so. Have I or Charles not made you welcome?"

"As if anyone could be unhappy with two such amiable people!" said Caroline, pressing Jane's arm. "It is true I have not been as cheerful as I am used to. With so many marriages taking place, I suppose, I have been considering my single state more than usual."

Jane smiled sweetly. "Well, that is over now. You have found someone worthy of you. You have waited patiently for the right person to come along, and I can see from your expression that it was well worth the wait."

Caroline shook her head. "When I consider how you had to be patient when Charles left Netherfield for London. How you must have suffered! And it was all our fault! But at least your patience was well rewarded."

Jane *had* suffered, and at their hands, though it had been Mr Darcy's idea to separate the couple in the first place. He had not approved of the Bennets.

"That is all forgotten," said Jane. "We belong together, and that is all that matters." She sent an affectionate glance towards Charles, who stood drinking sherry with Mr Darcy.

Captain Trewson was the last to join them. As always, he was perfectly turned out, his boots polished to the highest standard, the silver buttons of his regimentals gleaming.

"Oh, there you are!" cried Lydia, going to him and taking his arm. She turned to address the assembled guests. "Are you not glad that I brought you Captain Trewson?" she said loudly. "He is by far the handsomest officer I have ever met. If it were not for my naughty Wickham, I would set my mind to marry him."

Captain Trewson, clearly accustomed to such gushing sentiments, bowed gallantly. "Most certainly, Mrs Wickham. If your heart were not given to another, I would have run away with you this very minute, for you are by far the liveliest young lady of my acquaintance."

She giggled and led him to a seat, but he did not take it, and sat by Louisa instead.

"Let us have no talk of running away," said Mr Bennet. "We have had more than enough of that to last a lifetime."

"Do not speak of such things, Lydia," said Eliza sharply. Her voice was firm, and she sent an imploring glance to her father, whose face clouded immediately.

"Lydia," he said, tossing down his book, "I must have a word with you."

Lydia threw her father a rebellious glance. "I am a married woman now, Papa. You cannot treat me as a child any more."

"I will treat you as a child if you behave like one," said Mr Bennet. "Now come or I will not hesitate to drag you away."

Lydia rose and followed her father sullenly.

Captain Trewson watched this exchange with astonishment. "I do not understand why everyone has become so serious. We were simply exchanging pleasantries."

It was not up to Caroline to inform him that Lydia had ran away with Wickham before their marriage, and that the marriage had only taken place after Wickham had been paid to marry her. The Bennet sisters had been mere days away from total ruin. Eliza was quite right: It was no laughing matter.

"It is wrong for Lydia to exchange pleasantries when her husband has just left her," said Mary. "She should stay alone in her room, pondering her folly."

"Kitty," said Mrs Bennet, "I have told you many times not to cough like that."

"I am not coughing, Mama, I am clearing my throat."

"Well, stop whatever you are doing. Have some compassion for my nerves. I do not like loud noises."

Louisa put her hand on Trewson's arm and said something to him. He laughed, and the awkwardness of the moment disappeared.

Dinner was announced. To Caroline's surprise, Trewson came to her and offered to take her in. Instinctively, she glanced towards Mr Robert, but he was bearing Mrs Miles on his arm, and they were moving towards the dining hall, laughing playfully.

"Thank you, Captain Trewson. I would be delighted."

She regretted it a moment later, however, when she passed Louisa, who sent her an angry look that spoke volumes.

❧

Lydia and Mr Bennet rejoined the party presently. Whatever her father had told her seemed to have had some effect, for Lydia remained subdued throughout dinner and made no attempt to draw Trewson's attention. Caroline doubted he even noticed. He was much in demand, as the young ladies, including Georgiana, plied him with questions about his time campaigning with Wellesley.

"I was wounded, unfortunately, at Porto. We managed to defeat Soult at the Battle of Grijo, after fighting two days, and then marched to Oporto under Hill."

"You are far too modest. I am sure such a dry account does not do credit to your bravery." said Louisa. "Do tell us what happened."

Captain Trewson protested, saying that he did not want to bore everyone, for it was a very long time ago and not interesting in the least. So much had happened since that it was not worth recounting.

A number of voices pressed him to continue and he surrendered with laughter and good grace.

"If you must hear it, I will tell you. But do not blame me if you start nodding into your plates!" General hilarity met his remark. "There is really very little to recount that you do not already know. Soult blew up the bridges on the Douro river, and we could not cross without being fired on by the French, but then someone conceived of using the wine barges downstream, which took Soult completely by surprise, and he was soundly defeated. Word is we reached Soult's lodgings in time for Wellesley to eat the supper intended for Soult. I know they have accused Wellesley of not making an effort to rout the French, but if they had been there, they would not have said so. A number of us were sent after the French stragglers, in fact. But without knowing the terrain, it was an impossible task."

He paused, a pained expression on his face. "That is where I was shot—in the mountains. You can imagine what it was like, to be lying wounded, cold, wet, hungry, and completely alone, expecting a Frenchman or a Portuguese peasant to come looking for loot and put an end to me."

His audience held onto his every word, rapt with attention.

"Finally, however, I heard the welcome sound of English voices. 'Help me!' I managed to say. Until this day I still marvel that they were able to hear me, for my voice was quite faint with hunger. I tell you, I have never been happier to see their red coats in my life."

An animated buzz of excitement rose around the table. Captain Trewson waited until it died down to continue. "I did not know the two soldiers who helped me. I would not have blamed them if they abandoned me to my fate. But they prepared a makeshift litter and climbed down the mountain with me. They slipped more than once on the rocks, even dropped me on one occasion. But they did not abandon me. By the time we reached the main camp I was in a fever and unaware of my surroundings. And do you know, I never found out the names of those two men who sacrificed so much to bring me back? Were it not for them, I would have been left as carrion for the vultures in Portuguese mountains."

There were shudders and sighs from all the ladies at the table.

Robert Darcy, who was far more interested in whatever Mrs Miles had to say, remarked that Wellesley had gone on to other victories since then. "And a good thing, too. Eating Soult's supper was hardly enough to send Napoleon quaking in his shoes!"

There were wide protests at Mr Robert Darcy's heartless reaction.

"I should have liked to be a soldier," said Charles, wistfully. "It seems far more appealing than our humdrum existence here. Even if it meant being lost in the mountains and fearing for one's life."

"And I say it would have been a great deal *less* interesting for us if you had gone missing in the mountains. What then would have become of Jane?" said Mrs Bennet, quite put out by the idea.

Mrs Bennet had inadvertently lightened the atmosphere, and they were able to move on to less serious reflections.

But it was not long before Trewson became the centre of attention once more.

"If it were up to me," he said firmly, in response to some remark, "I would never have outlawed duelling. It is, after all, the only way a gentleman can repair a slight to his honour. Besides, banishing duelling has not put a stop to it at all. Far from it. I myself have fought two duels, and I know men who have fought as many as four."

"Really?" said Lydia, her eyes shining. She had quite forgotten that she was not supposed to draw Captain Trewson's attention. "You *must* tell us about it."

"It is hardly a topic one should discuss over the dinner table," said Mr Darcy, attempting to put a stop to a subject unsuitable for young ladies.

"Duelling, in my opinion, is just as much a sin as murder," said Mary.

"Come, Captain Trewson. Can you not tell us?" said Louisa.

"Well, I would not want to go against the opinion of my host."

"I for one," said Mrs Bennet, "would not object to hearing about a duel. As long as it did not involve Mr Bennet, of course, for he came very close to fighting one when my dear L—"

"Mama," interrupted Jane, quietly, distracting her mother from referring to that embarrassing event, "perhaps we should let Captain Trewson tell us his tale."

Mrs Bennet turned to him expectantly. "Yes, please do, Captain Trewson."

Mr Darcy, his opinion completely discarded, looked displeased.

"Well, if you insist. It was over a card game—a man I suspected of cheating. As the game continued, I grew certain that the same cards were making an appearance. Finally, I could stand it no more. 'I would like this pack looked at,' I said. But he refused and grew very angry, demanding that his honour be satisfied. Even then, I tried to find a way out. 'Perhaps there is some explanation, then?' I said, giving him a chance to bow out of the situation. But he was hot blooded and refused to mend the matter. "You have insulted me, sir,' he said. 'And I will not be satisfied until I draw blood.'"

Lydia gave a little gasp. "How perfectly *monstrous* of him! I hope you gave him a good hiding, sir."

"I did indeed. But it was not easy. He was a good swordsman. One of the best. There was a time during the fight when I thought myself done for. It was the worst moment of my life. But then, just when I was ready to give up all hope of emerging from the duel alive, I was given an opening. I did not hesitate. I lunged immediately and managed to wound him. I could have killed him, in fact, but I restrained myself. Just as I was about to walk away, he attacked me from behind."

"What villainy!" cried Louisa.

"I hope you taught him a lesson, for he certainly needed one," said Mrs Bennet.

"It was all I could to fend off his attack," said Captain Trewson. "I was taken by surprise. But fortunately I was able to rally round, and fight him off. He realized he had done something unpardonable, and when he saw I could not be brought down that way, he made his escape. I have not seen him since."

"It is often the case, I have noticed," remarked Mary, "that villains escape unscathed."

"I for one wish you had killed him while you had a chance," said Mrs Bennet.

Fortunately, it was time for the ladies to withdraw. Caroline had had enough of Trewson's gruesome tales, and she could not help agreeing with Mr Darcy that it was not an acceptable conversation over dinner.

But she soon found herself in the minority. The ladies' conversation focused on Trewson's adventures, and she was forced to hear the whole of his tales again when they were recounted to Eliza, who had remained in the drawing room, too fatigued to join the company at the table.

Eliza appeared much struck by the account, which was suitably embellished by Louisa, Kitty, Lydia, Georgiana, and Mrs Bennet. When they had finished, Caroline drew close to Eliza and sat on the edge of her armchair.

"I hope we are not tiring you," she said.

"No, on the contrary, I am vastly entertained," answered Eliza cheerfully. "It is rare that one gets to hear of such adventures as this."

Caroline sighed. "I find they are not much to my taste."

"That is because, Caroline, you are not inclined to be romantic. Those of us who are, however, delight in picturing such events."

She did not want to argue with Eliza, so she shrugged, and wandered off to amuse herself elsewhere. As soon as Louisa saw her on her own, she came to grasp her arm. "I am surprised Captain Trewson took you in to dinner, Caroline," she said. "Right under the eye of your Robert Darcy, too. I do not think it quite right."

"Nonsense, Louisa. One cannot be so strict about these things when not in public. This is a small family gathering, after all."

"But Captain Trewson knows that you are engaged," she said.

"I need not ask who told him," said Caroline drily. "Louisa, did we not agree that we would not reveal the engagement to strangers?"

Louisa dismissed her words with a gesture. "That is beside the point. What I wished to say was that it should not have happened."

"Are you censoring my behaviour," said Caroline, "or his?"

Louisa looked confused. "I am not censoring anyone." She stood listening to the others for a moment. They were all gushing over the handsome captain.

"He is charming, is he not, Caroline?"

Caroline looked at her sister in surprise. "He is, indeed. I cannot dispute that."

"And so very gallant," she said.

Once again, Caroline agreed.

"He has been paying me quite particular notice, you know. Did you see how he snubbed Lydia and came to sit by me?"

Caroline *had* noticed, and she agreed.

"And he addressed many of his remarks to me at dinner."

Since Caroline would not go so far, she refrained from saying anything.

"And his sister, Mrs Miles. Is she not the very image of fashion?"

"They are both perfection itself," said Caroline. "But may we speak of something else? I am quickly growing tired of singing their praises."

"Perhaps," said Louisa, "you are piqued because he did not pay *you* enough attention."

"He took me in to dinner," retorted Caroline, then wondered why she allowed herself to be drawn into this little game. She was indifferent to Captain Trewson. She was initially flattered when he had taken her in to dinner, but quickly lost interest in him. He was too accustomed to being the centre of attention. Charming as he was, and despite his flawless face, she preferred the company of someone who delighted less in attracting the ladies.

When the gentlemen rejoined the ladies, a table was set up for a game of loo. Robert and Mrs Miles declined, preferring to play whist, and Mrs Bennet, saying that she found loo too noisy, made to join them.

The play had hardly begun, however, when she withdrew. "I like a good game as much as anyone," said Mrs Bennet. "But I do not play for such high stakes." She turned to the group playing loo. "I hope you are not playing unlimited loo."

"Have no fear, Mrs Bennet," said Charles. "We are playing a very sedate game. Come, you must join us."

"I advise you to look sharp with my sister, Mr Robert," said Captain Trewson, who was playing loo. "She is a very good whist player. She never forgets a card. In fact, you would be well warned not to play with her at all."

"Not fair!" said Mrs Miles. "You should not have warned him. Then he would have been caught off guard, for he would not expect a lady to play so well."

"I am considered a fair player myself, so I believe I will rise to the challenge," said Robert Darcy. "And if I lose, then I will be delighted to lose to the better player, and to one, moreover, who is so beautiful."

"Do not say I did not warn you," said Captain Trewson. Louisa, who was his partner, tittered at his side.

By the end of the evening Captain Trewson's advice proved true, for Robert Darcy lost a considerable sum. But to judge from his laughter, he was taking great pleasure in the game, and regarded the loss well worth it.

Mr Darcy did not participate in any games and spent the evening writing letters and reading.

"I have never known such a fellow as you for writing letters," said Charles. "I do not understand who you can be writing to, now that Georgiana is with you. You were always writing to her, last year."

"I have many business matters I conduct by post when I am at Pemberley," replied Mr Darcy. "And I correspond with a number of my relations as well as friends. In fact, there is never enough time to write all the letters I ought."

Louisa let out a loud shout and collected her winnings. "Do not tell me you wish to split our winnings, Captain Trewson," said Louisa, "for although you are my partner, it was I who held the best cards."

"I would not dream of depriving you of your winnings, Mrs Hurst. As long as I can continue to partner you, that is more than enough of a prize for me."

Mrs Bennet implored him to stop wasting time and concentrate on the game. "For I intend to make up my losses, you shall see," she said. "And you need not look at me down your nose, Mr Bennet, for you know I have done it on many occasions."

"If I look down my nose, Mrs Bennet," said Mr Bennet, "it is because my eyeglasses are in danger of falling off."

The evening passed pleasantly, though Mrs Bennet seemed quite shocked at how much Robert Darcy had lost.

"Five hundred pounds seems an excessive amount," remarked Mrs Bennet to Caroline as they walked down the passageway to their rooms. "I do not think it quite right, do you?"

"Five hundred pounds? Surely he could not have lost so much in one sitting? And he does not even look perturbed."

"I suppose money is no object, when you have plenty of it," remarked Mrs Bennet.

But Caroline, though accustomed to the high stakes used for playing in London, could not help but feel that Mr Robert had been more reckless than she would have expected.

Chapter 13

CAROLINE HAD OCCASION TO MENTION THE LOSSES TO ROBERT Darcy the next morning, when she met him at breakfast.

"I am surprised to see you down so early," said Caroline. "I expected you to have a late night of it, since you were well and truly trounced when I left. Did you not attempt to win back your money?" she asked.

His mouth twisted wryly. "I was unlucky with my cards."

"It is more likely that you were too distracted by the lady." She had meant it as a joke, but when she spoke there was a touch of pique in her voice. "I am glad I did not play," she added quickly, before he noticed, "you were not the only one to lose."

"It is the nature of wagering," said Robert. "You can only win *some* of the time."

"Which means you are certain to lose *most* of the time."

He grinned. "Now there, I don't agree. It depends on your luck."

"I see you have the soul of a gambler."

He shook his head. "You are mistaken. At any rate, I am not devoted to betting and card games. I generally dislike gambling. And with business matters I never take a chance." He spoke earnestly.

Caroline smiled. "I am relieved to hear it," she said.

"Come, Miss Bingley, you need not look so worried. I will not be dragged off to debtor's prison for losing to Mrs Miles."

She was at the point of asking if it was worth it, simply to gain Mrs Miles's attention, but she held back. She did not want to appear peevish, and such a question might be misinterpreted.

"My cousin has proposed that we go trout fishing this morning," said Robert Darcy, "since the weather has been holding well, though it is late in the season. Perhaps we shall have fish for dinner."

"I am certain we will. For if anyone is bound to catch a fish, it will be you," she said. "Did I not hear that you are considered a Corinthian? Surely fishing well would be part of such a distinguished title?"

"You must not roast me, Miss Bingley," he said with a laugh. "My friend Mr Pole is attached to me and has an exaggerated sense of my sporting abilities."

"Well, in any case, *one* of the five of you at least should be able to catch something, so I can predict with every certainty that we will have fish for dinner."

"There are only four of us, I regret to say, which diminishes the chances. Captain Trewson has a dislike of getting wet. Or maybe he prefers to spend his time with the ladies."

Caroline smiled. "He can be assured of a welcome," she said, as an image manifested before her of all the young ladies—and Louisa—swarming around him.

"Surely you are not one of his admirers as well?" said Robert Darcy.

She threw him a saucy look and raised her brow. "You cannot really expect me to own up to such a thing. Experience has taught me that I ought not to reveal my most guarded secrets."

"Aha! So that is where the wind blows!" he said, playfully.

"Very well, I will allow you to guard your secrets. In the circumstances, though, I hope you do not expect me to tell *you* anything in return."

"Oh, that does not worry me. Your intentions are very clear." She was thinking of Mrs Miles.

"Do not be so very sure," he said, and to her surprise, his tone was serious.

The younger members of the party, egged on by Lydia, resolved to enjoy the good weather by walking to Lambton. Caroline did not care to traipse through country lanes and across fields, and when she was told that it was at least three miles to the village, she declined. Captain Trewson, who had just woken up and come downstairs, however, agreed happily to the outing.

"It is such a fine, sunny morning," he said. "A good walk is just the thing."

The young ladies were delighted to accompany him. Louisa, who had just refused to go, made as if to join them. But Caroline quickly asked her for help in the wording of a letter, and Louisa was forced to follow her.

When they had gone, Louisa turned on Caroline angrily. "Why are you trying to ruin things for me?"

"I am not trying to ruin things for you," said Caroline. "But surely Captain Trewson heard you refusing to go as he came down the stairs, and it would have been too forward if you had changed your mind once you knew he was going. Really, Louisa, you must be more circumspect in your actions."

Louisa glared at her, and was about to retort angrily when there was a crash of glass and a cry.

"One of the servants has broken a vase," said Louisa. "It is no concern of ours."

But Jane came hurrying in, her face full of distress.

"I have broken a china piece I believe to be an heirloom. I do hope Mr Darcy will not be upset." She wrung her hands. A trickle of blood appeared on the side of her finger, staining her jonquil yellow morning dress.

"Jane," said Caroline, going quickly to her. "Look out! There is blood on your dress."

Mrs Miles, who was passing by the drawing room, stopped in the doorway. "Is anyone hurt?"

"Jane has cut her finger," said Caroline. She searched for her reticule and realized she had left it in Eliza's parlour. "Do you have a handkerchief, Mrs Miles?"

"I am sorry to disappoint you, but I do not," she said. "Shall I ring for a servant?"

"I will fetch mine from upstairs," said Louisa.

Mrs Miles continued on her way. Caroline pressed Jane's cut to staunch the blood. "It seems to be quite deep," she said. "Does it hurt?"

"No, it does not," said Jane. "But I wish I had not decided to arrange the flowers for the dining room. I am sure Mr Darcy will be displeased."

"Mr Darcy has enough heirlooms. One more or less will make little difference, surely?" said Caroline.

Louisa returned with some salve and a fresh handkerchief, which they tore into pieces to bandage the cut.

"Thank you both for your help," said Jane, in her quiet way.

The three ladies settled down. From where she sat, Caroline could see the expanse of the Darcy lands, an undulating line of deep green hills and orange copses, with sheep dotting the landscape. "I would have liked to go fishing," she said, remembering her feeling of pride the first time she hooked a fish.

Jane shuddered. "Oh, I would dislike such a thing very much. I would especially not like to pull the hook from the poor fish's mouth and watch it die. I believe I would return it to the water. It is too cruel a trick to play on such an unsuspecting creature."

"Really, Jane," said Louisa. "Your sensibilities are far too delicate. Would you have no fishing and hunting, then? Would you live on vegetables all your life?"

"I have read," said Jane thoughtfully, "that there are people in India who do such things. They have forsworn meat and fish for religious reasons."

"Those are heathen ideas, and surely not for us to imitate," said Louisa.

Jane shrugged. "I know it is the nature of things for us to hunt and fish, but I cannot help but feel that, if I could choose, I would prefer to do without."

A sneer appeared on Louisa's face.

Caroline, however, wondered if it was indeed possible to live that way.

"Those condemned to poverty cannot eat meat or fish because they have no means of obtaining them," said Caroline, considering the idea. "They are more disease ridden and die younger than those of us who are more fortunate. Surely there must be some benefit to being able to eat meat and fish?"

"Of course there is," said Louisa in a scornful tone, "you would hardly wish to condemn us to such a fate, Jane."

Jane sighed. "Yes, I know. We are fortunate to have these things. I was not thinking clearly."

Jane was too good-natured to put up a fight. But for once, Caroline would have liked her to. She was disappointed at Jane's easy acquiescence.

"I sometimes think about the rightness of killing animals for our own benefit," she said. She knew Louisa would mock her, but she was determined to stick her ground.

But Louisa had already lost interest. "Oh, look," she said. "There is Mrs Miles, walking in the garden. I think I will join her."

She hurried away through the French doors, and for a moment it appeared she would catch up with the tall lady. Mrs Miles stood wiping her brow with a white handkerchief. But then she moved away, out of sight.

A few minutes later, Louisa returned from the garden. "I did not find her," she said, sitting down again. "And it is quite dull to walk in the garden alone."

⁂

The young ladies returned after a luncheon of cold meats and pies. Their trip had apparently been successful, for Lydia came in with lustrous eyes, Georgiana looked invigorated by the exercise, Kitty was quite cheerful, and even Mary seemed less sombre.

"You will never guess what happened, Mama!" said Lydia, as Mrs Bennet entered the drawing room. "There was a troop of militia in Lambton. They are on the way to Chesterfield, which is a pity, since we will not see them again, but they introduced themselves and they were very agreeable."

Caroline noticed that Captain Trewson had not returned with them. "What happened to the captain?" she asked.

"Oh, he stayed behind in Lambton," said Lydia. "It was very tiresome of him to abandon us so suddenly when I had counted on him introducing us to some of the officers, for nothing could be easier, since he is an officer himself. But when I turned to ask him, he had disappeared."

"I believe he found a friend," said Georgiana. "For I caught a glimpse of him later when we passed the inn. He was talking to a gentleman inside."

"I did not like the look of his friend," said Kitty.

Lydia turned on her. "You are forever taking a dislike to somebody or the other. I do not know how you are to be married, for you seem to find fault with everyone, especially the officers."

"I would not wish to marry anyone," remarked Mary, insistently, "unless I was convinced of his superior moral character."

Kitty snorted rudely and was scolded by Mrs Bennet for her unrefined manners. She retreated into a corner of the room, drawing Georgiana with her, and leaving Mary and Lydia pointedly behind. Lydia, glad to have her mother to herself, launched into a description of the officers she had met, and her mother listened to her with enjoyment.

Louisa's vision, Caroline noticed, strayed to the door continuously, no doubt in the hopes of seeing Captain Trewson return. Caroline considered it shabby of Captain Trewson to leave the girls to return unaccompanied, and she said so.

"Pooh!" said Louisa. "You have forgotten that they were originally to set out alone. He only joined them at the last minute, after they were ready to set out. You were not so concerned about them *then*, or you should have offered to go with them as chaperone. In the country things are done differently, and there is no harm in them walking to the village alone."

Louisa was right. Caroline did seem set on finding fault with Captain Trewson. She was at a loss to explain the reason. But the feeling persisted, and she determined to write to an acquaintance of hers in Newcastle whose husband was an officer, and ask her what she knew about Captain Trewson. Then she could set her mind at rest.

The door opened, and the butler announced Mr Bass.

"I hope I have not come at an inconvenient time," said the vicar, casting a quick look at the side-table to see if there was any food there. "But I did not want you to think that I was negligent, especially with such a large party assembled here."

"Well, I am sure you are very welcome," said Mrs Bennet.

"I have brought you a volume of William Carey's *Enquiry*, Miss Mary," he said, turning to that young lady with a smile. "I believe you expressed interest in it the last time we met."

"Yes, Mr Bass. I am grateful that you remembered."

"An elephant never forgets, Miss Mary," he replied, with a quick laugh.

"Your modesty does you credit, Mr Bass," said Mary. "I know it is your concern for my soul that prompted your memory."

"True, true," he said. "Young though you are, you are very wise," he said.

Kitty, who observed this exchange from her corner, groaned. Her mother advanced on her at once and ordered her in a loud whisper to leave the room, if she could not behave herself. Kitty, more than happy to escape, went into the garden, with Georgiana in tow, and was soon followed by Lydia, who yawned and remarked as she left that the company had suddenly become very dull.

As if Lydia's departure was a signal, the room began to empty. Louisa said she had some letters to write; Caroline recollected that she had promised to read to Eliza; Jane mumbled that she had something to tell the housekeeper. Only Mrs Bennet remained behind.

But Caroline had scarcely taken two steps when she discovered Mrs Bennet behind her.

"You are not leaving them alone, surely, Mrs Bennet?" said Caroline.

"Only for a few minutes while I bring down some needlework," she said. "There can be no objection. He is a man of the cloth, after all. I have nothing to worry about," she said.

It seemed hardly possible that Mrs Bennet was already match-making when Mary had met Mr Bass no more than a few times. Caroline refrained from further comment, and excused herself and went to join Eliza in the parlour.

To her surprise, she found Eliza busy making up lists and preparing for the party.

"I thought we agreed that you would leave all this to the rest of us," said Caroline, with some concern. Eliza's gaunt pallor was particularly noticeable today.

"There is so much to be done," mumbled Eliza, "and I am quite tired of lying back and doing nothing."

But her hand was shaking, and a blot of ink fell onto the paper in front of her. She stood up to go to the bell pull, but swayed even as she came to her feet, and Caroline was barely in time to catch her and prevent her from falling to the floor.

The door opened and Mr Darcy entered, still in the clothes he wore for the fishing expedition. Caroline looked at him in mute appeal, and understanding the situation immediately, he hurried to her side, took Eliza into his arms, and carried her to the sofa, where he laid her down carefully and covered her.

"You have been exerting yourself too much," he said, sitting by her side and peering anxiously into her face. "I warned you that this would be the case when you proposed having a house party."

"I am able to manage it."

He stood up and began to pace the room. "I can see how able you are to manage," he said. "That is why you are ready to swoon with the effort."

"But—" Eliza began.

"The party will have to be cancelled."

Eliza struggled to sit up. "No, no, we cannot," she said. "We have already sent out many of the invitations."

"Then they will have to be retracted. My secretary will write to express our regrets."

"But everyone will be so disappointed," she said.

"I care more for your health than for your family's disappointment," he said.

She reached her hand out to Mr Darcy and he came to her, taking it and looking down at her. They exchanged glances. She leaned back and closed her eyes.

"Perhaps I have been too ambitious. If we could have a very small party, with a small select group, surely that would not be too much trouble," she said, opening her eyes again. "And we could make their stay short, with my illness as an excuse."

"It is hardly an excuse," he said, "it is the truth."

He shot Caroline a disapproving look, as if she was to blame for the whole idea. She fought the impulse to object loudly that it was hardly her fault.

"Just a small party?" said Eliza. "I would enjoy seeing some of my friends again."

There was so much appeal in her face that his expression softened, and he relented. "Very well," he said. "A very small party. But you must promise to leave the preparations to everyone else."

She sent him a radiant smile, and he smiled back, their eyes meeting in a moment of understanding.

Caroline felt very much an intruder, and edged slowly to the door, trying to leave without attracting attention. She reached it just as Mr Darcy sat down beside Eliza, taking her fingers to his lips and kissing them.

Caroline closed the door behind her carefully, hoping the small click would not disturb them, and tiptoed quietly away.

She encountered the other gentlemen just as they entered the house, stepping heavily into the entrance with their muddied boots and smelling strongly of the outdoors and, inevitably, of fish. Mr Bennet went upstairs immediately to change.

"So?" she said to Robert Darcy. "Was your outing successful?"

"Of course. I caught the largest fish by far," he said, with a crooked smile.

"You did not," protested Charles. "Mine was the largest. Yours was merely the fattest, which does not count."

"How preposterous! Since mine weighs far more than yours, I definitely claim the honour of having caught the biggest fish."

Their good-natured banter prompted Caroline to answer in kind. "If I had been there, *I* would have caught the largest, and then neither of you would have won."

They turned to look at her. "You, Caroline? Surely you are not interested in fishing? You have never expressed such an interest," said Charles.

"I used to fish when I was little," she said, in a small voice.

"That was a very long time ago," replied Charles.

"My father took me and Charles fishing a few times," she explained to Robert Darcy. "But he died when I was eleven, and I never went after that."

"You must miss it, in that case," said Mr Robert Darcy, readily. "I would be happy to take you one day, if you wish to go."

"You must be funning. Caroline has grown too much a lady to wish for any such thing." There was an odd note in Charles's voice.

"I—" She was torn. Part of her was afraid that fishing was, indeed, too unladylike. But when she looked into Robert Darcy's eyes and found no condemnation there, she was able to say it. "I would like to go fishing," she said, firmly.

"Then we shall go fishing again tomorrow," said Robert Darcy.

Charles laughed, a joyful laugh that made him look like a boy again. He gave Caroline a quick thump on the shoulder, and she thumped him back awkwardly.

She turned and walked quickly to the drawing room, hoping Robert Darcy had not seen the tears that had sprung unbidden to her eyes.

Chapter 14

THE FISHING EXPEDITION DID NOT MATERIALIZE AFTER ALL. THE sky turned rock-grey, and the rain swept in, falling in vicious squalls, drenching everything in its path. The guests were confined to Pemberley for the next three days.

The confinement did not affect Caroline, who was quite busy. She offered Eliza and Jane as much assistance as was needed in running the household, and together they planned for the party. After that moment in the parlour, Caroline was more concerned than ever for Eliza, and was anxious for her to recover her strength. At times she felt it would have been better if they had not come, for surely Eliza would have recovered her strength more easily without the constant demands of so many people around her. But Eliza seemed to take pleasure in having company, and the idea of a party brought a sparkle to her eye.

Louisa's attitude towards the whole situation frustrated her, however. She made no effort to spend any time with Eliza and seemed to count herself as a guest. Often, if she was cornered into performing a task, she would evade it, with the consequence that it was left undone.

It was on such an occasion that Caroline happened upon Louisa unexpectedly. Caroline had come to ask for her help, but could not find her in any of the usual places. It was quite by accident that she heard Louisa's voice, and realized she was upstairs in the picture gallery. Caroline climbed the stairs, quite out of patience after such a long search.

They started apart the moment she came into view.

"Good morning, Captain Trewson," said Caroline, politely. She focused her attention on Louisa. "I am sorry to interrupt your conversation, Louisa, but you are needed," she said, keeping her tone level.

Louisa threw Captain Trewson a regretful glance and excused herself. Caroline marched away stiffly, leaving Louisa to hurry behind her.

"For goodness' sake, Caroline!" hissed Louisa. "What do you mean by interrupting us like that? You are really going too far now."

Caroline did not slow down. "There is a houseful of guests, and there are many things to be seen to. Did you not promise to do the flowers for the hallway and the drawing room?"

"It is *raining*, Caroline. You did not expect me to go out in the *rain* for some flowers, did you? Why must you always fuss? You and Jane are perfectly able to manage a small group of guests. How many of us does such a simple thing require? And there is Mrs Reynolds, the housekeeper, who is more than capable."

Caroline walked on. Behind her, Louisa's hand shot out to grasp Caroline by the shoulder.

"Surely you can understand that I would like to marry again. To have children?" said Louisa, breathing heavily. "I do not understand why you are so resentful." She waited for a response. When none was forthcoming, she went on. "Is it because you have remained single, while I was already married once, and now I'm likely to marry again? You cannot begrudge me my happiness."

Caroline turned on her heel and started to walk, afraid that she would say something she would come to regret.

"Captain Trewson has come to mean a great deal to me, Caroline."

Caroline halted so abruptly that Louisa, who had followed after her, collided with her. Caroline swung round, schooling her features, but unable to take the bite out of her words. "You have been acquainted with Captain Trewson no more than a few days. And the fact is, we know absolutely nothing about him. And now you are—kissing in the corners with him." It embarrassed her even to speak of it. "Why are you in such a hurry to reach an agreement with him? Surely if you really care for him, you would want to enjoy the relationship, instead of rushing into it headlong? It would not surprise me at all if he has made no mention of marriage."

"There you wrong him, Caroline. He *has* mentioned marriage. In fact, he is as eager to marry me as I to marry him. And you need not worry that something untoward has happened between us. He has been a gentleman in every possible way. My feelings for him are reciprocated. I do not see what reasonable objection you could offer. Especially since *you* became engaged to Robert Darcy after only a few days' acquaintance."

"My case is entirely different, as you well know. I did not do it from choice," said Caroline. "And at least we know something about Robert Darcy. We are very well acquainted with his cousin, who obviously holds him respect. But what do we know of Captain Trewson?"

"We know that he is a war hero and has fought against the French," said Louisa. "I cannot think of anything more noble than that."

Caroline knew she would be unable to make her sister see reason. She could not say what needed to be said. She did not think Captain Trewson's intentions were honourable. Why would he wish to marry Louisa, when there were so many young and beautiful ladies eager to throw themselves at him? But she could not say that to her sister.

"In any case," she said, since she had to be circumspect, "I am hoping that our ignorance will soon be remedied. I have written to a friend of mine and I am hoping she will tell me more about him. If I can be reassured on that score, I will wish you every happiness, my dear sister."

"Then I hope you will hear soon, because I do not feel the need to justify myself to you," said Louisa. And with that she walked away, back in the direction from which she had come.

Matters were moving beyond Caroline. What right had she to advise Louisa how to conduct her life? Not only was her sister more experienced than she was, especially since Louisa was a widow and knew the ways of marriage, but she was also older. Caroline leaned over the balustrade and stared down into the hallway below. She no longer knew what was correct. She had thought the rules very clear, but somehow they had grown confused along the way. Her certainty seemed to have deserted her.

"You take life too seriously," said a voice in her ear.

"Mr Robert! You startled me!" she said, reproachfully. Gentlemen did not, in her experience, creep up so close to ladies like that.

He grinned. "You looked so very stern, I could not resist the temptation."

"I would thank you to resist the temptation next time, if you please."

"I cannot promise you that," he said, unrepentantly. "I like to surprise people."

"Have you nothing better to do?" she said. "Where is your Mrs Miles?"

"Still fast asleep," he said. Then realizing from her indrawn breath how she had interpreted the remark, he added, by way of explanation, "We played cards very late into the night, and she has not yet come down. That is why I surmise that she is sleeping."

"Ah," said Caroline, ashamed that he had understood her reaction. "And did you sustain any more loses?"

"No more than I would have expected," he said.

Caroline was silent for a moment. "Have you told her we are engaged?" she asked, abruptly.

"No," he said, throwing her a searching glance. It made her uncomfortable, and she looked down into the hallway again. "Did you wish me to?"

"No," she replied.

"Why do I have the feeling you do not like her?" he asked.

Caroline tried to explain. "I do not dislike her. I just cannot feel comfortable with her. She is too ready to express her feelings in public. Her manners are impeccable, yet..." She searched for the right word, but could not think of one. "There is something too open about her," she said, lamely.

He stiffened. "You are very ready to condemn others for expressing their feelings, or for not falling completely in step with everyone else. In my mind, however, it is far better to be open, even to the extent of appearing imprudent, than to be so terrified of one's emotions that one does not even know they are there."

And with that he walked away.

Her two encounters threw Caroline into a morose state of mind. She could not easily dismiss the accusations of both Louisa and Mr Robert Darcy, nor could she explain why she had taken a dislike to the Trewsons. The more she thought about it, the more she reached the conclusion that her sister was right.

Her dislike had its root in envy.

In the wake of this conclusion rose the spectre of spinsterhood. When had she become the kind of person who could not endure the sight of other people's happiness? Caroline's own attempts to form relationships had not been successful. But was she really so embittered that she was all too ready to condemn those whose natural charm enabled them to form relationships with ease?

This new view of her character occupied her so much that, when she went to see Eliza that afternoon, she found it hard to concentrate on anything that Eliza said.

"You are very preoccupied today," said Eliza, after she had repeated a simple question twice before Caroline comprehended it. "I hope there is nothing wrong."

Caroline shook her head. "It is just that I am wondering how long Captain Trewson and Mrs Miles are planning to stay. I must admit I would be glad to see the last of them."

"I am surprised to hear that," said Eliza. "They seem very good company. Indeed, everyone seems quite taken with them."

"Yes, that is all very well, but I have my concerns. My sister Louisa seems to have conceived a *tendre* for Captain Trewson."

"And you do not approve?" said Eliza.

"I do not, but I cannot say why."

Eliza looked stricken and reached for Caroline's arm, her face full of concern. "Oh. Poor Caroline! This is all about Robert, is it not? He is paying court to Mrs Miles." Eliza frowned as she considered the implications. "I would never have thought him so inconsiderate, when you have only just been engaged! I call this shabby behaviour indeed!" She ended on an indignant note.

Caroline pulled away immediately, alarmed by Eliza's misconception. "Oh, no!" she cried. "I—"

"You are taking this very well. In fact, remarkably well. He is behaving badly, and you should not find excuses for him," insisted Eliza.

Caroline did not wish to wrong Robert Darcy. The situation *did* make him appear in a very poor light. After all he had done for her, however, she could not in all honesty allow the misconception to continue.

"It seems that I must tell you everything," said Caroline, sighing. "But you must promise not to breathe a word of this to anyone."

"You may speak freely. I will tell no one," said Eliza.

She had been waiting for days for a chance to confess and the words began to flow almost as soon as she opened her mouth. Before long, she had told Eliza her sorry story, but only after extracting a promise that she would not reveal a word to Mr Darcy.

Caroline hesitated only when it came to recounting Mr Darcy's high handed behaviour, fearing to cause offence. But Eliza found the account highly amusing, and before long they were laughing as Caroline described the confrontation between her and Darcy in detail.

"I am glad you stood up to him," said Eliza. "He is too inclined to think he has the right to decide people's future. This is not the first time he interferes this way." She smiled, apparently remembering something. "It is too bad this whole thing is to be kept secret; I would have enjoyed teasing him about it. For I am beginning to see that he resembles his aunt, Lady Catherine de Bourgh, more than I thought. I am sure you have had the opportunity to meet her, and you will know what I mean."

Eliza had not been as changed by her marriage as Caroline had imagined. *She* would never have presumed to compare the two.

But then, Eliza was known for her impertinence, and Caroline was not.

Caroline was awakened after a long restless night by the sound of loud voices from downstairs. Curious as to what could have caused such commotion so early, she dressed hastily and went down. Eliza, who rarely left her parlour in the morning, was in the drawing room, surrounded by servants.

"I do not know how the keys went missing," said Mrs Reynolds, the housekeeper. Her face was red, and she looked flustered, which in itself was unusual, since Caroline perceived her as the embodiment of tranquillity.

"Never mind that," said Eliza. "The main thing is to determine if anything has been taken. You must do a complete inventory, and report to me as soon as possible. We will discover who is behind this. You need not worry."

Mrs Reynolds left the room much reassured, followed by the others.

"What has happened?" Caroline enquired.

"Mrs Reynolds' chatelaine has gone missing, with all her keys, and is nowhere to be found," said Eliza. "I do not think it is a matter of grave concern however. No doubt someone planning mischief has taken them, and we will find them returned to their place by and by."

"What is Mr Darcy's opinion?" said Caroline.

"I have not yet involved him. He is partaking of breakfast, and I did not want to disturb him."

But it was not long before Mr Darcy came into the room, looking grim.

"Mrs Reynolds has spoken to me," said Darcy. "I intercepted her as she was coming to report to you. It appears there are several items of silver missing, as well as a number of valuable objects about the house, among them some of the china heirlooms. You would be well advised, my dear, to have your jewellery box checked, and to have the other guests look into theirs. Someone forced an entry into the house last night. A pane at the back of the house has been shattered, and the window opened to allow the thief to enter."

Eliza sank back on her seat. "Oh, this is bad news indeed," she said.

"I will send for the magistrate," said Mr Darcy. "He will pursue the criminal. He cannot have gone far after all."

The uproar that followed as rooms were searched and cupboards inventoried brought everyone downstairs. Eliza, too filled with anxiety to respond to their questions, recommended each of the guests to check their rooms and report any thefts.

Caroline's heart beat fast as she hurried to check her valuables. She had brought only a few items with her, and they were not her finest. She had not expected that there would be much call for wearing jewels at Pemberley, given that Eliza was unwell. But a favourite ruby chain and set of earrings was among them. She opened the drawer where she kept them. It was empty.

She tugged at the bell pull.

"Do you remember, Molly, where you put my jewels last night?" she asked, still unwilling to believe they were gone.

"Yes, Miss Bingley. They were right here." She pulled open the drawer and stared at the empty space where they had been.

It was terrible to think that someone had crept into her room while she slept, defenceless. She shuddered.

She pushed aside the image. She had not been harmed, at least. She cheered herself further by being thankful that she had not brought any family heirlooms with her.

"Perhaps we mislaid them, Molly,"

"Yes, it is possible, Miss Bingley," said Molly. Together, they conducted a careful search. But they were nowhere to be found.

She returned downstairs to report her loss.

Georgiana was already in the drawing room. Nothing had gone missing in her room. Presently Kitty and Mary, who shared a room, arrived in the drawing room and declared that all was well with them. Charles came down, and, looking indignant, said that the pocket watch he had left on the dresser was gone, but that Jane had suffered no losses.

By and by, Mrs Miles came down, looking quite pale. She announced in a stunned voice that a few pieces of her jewellery had been taken.

"I left them on the table beside my bed," she said. "I have no one to blame but myself, for I should not have been so careless as to place my jewels in plain sight. The jewellery box was well hidden, and the thief made no effort to find it." She covered her face with her hands, quite overcome. She moved blindly across the room, trying to find a seat. Robert Darcy stepped forward and, taking her arm, led her to one. "You may think me silly to make such a fuss, but two of the pieces were given to me by my mother on my eighteenth birthday, and I cannot bear to part with them. I do not really care about the others. They were trifles. But those two…" Clearly distraught, she drew out a handkerchief and blew her nose. Caroline noticed the initials RJ embroidered on them.

"They will be found," said Robert Darcy, grinding his teeth. "We will put out a description of the items, and make sure that the thief will find them impossible to sell."

"Can you do that?" she said, looking at him as though he had offered her salvation. "Oh, you give me some hope I may recover them, at least! If only you could! I will furnish you with a description immediately. Though I am sure *you* remember the pearl necklace I was wearing yesterday." She came to her feet with a sense of purpose, and sitting at the writing table, she began to write a list.

This public avowal brought a hint of red to Robert Darcy's face, but he quickly brought his expression under control. He did not glance in Caroline's direction.

The next person to appear on the scene was Captain Trewson, who announced that nothing had been taken from him, but that he thought perhaps there had been money in one of his pockets, and it was gone. He did not set much store by his memory, however, since he could not name the sum, nor could he be completely certain, so it was possible the thief had not come into his room. He looked enquiringly at his sister, who said quite simply and meaningfully to him, "Alas, it is the pearl necklace Mama gave me!"

Her pronouncement had a strong effect on him. He went quickly to her side and pressed her hand affectionately. "We will move heaven and earth to find it, Eleanor," he said. "We will hunt the culprit down and bring him to justice."

Mrs Bennet came into the room, supported by Lydia. The slump of her back and the lines in her face made her seem older and more fragile. "My necklace and earrings are gone. They were on the table by my bed, and they are no longer there," she said.

"You did search for them in the jewellery box, did you not, Lydia? I may have put them away and forgotten."

"I did, Mama." For once Lydia was looking grave. "They were not there."

It was a measure of her upset that Mrs Bennet said nothing more, but sat down and stared into space.

Mrs Miles, completely overcome by the whole situation, was determined to leave at once for London to engage the Bow Street Runners to pursue the thief and find the jewels. Captain Trewson, however, thought they could do better to search for him in the area. "I am all for setting out to follow his trail immediately. We cannot wait until the trail is cold."

"I have sent for the magistrate," said Mr Darcy. "The moment he arrives, we will conduct a thorough search. Believe me, Mrs Miles, no stone will be left unturned."

But Mrs Miles was too distraught to hear reason. Robert Darcy's words had convinced her that the thief would head for London to sell the jewels, and there was no changing her mind.

"What does the local magistrate know about such matters?" she cried. "You will be wasting your time looking for the thief here. Meanwhile, he will have sold my valuables and we will never find them again. No, we must go to London and engage the Runners to find him. *They* will know what to do."

"I can go to London alone, Eleanor," said Captain Trewson, trying to reason with her. "You do not need to be there. You can stay here and I will send you word as soon as I have any news. I am sure the Darcys will not object."

"Of course not," said Eliza. "You may stay as long as you wish."

Mr Darcy echoed her sentiment, and made a move to dissuade her from leaving. "You can serve no purpose going to London, Mrs Miles," he said.

"Yes I can. I want to be there when they find him," she said, vengefully. "I want him to know how much distress he has caused. I want him to hang for it."

Caroline was angry and troubled herself, though she could not feel so strongly about it, since the pieces held no special meaning for her. She could not wish a man to hang, but she did want him to be caught. And she wanted her jewels back.

Captain Trewson looked apologetically at the assembled company. "I am afraid nothing will do but to post to London immediately. We will send the Bow Street Runners here as soon as possible. Meanwhile, if you apprehend the criminal, or discover anything about him, please send us a message." He turned kindly to Mrs Bennet. "If you will provide me with a description of the items you lost," he said to her, "I will make sure to give it to the Runners."

"I, too, have had something taken," said Caroline. "I will furnish you with a description as well."

They departed shortly after, leaving their London address behind. Everyone wished them good fortune, urged them to write as soon as they had any news, and asked them to return as soon as possible. Louisa was overcome with tears at the parting and went up to her chamber the moment the carriage left. Mr Robert, too, excused himself, and withdrew to the library. Charles declared himself ready to go in search of the villain, but no one took him up on it.

A gloom settled over the house after their departure. Rain battered at the windows, and though candles were lit, the rooms were full of shadows. Mrs Bennet's loss was the worst, for Caroline knew she could ill afford to replace what she had. Even her husband, who rarely exerted himself on her behalf, sat with her, and made every effort to relieve her distress. And Lydia set aside her impatience in an effort to console her mother.

Mary was the only one unaffected by the robbery. She merely gazed at the ceiling and proclaimed in an imposing voice, "One should not be concerned about worldly goods. All is vanity, after all."

Mr Bennet's response was to rebuke her and send her out of the room. She left with her nose in the air, declaring that it was all a big fuss about nothing.

In the next few hours an inventory was completed. The magistrate appeared, bringing round several men who went about asking questions. A carpenter was hired to seal the broken window until the glass could be replaced, so the sound of sawing and hammering echoed through the house. Yet in spite of the noise, everyone crept around and talked in hushed voices, as if afraid of being overheard. There was no formal dinner—everyone chose to eat in their rooms.

Caroline retired early, though sleep hardly came her way. The moment she dozed off, she was plagued by nightmares in which she imagined someone in her bedchamber. At some point, in the dark, she grew convinced she could feel someone's breath on her cheek. She sat up with a start, her pulse beating frantically, and peered into the darkness. She was alone. It took her a long time, however, to convince herself that it was safe to lie back down again.

When she awoke, a pale, watery daylight filtered through the windows. She lay in bed, listening to the drumming raindrops, disinclined to do anything. But eventually she rang for Molly, who informed her of the latest news. There was such a number of things stolen that the thief would have needed a large cart to get away. The magistrates' men had searched the area, hoping to find the wheel tracks, but the rain had washed them away. Still, they were following any lead they could find, and they had no doubt they would bring the criminal to justice. All the gentlemen, except for Mr Bennet, had gone out to comb the area and ask questions. Mr Bennet had stayed behind with Mrs Bennet.

"She's in such a state, poor lady. She's taken to her bed, quite convinced she is going to die," said Molly.

Caroline shocked Molly by laughing and saying she was relieved to hear it.

Truth be told, she had been worried by Mrs Bennet's unnatural silence and was glad to hear she was her old self again.

When Caroline eventually left her room, Mrs Reynolds told her that Eliza wished to speak to her as soon as possible. She went to the private parlour immediately. Eliza was again at the writing table, and Caroline took her gently to task.

"You must not overtax yourself, Eliza, or you will never recover."

Eliza nodded and surrendered the pen to Caroline. "Yes, I know, only it was urgent. I have decided to cancel all our invitations after all. With the house in such disarray, and the magistrate's men in and out, and everyone so glum, it is hardly the right time for a party. But we must send out the letters today, otherwise they will not arrive before people set out. So you see, there is not a moment to be lost. Mr Darcy has sent for his secretary, but even if he were to come at once, he could not complete all the letters quickly enough by himself."

"Then there is no time to waste," said Caroline, in a no nonsense way. "You can dictate to me, and that way you can still accomplish what you wish without having to endure the discomfort."

Eliza relinquished her place at the table with a smile. "I am very glad you came to Pemberley, Caroline. I did not think we got on very well, but now that I know you better, I find I was much mistaken in my initial impression."

Her words made Caroline suddenly shy. She looked down at one of the papers in front of her, searching for the right words.

"I have always cared for Jane," said Caroline. "I thought you were too self-sufficient. That is perhaps still true, but I feel now that we can be friends."

Eliza nodded. "Yes, perhaps we can."

Caroline had always believed herself to have plenty of friends. Eliza's words, however, gladdened her and lifted her spirits. Perhaps she had lost something by coming here, but she had gained something more valuable.

Chapter 15

GLOOM HAD DESCENDED UPON THE HOUSEHOLD, THICK AND heavy as fog, affecting everybody except the irrepressible youngest Bennet girls. For two more days the rain continued to descend with dreary regularity, so there was no possibility of escaping from the house. Lydia, who hoped all day to go to Lambton in the carriage, was forced at last to concede that the rain was not likely to cease.

"Oh, this is so *very* boring! I wish I had not come!" cried Lydia, throwing herself onto an armchair. "It will never stop raining, I declare!"

"I have to agree with you, Lydia," said Mr Bennet, looking up. "I think it very likely that it will continue to rain until the whole world is flooded and we will be forced to ride in an ark. But I wonder if you would be allowed on it?

"The flood was sent to punish the wicked," said Mary, ominously.

"Yes, but none of us here deserves to be drowned," said Mrs Bennet. "Except for the thieving villain who stole my jewels. *He* deserves it above all others, and I hope he *will* drown. But I wish he would return my necklace and earrings first, for depend upon it, they will be carried away a long distance by the flood and taken up by someone else."

"There will be no flood," announced Kitty, in triumph. "The rain has stopped."

Lydia rushed to the window to look out. "So it has. Mama, may we go out walking?"

Meanwhile Caroline decided to make the best of their enforced confinement to speak to Robert Darcy, for she needed to settle matters with him. Her confession to Eliza had done away with her fear of disclosure, and it seemed altogether pointless to continue a façade which had began to crumble almost as soon as it was built. She saw no advantage to prolonging the engagement, particularly in view of his interest in Mrs Miles.

When she asked for his direction, Mrs Reynolds pointed her to the library.

"Miss Bingley," he said, with his usual smile. "Allow me to pour you some refreshment. Or would you prefer tea?"

"I will have sherry."

"Very daring of you, I must say! Are you certain?"

"You must not tease," she said. "I am here to speak to you seriously."

He made a face. "That is very ominous indeed. What are you to accuse me of this time, I wonder?"

"I promise you, I am not here to accuse you of anything."

"Then I promise in return to be serious. More serious, perhaps than you would wish." He gazed into his port bleakly.

"Does this unusually solemn mood have anything to do with Mrs Miles?" she asked, the words spilling from her mouth. It was not what she had intended to say at all.

Robert Darcy raised an eyebrow. "No."

Such a brief answer did not satisfy her. "Do you plan to meet her in London?"

He lifted both brows in exaggerated surprise. "Why, Miss Bingley! I think you are in danger of becoming quite human. I would never have imagined you could ask such a personal question."

Heat flooded up to her face and to the very roots of her hair. She cursed herself for her lack of discretion. What did she care about Mrs Miles, anyway? "I'm sorry…"

"For Heaven's sake! Surely you are not about to back out?" He took a long gulp from his glass. "She was a charming companion, and no, we did not spend the night together, just in case this new-found curiosity of yours provokes you to ask. She was charmingly open and free in her manners, which I found very refreshing. I may meet her in London, but I have not yet decided. Does that satisfy you?"

"Of course. You know I could not possibly have asked—"

"But you wanted to know, and I have told you."

"I did not wish to know."

He leaned forward and took both her hands in his. "Oh, Caroline, what will it take for you to be able to bare your soul?"

With her hands wrapped firmly in his, she could not think. "I cannot…" She hesitated, not at all certain what it was she could not do.

"No," he said, dropping her hands. "I know you cannot. Though I still believe that under that cold exterior there is a warm heart, waiting to be discovered."

She wanted to tell him that of course there was a warm heart. She was warm. Her brother thought her warm, surely. Jane did. Others did, did they not? Perhaps not her sister. Her sister would not think her warm. She would not wish her to be warm.

"I have thrown you into confusion," he said. "I should apologize, perhaps, but I will not."

Caroline stood up to leave. "I think today is not a good day to have our conversation. You are in a strange humour."

"On the contrary," he said. "It is an excellent day. I will try to refrain from making personal comments, though I do not promise to succeed. I seem to have this impulse, you see, when I am with you."

She took her seat again. She could not have left in any case. No one had ever spoken to her the way he did. It made her uneasy, and yet she could not walk away from it. She *wanted* to know what he thought.

"If you are not upset about Mrs Miles's departure, why then have you been in the doldrums since, Mr Robert?" She felt very daring, confronting him like this.

"If you insist on asking me questions of such a delicate nature, then you could at least call me Robert."

"Very well," she said. "But you have not answered my question, *Robert*."

"You have quite mistaken the matter. It was not Mrs Miles' departure which brought on a fit of doldrums. It was something else entirely. I have at long last received a letter from my family in Boston, for, as you know, with the hostilities between our countries in full swing, the mail service is not at its best. My mother is asking me to return. I have left my younger brother Frederick in charge of the family business. He is not alone, since two of my father's friends are there to lend him a hand. Nevertheless, Frederick is responsible for all decisions that must be made. Some business matters have come up requiring urgent attention. If I were there, I would settle them easily, but I cannot do much from here, not without being in possession of all the facts." He stared again into his glass, as though he expected to find a solution in the fiery dark liquid.

"I am trapped, Caroline, and that frustrates me no end. I do not know how they will manage. One false step is all it takes for the business to come crashing down."

"Is your brother too young, then? Do you not trust him to make the right decisions?" she asked.

"Frederick is only twenty-four. He is old enough, perhaps, but he does not have the experience, and he was not trained to the business as my father trained me. He is resourceful and very clever, but I do not know if he can take the whole weight of the business on his shoulders."

"You have to trust that he will do well, that is all," remarked Caroline. "Perhaps, because he has no choice, he will do what needs to be done."

Robert nodded. "That is a good way of looking at it," he said. "I think he may prove quite equal to the task. Perhaps it is just as well that I cannot go back. Who knows? Frederick might well come into his own during my absence."

It was the first time he had spoken about his brother. Caroline realized she knew nothing about his family at all. She did not even know how many brothers or sisters he had.

But that was not what she asked.

"Do you miss them?" It was certainly not what she intended to ask. Her tongue had acquired a mind of its own.

He had not expected her question, either. "Yes, I do miss them. I did not imagine that I would. The family has always meant the business to me. But now that I cannot know when I will see them again, I find myself thinking about them far more often."

"Do you have sisters as well as a brother?"

"I have two sisters." He smiled in recollection. "You would find them quite deplorable, for they are both real hoydens. Clarissa is now sixteen, and May is fifteen. And my youngest brother, Lawrence, is twenty. Lawrence has always had a tendency to get into all kinds of scrapes. That is one good thing about not being there: Frederick has to deal with it, thank heavens!"

Caroline noticed for the first time that one side of his mouth tended to curl up much further than the other when he smiled.

"What about your mother?"

"My mother is very proper. She was careful to raise us to take pride in our lineage, though my father never gave a fig for it. It was a constant source of friction between them. She never understood that he cared nothing for the Darcy name. And he never really understood that she had married him *because* of it."

He paused to put down his empty glass. "A sad tale, but not an unusual one. My father had a knack for commerce, which society would never have approved had he stayed here in England. It would have been considered beneath him, as a gentleman. So after he left the Navy, he began to work in shipping, and built a very good business for himself. Though I must admit he funded some rather strange inventions." He grinned and shrugged. "They *would* have been good if they had worked."

He entwined his fingers together and regarded her thoughtfully. "But you did not come here to ask about my family, Caroline."

"I am glad to have learnt about them."

He took up his empty glass. He did not pour himself another, as she would have expected. He just looked at it, then put it down again. Instead, he sat back and watched her.

"So tell me what you wished to discuss."

"I came to speak to you about an entirely different matter. I came to talk about... ending our engagement."

"Yes," he said, which was hardly helpful.

"How do you wish us to end it?"

"I told you before, that is your decision to make," he said. "We agreed from the onset that *you* would terminate it."

"I hoped to come to some agreement with you."

"*I* am not the one ending it," he persisted.

"I need your help," she replied, not understanding his mood at all.

"You do not need it. You are far more capable of knowing how to handle this situation than I am. It is you who knows all the social niceties. If I have learned anything lately, it is that I do not always understand the subtleties of English life."

His refusal to discuss the matter exasperated her. "I do not know why you are speaking thus. It is quite ridiculous."

"Why ridiculous?" he asked, equally annoyed. "Is that not what you have been saying all along? That I am not a true gentleman? That I do not truly belong here? That because I was not born on this soil I have no claim to be English?"

"I do not understand you," she said. "Why are you bringing up all these questions? I thought we had put them behind us when we declared a truce. I simply wanted to discuss our arrangement, and how best to deal with it."

"Everything is always simple for you, is it not?" he said. "If that is the case, I do not comprehend what you wish to discuss. You may do as you please. Why consult with me?"

She held on to her temper, reminding herself that when he had announced their engagement, he had helped her out of a bad situation. But she could not control her tongue. "You cannot disclaim responsibility. It was you, after all, who caused the muddle. I never *asked* for your help. No one consulted me *then* and asked my opinion. Suppose I *had* in fact circulated those rumours, hoping to force Sir Cecil to show his hand? And you stepped in, oh so gallantly, and announced our engagement. What am I left with now?"

She had not been aware that she still resented what had happened. That was the problem with Robert Darcy. All he had to do was goad her a little, and everything she was guarding carefully inside began to burst through, like a flood.

"You did not touch your sherry," he remarked, mildly.

"I dislike sherry," she muttered.

"I never offered you sherry. I hope you do not plan to blame me for *that* as well," he said, with a cynical gleam. "You asked for it. I know very well that you would prefer tea."

"You know what I dislike most about you, Robert?" said Caroline, taking up the sherry in a gesture of defiance, and swallowing it down in one go, "You always think you know everything about me, but you do not. You know nothing."

"I know more than you would credit me with."

A sense of perversity gripped her, and to prove him wrong, she poured herself another glass. She gripped the decanter by the neck and brought it with her.

"Be careful," said Robert Darcy. "You are not accustomed to drinking." He winced as she consumed another glass. "Especially so quickly."

"Sherry?" she said, indignantly. "You are worried about sherry?"

"I am worried about *you* drinking sherry," he insisted. "Since you are unaccustomed to drinking anything but a single glass of wine over dinner."

She was more than tired of his protective attitude. Who had given him permission to guard her like a snapping dog? No one. She tossed down the drink and poured herself another.

"In that case, I will not be responsible for your actions," he said.

"You are *not* responsible for my actions. Nor is anyone else. Why can't you leave me to my own devices?"

"Unfortunately, at this particular moment, I cannot," he said, leaning back in his chair, "since you are beginning to look distinctly unsteady."

Her head felt vaguely heavy, but she was *not* unsteady. "As usual, you are completely wrong," and to prove it, she took another glass.

He strode deliberately to the bell pull and tugged at it.

"What are you so worried about?" said Caroline, mischievously. "Do you think I will behave inappropriately towards you?"

"I think it highly unlikely," he said.

"What do you mean, *highly unlikely?*" she cried. "Do you think me such an old maid that I would not?"

She would show him how mistaken he was. She pulled herself up and began to advance towards him. She would kiss him, if it was the last thing she did.

"I think nothing," he said, keeping his distance. "I am merely ringing for someone to take you to your room. We will finish this dialogue later."

She continued towards him, intent on showing him that she was quite capable of behaving improperly. Mrs Reynolds, however, appeared very inconveniently in the doorway. Caroline was not so far gone that she would do anything rash in front of a person as dignified as Mrs Reynolds.

"Miss Bingley is rather unwell," said Robert Darcy. "I think it would be best if she were taken to her room."

Mrs Reynolds fussed over her, asking with concern what was wrong. Caroline had enough presence of mind to say that she felt dizzy—which was not completely untrue. Throwing Robert Darcy a glance that promised retaliation for his betrayal, Caroline went away with the housekeeper.

When she reached her room and Mrs Reynolds had helped her lie on her bed, Caroline reached a resolution. She was more than tired of attempting to deal with Mr Robert Darcy. In fact, she had no intention of dealing with him ever again.

With that resolved, she began to feel much, much better.

Chapter 16

CAROLINE GROANED WHEN SHE WOKE UP. THEN SHE TRIED NOT to groan as Molly helped her dress for dinner. She had made a fool of herself yet again with Robert. Why could she not have an ordinary, calm, sensible conversation with him without something untoward happening?

And now she had to go down and face him, haunted by the persistent memory that she had been on the verge of kissing him, before he rang for Mrs Reynolds.

Pemberley had a strange effect on her, she was now convinced. It was as if the house itself was a kind of presence that drove her to do things she would never do in her right mind. As if she had entered an uncanny realm where all normal rules were suspended.

Well, it was as good an explanation for her behaviour as any.

Meanwhile, Reality was waiting for her downstairs. If she could have hidden in her room and remained there for the rest of the stay, she would have. But she could not. Sooner or later, she would have to look Robert Darcy in the eye and know that he knew that she had tried to kiss him.

Caroline, if nothing else, had a practical mind. If something unpleasant had to be faced, the sooner the better.

Instead, she stayed in her room and hid, and pretended to read, and hoped nobody would come looking for her

Time passed slowly. She heard laughter from downstairs, and then voices as everyone passed through the hall and moved to the dining room.

That was what drove her downstairs at the last possible moment. For if there was anything worse than being too embarrassed to make an appearance, it was realizing that she had been completely forgotten.

She gained one advantage from her late appearance. The seating arrangements had been changed, so that instead of being put next to Robert, she was relegated to the bottom of the table, and seated between Georgiana and Kitty. At first she avoided looking down the table, afraid to catch his eye. But then he said something funny and chuckled, glancing towards her, and before she knew it she was laughing too, and all her dread had dissipated.

During the second course Caroline's long-awaited letter from Newcastle arrived. She took it from the silver salver and was about to put it away to read later when an intuition prompted her to open it. She skimmed the content quickly then, as her heart skipped a beat, she went back to examine it again carefully. Her reaction must have shown on her face, because conversation at the dinner table ceased as all eyes turned towards her.

"Oh, you have received bad news!" cried Mrs Bennet. "Pray tell us what it is at once!"

She read on. Part of her still wanted to believe that she had misunderstood, but she knew it could not be so.

Therefore, my dear Caroline, if it is in your power to summon the magistrate in secret, before they can escape, you will be doing us all a great service. For there have been several households here in Newcastle who have suffered losses from that infamous pair.

The letter concluded with hopes that she would not receive the letter too late. She put the letter down, and stared round at the expectant faces.

"The letter concerns Captain Trewson and Mrs Miles."

Mrs Bennet put a hand to her heart and gasped loudly. "Oh, no! They have met with an accident! What has happened? Tell me quickly! I cannot bear to think of it!"

Louisa turned as white as the tablecloth in front of her. Caroline felt profoundly sorry for her, and wished she could have broken the news another way. But she had no choice now but to continue. She struggled with her words, trying to reduce the impact on her sister.

"No, there has been no accident," she said, keeping her voice steady. "I have received a letter from a friend of mine in Newcastle. I wrote to enquire about the Trewsons. She has only now responded."

Caroline could not bring herself to say it, but she had to. She tried not to look at her sister. "I am afraid that we have found our thieves."

The blankness on everyone's faces told her she had not made herself clear. "I wrote to friend in the hopes of discovering more about the Trewsons. My friend did not respond at first, because she knew no one by that name. But I had described them to her, and something I wrote must have alerted her, for she soon put two and two together.

That was when she realized that the brother and sister known to her as Captain Cartwright and Miss Jennings were one and the same as our Captain Trewson and Mrs Miles. She in turn enquired about them from friends of hers who had suffered a robbery, which is why she did not write sooner. According to her information, when they last appeared in the vicinity of York, they were husband and wife by the name of Captain and Mrs Flemings, only they were darker and their appearance slightly altered. But there can be no doubt they are one and the same, for everyone is quite in agreement about their manners and behaviour."

Caroline cast a sideways glance at Robert. He had paled, and his fingers gripped the table tightly. She did not look at Louisa.

"In York, as in Newcastle, they have left behind them a trail of debt, stolen property, and broken hearts."

There were cries of outrage and anger. Lydia jumped up and stared with horror at the company. "Oh! It cannot be! And I actually thought them so kind to pick me up and drive me all the way here! When all the time they could have cut my throat and tossed me by the wayside!"

"And to think they seemed so charming and handsome," said Mrs Bennet, "and all the time they were ogling my jewels! It is not to be endured! Mr Bennet, how *can* you sit there so calmly eating your food at a time like this? You must *do* something."

"It would be a pity to waste such an excellent dish," said Mr Bennet. "And I cannot imagine what I could possibly do. They are no doubt disguised at this very moment under another name in a household similar to this, charming silly young ladies—and gentlemen, it must be said—with false stories about their lives."

"There must be something you can do to stop them! Oh, why must you always be so contrary? You are never willing to stir yourself on my behalf!" cried Mrs Bennet.

"I do not see what you expect me to accomplish, my dear. Besides, if we are to believe Captain Trewson, he is a practised duellist."

This statement had a powerful affect on Mrs Bennet. "No, no, my dear! You must not fight a duel! For you would be killed, and then that detestable Mr Collins will take your place."

"Then I hope I have your permission to continue eating, Mrs Bennet."

Mr Darcy rose, and with a word, brought silence to the general uproar around the table. "We must not waste a moment. The first thing to be done is to send for the magistrate. Now that we know that it is the brother and sister who are responsible for the theft, we have a far better chance of catching the culprits."

"At least we know one thing," said Robert, his voice dry and devoid of all inflection. "We know which direction they did *not* go. They did not go to London."

A clamour of voices rose to argue with him, with everyone wishing to contribute something.

Mr Darcy left the room, presumably to inform Eliza of the new development, and to send someone for the magistrate.

"How can we know that they are brother and sister?" said Kitty. "Perhaps it was simply part of their disguise."

The question was perceptive. Since everyone else ignored the remark, Caroline answered Kitty herself. "You are quite right. I suppose we shan't know unless they are caught," replied Caroline.

"What I would like to discover," said Robert, "is how they knew to escape before the letter arrived."

"I am to blame for that," said Louisa, bitterly. "I knew my sister had sent a letter, and I was unwise enough to inform Captain Trewson—or whatever his name was."

"I think that everything was already planned," said Kitty,

warming to the subject. "Remember our walk to Lambton? I said then that I did not like the man Captain Trewson met at the inn. They were planning the robbery at the time, I am certain of it. There was something stealthy about their movements. He must have provided the wagon to remove their goods. I told you, did I not, Lydia, that I did not like him? But you were too occupied with the officers to care."

"You can't blame *me*. How could I have known? And what concern was it of mine, in any case?"

"You were the one who brought them here," said Kitty.

"Stop, Kitty, at once!" said Mrs Bennet. "Do you not see we are miserable enough, without you making it worse?"

"I do not see how I could make it worse by speaking about it," said Kitty, unrepentant. "And it was Lydia who brought them here. If she had arranged for a proper escort when she left Newcastle, instead of relying on strangers, we would not be in such a basket."

Lydia burst into tears and fled from the room, with her mother close behind her.

Mr Bennet looked up from his food with a sigh. "Now we will at least have some quiet."

Even Jane looked shocked at his statement. "Papa, you *must* see that Mama is quite distressed."

"I hope you do not mean to harp on the same theme as well, Jane. I would have thought you had more sense," replied Mr Bennet.

"My wife simply wished to point out that Mrs Bennet is genuinely distraught, Mr Bennet." Charles spoke more sharply than was customary for him.

A tense silence followed. It seemed useless to continue at the dinner table, since no one, not even Mr Bennet, was eating by now. In the absence of both Mr and Mrs Darcy, Robert proposed that they should all retire to the drawing room, where they could each read the letter, and reach what conclusions they may from it.

Louisa excused herself and pleaded a headache. Caroline would have followed her sister to her chamber, but Robert held her back.

"She might need some time alone," he said. "Especially since the exposure of her friend was so public."

Caroline thought perhaps he was echoing his own sentiments. But he came into the drawing room with everyone else, and waited patiently for his turn to read the letter.

"Have I misrepresented anything?" she asked, worried that she had read the letter too quickly, and hoping that perhaps she had misunderstood.

"No, no," he said. "You have, if anything, expressed the matter very tactfully. It appears they are sharps of the worst order. And now that I think back on it, I realize that she won at cards far more often than was natural. It would not surprise me if the cards were marked." He looked profoundly unhappy.

"I am sorry," she murmured. "I know you had an interest in her."

He looked down at the ground. "I will admit I was completely deceived by her. I was duped by her easy going behaviour. I was tired of the hypocrisies of society, and thought her directness a refreshing change. I welcomed her lack of restraint with me, and her willingness to express her feelings. Or so I thought." He tousled his hair, then tried to smooth it down again.

"What is worse is that now I know nothing about her at all. Not her name, not her origin, and not even if she is married. It is quite a blow to discover that someone you liked is in fact a complete cipher, and you will never know if anything she said to you was true."

"I am sorry," said Caroline again, knowing it was inadequate.

"I do not even know why she singled me out for attention. She did not steal anything from me."

"It is not puzzling that she would single you out. You were the only available bachelor," said Caroline. "And the captain did not steal from Louisa, either. I wonder what they were about."

"We will only know the answers to our questions if they are caught. And perhaps, not even then."

❧✻❧

But Caroline was obliged to offer far more than guesses by the time the evening was out. She was summoned to the library to speak to Mr Benson, the magistrate, since everything depended on the letter she had received. Mr Benson raised an unexpected number of questions. When asked why she had written the letter in the first place, she was forced to give a circumspect answer, since she did not wish to involve her sister. And then there was the credibility of her correspondent to establish, and a number of other queries besides which left her quite exhausted.

Mr Darcy and Robert were both present at the examination. Mr Darcy gave her an encouraging smile as she began, and she took heart from it. She forgot him quickly as she struggled to recall specific events or circumstances. But she was aware throughout of Robert's gaze on her, and of his warm presence supporting her. He interceded several times when it was apparent that Mr Benson's questions were too delicate or too personal.

She was blameless, of course, but Caroline could understand that Mr Benson needed to be thorough. Since so much depended on it, he needed to determine whether she had any motive in attributing the crime to Captain Trewson and Mrs Miles. She did not resent his questions. As an officer of the law, he was doing what was required, and overall, she thought he did very well.

Finally, he seemed satisfied, and he and Mr Darcy made their way to the drawing room to speak to some of the others, in case they had anything to add.

Caroline was left alone in the library—not for the first time—with Robert. The familiar furnishings wrapped around her like a cloak, and she felt content.

"This is becoming quite a habit," she said, with a faint smile.

Robert's eyes lit up. "And no doubt you wish for a sherry."

"After all the events of the day, I would wish for something stronger." At his expression, however, Caroline burst into laughter. "No, you need not worry. I was not serious."

"Not serious? You! Impossible!"

Their shared laughter was a balm to her, and she felt some of her tension slip away. She sat back in her armchair, and, driven by the spirit of mischief, stretched her legs out as he did.

He observed her with interest. "Are you not becoming too lax in your behaviour? I cannot imagine that it is proper for a lady to be quite so comfortable as this, alone with a gentleman, without a chaperone in sight, her legs stretched out in a decidedly unladylike manner."

"There is nothing improper in my posture—it is merely *unceremonious*, which is not the same thing. As for your other remark, I cannot seem to avoid being alone with you, so I might as well accept it."

"I am glad to hear it," he said. "I have always thought myself irresistible."

"I see that your pride has rallied from the blow it suffered at Mrs Miles's hands."

"Not so," he said, turning serious. "My pride does suffer. It rankles that I did not see through her. I foolishly equated free manners with an open nature, and I have been stung as a result. When I think how taken in I was…"

He grimaced and fell silent. "Fortunately," he said, after a long minute of reflection, "my feelings were not engaged. It is only my pride that is injured."

"Then no great harm has been done," said Caroline.

"Oh, yes," said Robert Darcy. "Something else rankles even more. *That* is not a matter so easily forgotten."

Caroline hoped he did not intend to confess something very private. She waited uneasily.

"I cannot quite believe it, but *you* proved far cleverer than I. You *did* warn me that something was not quite right."

"Cleverness had nothing to do with it," she replied tartly, "*I* was not under her spell."

"You were not under the captain's spell, either," said Robert. "You were able to see through them from the very beginning."

She shrugged. "You may think me fanciful," she confessed, musingly, "but I feel an odd kinship with them." In the familiar depth of the library, with the shadows from the candlelight dancing around them, the world no longer looked quite the same. She sensed she could say this and not feel foolish.

"Sometimes I think that my whole life is a pretence, that I cannot know who I really am. I have been so shaped by my schooling and the expectations of others that I no longer understand what I was meant to be. And in that, perhaps, I feel some kinship to the Trewsons. They become what people expect of them."

"You bear no resemblance to the Trewsons, Caroline," he responded. "You do not dissemble to take advantage of others."

"Perhaps not, but does that make the pretence any more justified?"

Robert waved his hand impatiently. "You at least are not trying to be something you are not."

"I have spent such a long time trying to be a lady. But am I really one? Or is it only a mask that I wear, to cover up my awareness that I am not?"

He shook his head. "You are being too harsh, as always. I do not understand why you constantly malign yourself."

"Your cousin would disagree."

"It comes to that," he said softly. "It always comes to my cousin."

"No!" she said, knowing where his thoughts had taken him. "You mistake me. That is not what I speak of. I no longer have any interest in Mr Darcy's attentions. I realized that the moment I came to Pemberley. But I have been hurt by him in more ways than one. If I do still have an ideal of an English gentleman, it would be him. He has judged me harshly and passed his verdict: I am not a lady."

"I think it is you who have misjudged my cousin, Caroline, and you have read too much into his words," said Robert. "There are reasons for his conduct."

"What reasons could possibly account for his insistence on his—and your—superiority?"

For a moment Robert struggled, then seemed to reach a conclusion. "I should not speak of this, but I say it in the strictest confidence. I know I can trust you not to reveal it to anyone."

He paused. She waited.

"You must not be hard on Fitzwilliam," said Robert. "He is not himself. He has been very anxious about Elizabeth. No one must know of this, but the doctor has told him that it is very likely Elizabeth will never be able to bear children."

She put a hand to her mouth in dismay. Whatever she had imagined, it had not been this. "Oh. Poor Eliza! How devastating it must for her!" She reeled as the implications sank in. "When he spoke of you being his heir, I thought it hypothetical, because I thought them likely to have children." She closed her eyes. "And theirs is such a happy marriage."

Robert nodded. "So you see why you must not take his condemnation to heart. It is his way of railing against fate. It was unfortunate that you were the target of his vexation."

What Robert Darcy told her changed everything. She only wished she had learned of it earlier. But then, how would things have been any different? She had become friends with Eliza without that knowledge. And as for Mr Darcy, he would not have appreciated her pity.

"Sherry?" asked Robert, breaking into her thoughts.

She declined. A thought flashed into her mind, blinding in its clarity.

"Is that why *you* are railing against your fate?"

He frowned. "I am not sure what you are referring to, Miss Bingley." She was not Caroline any more. She was Miss Bingley. His voice was distant, and quite, quite cautious.

"If you are Mr Darcy's heir, then it has become very hard for you to leave England, has it not?"

For a moment he did not answer. "I am not prepared to talk about this at the moment," he said, finally.

"I will not press you to do so. One does not always want to bare one's soul." She paused. "And sometimes, if it is important enough, one does not even know how."

And with that, she left him to his brooding.

Chapter 17

On her way to her bedchamber, Caroline scratched on her sister's door. There was no light under it, however, and, after waiting a few minutes, Caroline continued with heavy steps to her own room.

The next morning, with allowances made for her sister's late mornings, she repeated her attempt. This time she found her sister propped up in bed, with a book in her hand. She did not return Caroline's greeting.

"Louisa, I am sorry. I wish I could have spared you this."

Louisa stared down at the book, motionless.

"I did not anticipate that the news would be so bad. I meant only to find out more about Captain Trewson."

Louisa did not respond.

"I should have waited until we were more private. I should not have broken the news as I did, over the dinner table."

Silence.

"For heaven's sake, Louisa, say something!"

"What do you wish me to say?" said Louisa, tossing down her book. "Everyone is mocking me downstairs. I am certain of it," said Louisa. She took a shuddering breath. "And they are right." She stared down at the bedcover. "Remember what Mrs Drakehill used to say, Caroline? That a lady should see the world from above, as though standing on the top of a tall mountain, with everyone else far below?"

Caroline remembered very well.

"And how she used to make us walk around with sharp pieces of wood sewn into our collars so we were forced to keep our chins raised?"

Caroline nodded.

"She taught us never to forget our status in life. Yet I set aside her teachings, thinking myself beyond them. Now I am reaping the seeds that I sowed. I was gripped by sentiment, and I allowed myself to believe—oh, I do not even know what it was. You, however, did everything that is proper. You did not step down from the mountain, nor did you once lose sight of our position. You set out, quite correctly, to investigate Captain Trewson's background. I, on the other hand, must pay the price of my folly. It is my punishment."

"But Louisa," said Caroline, "it was not from a sense of superiority that I questioned his motives. Nor was I primarily concerned with his status. My concern sprang more from distrust. There was something about the two of them I could not like, and that is what prompted my actions. Believe me, Mrs Drakehill did not cross my mind."

"And to think that I wished to marry him! When he is nothing more than a common actor and a thief."

"We know nothing about his origins. Perhaps he is a gentleman fallen upon hard times."

"No gentleman would behave as he did."

"We cannot know what he is, or was," said Caroline firmly.

Louisa stared at her as though she had acquired a distasteful disease.

"We *know* he is not a gentleman."

"How can we know that?" cried Caroline. "His manners and speech make it very likely that he is. That does not change the fact that he is a villain."

"What talk is this? You have been spending too much time with that fiancé of yours, listening to his seditious sentiments. Did they not have a Revolution in the Colonies, as they did in France? You must be careful not to be influenced by his coarse opinions."

Caroline threw her sister an icy look. "Once and for all, Louisa, I will not allow you to speak of Robert Darcy in this manner. He has helped me a great deal, and I have come to regard him as a… friend."

"If Mr Hurst were here, he would be alarmed at your conduct."

Caroline snorted. "You were not so eager to speak of Mr Hurst a few days ago. If Mr Hurst really were here, he would have most likely been asleep, since that was his favourite occupation."

"You are beginning to sound distinctly vulgar, Caroline."

Caroline rose to her feet. "I do not believe so. But if I am, then I rejoice in it, for it has helped me speak my mind."

She fetched her pelisse and went out to the garden. After days of rain, the sky was blue at last, and she needed some air to clear her mind. As she crossed the hall, however, the sound of an altercation reached her, and she drew back just in time as Mr Bennet advanced down the passage to the library, followed by Mrs Bennet.

"You can be quite sure, Mr Bennet, I will *not* return to Longbourn," said Mrs Bennet, rather breathlessly. "*You* may choose to ride ahead, but *we* will follow later. I will not leave now."

"I see no purpose in remaining, Mrs Bennet," replied Mr Bennet. "Eliza is recovering slowly and she is well enough to manage without our tender care. I do not wish to be a burden on her. And I am concerned about Lydia. She will do far better at Meryton. There is little to occupy her here, and she will soon find a way to cause trouble."

"But how can you be so insensible to Mary's situation? For *her* sake at least, we are obliged to stay."

"Mary's situation?" said Mr Bennet. "I fail to understand you."

"But you must know I'm expecting Mr Bass to offer for her."

"I cannot speak for your expectations, Mrs Bennet. But allow me to say I would be a very poor parent indeed if I allowed Mary to marry Mr Bass. Besides, you are presuming too much. Much as I esteem my daughter, I hardly think he will offer for her after such a brief acquaintance. I have bowed to your superior knowledge in the past, and you have done very well, for now both Jane and Eliza are happily married. But I will draw the line at having Mr Bass as my son-in-law. You will have to look elsewhere for a husband for Mary, my dear."

"But Mr Bennet—"

The squeak of a door opening and shutting signalled that the Bennets had gone into the library. Caroline could not help agreeing with Mr Bennet. She would not wish Mr Bass on anybody, even if Mary was something of a prude. It was possible she would grow out of it as she grew older, or that she would find someone who would capture her fancy and charm her out of all her pretensions.

But Mary was not her concern. It was Eliza who needed her consideration. Now that she was aware of Eliza's condition, Caroline understood why her spirits were so low. She could not betray Robert Darcy's trust, of course, and hint that she knew the truth, but she would try harder to bring Eliza out of her melancholy. It was, after all, her purpose in coming to Pemberley.

Eliza was reading when Caroline joined her in the parlour. She put down her book and held out her hand with a welcoming smile.

"My father has informed me that my family is planning to leave soon. It will be very quiet when they go. I hope you are not planning to leave as well. You and Jane have been so good to me, I do not know how to thank you."

"I have done nothing," said Caroline, touched by Eliza's praise. "I only wish you were better, and that we could do more things together. In any case, I will not leave until I am certain that you are in better health. We need to have you walking and riding again. You cannot stay indoors all the time."

"I have never cared much for riding. Jane is the rider in my family, not I. A turn in the carriage, however, might be just the thing."

An idea came to Caroline, partly propelled by her own curiosity, and partly by concern for Eliza. The more she considered it, the more the plan appealed to her. She could hardly wait to see if they could put it into effect. Eliza needed a change of atmosphere, and a short journey in the open air would do her some good.

She excused herself and, with mounting enthusiasm, went in search of Robert. To her disappointment, she discovered from Mrs Reynolds that he had gone to make some purchases in Lambton.

This did not deter her for long, however. Thankful for the pleasant weather, she requested the groom to saddle her a well-behaved horse, and was soon on her way to the village. It was possible that their paths were different, and that she would find when she arrived in Lambton that he had already returned, but she was glad to be out of the house.

The countryside was carpeted in crisp new growth, sprouting up after the prolonged rain, the air smelled sweet and unsullied, and drops of moisture on the trees sparkled in the sunlight. The rolling hills, the wide sky and the unfettered fields provoked in her a sense of elation.

All too soon, it seemed, she arrived in the village. The sense of elation died down. She found Lambton narrow, cramped, and crowded. She left her horse at the inn stables, and enquired inside for Mr Robert Darcy.

Caroline discovered him in the tap room with a chunk of cheese, a half-eaten loaf of bread, and a mug of beer, laughing with the innkeeper with the ease of long acquaintance. She paused at the threshold, observing him as he laughed and talked, and a surge of envy passed through her.

She could never be like him—so free and indifferent to his surroundings.

Since she was very young, she had been taught to hold herself apart from those around her. It was as if she walked inside a bubble, walled off from other people. Or perhaps it was simply that she was a woman, and as a woman such easy camaraderie was denied her. Even if she were to step out of the bubble, she could not sit and laugh as he did with the innkeeper.

Caroline knew the instant he registered her presence. She lamented the wariness that passed over his features, the stiffening of his back. Even the innkeeper noticed, for he followed the direction of Mr Robert Darcy's glance, and his gaze alighted on her curiously.

He came immediately to her. "A happy coincidence, Miss Bingley," he said. "What brings you to Lambton?"

"You do, actually," she replied boldly.

He gave her his lopsided smile. "I am generally perceived to be charming, and it is not unusual for the ladies to flock to me, so I should not be surprised you cannot stay away." He narrowed his eyes. "Why then do I find that difficult to believe?"

"It happens to be true," she said, with a smile. "Though not for the reasons you are hoping for, so you need not give yourself too much consequence."

"Be still my beating heart," he replied, with exaggerated fervour, putting his hands to his chest. "Do not wound me thus!"

He was playing the clown again. She would have preferred him to be as he was yesterday. But he made her laugh, and for once she was content. "I have a plan." When she had been on horseback, the plan had seemed perfectly reasonable, but with him before her, she grew reticent, and began to think that perhaps she was imposing.

"Tell me then why you rode all the way from Pemberley to find me. The reason had better be good, or I will suspect you of having intentions," he said.

"Hush," she said, swatting at him playfully. "Will you listen to me or not?"

"I will be happy to listen. Do you not wish for some refreshment?"

Caroline shook her head. "No, I would rather walk through the village. It is too beautiful a day to be indoors."

He paid the innkeeper and they moved outside.

"I have been thinking about Eliza, now that I know more about her condition," said Caroline, "and I am convinced she needs a change. She is spending too much time in the house brooding. I know she is not strong enough to travel far, but I think a small journey might be just the thing. So it occurred to me that perhaps if we were to take her to visit your estate, she may be coaxed a little out of her gloom, and that in turn may help her recover."

She flushed under his scrutiny. He would suspect, of course, that she was curious about his home, for he always seemed to guess her thoughts. Well, curiosity was nothing to be ashamed of.

But he gave no indication that he had reached that conclusion. Instead, his face lit up, and he began to elaborate on her plans eagerly.

"You have hit upon it, Miss Bingley. It is exactly what Cousin Elizabeth needs. A change of scene will speed her recovery, I am sure. I will issue an invitation. Under normal conditions, I would not expect anyone to stay, since it is within an easy enough distance. But given Elizabeth's delicate health, I will expect everyone to stay for two or three nights at least. It is just the thing. I will send ahead to my housekeeper, Mrs Elliot, and ask her to start preparations immediately."

"Not so fast," said Caroline. "You had better consult with your cousin first. He may have something entirely different to say about the scheme."

"Leave Fitz to me," said Robert. "I will bring him round. Come, let us ride back and break the news together."

When they returned to Pemberley, however, they discovered that their plan had to be postponed. Word had come that a party of Darcy's acquaintances were to break their journey at Pemberley on their way from London to the Lake District. They were expected the very next day.

"I am *so* glad we did not leave after all," said Lydia. "I hope you are planning to have a dance, Mr Darcy, for after all the unhappy events of the last few days, it is just what we need to cheer us up."

Mr Darcy was not enthusiastic. Charles, however, thought it was a capital idea.

"A dance is just what we need," he said. "We have grown quite dismal and dull these last days."

Mr Darcy turned to Georgiana, who was watching her brother hopefully. "I will leave the decision to my sister," he said. "What do you think? Should we have a small dance here tomorrow?"

"I would like it above all," she said, her face glowing, "for we have not had a dance here since before you married."

"Really, Darcy," said Charles, "how could you do such a thing to your sister? You have been so occupied by your new circumstances you have neglected her sadly. For shame!"

"No, no," cried Georgiana. "You must not slander him, for he is the best brother in the world. I have had my share of dancing and society in local assemblies and balls. I only meant to say that we have not had a dance in Pemberley for a long time."

"Although I cannot entirely approve of dancing," said Mr Bass, who had come to call on them, "I do not begrudge young people the opportunity to divert themselves, as long it is done under the watchful eyes of their elders."

"It appears things are settled, then," said Louisa, rather too brightly. Caroline did not blame her for wishing to distract herself, though she seemed to have forgotten she was still in mourning and could not dance.

Mr Darcy raised his hands in surrender. "There are too many of you, and too few of me. I bow to the superior numbers."

Darcy was hailed as a hero, and in the next instant became the object of a barrage of questions, the first of which involved the names of the guests expected. He named a party of eight, most of whom Caroline knew by name at least.

"And Sir Cecil Rynes," he concluded.

Both Louisa and Robert looked towards Caroline. She squirmed uneasily under the sudden scrutiny.

"All the guests, with the exception of Sir Cecil, were supposed to come to the original house party, before we postponed it," said Darcy. "No doubt they were about to set out when they received our note, and decided to travel to the Lake District instead."

Just a few weeks earlier she would have been delighted at the prospect of seeing Sir Cecil. But she could not summon any enthusiasm over the prospect now. It was as if she had known him in a past so remote she could recall it only with an effort. She felt no interest in the other guests, either. Nor at the thought of hearing the latest gossip from London.

In fact, she could barely summon up any interest in receiving them at all.

❧

As soon as the ladies had left the gentlemen to their port after dinner, Louisa sidled up to Caroline.

"How unfortunate it is that Sir Cecil is one of the party!" She said, "It will be quite embarrassing for you. Perhaps you should explain to him the reason for your engagement to Robert Darcy."

"I see no reason for embarrassment. We do not know how he reacted to the news of my engagement, nor indeed if he has even heard of it."

"He will have heard of it, certainly. But now that I think of it, this is an opportunity you should not miss, Caroline. Sir Cecil on your very doorstep! You cannot let him go. He is a far better catch for you than Mr Robert Darcy could ever be."

Louisa's words were a timely reminder. She was beginning to slip into a comfortable way of thinking, as though she really was engaged to Robert, and did not need to exert herself to find anyone else. Here in Derbyshire, away from London, she was losing touch with what really mattered. She was content to let life pass her by. And there was something in the air of Pemberley that seemed to encourage this.

Sir Cecil's visit jolted her out of her torpor. Providence was serving her another sleight of hand. If Caroline did not care to go to London, London Society would come to her.

"You *must* secure your interest in Sir Cecil," continued Louisa. "He was so close to asking for your hand in marriage. Think, Caroline! It was what Mama hoped for. It was her life's dream that we would marry into the peerage."

Caroline thought of the mother who had died before she had a chance to see her daughters married. If Mama were alive, she would be disappointed in her for not yet having secured a husband.

"In fact," said Louisa, with sudden excitement, "your engagement may be the very reason he is here! He must have heard the news, and intends to confront you about it." She gave Caroline a tight hug. "Oh, it is simply wonderful! It is just as we thought. It can hardly be a coincidence that he is coming now when he was not even invited originally. No doubt it was he who urged the group to stop here on the way. I am convinced he is indignant to know that you are thinking of marrying someone else, and has come here to dissuade you."

It had never occurred to Caroline to think of Sir Cecil in this manner, but it was possible. What could be more natural for a suitor who felt himself pushed aside by a rival than to hunt down the object of his interest and ask for an explanation?

An uneasy guilt crept over her. She had never wondered for a single moment how Sir Cecil would receive the news of her engagement. She had not even had the courtesy to write and inform him.

How could she have been so neglectful? She had been so vexed about her own part in the muddle, that she had not spared a moment for him. Granted, Sir Cecil was not the kind to fall deeply in love. But he was proud, and he did not deserve to be treated so indifferently, without even a word from her. If he had determined to marry her, she had done him a bad turn. She could hardly blame him for coming to Pemberley to seek her out.

The more she thought about it, the more she dreaded his arrival. The idea of the confrontation that would inevitably take place worried her so insistently that when a game of whist was set up and she agreed to play, she discovered she could not focus on the cards, and had to be prompted constantly to remember her turn in the game.

"Oh, Caroline, I wish you would pay attention to the cards," said Kitty, who was her partner. "I know you think us tedious rustics, but it does not mean that our game is so very boring. We might not have lived in London, but whist is whist, whether it is played in London or in Longbourn."

Caroline wanted to tell Kitty that there was, in fact, a huge difference, since the stakes in London were frequently impossibly high. But she realized that her own incivility had prompted the remark, and she did not want to quarrel with Kitty. "I am sorry. I am not at all bored by your company. It is just that I am thinking of the London party who will be arriving tomorrow, and I cannot seem able to concentrate on the game."

The relief that showed on Kitty's face made her glad she had not answered unkindly. She took advantage of a break in the game, however, to excuse herself and retire for the night.

As soon as she had snuffed her candle, however, she regretted her decision to come upstairs. For as long as she was surrounded by company, she could deceive herself into believing that Sir Cecil's arrival did not overly matter.

But in the darkness his disillusionment at her neglect lurked in the corners of the room like a palpable presence. The more she pondered, the more certain it became that she would be forced to endure a very unpleasant encounter. And for that, she only had herself to blame.

Chapter 18

"So your suitor is going to be here," said Robert the next morning. "Now, I call *that* a lucky event."

Caroline busied herself in her task of arranging the flowers. The house was in complete upheaval. It could have been forty guests who were coming to stay rather than eight. But surprisingly, Louisa had thrown herself wholeheartedly into the effort, resolved to make everything perfect for the London arrivals, while Caroline lagged behind, her energy flagging.

The guests were due any moment and she really needed to go up to change. She had scarcely slept the night before and, after a long night of reflection, mingled intermittently with troubled dreams, she had come to see Sir Cecil's arrival in the light of a nightmare. For what explanation could she possibly give that would appease him?

"I have no time to linger," she said. "The guests are almost upon us, and we are far from ready."

Robert took up a clementine from a dish on the table and began to peel it.

"I cannot have enough of clementines. They are my favourite fruit. It is indeed fortunate that Darcy has a plentiful supply. We are not so lucky in Boston."

"He is indeed lucky to have an orangery," said Caroline, wishing he would go away.

"Are we no longer friends, then?" said Robert. "Now that your prospective fiancé is coming? I admit I am curious to meet the man you held up to me as a paragon of virtue."

She ignored him as she realized she had cut the flowers much too short and that they were past redeeming.

"You will slaughter those poor flowers if you do not sit down for a minute and take a rest," said Robert.

Reluctantly, she allowed him to tug her by the elbow and draw out a chair for her to sit on. He placed a peeled clementine in her palm. The sweet tangy fragrance revived her and without even noticing, she tore off a slice and bit into it.

"With some advance notice of the visit, we might have been able to do things differently. But it occurred to me that this might be a very good time to end our engagement, before Sir Cecil arrives. Then you can explain to him that it was all a mistake, and everything will be resolved."

She could not rid herself of that feeling of oppression. If anything, it seemed to be growing a great deal worse.

He waited for her answer, his gaze boring into her face. She studied the fruit she held in her fingers, a small part of her mind marvelling at all the tiny segments that had come together to form just one slice.

"I hardly think it wise," she said. "Breaking off our relationship now would provoke a reaction, and Sir Cecil would arrive amidst the torrent of gossip that would inevitably follow."

Robert peeled another clementine and gave her half. "I have spoiled things for you, have I not? You were right about that," said Robert, ruefully. "My only excuse is that my intentions were good."

She managed to give him a quick half smile, but she was too tired to answer.

"How do you wish me to do things, then, at the dance? Do you wish me to lead you in, as your fiancé? Or shall I disappear into the library, and hide myself out of view?"

"Of course you should not disappear," said Caroline, crossly. "You do not need to skulk and hide. You have done nothing wrong. I, on the other hand, have much to answer for."

"Sackcloth and ashes again? My, my, Miss Bingley, you carry a heavy burden of guilt."

She knew he was trying to cheer her, but she was too apprehensive to respond. "You can joke with me tomorrow, once this day is over," she said. "But it is no use trying today. Your attempts will only fall on deaf ears."

He nodded in acknowledgement. "Then I will make you laugh tomorrow. Today, we must be solemn as Mr Bass, who is right now coming in our direction. Excuse my sudden disappearance…."

She schooled her expression carefully as Mr Bass approached her. "I wonder if you can tell me where I can find Mrs Bennet?" he said, peering at her with his large eyes. "For I have looked up a quotation which I brought to her attention yesterday, and I am sure she would be delighted to hear it."

Caroline was certain Mrs Bennet would not thank her for giving him her direction. So she said, quite unrepentantly, that she believed Mrs Bennet was taking a walk in the garden, even though she had seen her not five minutes since going up the stairs.

By the time she went up to dress, she was running out of time. This did not diminish her desire to appear at her absolute best. However, she fussed so much over what to wear, and how to have her hair done, that Molly began to run out of patience.

"If you wish to be dressed by the time the gentlemen arrive, Miss Bingley, I would suggest that you decide on the emerald green, or I cannot promise I will have your hair dressed in time."

Molly's unusual sharpness served its purpose. Threatened by the prospect of not being ready when Sir Cecil arrived, Caroline restrained her fidgeting and submitted meekly to her maid's ministrations.

And so it was that, when two carriages drove sedately into the entrance and came to a standstill, she was ready, with not a hair on her head out of place.

The rest of the assembled guests were a blur. She knew them, and she exchanged civilities with them, she supposed, for no one appeared offended, but her eyes were only for Sir Cecil. He came towards them with a friend of his, a stocky young man with high starched collars and a haughty expression who was introduced as Lord Alfred Snighton, Baron of Dedton.

"How do you do?" drawled Lord Dedton, looking her over and dismissing her immediately.

She curtsied cordially, and turned to Sir Cecil. She noted the elegance of his clothing, his coat perfectly fitting his broad shoulders, his cravat impeccably knotted, as if he had just now come from the attentions of his valet. She wandered how that could be, when he had been on the road for hours.

"I am very glad to see you, Sir Cecil."

"Yes, it has been a while," he said, bowing over her gloved hand and kissing it. He said nothing about her engagement, which only increased her tension. Surely it would be the perfect moment to offer his congratulations?

But he moved on, and the moment was lost as the party entered the house and were guided to their rooms amidst a commotion of requests, commands, and demands.

Dinner was a formal affair, with so many guests assembled. Caroline worried that she would be seated next to Sir Cecil, and dreaded the awkwardness between them. They had exchanged a few polite phrases, but nothing more, and Caroline was more than ever sensible of the fact that she had hurt him with her carelessness. It was with relief, therefore, that she found herself next to Robert, and she gave a prayer of thanks for the rules of precedence that placed Lord Dedton and Sir Cecil at the top of the table.

"I have promised not to joke today," was the first thing Mr Robert said to her. "Though I must admit I am hard pushed to find a topic of conversation."

"The weather is safest," she remarked.

"I do not consider that topic safe at all," he said. "Look what happened when we last discussed it. Your idea of safety differs from mine entirely. But then, *you* didn't get wet."

She shook her head at him. "You must not make me laugh, Mr Robert. I am *not* enjoying this occasion at all."

"All the more reason why you should laugh. That is what I do. Look at me. Here I am, a savage among civilized people, some of whom barely tolerate me. Do I frown and look morose? No. I laugh. Believe me, it is the only way to deal with life."

Despite herself, Caroline chuckled. "I cannot easily subscribe to your philosophy," she said, "since a good part of my education was spent on learning *not* to laugh. But I admit it has its uses."

"Oh, I disagree that you were taught not to laugh. I think you were taught to laugh at others, which is another thing entirely."

She flushed at the implication of his words.

"Oh, do not get on your high horse, Caroline. I am not here to quarrel with you. It is also useful to laugh at others. But I would not recommend it. If I were you, I would simply concentrate on eating as elegantly as that gentleman over there."

Lord Dedton was eating his food fastidiously, rather as if it was a disagreeable task. He held his fork and knife by the tips of his fingers and nibbled at his food with pursed lips.

Caroline brought her napkin to her mouth to cover her smile. "You really are quite wicked, Mr Robert. Now I will be unable to look in his direction for the rest of the evening."

"But I only singled him out because I am envious, for I am afraid I tend to shovel food into my mouth quite gracelessly, and I am desirous to learn proper conduct. He is an example to us all."

"Oh, hush," she said. "Someone will hear you."

As if to mark her point, Eliza, who had made the effort of attending the dinner that night, looked towards her, her eyes twinkling mischievously. Caroline ducked behind her napkin, certain they *had* been overheard. She wished now that she had been seated as far away from Robert Darcy as possible, for he would not be content until he had landed her in trouble. She pointedly ignored him, occupying herself with Mr Fallow, a young gentleman she knew, who was seated on her right side.

"Charming countryside around here, Miss Bingley," said Mr Fallow. "I suppose Mr Darcy enjoys good hunting."

"I suppose so," said Miss Bingley. "I know he enjoys fishing."

"I have good fishing on my estate," said her companion. "But I am not very fond of it. Don't you know—muddy boots and wet feet, I don't feel it can be quite right. Hunting's the thing. I am considered a very good shot, if I say so myself."

"Indeed," said Miss Bingley.

"Good with pistols, too. I always say it's too bad they've outlawed duelling, for I would be sure to win every time. Not that I have had occasion to fight a duel, of course, but one never knows."

"But now that it is illegal, the occasion will surely not arise?"

"A man has to defend his honour," said Mr Fallow. "They cannot deny him that."

"But is a man's honour worth so much that you would kill someone for it?" asked Caroline.

"Men are killed for lesser reasons," said Mr Fallow.

"Do not tell me, Miss Bingley," said a young man from across the table, interrupting their conversation and breaking the rules of etiquette, "that you think there can be anything more important that a gentleman's honour? Take that away from him, and we become savages."

"But to kill for honour, Mr Maine? Would you rate your honour above the very existence of another man?"

"Without honour, a man might as well be dead," said Mr Maine.

"It is difficult for a lady," said Mr Fallow, with a condescending smile, "to understand such matters. Only a man can fully comprehend the meaning of honour."

"I understand full well the meaning of honour," said Miss Bingley, coldly. "But I still do not think it acceptable to destroy a life, as well as the lives of that gentleman's family, just to satisfy honour."

"Those who passed the regulations making duelling illegal obviously hold the same opinion as Miss Bingley," said Robert Darcy.

There was a momentary pause in the conversation, until someone mentioned Napoleon's defeat at Leipzig, and the conversation took another direction.

While the gentlemen remained to smoke and drink their port, the ladies hurried to prepare for the dance. Though the dance was meant to be informal, a small orchestra had been hired and, as the musicians tuned their instruments, Lydia, Georgiana, and Kitty waited with growing impatience for the dancing to begin.

By and by the gentlemen returned to join them. Robert came across to Caroline. Mr Darcy had already requested Robert and Caroline lead the first dance instead of the Darcys, since he was uncertain of Eliza's health. The opening dance being a minuet, Caroline chose a slow, stately step, though she had to endure many droll remarks from Robert about ladies who liked to *crawl* around the ballroom.

She sat out the next set, expecting Sir Cecil to find an excuse to speak to her, but she discovered him leading a thin young lady, Miss Enlow, onto the dance floor. She was even more put out to see her sister dancing with Lord Dedton. Upon reflection, however, she supposed that, since the dance was informal, no one could raise any real objections, and she was glad to see Louisa smiling and flirting again. It was to be hoped that, with some distraction, Louisa's disappointment over Captain Trewson would soon be a thing of the past.

As the next dance ended, Caroline sought out Sir Cecil. He was leaving the ballroom. Casting a quick look around to make sure no one would notice, she followed, planning to slip out behind him. They had not had an opportunity to talk, and she owed it to him to provide such an opportunity.

Lord Dedton was in the hallway, however, so she drew back behind the door, expecting him to step back into the ballroom. But Sir Cecil stopped him.

"Enjoying the party, Rynes?" said Lord Dedton.

"Hardly," remarked Sir Cecil. "Rather insipid, wouldn't you say?"

"Oh, I don't know. I think I may be onto something," said Dedton.

"If you mean your attention to Mrs Hurst, it *is* very marked, wouldn't you say? Allow me to point out that you are quite wasting your time. She is not the kind of lady to let a man between her sheets."

"Oh, that is not my purpose. She would need to be more attractive for *that*."

"Then what could it possibly be? Surely you are not contemplating marriage? Not with Mrs Hurst!"

"I am in need of money, Rynes. She has quite a neat fortune to her name. And she doesn't seem too particular. Most of the unmarried ladies are not allowed near me, you know. Everyone knows my pockets are to let, and I'm too close to the debtors' prison for comfort. You know how it is with cards. If I could get my hands on a decent sum of money, and pay off what I owe, I plan to leave gambling behind me for good."

"I congratulate you on your resolution. A rich wife would do very well. But your mother would certainly not approve a marriage to Mrs Hurst."

"Because she was married before? I care little for *that*. She's not the type to cuckold a man. Rather a quiet little thing. Hurst always said so. Beside, I don't have much choice."

"Even so. You can do far better. She smells of shop—whole family does. Shipping. The father made the money himself. He did well by them and educated them at a select seminary, so you could never tell. But they still smell of shop.

"Good Lord! You're quite right. My mother would suffer an apoplexy. Why didn't I know of this before?"

"They are understandably reticent about it. No one mentions their family. Mind you, the family *is* respectable—nothing troubling in their background. Just not—you know." Sir Cecil clapped Lord Dedton on the shoulder, and they began to move down the hall together. "You look disappointed," said Sir Cecil. "I hope I have not spoken out of turn."

"No, I'm very grateful, in fact. Saved me a lot of time and trouble, Rynes. I'll have to find someone else, of course. There was some rumour, a while ago, that you were interested in Miss Bingley for yourself."

"Shouldn't believe rumours. She was after me and I admit I was briefly tempted by the money. But I would never marry beneath me. Plenty of fish in the sea, you know. Now Miss Enlow, on the other hand—"

"No, not her! She's all sharp angles, and has a nose like a turnip."

"But she has a fat fortune to match it," said Sir Cecil. "If I were you—"

Caroline did not wait to hear Sir Cecil's advice. She walked slowly into clamour of the ballroom. She heard Lydia's laughter, a little too shrill, as though she was trying too hard to be merry. She saw Robert, skipping briskly down the line with Georgiana. She noticed Mary, who generally did not dance, solemnly joining hands with Mr Bass as their turn came.

She could understand now the clergyman's need to provide quotations for every occasion. She clung to a line of verse that popped into her head like a lifeline, deriving a strange comfort from it. *All the world's a stage, and all the men and women merely players.*

She would play. She would *not* leave the ballroom. She would not let Sir Cecil's remarks upset her, though when she looked down at her hands she found they were shaking.

His opinion did not really matter.

Some of her turbulence eased. But then she heard her sister's laughter again and everything returned. With a word he had destroyed Louisa's chances. His very manner of speaking jolted her. She could not forgive him his callous deliberation and heartless summation of Louisa's prospects.

And she had seriously considered being tied to him for life.

Bitter laughter soured her throat. As if it mattered that *she* had chosen him as a prospective husband. Clearly, she had once again chosen badly, blind to her position in society. Had she really thought that by dressing well and speaking well she could become part of Sir Cecil's circle?

The clink of a glass close by returned her to her surroundings. She could not stand like this in the middle of a ballroom, looking like her world had just fallen apart.

She smoothed down her skirt, and, pulling herself together, pasted a smile on her face. She moved towards the dancers, determined to join the next set.

As luck would have it, Mr Maine asked her to dance. It was a country dance and to her surprise, Mr and Mrs Darcy took their place at the top of the room. Caroline was distracted from her own worries by concern for Eliza, who was calling the dance, but after several minutes passed and Eliza displayed no sign of fatigue, she was able to relax. She herself had quickly regretted her impulse of joining in, for she could not focus, and stumbled a few times, which was quite apparent when there were so few dancers. The dance was slow, and Mr Maine's lethargic dancing did nothing to satisfy her need for a more turbulent dance to match her mood. A reel would have served the purpose far better.

She recalled the reel she had danced with Robert. The memory lightened her spirit, and she looked over towards him. He caught her glance and waved, though he was in the middle of dancing. How very like him.

Finally, the music drew to an end. Caroline exchanged a few polite words with Mr Maine, then excused herself, drifting over in the direction of the refreshments and pretending to procure herself a drink.

"Having a pleasant evening?" said the familiar voice.

He would know within a few seconds that she was not. She resolved not to burden him, for he looked to be enjoying himself. She pretended to be engrossed in pouring herself some ratafia, but her hand shook and she spilled some over the side.

He took the glass from her. "Caroline! Whatever is the matter? Are you ill?"

She had hoped for her distress to remain undetected, but she should have known that Robert was too discerning not to notice.

"Too much sherry?" she said, attempting a smile.

"Come," he said, taking her arm.

"Not to the library." she said.

"Not to the library. But only because I happen to be aware that it is occupied." He led her up the stairs to the small parlour where Eliza spent most of her days.

"Tell me what has happened to upset you so badly."

She was more than reluctant to tell him. Her mind went back to those discussions they had had when she first met him, and her face burned with shame when she thought of how she had held up Sir Cecil as the model of a gentleman. Robert Darcy would surely despise her now completely.

She should not have come up to the parlour with him. She could *not* tell him what happened. "I am tired. I have been sleeping poorly for several days now. I think my exhaustion is catching up with me."

"I think I know you well enough to know when you are being elusive," he remarked.

The flash of anger his remark provoked gave her the excuse she needed to turn him away. "Why do you always presume to know me? What do you really know about me? About my hopes and my dreams? About my childhood? About my family? About my schooling? You know nothing. You do not even begin to know who I am."

She stopped herself. She should not be lashing out at Robert. He was hardly to blame.

The bottom had fallen out of her world. How could she explain that without earning his contempt? After all their talk about Sir Cecil being her suitor?

No, she did not want to tell him.

"I am sorry, I should not have come with you here."

She was seized by an intense yearning to put her head on his shoulder and cry her eyes out. But of course, she could not.

She had to leave. If she stayed too long he would find a way to discover what had happened. She moved towards the door, but he intercepted her.

As if he had read her thoughts, he drew her to him. She wanted to resist, but her hands reached out of their own volition, and circled his neck. Her face nuzzled the hard warmth of his chest. He stroked her hair, his hands moving backwards on her head in gentle sweeps. She did not sob as she expected. Instead she became aware of the swift beating of his heart, the whiff of clean soap from his dark coat, the solid pressure of his arms against her back, the firmness of his body against hers. She breathed in the scent of him.

She tore herself away.

"I need... to go," she said. "Please make my excuses to Eliza and Mr Darcy. I need... to think."

And she fled, before the words poured out of her throat.

In the ignominy of her chamber, she struggled to bring her turbulent emotions under control.

The insult she had received at the hand of Sir Cecil smarted like an open gash, and, for the first time in her life, she understood duelling. If she were a man, she would have challenged him for such a blow to her pride. But she was not. She did not have the chance to flourish her sword and teach him not to speak of her family this way.

But her anger towards Sir Cecil was nothing compared to her confusion at behaving as she had with Robert. She had never truly forgiven him for witnessing her outburst on that fateful day when she had first met him. He had seen her at her weakest moment and part of her still resented him because of it. Yet time and time again she had been stripped of her defences before him, as though, having done it once at the beginning, she was doomed to repeat it, like a theme with variations in a musical set.

Today, it had gone too far. She could no longer answer for the consequences.

She had to be alone, as she had not been since this outlandish trip to Pemberley began. She had to sort out how to proceed with her life, having discovered now what she could expect from society. And she had to decide what to do with Robert, who had invaded her life, but who was not there to stay.

Perhaps she would take advantage of Mrs Germain's kind offer to stay with her in her London town house. There was her brother's town house as well, of course, but she would not be comfortable there alone. She did not want to go to a silent house. She wanted time to reflect so she could regain her sense of reality.

The idea of being with Mrs Germain comforted her. She would spend some time in London, outside her usual circle of friends. She would slowly recover herself. She did not like the country. She understood now why poets such as Wordsworth and Coleridge spoke of the country in the way they did. In the country, one could lose the civilizing affect of town life. In the country, if one was not too careful, one could lose oneself.

Having formed that resolve, she felt considerably more tranquil. She went to bed with a sense of purpose. She slept heavily through the night, waking more refreshed than she had for a long time.

It was time to build her defences differently, and to start her life anew.

Chapter 19

CAROLINE WAS HEARTILY GLAD THE NEXT MORNING TO BE RID OF the London party. She had never met with such insufferable self-importance. She took a particular aversion to Lord Dedton's high starched shirt points, which reached up to the middle of his cheeks. How he was able to see anything around him when he could hardly move his head was beyond her.

It would not do, of course, to reveal her distaste, so she took her leave of them all with every sign of civility, and even agreed to see some of the ladies on their return to London.

"I am very sorry to say good-bye to Lord Dedton," remarked Louisa, as the carriage departed and they walked back into the house. "He paid me a great deal of attention. I found him very agreeable."

"Well, I did not," snapped Caroline. "You would do well to stay away from him. He has a reputation for heavy gambling."

"You cannot mean it, Caroline!" said her sister, staring at her. "I have heard nothing of the sort."

"Allow me to know what I am talking about. I was right about Mr Trewson, was I not? Believe me when I tell you I am right in this as well," she said, steadily. Louisa's eyes reflected her distress. Caroline sighed. She wished she could tell Louisa what she had overheard. But she knew it would hurt her sister far more to know the truth. She would not accept it.

She would spare her that knowledge, but she could not allow her to harbour any illusions about Lord Dedton.

"You are a cold person, Caroline. I do believe you have no feelings at all."

Caroline remembered Robert's words. Did she really come across as so cold and unfeeling? "You are probably right," said Caroline, with another sigh. "But I care enough about you to prevent you from making another mistake." Louisa winced, and Caroline, wishing things were otherwise, added gently. "You must trust me in this, Louisa."

Louisa left her abruptly and returned to the drawing room. Caroline had not told her yet of her decision to go alone to London. She would have to tell her, of course, but she did not care to open a Pandora's box. Louisa would insist on coming with her. Then Charles would insist on opening up the town house and would not hear of her staying with Mrs Germain, who was virtually a stranger. And Eliza would wonder why Caroline was leaving after she had explicitly asked her to stay.

Why did everything have to be connected with everything else? Why were the threads of her life so entangled?

She climbed to her room to supervise the packing. She had already instructed Molly to begin packing the moment she had woken, and there was very little left to do. Caroline had always admired Molly's bustling competence, but today she appreciated her more than ever. She thanked her for her hard work, then went in search of Eliza.

Caroline did not want to disappoint Eliza, but she had no choice. Hopefully, Eliza would understand. She had come to value her friendship and did not want to jeopardize it. She had discovered Eliza to be good-natured as well as intelligent, and Caroline knew she would be a good influence on Mr Darcy. She already was, in fact.

Eliza's reaction was just as expected. "But why this sudden decision, Caroline? Did anything untoward happen? I had really hoped you would stay. I did not ask you out of politeness, you know," said Eliza, when Caroline had told her of her intentions.

"Yes, I am aware of that. But I really need to go."

"But why alone? Mr Darcy has not said something to offend you, has he?"

"No, not at all."

"Is it anything to do with Robert, then?"

"No. Nothing like that. It is just that I have some decisions to make, and I cannot think clearly surrounded by a houseful of people."

Eliza nodded. She still had blue shadows under her eyes, but a touch of pink now coursed through her cheeks. She was on the road to recovery. "Well, if I cannot change your mind, all that remains is to wish you a safe journey. You will be missed here." She hesitated. "Will you be telling my husband about the end of your engagement? You have not told him the truth yet, I believe."

Caroline closed her eyes. Eliza was right. She could not go without explaining the situation to Mr Darcy. And then, yes, she would have to end the engagement. The illusory engagement. "Yes. I think it would be better to do so. In fact, I will speak to him without delay, if he is not too occupied to see me."

She went in search of him. She discovered him poring over papers with his overseer, but her business could not wait. "I will not take long, Mr Darcy, but I particularly wish to speak with you privately. I have come to bid you good-bye."

The overseer excused himself, saying he would return later.

"So you are leaving us?" said Mr Darcy, in a quite friendly manner. "I believe Eliza will miss you."

She smiled. "Yes, we have become friends. But I have stayed long enough, and London beckons." She held back, uncertain how to begin, then took the plunge. "I have an announcement to make as well, which is why I wanted to speak to you alone. I believe this will be good news for you, since it is what you wished. My engagement with your cousin is at an end."

His smile disappeared. He was stunned. She had expected him to be pleased, or triumphant, or to gloat, even, but instead he looked dejected.

"May I ask for the reason for this change? For I have observed that you and my cousin seem to deal tolerably well together," he said, regarding her intently. "I hope nothing that I said—I overstepped my boundaries the other day."

"No. Rest assured that it was not that. It is just that I have realized we will not suit, especially since I believe he has every intention of returning to Boston."

"Did he say that?" said Darcy, again looking quite struck.

"He led me to understand that he missed his family, and would have gone, were it not for the hostilities between our two countries."

Darcy paced up and down the room, with an air of agitation that bewildered her. It had never occurred to Caroline that he would receive the news with anything but relief. It struck her as she watched him, however, that she had blundered again. The excuse she had given, which they had agreed upon from the beginning, was unfortunate, considering that Robert was Mr Darcy's heir. She cursed herself for not thinking ahead. Of course Mr Darcy would not want his heir to leave England.

"I can understand your reasons," said Mr Darcy, "if that is the case, although my cousin has never led me to expect such a thing. But I want you to assure me that my words—my initial reaction to your betrothal—have had absolutely no bearing on your decision."

Was he feeling guilty? Was he regretting his harsh judgement? She found it difficult to believe. After all, she had now discovered that he was not alone in condemning her background.

"Your words had no bearing whatsoever on my decision, Mr Darcy. You must believe me when I tell you that, had I truly wished to marry your cousin, I would not have allowed anyone to influence my decision."

He inclined his head in acknowledgement. "In that case, I can only wish you luck, and hope you will not live to regret it," he replied gravely.

"I will not," said Caroline. She held out her hand to him and marvelled that his brown eyes were just that. The brown eyes of Mr Darcy. They were fine-looking eyes, but they had no effect on her. He was a handsome man, she could not deny it, but he had long lost the power to move her.

He bowed and she turned to leave.

"We—Mrs Darcy and I—hope to see you in London in the near future. We will come down as soon as she is recovered enough. I am certain Mrs Darcy would like to resume your friendship."

"I will look forward to it with pleasure," she said, meaning it.

She could feel his gaze on her back as she walked to the door and wondered what he could be thinking.

The news of her departure let loose a flurry of questions, requests, objections, and assumptions about the reason for her journey.

"But why such a sudden departure, Miss Bingley?" said Mrs Bennet. "You said nothing about it before. I am sure Eliza will be quite disappointed. She has come to rely on you. And now that we are leaving…"

"Jane will be remaining here as well as Louisa. They can care for her, Mrs Bennet. We are not all abandoning her at the same time."

Lydia's objections took a different direction. "You cannot mean to go to London when I am going to Meryton! You *must* convince Mama and Papa to let me travel with you. I would be happy to come as your companion, and I can keep you entertained along the way."

Mr Bennet put down his novel and threw his daughter a dark look, but if she noticed, she gave no sign.

"I was in London for a while, you know," she continued, quite undaunted by her father. "That was when Wickham and I first married, and I liked it above all else. I would love to spend a longer time there, for I am sure it is the most exciting city in the world."

"Then you are doomed to be disappointed," said Mr Bennet, deciding it was time to intervene. "You are prohibited from going to London, Lydia, unless I accompany you. And since I dislike London exceedingly, and have no intention of going if I can help it, it is very unlikely that you will go there in the near future. For I have learnt my lesson, you know. I will not let you out of my sight, not unless your foolish husband comes to take you off my hands."

Kitty clapped her hands gleefully and said it was just what she deserved for behaving so thoughtlessly, and very soon the two sisters were quarrelling.

"I have no great love of London myself," remarked Mrs Bennet. "But I understand that it is all the rage, and it is the place to go if you want to be dressed in the latest clothing. I myself have no such aspirations. We do very well in Meryton. I dare say my dressmaker can fashion a dress from the latest fashion plates as well as any London *modiste*, and at half the price, and without having to put up with their French airs. But I suppose *you* think only a London *modiste* would be good enough."

Louisa, who had just come in, wanted to know immediately why they were discussing London *modistes*.

"Caroline is leaving for London."

Caroline, who still had to inform Charles, Jane, and Robert of her departure, came to her feet and excused herself, saying she had to oversee the packing. She did not doubt for a moment that Louisa would follow.

"I cannot believe it!" hissed Louisa, as the door closed behind them. "What do you mean by taking up and leaving so suddenly? And without even mentioning it to me?"

"The fact is I am planning to go alone to London."

"I, too, wish to go to London."

"I am going alone, Louisa. You may follow me later if you wish, but remember that you have not completed your full mourning period yet, so you cannot be out and about. And you would find nothing of interest there at this time of the year."

"You are being ridiculous, Caroline. If there is nothing of interest in London, why are you going? Besides, it would be far better for us to travel together than for me to follow later. And I am no longer in full mourning."

"I am going alone," said Caroline, again, resolutely. "And you cannot come with me, because I intend to stay with Mrs Germain. She has invited me to visit."

"Are you mad, Caroline? Stay with Mrs Germain! Whatever for? She has nothing to recommend her. She does not even move in fashionable circles. You cannot mean to go all the way to her house to play a game of chess!"

"She has invited me, and I have my reasons for accepting," said Caroline.

"Ah!" said Louisa, looking quite cunning "She has promised to introduce you to someone! That would account for it! But who could it be, I wonder?"

Caroline shook her head at her sister. "You are quite the hopeless case, Louisa, if you but knew it. I have not even broken off my engagement with Mr Darcy, so I do not see how you can suggest such a thing."

"Does Charles know of your departure?" asked Louisa.

"Not yet, but I do not see that he can object."

"No, that is true enough," said Louisa. "Unfortunately my brother is too good-natured to take a firm stand on anything." She examined Caroline at length as though willing her to reveal her reasons. Then, unable to make out anything, she shrugged. "These days I feel I do not know you any more. You have changed, Caroline; I cannot guess what you are about. But whatever it is, I hope you do not regret it."

Who would have thought Louisa and Mr Darcy had anything in common? What did they think she would regret?

"I do not see what is so unusual about wanting to be in London," remarked Caroline.

"It is not that," said Louisa. "It is the manner in which you go about things that has changed. But I will not stand in your way. You have always done what you wished, in any case."

Caroline shook her head. "I have never done what I wished," she said. "But perhaps I am learning how to do so now," she said with a half smile. "Come, Louisa, let us be friends."

"I have never been your enemy," said Louisa, with a quick peck on the cheek. "I would be happier about it if you took me with you, but as you said, London at this time is quite drab, and most of our friends are away. I will follow later, with Charles and Jane. As for being friends, we are sisters, after all." And she returned to the drawing room.

Charles, as expected, raised no objection, saying only that she would be missed, and that he and Jane would join her in Town as soon as Eliza was well enough. Jane embraced her affectionately, saying she did not blame her for wishing to leave. "For we are very uninspiring company, I know, and you must be craving more excitement than you can find in Pemberley. No doubt Mr Robert Darcy is planning to join you later?"

The moment was upon her. This was the right time to announce that their betrothal was over. But she could not do it. For one thing, she could not tell her family anything before she spoke to Robert. True, she had informed Mr Darcy, but she did not expect that he would announce it to all and sundry. Besides, it was hardly fair of her to deliver the thunderbolt, then leave Robert behind to face a horde clamouring for answers.

"No, not at the present time. I have some things I wish to do in London," she replied, eventually.

Jane laughed. "Now you are being mysterious. Perhaps you are going to have some new gowns made? A bridal gown, maybe?" she remarked, with a hint of mischief. "I do not blame you in that case for going alone. That is something gentlemen do not seem to like—shopping for new clothes."

"Yes, I dislike it above all else," said Charles. "I do not understand how ladies can derive any enjoyment from it. I own I do not object to shopping for my own clothes, but to be constantly consulted about the colour of ribbons or the pattern of a piece of lace or which feathers would suit is far beyond any patience I might have."

"Oh, Caroline!" cried Jane, as a thought struck her. "I was not thinking! You should not have to put together your wedding clothes all by yourself. I have neglected you badly. I should be coming to your assistance, since you have no mama to do that for you."

Caroline assured her that she was quite happy buying clothes by herself, since that way she would not have to consult anyone but herself.

"I suppose that is an advantage. Besides, your taste in clothing is far superior to mine, and I would have little enough to contribute. In any case, I cannot leave Eliza just yet." She put her hand on Caroline's arm. "I hope you will forgive me, but if you should need anything— "

Caroline, moved by Jane's concern, was sorely tempted to tell her sister the truth, for she did not like continuing the deception. But she really ought to notify Robert first.

Alarm shot through her. She had not alerted Robert that she had spoken with his cousin, nor was he aware she was leaving. She needed to find him immediately, before Mr Darcy pressed him for an explanation. She excused herself and left the room in a hurry.

He narrowly missed colliding with her in the hall. "You could have warned me!" he said, the instant he set his eyes on her. "You placed me in a very awkward situation, Miss Bingley. I appeared positively cork-brained when my cousin began to question me about my future plans, since I had no idea what you had told him."

"I am really very sorry," she said, contritely. "I informed your cousin that we were ending our engagement. I am leaving for

London, and I felt in all fairness I could not go away without making matters clear to him. I stuck to what we agreed upon initially, and only realized too late that he would not welcome *that* news."

"Still, I would have preferred—" Her words sank in, and the angry spark in his eyes died down, to be replaced with a puzzled frown. "Leaving? For London? But you said nothing of that yesterday."

Caroline gave out an exaggerated sigh. "I do not know what is so strange about my going to London," she said, in a bright, brisk tone, though she avoided looking at him. "Everyone is talking of leaving. Yet somehow everyone expects me to stay."

"Well, then," he said, his face impassive.

The events of the day before rose up between them like a ghost. They stood very still in the middle of the dark corridor. Then a door opened somewhere and they moved apart.

"So do you wish to make a general announcement? About us? To everybody?" he asked blandly.

"My courage fails me," she said, smiling ruefully. "I cannot bear all the questions and remarks and remonstrations." She paused and wrinkled her nose. "It is cowardly of me, I know, but I will write it in a letter," she said. "I will say that I went to London to think things over and came to a decision there."

"Did you tell my cousin that the engagement was just a travesty?"

"No. I simply said that I did not wish to go to Boston, and that we could not come to any agreement on that point."

"I see," he said. "I will encounter you in Town then, no doubt, when I am there," he said.

"Yes." She hesitated. "I am sorry I fled so suddenly last night. I was distraught. I—I did not mean to offend you."

He shrugged. "You need not worry," he said, his smile lopsided. "I have alligator skin." He pulled back his sleeve as though to display the texture underneath.

She shook her head and smiled faintly.

"Then I shall see you in London."

He nodded, and with a quick bow, turned to stride away.

"Robert," she said.

"What is it?" He paused, but did not turn back towards her.

"Thank you," she said, to his back. "Thank you for everything."

He did not reply.

❧

Everything was in place for her departure the next morning. But she was not destined to go to London alone.

Later that morning a rider arrived with a pressing letter for Mr Darcy. It was from Colonel Fitzwilliam, urging them to go to London immediately.

George Wickham had been shot and was not expected to last the night.

Chapter 20

A MEETING WAS CALLED IN ELIZA'S PRIVATE PARLOUR, TO THE exclusion of the younger ladies, and of Mr Bennet, who had already been apprised of the situation, and had the unpleasant task of informing Lydia.

"Oh, Mr Darcy!" said Mrs Bennet. "Tell me at once! I cannot wait a moment longer! Tell me what has happened? What have you learned? If he is a war hero, it will go very well, for then Lydia will have reason to be proud of him. But how could he be a war hero, when he was not even posted to France? Oh, you must tell me immediately."

Jane moved to her side. "Mama," she said, leading her to a seat. "Mr Darcy cannot begin until you cease questioning him."

"But—"

"Madam," said Mr Darcy, coldly. "I insist on being allowed to inform everyone of the content of the letter."

Mrs Bennet threw him a wounded look, but was sufficiently impressed by his air of authority to keep quiet.

"The news is of the gravest kind. It is doubtful that he will survive the wound."

"But what brought it about?" enquired Caroline. She dreaded the answer. He must have been involved in a brawl. It could be nothing else.

"A duel," replied Mr Darcy. He did not need to say more. They all knew what a duel signified. He had run away with the wife of another man, after all.

Mrs Bennet collapsed backward on her chair. "Oh, the scandal! How will we survive the scandal?" she said, mopping her brow with a handkerchief.

"I will leave for London immediately," said Darcy. "I will endeavour to hush the scandal and to see what can be done for Wickham. I am sure Colonel Fitzwilliam has brought him the best of physicians, but I will call in a second opinion. He might perhaps still recover. My cousin Robert and I will set forth immediately—in fact, Robert is already waiting downstairs with the horses—while those of you who are planning to join us can follow behind. I need not say that speed is of the essence."

He paused and looked around the room at the grave faces assembled there.

"Mrs Bennet, you would be very well advised to inform nobody of these circumstances. Indeed, I must require complete secrecy from everyone in the room." Caroline thought he cast Louisa a severe glance. "We must all say that he met with a carriage accident. It will be believed, for he was known to seize the reins and to drive recklessly. Mrs Hurst, I will rely on your discretion. Charles, I hope you and Mr Bennet can accompany the ladies and see to their comfort along the way? And Miss Bingley, may I entrust you to make sure our baggage is sent after us? My man will know what to pack. And can I hope that you and Jane will remain here with Mrs Darcy? I know you were planning to leave, Miss Bingley, but if it is not something urgent—"

"I will be happy to help in any way I can. I do not have any fixed engagements."

"Good," said Darcy.

He cast an eye on Mrs Bennet, who was sniffling heavily into her kerchief. "I will leave it to you, Mrs Bennet, to ensure that everyone has the proper mourning clothes, in case the worst should happen."

At that Mrs Bennet gave a cry and burst into tears. Darcy, with no time to spare, left the room, and a short while later the sound of hoofs indicated that he had set off with Robert.

There was no reason to remain in the parlour. The group dispersed, each trying to assess what the situation would mean to them.

"Come. Let us leave Eliza to rest," Caroline said as gently as she could to Mrs Bennet. "I will order you some tea in the drawing room. It will help you recover a little from the shock. Then we can sit and plan your journey."

But Eliza had other ideas entirely. "It is all very well for everyone to treat me like a helpless invalid, but I cannot simply lie here and rest," she said, throwing off her covers, "I never agreed to stay behind. My sister's husband lies dying. I must come too."

Mrs Bennet stopped crying to stare at her offspring. "You cannot be so silly as to think you will be needed," said Mrs Bennet, quite firmly. "You had better stay here and recover from your illness. I will not answer to Mr Darcy if something were to happen to you. Instead of facing one funeral, we will likely be saddled with two."

Mrs Bennet's extreme assessment had no effect at all on Eliza, who was used to her mother's manner of speaking.

Caroline was forced to add her entreaties to those of Mrs Bennet. "The consequences may not be so dire," she said, "but your mother is right. If you were to fall ill as a result of the journey, you would hardly be helping anyone. Then we will have two invalids on our hands instead of one."

But a stubborn expression settled on Eliza's face, and Caroline could see she would not be swayed by any argument. She had always been headstrong. And Caroline recalled that Eliza had liked Wickham at one time. She had even preferred him to Mr Darcy.

"Mr Darcy would certainly not wish you to go, Lizzy," said Mrs Bennet. "You should not go against your husband's wishes in this. There will be a huge uproar when you arrive in London, and I am sure I will be blamed for letting you travel!"

"Fiddlesticks!" said Eliza.

Caroline tried one more approach. "But Eliza, you cannot think that you will be needed in London. Everyone will be tending to Wickham, and nobody will spare any time for you. You will be completely abandoned."

"I will be needed, I am sure of it," replied Eliza. "My father, at least, is accustomed to rely on me in situations such as these. And I do not care the least about being abandoned, if there is a reason for it." She reached over and patted Caroline's hand. "I am not being foolish with my health, I promise you. I am quite well enough to travel. But I cannot be left behind when everyone is in London. I will be torn with anxiety over what is happening, and waiting every minute to hear news. I would be far more likely to fall ill under those circumstances."

Mrs Bennet seemed much struck by this. "True, my love," she said. "There is nothing worse than waiting for bad news. You must come with us. And I know you will be a support for me, as you always were the level headed one. For if Wickham dies, Lydia will be broken-hearted, poor lamb, and I will not know how to console her."

They arrived downstairs just as Lydia emerged from a small sitting room where she had been closeted with Mr Bennet. "Oh,

Mama!" she said, sailing across the corridor and into Mrs Bennet's arms. "Oh, I so hope Wickham does not die!"

"There, there, my love," said Mrs Bennet, "I am sure he will recover. He just needs you to nurse him and he will be back to his usual self."

Lydia recoiled. "Nurse him! But how could I nurse him? Surely I will not be expected to do so! I know nothing of the sick room."

Mrs Bennet started to say something, but Eliza interrupted. "Of course you will be expected to nurse him," she said, firmly. "He is your husband, and you have promised in your marriage vows to be by his side in sickness and in health, and so you *shall* be."

"But I cannot!" wailed Lydia. "For I cannot endure the sight of blood, and I am sure his wound will fester, and then how could I bear to change the dressings when they are—ugh!"

Even Mrs Bennet was speechless. She did not try to persuade Lydia. She muttered something about needing to pack and quit the room quite suddenly. Eliza spun Lydia around by the shoulder and marched her away, no doubt to talk some sense into her.

"I wish you luck, Lizzy," said Mr Bennet, pausing as they passed him. "But I suspect you will be no more able to convince her of the seriousness of the situation than I was, and I can assure you I tried."

Charles tried to talk Eliza out of travelling, but failed. Jane made a half-hearted attempt. Her father, perhaps wisely, did not even make one. After that, everything descended into predictable disorder as the household prepared for the departure of eleven people. The two gentlemen's boxes were sent forward, and the carriages made ready. The Darcy carriage was brought out, and a second carriage hired. The old Darcy coach was prepared for Eliza to travel in, since it was heavily padded and comfortably upholstered, though not as well sprung as it could have been. It was also the slowest, and could not be used for those of the party who needed to reach London more quickly.

It took some time to organize the details, but it was ultimately determined that Charles, who was to be on hand to arrange for accommodation and horses, had to travel with the faster party.

"I hope you do not mind, Caroline," said Charles, "if I ask you to travel with Mrs Darcy and Miss Darcy in the coach? You are quite sensible, and will deal with the arrangements well, I am sure."

"I do not mind at all," said Caroline, her lips twitching. "If I had had the choice, I would have chosen exactly that."

"I can always depend on you," said Charles, gratefully. "You need not worry about sleeping arrangements. I will send ahead and bespeak the inns for you for on the way."

The carriages were loaded, and everyone prepared to set off as quickly as possible. Caroline was just talking to John Coachman when she heard her name called.

Lydia waved down at her from the window excitedly.

"You see, Miss Bingley," she said, leaning out precariously. "I am coming to London after all! What an adventure this is!"

"Have you no feelings?" cried Kitty from behind her. "Poor Wickham may well be dying at this very moment."

Lydia pouted. "I am sorry for poor Wickham. But I cannot pretend to care too much, for he ran off with another woman, and was shot for it, so I cannot be as sorry as all that."

It was the most rational thing Caroline had heard Lydia say for some time, and she could comprehend her sentiments.

As soon as Caroline re-entered the house, Kitty, who had hurried down the stairs, took Caroline to one side. "I wish you would allow me to ride in the coach with you, for I am the end of my tether. Lydia speaks of nothing but her excitement about going around in London, and talks of the theatre and rides in the park and visiting the Vauxhall Gardens. She will not listen when I tell her that it will be impossible. She insists that she will attend the theatre, even if she is to go in disguise. The worst of it is I cannot complain to Mama, for *she* thinks Lydia can do no wrong."

"You have my sympathy," said Caroline. "I am sure it is very difficult, but you cannot ride with us, for we cannot cram the coach and make Eliza uncomfortable, and we would have to remove Georgiana's boxes and replace them with yours, which will delay everything. Besides, what excuse can we give for separating you from your sisters? You must agree that it will be awkward to explain." Kitty looked so unhappy that Caroline squeezed her hand consolingly. "The journey will not be too long, and I am sure you will sleep part of the way, so it will not be so very bad. And your mama might need you when you arrive."

Kitty sighed. "I suppose you are right. It is just that I am no longer accustomed to spending any time with Lydia," she confessed. "I had forgotten what she is like. I must admit I was glad to have her married and removed far away, for I had more time to myself. Now I cannot escape her company, and I cannot imagine how I used to think her so much fun at all."

"That is possibly because you have grown into a sensible young lady," said Caroline, and was happy to see Kitty's crumpled frown change to a smile. She was really quite pretty, reflected Caroline, and she had indeed grown into an agreeable companion. Something might be made of her after all.

The coach reached the Darcy town house in Berkeley Square after nightfall. Darcy was not there, so they were spared his reaction to Eliza's arrival. Robert appeared in the doorway as soon as they descended from the carriage. He smiled cordially at Georgiana and Caroline, then hurried to assist Eliza up the stairs and indoors despite her protests, asking anxiously about her health. She had fared better than Caroline had expected, and though tired, did not harbour any ill effects from the trip. Eliza dismissed his enquiries and begged him to tell her instead the latest news about Wickham.

"He is still alive, but the fever has taken hold, and he does not recognize anyone. The wound is quite infected. The Bennets are with him. So is Fitz. He was his childhood companion, you know."

"Yes, I remember very well," said Eliza, exchanging glances with Jane.

"Well, there is still hope," said Caroline, "if he has survived until now."

"There is always hope, when there is life," said Robert. "If you are not too tired from your journey, after you have changed and taken some refreshment, I will take you to see him. He is at the Gardiners'. He was brought there when he was first wounded and, though Fitz wished to bring him here, we were advised not to move him."

"You remember the Gardiners, do you not, Caroline?" said Eliza. "My uncle and aunt?"

"Yes," said Caroline. "I had the opportunity to call on them in Gracechurch Street when Jane was in Town last year."

"Did you really?" said Eliza. "I wonder she did not mention it." The twinkle in her eye contradicted her statement. Caroline flushed, for she had been quite uncivil to Jane on that occasion.

Prompted by her wish to please Mr Darcy, she had followed that gentleman's directions, doing what she could to prevent Jane from marrying her brother Charles.

"It is best forgotten, I think," said Caroline.

"Shall we set out then?" said Robert.

"Yes. I for one do not wish to delay. We did not travel all the way here to stand around," said Eliza. She turned to Caroline. "Caroline, you are not obliged to concern yourself with Wickham. He means nothing to you. I am sure you would prefer to stay here and relax after the journey."

"Yes," said Jane. "You are under no obligation to come with us. I would like you to, if you wish, for you have a steady head and can see things clearer than I do, but I would understand if you are tired."

"Of course I will come. He is your brother, Jane, after all, which makes him a relative, though a distant one. And I will be happy to assist in watching over him if I am needed. Then there will be enough of us so we can take it in turns. Though I do hope you will be sensible, Eliza, and not plan to watch over him at night yourself."

Eliza gave a slight smile. "No, I will not exert myself that far, though I wish I could. I grow quite tired of my weakness."

"Come Lizzy, you know you have already improved a great deal," said Jane. "You cannot expect miracles."

"I know," said Eliza. "And it does seem selfish of me to think of myself at such a time. It is only that I would like to do something."

"Let us go to the Gardiners," said Robert. "That is the best we can do at the moment. It is growing late."

The Gardiners welcomed the newcomers and did their best in the circumstances to make them comfortable. Eliza greeted them with evident affection. Georgiana was immediately claimed by Mary and Kitty. *There* had been no change in Wickham's condition, and Caroline and Eliza were ushered in to see him.

It was impossible to tell if Wickham would survive his wound. Caroline pitied him as he flung himself from one side to the other, struggling against demons only he could see. Flushed by fever, he was not aware of his surroundings, and seemed in considerable pain. He was fighting to stay alive, but unless his fever turned soon, he would become too weak to sustain the battle.

Caroline even felt some compassion for Lydia. The young girl had not exaggerated when she said she could not bear the sick room. It was clear that she was not suited to it at all, as she was too faint-hearted to be of any use. Her hands shook, and she dropped everything she was asked to hold. She cringed from holding Wickham up while his pillows were plumped, avoided looking at his wound, and then sat at the furthest corner of the room from him.

It was Mrs Bennet who bathed his brow with cold cloths, and tried to feed him some broth, and fussed over him. She was everything a nurse should be. In the sick room, she set aside all her sentiments and concentrated only on her charge. She even spoke quite cheerfully, whispering to Caroline that she believed his fever was likely to break any moment, and that she had high hopes of seeing Lydia and poor Wickham reconciled and living happily together again.

That was of course, the best possible outcome, but Caroline could not imagine that it would bring Lydia much happiness.

Chapter 21

CAROLINE DISCOVERED TO HER SURPRISE THAT SHE WAS TO STAY with the Darcys in Berkeley Square. For convenience's sake, the party had already been divided up before they arrived, with Lydia and Mrs Bennet staying with the Gardiners and their four children, and the rest of the Bennets as well as Louisa residing with Charles and Jane.

"I hope you do not mind staying with the Darcys," said Charles, apologetically. "It is just that the town house is very crowded. Unfortunately, the Bennets arrived before you, and our house is more conveniently situated to reach the Gardiners, and I would not wish to turn anyone away to give you their room."

"Do not concern yourself, Charles. I am perfectly content to stay with the Darcys."

She encountered Louisa briefly at the Gardiners'. She dropped in dutifully to enquire after Mr Wickham, but did not stay above ten minutes. Under the cover of another conversation, Louisa turned to her sister. "I came tonight because I wanted the chance to see you. I wrote yesterday to tell a friend of mine I had arrived in Town, and she has arranged for me to attend two or three intimate gatherings, with just a few friends, nothing formal. She is holding a small card

MONICA FAIRVIEW

party in her home tonight, and she has asked me to stay with her. Since Mr Wickham is not really related to me, do you think it would be improper for me to attend these events?"

Caroline wondered that her sister had troubled herself to consult her. She reflected for a moment, then shook her head. "As long as you are discreet about it," she said slowly, "I see no reason why you should not enjoy yourself if you can."

"I heard you speaking of watching over Wickham. That is not required of you, surely?"

"No, it is not. I offered to do it because I wish to help, not because it is required," said Caroline, decisively. "Go then. You have been confined with us all for long enough. If you will give me your friend's direction, I will send a note round to you if anything changes."

When Caroline returned to the house in Berkeley Square with the Darcys, Robert, and Georgiana, a late supper was ready for them. It was a very informal affair, since the Darcys retired immediately to their room and asked for their meal to be sent up. With only three of them at the dinner table, and Wickham's condition weighing upon them, the conversation did not flow easily. Georgiana was anxious about Wickham and asked Robert several times if he would survive. Caroline was tired, and though she made an effort initially, she found herself lapsing into silence all too easily.

They set up a card table, but the game quickly came to an end. Caroline played with only half her mind on the game, the other half straining to listen for any sound at the door. She was in constant dread that a message would arrive to inform them of the worst.

280

By and by, Georgiana started to yawn and, excusing herself, went up to bed.

Left alone with Robert, Caroline gave him a wry smile, which he returned.

"Her intentions are kind," said Caroline. "She is trying to help us, by giving us this chance to be alone together."

He rose and rang for some glasses.

"I am coming to dislike this deception," said Caroline. "It is really time to end it, but how can we break the news at such an inopportune moment?"

"It never seems to be the right time, does it?" he asked. He looked tired, his face drawn.

Darkness settled over the room. Some of the candles had burned out, leaving an acrid trail of smoke behind. Those remaining were pinpricks of light in a large space full of shadows. Caroline shivered as a cold draught touched her shoulders. She drew her shawl around her in an effort to stay warm.

"We will have to resort to our usual habit," said Robert.

"Which is?" she asked absently. She was listening to the sound of shuffling footsteps at the door outside the house. She waited, completely still. But the knock she expected did not happen, and in a few moments the footsteps shuffled away. It was only the night watch passing by. A moment later he called out the hour.

"You have forgotten already?' said Mr Robert Darcy. "How could you?"

Caroline, who had no idea what he had been saying, threw him a puzzled look.

He raised the decanter. "Sherry for you?"

The puzzle was solved. "I am resolved to give up sherry," said Caroline, with a grimace. "I prefer to stay lucid."

"Then I can offer you nothing," he said. "It is too late for tea, and I do not think there is any ratafia at hand. And I am certain you will not take brandy."

She shuddered. "No. Never!" She considered going up to her room, but knew she would not be able to sleep just yet. "Very well," she said. "One glass of sherry will not kill me." She winced at her own words, thinking of Wickham. Robert handed her a glass without comment.

By unspoken agreement, they drew closer to the fireside, huddling by it for light and warmth. Neither of them spoke. The fire sputtered and sighed. The only other sound was the steady onward ticking of the clock. They sipped at their drinks. Caroline contemplated the yellow firelight as it ebbed and flowed through her glass, breaking up into a thousand pieces among the crystal.

He sat with his legs extended, as was his habit, but he did not look relaxed. "I hope for Lydia's sake he survives. It will be a difficult storm to weather, otherwise, even if Fitz tries to restrain some of the gossip. There are more people involved than just the Wickhams."

"I wonder what has happened to the man who fought the duel with him?" said Caroline. "If Wickham dies, he will be forced to flee. And what of his wife? She must be a giddy woman, indeed, to leave her husband and go with him. Such a senseless thing to do! What did she imagine would become of her?"

"When people are in love, they grow carried away by passion and forget anything else."

"I cannot imagine that," she said.

"Can you not? I can," said Robert.

Caroline did not know what to make of this.

"I never met George Wickham," said Robert. "He must be exceed-ingly charming if he can manage to make women so smitten with him."

"I have never understood his appeal. I met him when I first came out, for he visited Mr Darcy often in those days, but then Darcy and he quarrelled, and I did not see him any more until he appeared with his regiment in Meryton. I never thought him of particular interest."

"You were occupied with other matters," said Robert Darcy, pointedly. "I hardly think you qualify as a judge."

Of course he would remind her of her obsession with Mr Darcy.

She put down her glass and stood up. "I think it is time to retire. Who knows what tomorrow will hold for us?"

He looked surprised. "You are going to sleep?"

She blinked. "It has been a long journey, Robert. I am tired."

"Very well, then," he said. "I hope you have restful dreams."

It was inevitable. Caroline was, of course, unable to sleep. Every time there was some unaccustomed noise in the street, she would spring up and go to the window, convinced news of Wickham's death had arrived.

She finally drifted into a turbulent sleep, with fragments of dreams tossing in and out of her mind... *She lay in a grave, the dank odour of earth filling her nostrils. A spade scraped as they tossed the earth onto her. Except it was not her. It was her mother. And she was crying. Crying and asking to be taken out...*

Caroline opened her eyes and willed the nightmare to go away. She had not dreamt of her mother like this for a long time, though at one time she had had the nightmare every day.

She peered into the darkness for a long time, until sleep overtook her again and she sank into it... *The man had fallen face downwards into a puddle. She reached down to touch the water. But it was not water. It was thick and dark. And instead of his shoulder there was* a *great gaping wound. She gazed at her fingers. Blood...* She could not see her hands in the darkness. She fumbled for the candle, but it dropped to the floor with a thud. She fell back into her pillows, urging the dream from her mind. But sleep refused to return.

She resigned herself to remaining awake. She reached for the flint box and found it on her dresser, then went to her knees to grope for the candle. It had rolled under the bed. She lit it and looked around her. The room appeared strangely normal, the furniture stable and steady.

She picked up her shawl and, draping it round her arms, went down to find a book. The candles were still lit in the drawing room when she passed by. Robert was still awake, then. She paused and considered going in to talk to him, to tell him of her nightmares. He would make her feel better, she was sure of it. But after a moment's hesitation she crossed the hallway as silently as she could and went down the stairs. She was not a child. She did not need someone to soothe away her fears. A book was enough. She simply needed something to distract her in the long night that extended before her.

She reached the library and hesitated again for an entirely different reason. This was the library where she had met Robert Darcy.

Everything returned to her in a jumble of images. Herself on the ground, sobbing. And then Robert, sitting there, as calm as though she had done nothing more than said good morning. She turned the knob, afraid of stepping back into that moment.

Robert was there.

She recoiled. She stood there, a candle in her hand, her shawl only loosely covering her. This time he left her in no doubt that he had noticed her entrance. His eyes swept over her, examining her from the top of the nightgown she had not fully fastened to her exposed calves and ankles.

"Ah! You again!" he said. He had been drinking alone for some time, she guessed, for there was an empty decanter on the tray in front of him, and an empty bottle next to it. If it were her brother, or Darcy, she would think nothing of it. But she had not yet seen Robert drink so much. He had already declared to her that he had no head for drink.

"I just needed a book," said Caroline, lamely, pulling the shawl around her as well as she could with only one hand free.

"Did you, I wonder? Why then did you come in when you saw the light under the door? Surely you knew someone was in here. You were clearly not expecting me. Were you were hoping to find my cousin here? Your Mr Darcy?"

"You are being absurd, Robert," she said, with an uneasy laugh. "You have had too much to drink, and you do not know what you are saying. It is certainly true that you cannot hold your drink. I now have confirmation of it."

"Can you deny that you loved him?"

"I am not going to deny anything, because I do not need to. I shall be leaving."

"Don't go," he said.

She eyed him uncertainly, wondering if she would be wise to stay.

"You have the damnedest eyes, Caroline," he said. "Soft brown eyes that look out at the world as though trying to pry open its secrets. They glow like a cat's in the candlelight. Did you know that?"

She stood frozen, her eyes locked in his.

"No, I would wager you did not."

His gaze dropped to her lips, and the corner of his mouth curled up. "And you have a habit of biting your lower lip when I say something you do not like. As you are doing now. You give yourself away, always. I know when you are preparing yourself to give me a set down. As you are now. When you do that, you draw attention to your mouth, which is soft, and rounded, and wonderfully tempting."

She made a sound of protest. "Robert, you do not know what you are saying. I beg you, please stop. You will regret this tomorrow."

"Why, when I am only telling you the truth? I am not saying anything shameful. I am only describing how I see you."

The flame of the candle leapt up as it trembled in her hand.

"I hope you are not planning to throw that candle at me," he said, with an exaggerated grimace.

"I have never thrown anything at you," said Caroline, "and if I did, I would not start with a candle."

She put down the candle on the mantel piece. It would be far safer there.

"No, you have too much sense for that. I am sure you have never thrown anything at anyone." He chortled to himself. "I have something to point out to you, because you may not be aware of it either, but your nightgown is quite transparent."

She pulled her shawl around her protectively. "You have gone quite far enough, Mr Darcy! If you will excuse me, I will fetch my book and go upstairs."

"Oh, I am far from going quite far enough," he said, then puzzled over his words. "I do not think that made sense."

"None of what you said made sense. I would advise you to go to bed and sleep it off."

"Are you proposing to put me to bed, then? That would be beginning to go far enough," he said, grinning widely. "Perhaps not as far as I would like, but beggars cannot be choosers."

She shook her head at him.

He followed the movement of her hair with his eyes. "You have let your hair down. It ripples like waves. I crossed the ocean to come here," he said, apparently veering off in a different direction, and she sighed with relief. "I watched the waves rise and fall day after day before we finally came to land. In the evening, the sun would set, and the waves would shimmer and reach up as though trying to catch the last of the sun and hold it." He seemed for a moment lost in the memory, then he smiled at her. "That is what your hair is like."

The words struck a chord in her. They were whimsical, nonsensical words, but somewhere inside her they resonated, reaching a part of her that went beyond language. She had once heard the sound of a gong that an old school friend had acquired from China. It was a plain, round, brass thing, holding little promise. She did not understand why someone would take the trouble to bring it all the way to England. But when her friend struck it, the sound rang out full and unfathomable, vibrating through her very bones. And the sound had continued on and on until the very air quivered with it.

"I am cursed with a romantic sensibility, as you can see, Miss Bingley, and you do not approve of such a thing. You will laugh, and you will dismiss my words and you will think them merely the implausible ramblings of one who has drunk too much."

He picked up another bottle and poured himself a glass, splashing the ochre liquid onto the carpet. "Go, then, Miss Bingley. Go and get some sleep. You need not pretend polite interest in my meaningless ranting any more."

Caroline hesitated. She wanted to tell him that she did not think his words meaningless. And that she would *not* laugh at them. But he had retreated into a world of his own.

"Good night, then," she said, taking up her candle.

He waved the bottle at her and grinned. "No, wait," he said. She stopped. "Are you sure you would not like to help me up to my bedchamber?" He began to laugh.

She did not stay to hear more.

His words continued to resonate as she returned to her room. She examined herself closely in the mirror. She swept her hair forwards and tried to see the waves he had spoken about. She ran a finger across her lips and tried to feel the roundness he had described. She moved the candle back and forth in front of her eyes and tried to catch the cat glow he had mentioned. She saw none of those things. She had expected to see someone entirely different, a captivating creature with molten eyes who danced on the waves and drew men to her like a siren. She expected far more than she saw.

She saw only Caroline Bingley in front of her, gazing back at her from a rectangular mirror framed in painted wood and hanging on a flat wall.

She repeated his words to herself. Charming words, capricious words that made her smile. Even his indecent proposal did not shock her, but amused her instead.

They amused her because she did not believe him serious. She was too anchored in reality to believe that he could possibly perceive her that way.

And because Caroline was a practical person, she snuffed out the light and prepared to go to sleep.

The next morning she awoke very late, stretched luxuriously in her bed and smiled drowsily at Molly, who had been calling her name.

"I'm sorry, Miss Bingley," said Molly. "It was that hard to wake you up, I thought I would have to shake you to make you hear me." She drew back the curtains, allowing the sun to pour brightly into the chamber. "It's not like you to sleep so late. I hope you aren't coming down with something." She examined Caroline's face carefully. "Hmm. Those dark circles will need covering with rice powder," she said. "You've had a bad night, I'd say."

A bad night was *not* the word for it. She had lain in the dark and—imagined. If she was a siren, then Robert surely was Neptune, springing from the foam. She had played that game and laughed to herself in the blackness around her. And then she had fallen asleep and dreamed of gliding over water, her hair floating behind her, her eyes gleaming in the dark like coals.

"I wouldn't have woken you if it wasn't for Mrs Darcy asking me to do it."

Caroline returned to reality with a crash as the saucer of her hot chocolate toppled onto the table. "Has Wickham—has something happened to Mr Wickham?" she asked, the breath catching in her throat as she listened for the answer.

"No, there's no news yet," said Molly. "But Mrs Darcy said you had agreed to go and sit with him this morning."

Caroline put down her cup in her tray with a loud clatter. "What time is it?" She buried her head in her hands. Guilt whipped through her. How could she have been allowing herself to indulge in such ridiculous, trifling fancies when Wickham was lying sick and tormented and possibly on his deathbed?

And to think that it took only a few words from a gentleman who was quite drunk to make her lose sight of reality so completely! Someone who by this morning would already have forgotten what he had said.

She could no longer lay the blame on Pemberley and the country-side of the poets. She was in London now.

It was time to lay the blame where it belonged. But, try as she would, she could not decide who was to blame, Robert Darcy or herself.

Caroline's immediate reaction when she saw Wickham was that his will to live was fading. He still burned with fever, and he shifted and turned, but his motions were sluggish, and there was a grey tinge to his complexion.

Lydia sat on a chair, staring fixedly out of the window, and did not greet them when they entered. But when Georgiana joined her, Lydia drew another chair next to hers, and launched into a long whispered monologue.

Mrs Bennet's face was drawn and her eyes shadowed. Though she welcomed them cheerfully enough, Caroline could detect her anxiety.

"I have sent the girls out to take some fresh air with Jane and Mrs Gardiner. The physician has just left, and has consulted with Mr Darcy and Mr Bennet, but I do not think they hold out much hope. The trouble is, I cannot get him to take any broth, and he is growing weaker by the hour."

"Surely you have not been with Wickham all the time?" said Caroline.

"No, we have taken it in turns, Mrs Gardiner and I, and Kitty has also done her share. She has a steady head on her shoulders, that Kitty, though you wouldn't think it."

"Well, you can rely on me to stay with him for a while. You may go and rest."

"Will you?" she said. "I do not plan to sleep, but I admit I am rather hungry, and I could do with some fresh air."

"I will stay, too, Mama," said Eliza. "You need not hurry back."

Caroline sat by the bedside, looking at the sallow visage pitching against the pillow. His skin was dry and burned with heat. The cloth on his forehead was warm.

She reached for the basin and wrung out the cloth, hoping the coolness would make him more comfortable, but he continued to move his head from side to side, uninterrupted. She doubted he was even aware of the cloth. A sense of futility gripped her, but she struggled against it.

"I do not know how to help him," she murmured to Eliza, who sat at the other side of the bed.

"I could read to him, for perhaps that may soothe him," replied Eliza.

"Oh, he has always hated being read to," said Lydia, overhearing them. "He never could abide people who liked books. So you need not bother. If anything, reading to him might cast him into the fidgets."

Caroline was forced to content herself with wringing out the cloth every time it grew warm, wondering if it made any difference.

By and by, Mrs Gardiner came in.

"Refreshments have been laid out," she said. "You must go and help yourselves. I will sit by his side."

Though she would not have admitted it, she felt relieved to relinquish her useless task. Eliza, too, seemed glad to escape the sick room.

"I don't think I could eat anything," said Eliza. "Poor Wickham. He was so full of high spirits."

"He may yet recover," said Caroline, trying to hold onto a shred of hope.

Eliza made an effort to appear cheerful. "Yes. You are right. I do not know what I am saying. The fever may break at any moment."

Caroline, feeling that her presence at the Gardiners' served no useful purpose, excused herself as soon as she could and returned to Berkeley Square.

The butler had barely opened the door for her when Robert appeared, signalling her to join him in the library. He had clearly been listening for her return. Caroline felt it more important than ever to avoid being alone with him. Before she could say anything, however, he had already vanished into the library.

He closed the door behind them after she entered. She eyed him warily, wondering at his intentions. Deliberately, she built a wall around herself to prevent him from captivating her, the way he had last night.

He leaned back against the door, keeping his distance, his fingers combing through his hair.

"I need to apologize, Miss Bingley. I do not know what came over me last night." His voice was smothered, and he kept his gaze on a point just beyond her shoulder. "I admit that I had a little too much to drink yesterday. But that is absolutely no excuse. My behaviour towards you was entirely unacceptable."

"We were both in the wrong," she said, her face flaming. "I—should have left the room as soon as you began, but I did not. If anything, much of the fault is mine. I should not have entered the library, dressed as I was, knowing that in all likelihood there was a gentleman there."

She expected him to say "sackcloth and ashes." When he did not, a frisson of alarm swept through her. Had last night changed his attitude towards her? He had apologized, yet his manner was detached, with more than a hint of frost. Did he think the worst of her for not putting an immediate stop to his indelicate suggestions?

"I have confessed my guilt," she said, hoping to reach the familiar Robert Darcy rather than this stranger who stood before her. "Now it is only fair that you should tell me what has brought on your fit of the sullens."

"Fit of the sullens!" he said, indignant. "When I told you how much I regretted what I said yesterday?" A lock of brown hair fell forward to cover his eye, and he brushed it aside impatiently. "The devil of it is that I do not really remember everything I said. I hope I did not say something unpardonable."

She smiled mischievously. "Are you asking me if you revealed any of your dark secrets to me?" she asked. "I suspect your purpose in speaking to me was not to apologize at all. You wanted to discover from me if you said anything revealing."

He raised his left eyebrow and regarded her with mistrust.

She grinned triumphantly. "You can see now that I have come to know you very well."

"Ha!" he said. "That is beyond anything! When just a scant few days ago you argued—and I remember your words exactly—that I did not know *you* at all."

"It does not follow that if you do not know *me*, then I do not know *you*. I have never pretended to be open with you, whereas you have always advocated complete honesty and held it up as an ideal."

His eyes crinkled up with amusement. "If I were a gambler I would say, as they do back home, that you were calling my bluff."

"Perhaps I am," said Caroline, with a challenging smile.

"Then answer me," he said, trapping her gaze in his. "If I were to gamble and say that I did not want the engagement to end, where do you think I should lay my chips? Should I wager that you do not wish it to end either? Or should I wager that you will be glad to know it is over? What do you think?"

His face was bland.

She studied him uneasily. His tone was light. Not a muscle in his face gave any hint of whether he was joking, or whether he was deadly earnest. His eyes glinted, refracting like two sapphires, giving nothing away.

It could only be a trap.

He had told her at the beginning that he would not continue the engagement. And he had given her very clear reasons. She would not lay her pride on the line by answering wrong.

"I would say you are forcing me to play blind, for I do not know which cards you are dealing me," she replied, firmly. "I would say Brag is a gentleman's game, not a lady's, which gives you an unfair advantage, for I have never learned to bluff. And I would say that your stakes are too high."

She shrugged, abandoning that particular game.

"If you must have a response, I would say you are gambling that I have forgotten what we agreed upon at the very beginning. But I have not."

His lips curled upwards, but his eyes were opaque stones. "Then I would answer that you do not know me at all," he said. "You have forgotten that I do not like to gamble. I would certainly never gamble with my life."

And with that he moved to the door and opened it.

Frustration lanced through her. "For one who advocates open-ness," she called out to his retreating back, "you are remarkably good at hiding behind your words."

He did not look back.

Caroline was given very little time to determine the meaning of his strange challenge, for barely a half hour later, Colonel Fitzwilliam came to the door.

George Wickham had breathed his last.

Chapter 22

CAROLINE WANTED BADLY TO SPEAK TO ROBERT, BUT THE circumstances made it impossible.

For one thing, he moved from Berkeley Square to private rooms of his own, and the Bennets moved in.

Which left Caroline with a dilemma. Now that there was room for her at her brother's house, she should return there. Indeed, she would have preferred to. And it made perfect sense to rejoin Jane and Charles rather than stay with the Bennets. Surely it was time to start slowly picking up the threads of her life again.

However, she could not feel comfortable abandoning Eliza to her own devices, with a houseful of people and the funeral feast to plan for. Nor could she be certain that Mrs Bennet would shoulder the burden. She could not come to any conclusion, for she could ask neither Eliza nor Mrs Bennet without seeming indelicate. And as long as she could not reach a decision, she could not leave.

One more thing prevented her. Robert Darcy. Their last conversation had thrown her into turmoil, and the only way to set her mind at ease was to talk to him. But her only chance of meeting him was in Berkeley Square, for surely he would come to call on his cousin?

It was really quite exasperating, for Robert's question would not leave her head, and she slowly grew obsessed with the need to ask him what he had meant. Now that the words had been spoken, they clung tenaciously to life, and gripped onto her so powerfully she could not shake them off.

Why had he said what he said? If it was to tease her, he had certainly fulfilled his goal. He had certainly proved that she did *not* know him. Or was it to mock her lack of resolution in bringing an end to their engagement? Was he ridiculing her cowardice?

And then there was that half whispered thought: what if he had meant what he said? What if he meant everything he said, even that night when he was drunk? What if he really did not wish to end the engagement?

Then, if that was the case, why could he not have simply stated it outright? Why present it like a riddle and force her to try and puzzle it out? She had always hated charades. She did not enjoy riddles.

Oh, why had she not stopped him right then and there and asked him to explain himself?

※

"I *so* detest black," said Lydia, examining herself critically in the library mirror. "It is the least becoming colour in the world. And in the candlelight, I might as well disappear."

"It is not meant to be flattering," said Kitty. "These are widow's weeds, Lydia. You are in mourning for your husband and will remain in full mourning for a year, so you might as well get used to it."

Kitty lost Lydia's attention before she even completed her sentence, for just then Colonel Fitzwilliam arrived, and Lydia ran to receive him. "Is it true, Colonel Fitzwilliam, that your regiment is leaving for France?"

Colonel Fitzwilliam, who had come prepared to offer his condolences, was taken aback, but he answered, quite civilly, "Yes, we are indeed leaving. We expect to depart on Monday."

"Oh, I am glad," said Lydia. "For then you can attend poor Wickham's funeral on Sunday. Perhaps if you bring some of the officers with you, I will have a chance to say good-bye to them. Though I would have much preferred to wave them off."

Colonel Fitzwilliam was quite at a loss as to how to reply to such a clearly inappropriate remark. He frowned, but answered in clipped tones that he would see what he could do. His answer seemed to satisfy Lydia, for she went immediately in search of Georgiana, to tell her the good news.

Wickham had been moved to Darcy's house, and was now displayed in his leaden coffin on trestles in what was normally the breakfast room. But since he did not have many friends in London, and they had not made a public announcement, no one had yet come to pay their condolences, so the room did not see much traffic, and was kept shut.

Mr Darcy had made a half-hearted attempt to convince Lydia that she should keep watch by her husband's body, since it was customary. But she had protested so vehemently that he had backed down, and contented himself with advising Mrs Bennet on the proprieties.

"I am well aware of the proprieties, Mr Darcy," said Mrs Bennet. "But I must admit I see no call for Lydia to be shut up in that room with a coffin when there is no one to witness it."

Caroline could not help but agree. It did seem senseless for her to sit there, hour after hour, when she did not really mourn him. There was no sense in maintaining appearances, if they were to receive no callers.

"It would have been entirely different if an announcement had been placed in the paper," continued Mrs Bennet, warming to the subject, "for then everyone would have known, and we would have had people coming and going. *Then* Lydia would have been glad to sit with him, and to receive people's condolences."

Mr Darcy said nothing more, and moved away. Mr Bennet reminded Mrs Bennet once again of Lydia's uncomfortable circumstances. "You must remember, my dear, that we are trying very hard to avoid scandal, so it would hardly serve to announce Mr Wickham's death to the world. And there is Captain Finchley to think of. It was he who fought the duel with him."

"I do believe you care more for Captain Finchley, who is a stranger, than you care about poor Wickham. In any case, he has fled the country," said Mrs Bennet, "so why should it matter?"

"Captain Finchley has gone to fight in France," said Mr Bennet. "And may yet return, if he is not killed in the fighting. I am sure you would not wish him to hang, for it was hardly his fault that Wickham stole his wife."

But Mrs Bennet was not to be appeased. "I cannot help but think it wrong that such a handsome young man has no one to mourn him!" she cried. "It is really too bad!"

Lydia, who had already been confined for three days in the sick room, was growing so restless that she threw herself onto the sofa, and declared herself ready to escape from the window if she would not be allowed to go out. "For here we are in London," she said, "and we might as well be in the middle of nowhere, for I have seen nothing of London at all!"

Kitty looked appalled. "Lydia, you cannot speak so, not when Wickham is lying cold under this very roof!"

"I am very sorry for poor Wickham. It cannot be pleasant to lose one's life, though a duel is surely the most romantic way to die—if you must die, that is. But he did not care for me, and now he has left me a widow, and I will be forced to wear these ugly clothes for a whole year. Oh, it is the worst thing in the world! Why is it only women have to wear mourning and forsake society and not men? It is really most unjust!" She looked round the room defiantly. "And if you really want to know what I think of Wickham—I positively *hate* him for doing this to me!" And with that general announcement, she sprang up and left.

Mrs Bennet came immediately to her feet. "She is taking it very badly, poor lamb," she said. "I must go to her. It is really very hard to lose a husband when one is only seventeen."

They were destined to receive *one* visit of condolence, at least. Louisa made an appearance late in the afternoon. Though she was not really a stranger, a big fuss was made of taking her to see Wickham's coffin, and Lydia brought down her veil over her face, and sniffed into her handkerchief. The visit did not last long however, and the household once again settled into muted restlessness.

As it turned out, Caroline did not see Robert until the funeral itself, for, contrary to her expectations, he did not call on his cousin. A funeral was hardly a place to discuss a personal matter, but she hoped at least to set up a time to meet with him.

The funeral went as well as could be expected, with a minor crisis occurring when Colonel Fitzwilliam arrived without the expected officers. Fortunately nothing marred the solemnity of the moment, and Lydia was actually moved to tears by the words of the officiating clergyman. Caroline was immensely relieved when it was over, for she was gripped throughout with fear that Lydia would say something entirely unacceptable.

An opportunity to speak with Robert materialized when everyone filed out of the church. The women began to drift back to their carriages, while the men waited for the hearse to be brought out so they could continue the ceremony at the burial site. Caroline spotted Robert standing with Colonel Fitzwilliam. She started to move towards him, but Mrs Bennet called her name.

"Did you not think this a most splendid funeral, Miss Bingley?" she asked.

Caroline answered briefly and excused herself. By then, however, Robert seemed to have disappeared into thin air.

There was nothing to be done except shuffle to the carriage and return to Berkeley Square, where the funeral feast awaited them, and a table with cold meat, pies, and cakes had been set up. Caroline positioned herself in such a way that she could see the door, for she quite expected Robert to walk in at any moment.

Meanwhile Mrs Bennet exclaimed over how imposing the funeral had been. She admired the funeral procession, marvelling at such finely decorated black horses, with their magnificent ostrich plumes, and such an impressive hearse, and so many mutes and pall bearers with their batons looking very grand indeed, and such a number of hired mourners behind. And she praised Mr Darcy's generosity, for Wickham had been buried outside London, in a country cemetery, which was so much better than being buried in a church vault in town, for she had heard such bad things about them, and how crowded they were. She continued to talk about the unsavoury conditions of the vaults for a long time, until finally Mr Bennet took her by the elbow and told her she must not continue that way, for she was distressing everyone.

Mrs Bennet accepted her husband's reminder, and restrained herself with an effort. She rallied a moment later, however, by saying that she was merely expressing her gratitude to Mr Darcy, for he had paid for everything, otherwise how could they have afforded such a grand funeral?

"I have entirely forgiven Mr Darcy for not making an announcement in the papers," she whispered to Caroline, "for he has more than made up for it by arranging such a handsome occasion. In fact, I can hardly wait to return to Longbourn, to describe it all to Mrs Philips and Mrs Long, for they are sure to be impressed, as they have never seen anything like it. I paid particular attention to everything, though I am afraid I am likely to forget some of the details, for there were so many to remember."

As the food in the plates diminished, and conversations turned away from the funeral to more general matters, it became increasingly doubtful that Robert was coming. Caroline's head was beginning to throb, and she excused herself. She did not feel quite herself, so she lay on her bed, hoping a short rest would refresh her.

She meant to rest for a few moments and then go back down, but to her surprise she fell into a deep sleep, and when she awoke she discovered it was already the next morning, and Robert had come and gone long since.

Now that the funeral was over, there was no call for the Bennets to stay in London. With Lydia complaining insistently about not being allowed to see anything, Mr Bennet decided that the sooner they left, the better. The only objection came from Lydia. Both Kitty and Mary seemed quite content to return to Meryton, and Mrs Bennet was fairly bursting with the news and could scarcely wait to get there.

"I can hardly believe I will see all my friends again, and my dear sister Mrs Philips. I have so much to tell them!"

Mr Bennet shook his head despairingly. "Well, my dear, if I had thought a funeral would make you so happy, I would have arranged for one much sooner."

"And whose funeral would you have arranged, Mr Bennet, I would like to know? There is no one I could think of that I would not miss."

"Mine of course," he said. "Then I would be able to rest and be done with all this nonsense."

Mrs Bennet gasped, and brought a hand to her mouth. "Oh, Mr Bennet! This is really too bad of you! You cannot possibly mean it, since we all know what Mr Collins will do if that happened. We will very likely end up in a poorhouse!"

"Now I wish I had not joked about it," said Mr Bennet, "for you will speak of nothing else the whole way to Longbourn, and it will be Mr Collins this and Mr Collins that. Even though you know very well that neither Jane nor Lizzy will allow you to starve."

His statement cheered her up considerably, and she began to talk immediately about how clever she was to have married her girls so well.

Lydia, however, was not so pleased. "Jane and Lizzy have married well," she said. "But what about me? What am *I* to do? I might as well not have married, for what did I get from it? And now I cannot even marry again, for who will find me appealing in this drab clothing?"

"*That* does not signify," remarked Kitty, "since nobody will see you. Do not forget that you will not be attending parties and dances either."

Lydia rounded on her sister. "I hope *you* will have to suffer a fate like mine, then you will know what it feels like."

"I would not marry someone like Wickham for the world," said Kitty, "so it is unlikely I would suffer a similar fate."

Caroline put her hand on Kitty's shoulder. "Hush, Kitty," she said, soothingly. "You must not be unkind. This *is* a very difficult time for Lydia. For you must realize that while *you* will be free to come and go as you please, *she* will be very restricted. There is no need to make things more trying for her."

She thought Kitty would brush off her hand and sulk, but instead she took it and smiled. "You are right," she said. "But it is so easy to provoke her that I cannot stop doing it. It is very bad of me, I know." She leaned over and gave Caroline a peck on the cheek. "I used to think you a conceited, disagreeable person. I am sorry for it now, for you have been very kind. I hope I will see you soon in Meryton."

With that she skipped away without waiting for an answer. Caroline understood now what people meant when they said *you could have knocked me down with a feather*, such was the impact Kitty's words had on her. She stood watching the young lady bound up the stairs and marvelled that so much had changed in such a short time.

Caroline undid the stitches on her embroidery once again, for she had pulled the thread too hard and crumpled up the whole design. She sat in the drawing room with Charles and Jane. With no more reasons left for her to stay at Berkeley Square, she was now once again established in the Bingley town house. It seemed unnaturally still. She would never have expected it, but Caroline missed the clamour and clutter of the Bennets.

Jane had brought down a basket of things to mend and was quietly intent on her work. Charles was at the writing table, struggling to add up some figures in a ledger. He was beginning to sigh and rub his cheek with his palm. In a moment, Caroline predicted, he would abandon the task and ask her if she could do it.

"It is strange how things have worked out as I would have wished," said Jane. "Though not of course in the case of poor Wickham," she added hastily. "For the fact is, I can now help you pick out your wedding dress, and you can consult me about your wardrobe—that is, if you would like to. Just say the word, and I am ready to do the rounds of the *modistes*. I was never happy knowing you were doing it all alone."

"Oh, Jane. You are so good to me." Her conscience twisted inside her as Caroline recalled that Jane and Charles knew nothing of what had occurred between her and Robert.

"I wonder why Robert Darcy has not called on us," said Charles. He thrust away the ledger impatiently. "I really cannot get these figures to add up!" he exclaimed. "Caroline, you are the one with the head for figures. Perhaps *you* might make sense of them."

Caroline smiled, though she did not feel like smiling at all. "I will do my best," she said. "I will apply myself to them after dinner."

For a moment, the image of herself ten years from now, having the same conversation with her brother, flashed through her mind. She pushed the image aside. Surely she would not become an old maid, just because Robert would not have her. There would be plenty of other opportunities. She would meet someone who would suit her far better, and she would form a sensible alliance.

She did not want a sensible alliance.

A future without Robert stretched endlessly before her, desolate as the moors on a wintry day. An icy bleakness gripped inside and squeezed so hard she felt her lungs would crack.

It was useless to think of other opportunities, when it was only Robert she cared about.

"Do not worry," said Jane, "he will call on you soon, no question about it."

But there *was* a question about it. A very big question. One that she was not even sure he had asked.

She had had quite enough. She would *not* let him get away with toying with her feelings in such a manner. She would speak to him, and she would know once and for all.

"Do you know his direction, Charles?" asked Caroline. "Robert Darcy's?"

Charles looked startled. "No, I do not. He may have taken up a set of rooms in Albany, but I cannot be sure. Things have been so busy I did not think to ask. Did you plan to write to him? Darcy will furnish you with his direction, if you ask him."

She put aside her embroidery and sprang to her feet, only to find both Jane and Charles regarding her curiously. "I am in need of some exercise. I will walk to the Darcys' and obtain his direction."

"Would it not be better to wait until he calls?" reproved Charles mildly.

Caroline cast around wildly for an excuse. "I—we have quarrelled," she burst out. "Robert Darcy and I have quarrelled, and I need to communicate with him urgently."

It was a relief to tell the truth, or at least a partial truth.

She needed to communicate to Robert that she did not want to terminate the engagement, and she wanted to tell him why. He had asked her to bare her soul. She would do it.

"Caroline! I did not know. And here I was prattling about the wedding dress," said Jane, putting down her embroidery and looking troubled. "Oh, then you must go! I know what it is like to expect to see someone and be condemned to wait in vain." Jane looked towards Charles, who coloured a little, for she had come to London to see him and waited for him to call on her for weeks, and he had not even known. "However, I am sure things will work out, as they did with Charles and me," she said encouragingly, exchanging a special smile with him.

Their evident happiness only served to fuel Caroline's agitation.

"I must go," she said, unable to wait a moment longer. Stopping only for her pelisse, she left the house and set out for Berkeley Square.

When Caroline was admitted to the parlour, she found both Eliza and Darcy there. She was taken aback, for she had intended to speak to Eliza alone, but she could not very well ask Mr Darcy to leave the room.

An awkward moment followed in which Mr Darcy asked about Charles and Jane, and Caroline asked Eliza about the Bennets. Conversation slowed to a halt as they waited for her to reveal the reason for her visit.

She took the plunge. "I have come to obtain Robert Darcy's direction," she said. "I wish to communicate something to him rather urgently."

Eliza shot a look of distress at Mr Darcy, who frowned and looked acutely uncomfortable.

"I am sorry to say I cannot give it to you—"

"Do you mean he has forbidden it!" cried Caroline, interrupting quite uncivilly, and coming to her feet.

Mr Darcy raised his brow. "No. That is not it at all. As I was about to explain to you, I cannot give you his direction because he has none."

"I beg your pardon?" asked Caroline, thunderstruck by this information. "Has he left his lodgings?" she asked.

"He has been called away," said Mr Darcy. "An important letter from Boston arrived with news from his family a few days ago. Difficult as it was to arrange it, he was able to find a ship that will convey him back home immediately."

Every bit of blood in her face drained away. She sank down into her seat as her mind grappled with this unexpected occurrence.

"He is leaving?" she said, scarcely able to breathe.

Mr Darcy threw her a hard look. "That is hardly surprising," he said frostily. "*You* were the one who told me that he planned to leave."

"Oh, come, Fitzwilliam," said Eliza. "Cannot you see she is upset?"

Caroline came to her feet. She was still unsteady, but she did not want to stay a moment longer. "I have to go," she said.

Her steps faltered. She scarcely knew how to get to the front door. Eliza came after her. "At least wait until I order the carriage."

"I will walk," said Caroline.

"No, Caroline, not when you are in such a state."

But she could not wait. She pulled open the door, ignoring the footman, and rushed outside.

"If you are walking," said Eliza, "then I will walk with you."

Caroline continued on her way. She could not have stopped if an earthquake had torn the ground from under her feet.

He was gone. The words echoed inside her, as though she had become a vast, empty, hollow cavern.

He would not have left, he would not have been so indifferent to the dangers of such a trip, if she had somehow managed to communicate with him. She had let him believe she did not care, and that she was not prepared to take him seriously enough to consider a real relationship with him. She was too concerned with guarding her own feelings to care about his. And now he would return to his country, and he would never know what he meant to her.

"Wait, Caroline, you are walking too fast," said Eliza.

"Then go home," she said. "I did not ask you to walk with me."

But the footsteps continued, just behind her.

The rattle of a carriage neared, then stopped beside them.

"Get in, for heaven's sake!" It was Mr Darcy. "Miss Bingley, what do you think you are doing? Elizabeth, are you out of your mind?"

Caroline had no choice but to climb in or risk a scene, and she did not want to cause trouble for Eliza.

"You did not know that he was leaving?" said Mr Darcy, examining her closely.

She was beyond words. "No, I did not," she answered, flatly.

"You care for him." It was a statement, not a question.

She did not reply.

"I would think that is very clear," said Eliza.

"Then perhaps we can prevent him from taking such an irrevocable step," said Mr Darcy.

Caroline gaped at him.

"What do you mean?"

"I mean," said Mr Darcy, with a dazzling smile that reminded her how much he resembled his cousin, "I mean that we—the three of us—are about to embark on a journey."

Eliza gasped, then began to laugh. "You cannot mean—"

"It is exactly what I mean," said Mr Darcy, and they both began to laugh.

Caroline stared at the two of them, giggling like children. The world has gone mad, she thought, completely mad.

"Coachman," said Mr Darcy, bringing down the window to shout. "Take us to Portsmouth!"

Caroline could think of a number of objections to Mr Darcy's scheme, the first one being that she could not leave without informing Jane and Charles. The second that Eliza was not well enough.

When she voiced her objections, however, Mr Darcy already had an answer.

"You need not worry about your brother," said Mr Darcy. "I have sent word to let Bingley know you are with us and will be staying the night."

"Thank you," she replied.

The second objection was shrugged off by Eliza.

"If I could travel all the way from Pemberley," she said, "then a short trip to Portsmouth will hardly matter."

Caroline dismissed all other objections. What did they matter, after all, if she would be able to reach Robert in time to prevent such a drastic step?

It was a wild drive through the darkness. The horses galloped relentlessly onward, giving her hope that they might, indeed, be able to catch him. Providence seemed to smile upon her, for the night was clear, and a silvery moon shed light upon the road in front of them, otherwise Caroline would have feared for her life. Mr Darcy held Eliza against him, and she snuggled into his arms.

"Robert's ship, *The Budleigh*, is sailing early tomorrow morning," said Mr Darcy, as though he ought to give an explanation, though Caroline had not asked. "We managed to find a friend of mine who is captain of a merchant vessel trading in Boston, and he agreed to take him on, provided he would not be in their way if they ran into trouble. My cousin would have agreed to almost anything, as long as it took him home."

Caroline shook her head in confusion. "But why so suddenly? He could have at least—"

Mr Darcy finished the sentence she had begun. "He could have at least told you. Yes, he could have. I do not know why he did not. My impression from him was that you had quarrelled. I can only say that the letter he received prompted him to move quickly, though he did not confide its exact contents to me. I suppose you will learn soon enough, once you have spoken to him."

Caroline allowed that thought to comfort her. She *would* speak to Robert, tomorrow morning at the latest. She could not predict the outcome, but she could at least try to clear up any misunderstandings between them.

Across her, Mr Darcy sat with his eyes closed, Eliza huddled up beside him. Caroline tried to determine what had prompted Mr Darcy to help her. He opened his eyes and caught her watching him.

Embarrassed, she asked him the question that was on her mind. "You are going to a great deal of trouble, Mr Darcy. Why?" she asked.

He looked down at Elizabeth, who grinned at him.

"My cousin belongs here, in England," he replied, very gravely. "He is my heir, after all."

Eliza seemed to find this quite funny. Caroline failed to see what was so amusing.

She waited to see if he would explain further, but he said nothing more. She sat looking out of the window, staring into the darkness, and thinking of lost opportunities.

What had Robert expected from her? Had he really thought his words were enough to seal everything between them? He had given her no more than a few seconds to think before turning around and walking away.

Oh, why could he not have given her a few days at least!

Of course, there was also the possibility that he did not care about her at all, and his enigmatic utterances had been nothing more than a joke at her expense.

"If I were you," said Mr Darcy, breaking into her musings. "I would take the opportunity to sleep. We will be arriving in Portsmouth very late, and we will have to wake up at the crack of dawn. I do not know where he is lodging, but I know the name of his vessel. We will need to discover where it is anchored so we can reach it before it sets out."

Sleep was the last thing on Caroline's mind. There would be time enough to sleep afterwards. Now she needed to think of what to say to convince Robert Darcy to stay.

She was ready to leave long before the first hint of dawn appeared on the horizon. She had removed her dress before lying on the bed, with the help of a maid at the inn, wishing to avoid crumpling it. In the morning, however, she regretted this, for it was extremely difficult to dress by herself, and she could not wake the maid so early. Her precautions, in any case, had been pointless, for she had not slept at all, and she would have been better off sitting in the armchair. She crept down the corridor to the Darcys' chamber and scratched at the door, hoping they would hear her, and that she would not be forced to wake half the inn's guests in order to rouse the Darcys. Her fears proved unfounded, however, for Mr Darcy came quickly to the door, already dressed.

"Eliza is still sleeping," said Mr Darcy, softly. "I would rather not wake her. Stay here, and I will bring Robert to you."

Caroline, having suspected something of the kind, refused. "We came here because of me. You cannot seriously think I would agree to be left behind."

Mr Darcy smiled, briefly. "No, I did not. But I thought it worth a try. Come, then, if you wish to speak to him, but you must make haste. There is no time to be lost."

The inn was at the waterfront, by the dockyard. They entered through Victory Gate, passing the Porter's Lodge. Mr Darcy, with Caroline following, moved down the docks searching for *The Budleigh*, but could not find her anywhere. They finally returned to the porter.

"I am certain he said he was sailing from Portsmouth," said Mr Darcy, baffled by this turn of events.

The porter was more than willing to provide the information. "*The Budleigh*. Yes, of course. I wish you had asked, sir, before you went tearing around looking everywhere for it. I was wondering what you were about," he said. "Left unexpectedly, you could say. I suppose they received new orders, what with the blockade and privateers lurking about everywhere. I'm sure if you speak to them at the Admiralty they'd be able to tell you more. She sailed yesterday."

Caroline gazed out at the empty sea, out to the horizon. There was no sign of the vessel, of course. It was long gone.

And with it, Mr Robert Darcy. The man she was engaged to marry.

Chapter 23

CAROLINE REACHED HER BROTHER'S HOUSE AGAIN IN THE LATE afternoon. Jane and Charles were both in the small parlour when she entered. One look at her face must have revealed how she felt. Jane came and embraced her warmly, and Charles patted her awkwardly on her shoulder and said that no doubt things would turn out for the best.

"He has sailed then?" said Jane. "Were you unable to convince him to stay?"

"I did not manage to speak to him. The vessel departed earlier than expected."

"That is certainly unfortunate," said Charles, frowning. "For I am sure if you spoke to him he would have delayed his departure. I wonder he said nothing to you at all about leaving."

"I believe it all happened very suddenly."

Charles and Jane were expectant, waiting for her to clarify the situation. She sighed. It was the last thing she wanted to do, but there was no avoiding it, unless she escaped to her room, which would hardly be a fair reward to their kindness. No, tempting as it might be, she owed them something.

Before long, she had launched into a complete account of her relationship with Robert. At least, whatever she could tell them without revealing her numerous library encounters. *That* would have been taking her newly developed sense of openness too far.

A long sleepless night brought her to the only conclusion she could possibly reach: there was nothing else to be done but to follow him to Boston. The idea would be perceived as the height of folly, and she would face opposition, but she knew she had to do it.

She informed Charles and Jane of her decision after luncheon, as they sat together.

"Remove that idea from your head, Caroline," said Charles, with unaccustomed resolution. "You cannot be serious. This is wartime. What good are you to Robert Darcy if you are taken prisoner, or if your ship is fired upon?" He examined her obstinate face and added gently, "There is really nothing for you to do but to wait and see. He may send a letter when he arrives, explaining his departure. He may be intending to return. Who knows? You must be patient."

"I will *not* be patient," said Caroline. "I have no intention of sitting here and doing nothing, playing the love-struck lady. As long as there is something to be done, I will do it, whether you approve or not. I will not have my future decided by chance."

"But at least think about it," said Jane, in a sensible voice. "There is no hurry to leave, after all. One day more or less will not make a difference. This is not a decision to be taken lightly. It is a very big step and wrought with obstacles. Think about all of the danger."

"I have thought of the danger," said Caroline. "I think about it all the time. I am afraid something has happened to him."

"You cannot prevent that by taking a dangerous trip across the ocean. You will only compound the problem," said Charles. "Be reasonable, Caroline."

"I have been reasonable all my life, and it has lead to *this*," she said. "I am no longer interested in being reasonable."

"No," said Jane, "you have not been reasonable, you have been guarded. Now you are allowing your emotions to rule. It is more than understandable given the situation, but what you are thinking of doing has nothing to recommend it. It has no advantages that I can see, and has plenty of disadvantages."

"The advantage is clear," said Caroline, "and it outweighs all else. I will be reunited with Robert."

Charles was growing more impatient by the minute. "I am sorry, Caroline, but that is complete nonsense. There are too many uncertainties for you to proclaim that as an advantage. What if you find yourself in Boston, and Robert has not arrived there safely? How will you introduce yourself to his family, if he has said nothing about his engagement—if in fact, there has been no engagement? How do you think they will receive you? And if he does appear, and you were mistaken in assuming he cared for you, what kind of position will you put him in? You may force him to marry you to safeguard your reputation. Is that what you wish? And if he does not arrive, how will you manage? Do you expect to throw yourself at the mercy of his family, when they have never heard of you? These are the realities, Caroline. You must think before you act or you will live to regret it bitterly."

Charles's words were rational, but they were not enough to convince her. Caroline decided that she would follow Jane's counsel, at least. She remained determined to go, but a delay of a few days would not matter much. And it would not hurt to consider all the possibilities, and to plan for them.

The immediate consequence of her delay was that she had time to think. The more she thought, the more she feared for Robert. Reports of American privateers attacking British ships were widespread, and though she had paid them little attention before, they now loomed large in her mind.

And then there was the pain of his absence, which rubbed her raw. Caroline tried to find consolation by reading any love poems she could find, but they conveyed nothing of the gaping emptiness Robert had left behind.

She had not conceived of love as being such a powerful emotion. She had always thought it a whim dreamed up by young girls in the schoolroom, or by empty-headed young men mooning over every beauty that came their way. She would never make that mistake again.

If only her new-found knowledge did not come at such a high price.

Caroline was sitting at the window, looking out onto the street, her mind miles away, when Louisa entered the parlour. Her sister was still staying at her friend's house, so Caroline had seen very little of her since Robert had gone.

"My dear Caroline," said Louisa, surveying Caroline at the window, "why are your spirits sunk so low? You cannot mean to tell me that you fancy yourself in love? I can understand that you may have a *tendre* for Mr Robert Darcy, but I cannot accept that you mean to mope and pine for him in this girlish manner."

"Well," said Caroline, annoyed by Louisa's lack of sympathy, "considering how you felt after Captain Trewson abandoned you, I would think *you* of all people would understand how I feel."

"I?" said Louisa, her brow puckering, "I admit that I was somewhat put out. But that is perfectly natural, when one comes to discover such villainy from a person you thought you knew. However, I was not the only one to be deceived by him, so I did not need to feel so very bad about it."

"But did you not care for him at all?"

"How could I," said Louisa, "when dear Mr Hurst had barely been gone a year, and was still alive in my memory?"

"I suppose it was too much to hope for sympathy from you," remarked Caroline, bitterly.

"You cannot expect me to feel sorry for you at all, when you know very well that it was *you* who put an end to two of my potential matches."

Caroline gasped. "How can you say such a thing? I only intended to help you."

"You cannot deny that you took pleasure in seeing me humiliated!" said Louisa.

"I felt no such thing! On the contrary, I was pained by both situations, and more than sorry to be the bearer of bad tidings."

But her sister's confident certainty told her there was no point in pursuing this conversation. Caroline rose and stared glumly out of the window at the damp cobblestones and the drooping trees. "If only the rain would stop."

Louisa laughed. "How can you be so ridiculous? You sound like Lydia! It only started raining this very morning."

She folded her arms and regarded Caroline pityingly.

"This will not do at all," she said. "We will have to find a way to bring you out of the doldrums. What you need is more entertainment. Mr Wickham's death was enough to drive anyone to distraction. That is why I removed myself from the scene. If you had done the same, you would not now be in such poor spirits."

Caroline followed the progress of a rain drop as it drifted errati-cally down the window pane. "You think entertainment will be the solution?" she said, dully.

"Undoubtedly," said Louisa. "In fact, the sooner the better. We have an invitation to the Montford ball tonight. You know how coveted their entertainments are. I will pen Lady Montford a note to say that you are coming."

"Very well," said Caroline, with complete indifference.

Perhaps Louisa was right. A social occasion might be just the thing. Charles and Jane were dining out in any case, and staying at home would only mean indulging in self-pity. She could not conjure up any eagerness in the prospect, but anything was better than going over everything Robert had ever said in excruciating detail.

❧

The moment they arrived at the ball, Caroline knew she had gone from the frying pan into the fire. For the first person she encoun-tered after passing through the Montford receiving line was Lord Dedton, and beside him, Miss Enlow.

Lord Dedton inclined his head at them, careful not to disturb his shirt collars.

"Oh, Miss Bingley. We have not seen you since Pemberley!" said Miss Enlow. "I hope you have been keeping well?"

"Very well, thank you," said Caroline. "I had not thought you would return to London so quickly. You were touring the Lake District, were you not?"

"Oh," said Miss Enlow, "we quickly grew tired of hills and lakes and trees. There was really nothing to do there but gaze at them, so we returned to Town. It is so good to find oneself back in civilization. It is all very well for Mr Wordsworth to praise the daffodils," she added, with a giggle, "but there was not a daffodil to be seen anywhere."

"I suppose it would have been better to go in the spring, if that was the object of your trip," remarked Caroline, blandly.

Miss Enlow snickered. "Oh, I have seen enough of the Lake District to last a lifetime. I will not be going there any time soon. Would you not agree, Lord Dedton?"

"It was perfectly insipid, I assure you, Miss Bingley," he drawled. "I would advise against going, if you were planning to do so."

Caroline murmured something about wishing to judge for herself and was about to move away when they were interrupted.

"A pleasure to see you again, Miss Bingley," said Sir Cecil, coming up to them, his thin lips drawn out in a smile. His appearance conveyed the impression that he had been forcibly crammed into his dark evening coat. Why had she never noticed before?

"Yes, indeed," she replied. But when Sir Cecil began to criticize the dress of a young debutante and mock her pretensions, she could not wait to get away. "Excuse me," she said, not caring if they considered her rude. She could be as rude as she wished. After all, she came from trade, did she not? "I see someone I particularly wished to speak to."

She moved away in time to see Louisa fluttering her eyelashes at Mr Fallow, who had also joined the group. *Good luck, Louisa, with landing that particular fish*, she thought. She certainly had no intention of interfering.

She wandered across the ballroom to a quiet corner. She had no one in particular to talk to, but she would rather sit to the side like a wallflower than endure Sir Cecil's company.

Eventually, if she did not encounter anyone she liked, she would return home.

The ballroom was oppressively warm. A very young lady she had met once, and whose name she could not recall, came and sat next to her, fanning herself vigorously.

"It is so stiflingly warm in here!" she said, tittering, "And to think there are some ladies in long sleeves, too! Though 'tis the fashion, I do not know how they can endure it." She glanced at Caroline's dress and laughed nervously. "Oh, *your* sleeves are long! I did not notice."

The girl was looking embarrassed enough that Caroline felt sorry for her, so she spent a few minutes assuring her that she was not at all offended and trying to put her at ease. Caroline thought she must be growing old, for could it really have been such a short time since she had been young and careless as this girl was? Had she ever, in fact, been like that? Possibly not. It was more likely that she had been as unbending and dry as a stick.

The young lady, reassured that she had not committed an unpardonable faux pas, excused herself and fled back to her chaperon.

The heat *was* oppressive. Caroline's palms grew damp, and her hair began to droop and cling to her head. She looked around for an open window and went to stand next to it, hoping to cool down. She would not, of course, make the mistake of going out into the garden, however, especially without a shawl. She smiled to herself at the joke, wishing Robert was there so they could both laugh about it. A sharp pang wrenched at her as the events of that night—the night of Colonel Fitzwilliam's proposal—flooded into her mind. It was incredible to believe that the Loughs' dance had only occurred a few weeks ago. So much had changed since then.

As if conjured up by her thoughts, a tall, broad gentleman dressed in an old-fashioned powdered wig materialized before her.

"My dear Miss Bingley! Delighted to see you again," he smiled broadly.

Mrs Olmstead, who had stopped on the way to greet someone, spotted Caroline and came to join her husband, a wide smile on her round face.

Caroline felt some of her oppression lift. "Mr and Mrs Olmstead! How lovely to see you!"

"What have you being doing with yourself, my dear young lady?" said Mr Olmstead. "You look quite pinched and pale, does she not Mrs Olmstead?"

Mrs Olmstead took her hand and regarded her closely. "Yes, Mr Olmstead, I really must agree with you. The bloom has gone from her cheek. Perchance it is this London air. "

"Or perchance some problems in love?" boomed Mr Olmstead.

Squirming, Caroline darted a quick look around to make sure no one had heard.

"Mr Olmstead, I fail to see how you can say that, when you know very well she is to marry Mr Robert Darcy."

"I know no such thing," said Mr Olmstead, examining her shrewdly. "Since I was there, and I know exactly how the engagement came about. You have not been fool enough to cast him off, have you? I can't say that I approve of ladies who break off their betrothals. But considering how it happened, I daresay you have the right of it."

Caroline was only too aware they were in the midst of a ball, surrounded by crowds that would happily repeat the slightest whisper of gossip. And here was Mr Olmstead, trumpeting her concerns to the whole world.

"I am *sure* you ought not to pry into this young lady's concerns in such a manner," came another voice. "This is hardly the place to discuss such things."

Caroline turned gratefully to the source of the intervention. A turban with three vast plumes swaying above it greeted her, and under it, Mrs Germain's laughing face.

"Oh, Mrs Germain, I am so glad to see you!" she said, earnestly.

"So glad that you did not even bother to call on me? When I have it on good authority that you have been in London for more than two weeks?

Caroline winced. "Truly, ma'am, I fully intended to call on you," she said, feeling guilty. How had it slipped her mind? "Unfortunately, however, we had a death in the family, and—"

Mrs Germain's jowls shook. "You need not sound so sorry, child. I have survived well enough without your visit. I hope it was not someone close to you."

"He was a distant relation by marriage," she replied.

"In that case, since *that* is not the reason, you must tell me why you look so wan and gaunt."

"That was precisely what I was trying to determine when you admonished me," said Mr Olmstead. "I suppose you claim the privilege of your sex, Mrs Germain, and mean to leave me out of it."

Mr Olmstead opened his snuff box and brought a pinch to his nostrils.

"It is one of the few privileges we possess," remarked Mrs Germain.

"Aha! Now we come to it! I can see you want me out of the way," he replied good-naturedly. "I would be quite happy to debate with you, Mrs Germain," he continued, "but I must excuse myself. For I see Captain Johnson over there, and I wish to ask him about a hunter he is selling. Would you like to join me, Mrs Olmstead?"

"I certainly would," said Mrs Olmstead, "for I would not like you to buy a hunter without me."

And with that the Olmsteads walked away, arm in arm, leaving Caroline alone with Mrs Germain.

"I do not expect you to confide in me, my dear, and certainly not here, but if you should ever need to talk, I would be happy to receive you. We could have a tête-à-tête, if you wish. Or we could play another game of chess. I have acquired a new chess board which I think you would like, but I have no intention of giving it to you this time, so do not hope for it!" She wagged her finger playfully. "Meanwhile let us see if I can introduce you to some young buck who will take your mind off things."

She craned her neck and peered into the crowd, seeking someone eligible.

Caroline hung back, unwilling to enter into any kind of social interaction, especially with complete strangers.

"Come," said Mrs Germain, "it is no use standing there like a rabbit about to be shot. A few lively dances will lift your spirits."

Caroline shook her head. "I am sorry, Mrs Germain, but I find I have—a headache," she said. "I am quite ready to leave now."

Mrs Germain's gaze bore into her knowingly. "You no more have a headache than I have the pox," she said. At Caroline's horrified expression, she chuckled. "There. *That* captured your attention."

Caroline smiled limply. Mrs Germain noted the smile and nodded once.

"That was a milk-and-water smile if I ever saw one, but better than nothing. If you are planning to leave in any case, then I suggest that you accept a ride to my house, young lady, where I can keep you company for an hour or two, then you can be on your way. I hope you do not imagine I am going to allow you to go home and fall into a fit of megrims."

The tea things were brought to the parlour and the tea poured. They settled by the fire with their cups and saucers and the Shrewsbury cakes Mrs Germain insisted Caroline had to eat, "to put some flesh on those bones."

"Come, my dear," said Mrs Germain, "we shall be quite cosy here together, and you may tell me your troubles."

Caroline had not really planned to disclose her problems to Mrs Germain, but one look at Mrs Germain's kindly face and the whole sorry story poured out.

"And so I have no other possibility but to find a ship that will take me," she concluded.

"I applaud you on your decision. For who could be more determined than a lady who is prepared to brave an ocean in the middle of a war to find the man she loves? If I had had half the resolution you have, I would have married your father and made something of my life."

She took up a cake and nibbled at it absently.

"That aside, however, it seems to me a far wiser course to find a ship that will convey a letter to him, and try to gauge his reaction to the idea, before you set sail and start a whole chain of events that you may or you may not be able to control."

"Letters take a long time," remarked Caroline, bleakly. "I will be on tenterhooks waiting for a reply, and if I do not receive one, I will assume the worst, when it might simply be that the letter was lost. No. I must travel there myself and confront the situation, whatever it is."

Caroline put down her teacup with a rattle. Mrs Germain immediately poured her more tea, and balanced another Shrewsbury cake on the saucer next to the cup.

"I do not believe such extreme measures are necessary. If he loves you—" said Mrs Germain, "—and I said *if*, he will come back for you. If he does not, then there is no point to sailing across the ocean only to be rejected and having to turn tail and come back. I am not against your plan, Miss Bingley, I simply wish you to spare yourself the pain of a useless journey when you are uncertain of his feelings."

"So you, too, advise me to do nothing but wait? I had hoped for support from you at least." She sank back into her chair and covered her eyes with her right forearm. "I do not know how I will convince anyone to help me find a ship, when everyone is so opposed to the very idea. One would think no lady has ever crossed the ocean before."

Her anxiety was a pointed stick prodding her back. She could not remain seated. She stood and began to stalk through the room like a caged animal.

"Caroline—I hope you do not mind if I call you Caroline, for I think of you like a daughter— I am not against the idea. I only think you are being too hasty. Wait! Give the whole thing time. Perhaps Robert Darcy himself needs the time and distance to consider the situation. And who knows, maybe the war will end soon and you will be able to travel easily, without the danger and inconvenience that you would suffer if you left now. What do you think?"

Caroline bowed her head. "I promise I will think about it, Mrs Germain," she said, sitting down again. "Oh, if only I had done more to fix his attention, I would not be in this situation now," said Caroline, regretfully. "I have gone about it all wrong. I doubted him and confronted him and questioned him at every turn when I should have flattered him and cajoled him instead. For I *know* that is what gentlemen like."

"Whoever told you such a thing?" asked Mrs Germain, astonished.

"Mama, for one," replied Caroline. "And Mrs Drakehill." At Mrs Germain's look of enquiry, she explained, "She was the director of the Seminary I attended with my sister."

"And she was the fountain of wisdom who advised you on how to treat men?"

Caroline blinked. "Yes, I suppose so."

"Did you ever stop to wonder," said Mrs Germain, "how she knew so much about gentlemen's needs?"

Caroline's eyes widened. "Well, I assume she was married at one time."

"Then I suppose that is all the experience she could have needed. Your sister was married at one time, too. Do you think she is qualified to advise you?"

Caroline shuddered as she thought of her sister's constant misjudgements. "No, certainly not!"

"Then I would suggest, Caroline, that you stand on your own feet, and take your own counsel," said Mrs Germain severely. "Despite my marriage, I cannot claim to be an expert on what gentlemen prefer. But I am old enough to have seen many matches among the people around me, and I have formed some opinions over time. Based on that, I find it is not advisable to play games, for they inevitably come back to haunt one. It is something I have seen too often, not just in love, but in other things as well."

She stirred some sugar into her cup. "I would not presume to give you advice, but I *will* tell you my opinion. If Robert Darcy comes back to you, you must wear your heart on your sleeve. If that fails, then it will not be for lack of trying."

Caroline tightened her lips. "You are assuming he will come back."

"He will, if he cares for you. If he does not care, then there is nothing you can do, is there?"

The prospect filled Caroline with desolation.

"But enough of that," said Mrs Germain, cheerily. "Now you must tell me more about this Mrs Drakehill. I would like to know what other gems of wisdom she imparted to you young ladies."

Caroline would never have thought it, but by the end of the evening she was laughing loudly as she recounted tales from her schooldays with Mrs Drakehill. By the time Mrs Germain had called the carriage for her, she had cheered up considerably, and the impulse to leave for Boston immediately had left her.

Caroline arrived home a little after one o'clock, in a far better mood than when she had left. Thunder rumbled as she ran up the steps, and just as she entered, lightning ripped the sky and rain began to gush down.

"You have arrived just in time, Miss Bingley," said the butler, Welding—not their usual butler, but someone who had been hired when the house had been opened up so suddenly because of Wickham—as he took her pelisse. "A moment later and you would have been quite drenched."

She nodded, shaking out her dress. "Yes, it is certainly fortunate. Have Mr and Mrs Bingley returned yet?"

"No, miss," he replied.

"Then I suppose *they* will be drenched," she remarked.

She really was feeling better, if she was standing in the hallway chattering with the butler.

"If no one is here, then, Welding, I believe I shall retire. Good night."

"Good night, Miss Bingley. And, oh, Miss Bingley," said Welding, remembering. "Mr Darcy called about an hour ago and asked for you."

Caroline stopped in the process of removing a glove. She stood there, completely immobile, trying to come to terms with the information. What could possibly have prompted Mr Darcy to call on her at such an hour? She questioned the butler, but he had no more information to give her, and after asking if she would be needing anything, withdrew with an elegant bow.

Caroline remained rooted to the spot. Had Mr Darcy received a letter from Robert? No, that was absurd. Robert could not send a letter from on board a ship. Besides, Mr Darcy would have forwarded it to her with a note rather than coming round to see her.

All her good humour evaporated, and her fears returned threefold. Only dire circumstances could have prompted Mr Darcy to seek her in person rather than sending word. Something must have happened. She could only assume the worst.

She wished she had not sent Mrs Germain's carriage back, for she could have used it to travel to the Darcys'. She considered hiring a hack and going over to ask Mr Darcy what had happened, but he may already have retired, and it would hardly do to awaken the whole household. It may not be an emergency, after all. Perhaps he had stopped to see her on his way from his club.

That was extremely unlikely. Married gentlemen did not call on single ladies on their way back from their clubs without a reason.

If only she had not gone to Mrs Germain's house! She would at least have been spared the misery of suspense.

She stood in the entrance for a long time, weighing her options. Finally, she tossed her gloves onto a table and began to slowly ascend the stairs.

She had no options. There was really nothing to be done but brace herself, and wait until morning.

Chapter 24

Caroline presented herself in Berkeley Square as early as she dared. The skies roiled with granite clouds, but there were patches of blue. After the hard ruthless storm the night before, Caroline was relieved that the rain was holding back.

She waited in the hall, since the butler was reluctant to say whether Mr and Mrs Darcy were in. Ten minutes later, she still stood there. Her tense impatience reached such a level that she thought of running upstairs and seeking Eliza herself. But the risk of finding her with Mr Darcy in her bedchamber was too great.

She had no one to blame but herself, after all, for arriving too early for a morning visit.

But to her surprise, the Darcys presently appeared from the direction of the breakfast room, and began hastily to put on their outdoor clothing.

"I am sorry, Miss Bingley, but we cannot receive you at the moment," said Mr Darcy, his manner civil but reserved. "We have an extremely pressing matter to attend to. But if you would care to wait in the drawing room, we will return as soon as we can, and I will endeavour to explain what this is all about."

Caroline looked towards Eliza, hoping to discover more from her. But Eliza's eyes were cast down as she secured the buttons on her pelisse, and she refused to look up.

"What is it that can be so urgent?" cried Caroline. "Pray tell me! Why cannot you tell me now?"

"You will know by and by. I am afraid we must leave immediately. It is inadvisable for us to speak now," said Mr Darcy, obscurely, his gaze fixed on the door. "But we will—we will return very soon. Sooner than you would wish."

And with that unfathomable remark, he ushered Eliza quickly out of the house.

The ominous words rang in her ears. They did not bode well at all. Clearly Mr Darcy wished to avoid talking to her. But what could be so terrible that neither he nor Eliza could inform her immediately? Why could they not reveal the truth?

There was only one possible answer. Mr Robert Darcy had been killed.

Her worst fears had come to pass. His ship had been attacked by privateers. Caught in the fighting, with no military training, he had fallen in battle.

Tears flooded her eyes. If he had died—

But no! She could not even complete the thought.

Murky confusion enveloped her like mist. She could see nothing at all. Moving as if blindfolded, she found her way to the drawing room by touch, tripping up the stairs, then fumbling against the walls until she located the door. If she were not so familiar with the house, she could never have reached it.

She tore open the door and stumbled in.

A footman caught her by the elbow as she toppled forward. "Are you well, Miss Bingley?"

"Yes, yes," she said, righting herself, seeing him only as an outline in the fog.

She shut the door behind her, and leaned against it. Why had the Darcys not revealed the truth? How could they walk out and leave her like this? Did they have no mercy? Cowards, both of them! Could they not face her and tell her?

She lurched forward again, heading unseeing to the sofa. She had to lie down. She had to—

She tripped over an object in her way. She righted herself and continued on her course.

"What the devil!"

The fog cleared. Her vision returned, and she found blue eyes—familiar blue sapphire eyes—looking up at her. His legs—outstretched in that familiar insolent manner—had obstructed her way.

She halted, transfixed by the sight of him. She had forgotten how gloriously handsome he was. Forgotten how his eyes could look into her and see her very soul.

Except that his eyes were hard as pebbles and distant as the sky, and while she took a step forward, he came rapidly to his feet, and moved away from her to stand by the window.

For a moment they both stood there, doing nothing at all. She struggled to shape coherent words. But her brain suffered from a gaping void where words should be, and she could not find any.

He continued to look at her, in a severe, disagreeable manner. She had to say something, since he was unspeaking and she could not endure it for a moment longer.

"I see you have returned," she said, finally falling back on polite social chatter. "This is quite unexpected."

It is not what she would have wished to say at all. Now that language had returned, she could think of a hundred other things that she could have said first. But she had not.

"Yes," he replied, his voice frosty enough to turn the air around them into ice.

"Was your ship attacked?"

"No," he said. "The winds were unfavourable, and we were blown off course to the coast of France. The ship suffered some damage. I was forced to find my way back."

A muscle flickered in his cheek.

That tiny motion gave her the courage to brave the cold. She licked her lips as she struggled to find a way to communicate. His eyes followed the movement.

"I am glad that you have returned," she said. The words were wholly inadequate, but she could not go further, not before he gave her the chance.

"Indeed?" he said, raising an eyebrow with casual disdain.

She tried to pretend to herself that his contempt made no difference, but it did. It was a knife, chiselling away at her insides. But she continued, because it was her responsibility to clear things between them, and because to say nothing would have been far worse. "When did you return?"

"Last night," he said.

Last night, while she had been at Mrs Germain's house? The butler had said that Mr Darcy had called. But it had been Robert.

The thought set her pulse galloping so hard she was convinced he could see it. Without thinking, she pulled down her sleeves to cover her wrists.

"Did you come to our house yesterday?"

"Yes."

The single syllable told her enough. She knew what he was not saying, and began to understand the ice in his eyes. He had returned, thinking she would be distraught, wanting to speak to her, only to discover she had gone out to a ball, of all things. It was enough to convince him, yet again, of her complete indifference.

"Last night," said Caroline, "Louisa convinced me to go to the Montford ball. I was there for only a short time and I did not find it to my taste. I spent the evening with Mrs Germain instead."

He did not comment. He watched with ice-hard eyes.

Perhaps she had been wrong. Perhaps she had misread him and had allowed her imagination to build with no foundation. Perhaps she did not matter to him at all. She did not want to reveal her feelings to him. She could not possibly bare her soul before him.

You must wear your heart on your sleeve, Mrs Germain had said, *if he comes back.*

She took a deep breath. If there was ever a time for her to do it, this was the time.

"I am glad you have returned," she began. It was excruciating, this baring of her soul, especially since he could have been an ice statue. Who could have known it would be so painful?

"Because if you had not," she continued, taking a deep breath, and shivering inside, "I would have found a way to come after you."

He moved.

"A way to come after me?" he repeated. His voice was thick.

"I was planning to follow you to Boston."

"Why?"

The blunt question left her no choice at all. If she was wrong about him, if she had misunderstood the signals, if she was to be exposed—

She had been granted another chance. She could not protect herself now.

Very well, if he had to hear it— "Because I love you," she said. If her words sounded shrill, well, what could he expect when she had never said those words to anyone?

He strode forward, clutched her hands and hauled her to him. She dropped her face shyly, sank it into his shoulder, filling her lungs with the sweet familiar scent of him. She grasped him fiercely to her until he started to laugh.

"Is there something funny?" she asked, irked that he could laugh at such a moment.

"Yes, there is," he said, sliding his finger under her chin and raising her face to him. "You. You make me laugh." he said. "And do not bite your lip, for I will make you pay." She tried to draw back, but he held her fast. "Oh, Caroline, don't get angry, not now, love. You make me laugh, in many different ways. And I love you for it, my beautiful cat-eyed, sharp-clawed, very proper English lady."

He ran a thumb against her lower lip, and his touch sent ripples of joy reverberating through her. "I have wanted to do this for a long time," he murmured, "if you will permit me."

"Yes."

He bowed down and brushed his lips against hers. They were tender and gentle and everything that was Robert. They asked of her only what she was willing to give. Humbly, faltering in this new language, she answered, promising her love.

Loud footsteps sounded outside the drawing room. Caroline pulled herself languidly into the world of reality. Robert groaned in protest as he slowly relinquished her.

The voices of Eliza and Mr Darcy reached them distinctly. Caroline stepped away hurriedly as the door of the drawing room swung open.

Mr Darcy marched in, followed by Eliza, whose face glowed with mischief. "Did we stay away long enough?" said Eliza.

"It appears we are just in time," said Mr Darcy, rigidly correct. "The situation has gone quite far enough."

"Considering that they are engaged to be married, however— " said Eliza.

"—perhaps they have committed no major breach of propriety," said Mr Darcy.

"Cousin Fitz," said Robert.

"Yes, Cousin Robert?"

"You may go to the devil!"

Caroline flinched and threw Mr Darcy an apologetic glance.

But to her surprise, Mr Darcy began to laugh. Eliza, by his side, laughed as well. Robert, deflated, allowed his tension to disperse. Caroline, with the heady beat of her pulse now under control, slipped her fingers between his and gave his hand a tight squeeze.

"I warned you we would be back sooner than you wished! You cannot complain," said Darcy, addressing Caroline.

"You could have told me he was here. You knew I was filled with anxiety," said Caroline. "That was not well done of you."

"If we had told you, it would have spoiled the surprise," said Eliza. "But it has all turned out for the best, has it not? Surely you do not intend to hold a grudge?"

"You will not escape so easily," said Robert, "I will see my chance, one of these days, and I will take my revenge."

"Do so if you dare!" replied Mr Darcy. "Meanwhile, I think a celebratory drink might be in order. I shall ring for my best bottle of claret. And for the ladies?"

Caroline exchanged glances with Robert. "Sherry," they said, at the same moment, and fell into a peal of laughter.

Darcy and Eliza did not make it easy for them to excuse themselves. Since the Darcys were clearly delighted that matters were finally settled, it seemed disloyal to leave. But as the hour came closer to luncheon, Caroline jumped up, saying she needed to let the others know their good news. Robert, who was quite content to remain where he was, followed her rather sheepishly.

"Do you not want to spend any time alone with me?" she asked, astonishing herself with her brazen behaviour.

In answer, Robert raised her hand to his lips. But it was distinctly unsatisfying, since she was wearing gloves.

"Where do you wish to go?" he asked.

"To a park," she said. "I would like to walk with you in the park." She was thinking of the hills in Pemberley, and of the time they were there together.

Eliza, who had come out to say good-bye, let out a gurgle of laughter.

"I am beginning to distrust that laugh of yours," said Caroline, tying on her bonnet. "What is it that amuses you now?"

"Nothing," she said, with exaggerated innocence.

But as the butler threw open the door, Caroline groaned in disappointment.

The rain was hurtling down in heavy torrents, and the ground was a treacherous mire of pools and flowing waters.

"I suppose," said Eliza, "that you have changed your mind about the park. Shall I have places set for you for luncheon?"

Caroline shook her head at her. "You could have spared me putting on my pelisse and bonnet, when you knew the weather was so very dreadful."

Eliza's eyes danced. "But you looked so happy, all prepared to go walking with Cousin Robert. I did not want to be the one to disappoint you."

"You have a wicked sense of humour, Cousin Eliza," said Robert. "It will land you in trouble some day soon."

She leaned back against Mr Darcy, who had joined them and now stood behind her.

"I know," she said, smiling at her husband. "It already has."

Caroline stayed not a moment longer with the Darcys than she had to, for she had left home early, and Charles and Jane did not know her whereabouts. Besides, she was eager to impart the news to them as soon as possible. The moment the rain stopped, she set out with Robert, brushing aside Mr Darcy's offer to send round for the carriage.

One look at Caroline and Robert's radiant faces told Jane and Charles everything. They received him with obvious pleasure. Charles was so overjoyed that shook Robert's hand vigorously for several minutes.

"You cannot believe how glad I am you have come back," said Charles. "I tell you I was at my wit's end trying to convince Caroline not to follow you. Your arrival has saved my sister from a wild goose chase across the high seas." He let go of Robert's hand and thumped him cordially on the back. "What on earth obsessed you to go rushing off like that without a word to anyone? Come, you must tell us everything."

Caroline thought it was a good thing she had resolved matters with Robert before they saw her brother, for Charles had spoken far too freely.

"Before I start answering questions," said Robert. "I think you should know that Caroline has accepted my hand in marriage."

Jane and Charles heartily congratulated the happy couple. Louisa who had just stepped in, heard the laughter, and entered the room just as Robert had settled down next to Caroline on the sofa.

"Oh," she said to Robert. "You have returned."

"Yes," said Charles, beaming and rubbing his hands, "is it not wonderful news? They are to be married."

Louisa congratulated them in a lukewarm fashion, saying that she did not know what the fuss was about, since they had been engaged for quite some time now, and it was more than time that they announced it in the papers. "Not that it really matters. It is already old news, and everyone has heard about it by now. I suppose the announcement will make it official."

Robert exchanged an amused glance with Caroline.

"But you do not yet know the purpose of my visit," said Louisa, growing animated. "If you knew, you would be *quite* surprised, for it is *quite* out of the ordinary. I had to come over to tell you. You will never guess!" She paused to make sure she had everyone's attention. "Sir Cecil Rynes has announced his intention of marrying Miss Enlow! Everyone is talking about it, for Lord Dedton was pursuing her for himself, and he is quite put out. It is said, in fact, that he almost called Sir Cecil out, for he accused him of stealing a march on him. There was a most appalling row, but fortunately, they were able to prevent Lord Dedton from insisting on a duel. I wish you had been there, Caroline. You would have laughed so! Miss Enlow is worth thirty thousand, you know. And he is a good match for her, too, for she will be marrying into a title."

A carriage drew up in front of the house. Louisa stopped speaking and went quickly to the window to peer out. "Oh, that is Mr Fallow's barouche. I told him to call on me here. I must leave you now, for I promised to accompany him to Hyde Park."

Caroline went to the window and watched as Mr Fallow escorted her down the steps. Louisa draped herself elegantly over his arm and smiled up at him as they walked together and entered the carriage.

"Well," she said. "I wonder if Louisa is serious about Mr Fallow."

Nobody thought the question of any consequence.

Instead, Jane and Charles were eager to know what had happened to Robert, and they plied him with questions, all of which he answered with good-natured ease.

The conversation quickly turned to discussing the wedding. Despite the Bennets' bereavement, everyone agreed that it should not be postponed too long, and should be planned as soon as possible after the Christmas festivities were over. Neither Caroline nor Robert wished to delay it any more than necessary, for after they were convinced they had lost each other, neither one wished to risk anything coming between them. The date was set for the beginning of February and preparations began.

In the middle of January everything came to a halt when Colonel Fitzwilliam was sent home from France with a leg wound which threatened to fester. In the general anxiety over his condition, wedding plans were set aside, and there was talk of postponing it. Fortunately he recovered quickly, and the wedding took place at the appointed time. He was so far improved by then that he was seen dancing with a pretty young lady who appeared quite smitten with his uniform.

All in all the wedding went very well indeed. Only one thing marred the occasion.

On the day of the wedding they received a long letter from Lydia Wickham in which she expressed her anger at their lack of consideration towards her, and deplored their tactlessness in holding the wedding when they knew she would be unable to attend.

Chapter 25

THE HONEYMOON IN WALES WAS SHORTER THAN THEY HAD planned. After just three weeks, it was interrupted by news from Darcy that a letter had arrived from Boston.

"Why could he not have just forwarded it?" asked Robert, pacing angrily about the bedchamber. "Now we will have to chase after him, for he says in his letter that they are leaving London and returning to Pemberley."

"That is certainly odd," said Caroline. "I thought they had meant to spend the season in Town."

"One can never tell with Fitz," said Robert.

"I am certainly aware of that!" said Caroline, her eyes twinkling, but she refrained from adding anything else.

"So," said Robert, "which road do you think we should take? The Great North Road?"

Caroline laughed and shook her head. "Hardly! Not if you wish to find out the content of that letter any time soon."

Robert sighed. "Yes, I suppose it would be too circuitous. Though I think I would rather like to go to Stamford. And I am starting to acquire a taste for Stilton cheese."

They did not take the Great North Road, of course. But on the toll road to Warwick they passed a mid-Lent fair.

"Oh, look!" said Caroline. "Don't you love fairs?"

"It does not look quite the equal of our Nottingham Goose fair," said Robert.

Caroline, however, had spotted a small fortune teller's tent that had a familiar look to it, though perhaps, she thought, they all looked much the same.

"Let us stop," she cried. "I must have my fortune read."

A woman emerged from the tent when they approached it. Caroline felt a strange prickling as the woman's eyes alighted on her. She knew her immediately, for there was no mistaking those eerie blue eyes and night-black hair. She stepped inside hesitantly.

She gave her hand to the fortune-teller, who peered at it, then handed it back. "I see you have found yourself," she said gravely, in the same mysterious voice as before. "Now you will be content. Go, enjoy yourself, before the children come."

The woman rose, the interview at an end. Caroline blushed at the thought of children, and moved to generosity, gave her a large coin. The woman pocketed it silently, but a slight smile touched the corner of her mouth.

They arrived in Pemberley in the late afternoon. The sun was beginning to draw towards the horizon, and the hills and dales were etched against the sky. Caroline had wished to be mistress of it once, but now she loved it only because it was where she had grown to know Robert.

"I cannot wait to take you to my estate," said Robert. "Our estate," he corrected, with a tender smile. "It is difficult to believe you have not even seen it yet. It is not as grand nor as large as Pemberley, but I think you will approve of it."

She smiled. "I would like it, even if it was a hovel," she said.

Robert laughed. "Now you go too far, love. If there is one thing I know about you, it is that you would *not* like to live in a hovel. Alas, I do not value my charms so high. I will not forget how long it took for you to consider me a gentleman."

She hid her face in his coat, embarrassed at the reminder. "Must you always throw my words in my teeth?" she asked.

"Always," he said, "for that is the only way I can keep the upper hand."

The carriage came to a halt. "Come then," he said. "Let us face whatever news Mr Darcy is concealing from us. He has made us wait long enough for it."

The door opened and two footmen emerged. Eliza was framed in the doorway, wearing a pretty sprigged muslin dress with coquelicot ribbons and a Forthe shawl on her shoulders. Behind her Mr Darcy stood, tall and elegant as always.

Arm in arm, Caroline and Robert walked slowly to the entrance. Despite his nonchalant appearance, Caroline could feel Robert's tension in the tautness of his arm against hers and the rigidity of his frame.

"Welcome back to Pemberley," said Eliza, embracing Caroline warmly.

"You are looking well, Eliza," said Caroline. "You have put on some weight, thank heavens, and are much improved since I saw you last."

They were obliged to go through all the civilities, though Robert was obviously chafing at the bit, wishing above all to speak to Darcy.

"Would you like to refresh yourselves?" asked Eliza.

"No!" Robert's emphatic statement resonated loudly in the hallway. Realizing that it was too uncivil, he modified it. "No, thank you, Cousin Eliza."

"Then we can retire to the drawing room, and I will ring for some tea and cake."

"Perhaps the tea can wait," said Caroline, knowing that with the fuss of bringing in the tea things and the cakes, it would be a while before they could speak privately.

Mr Darcy threw her an appreciative glance. "Very well," he said, with his habitual politeness.

The moment the door of the drawing room closed behind them, Robert spoke. "Fitz, if you please. I will have my letter."

Darcy went to the drawer of his desk and opened it, handing him a thick packet of papers.

"As you can see," said Darcy, "I could not send you such a large packet, or I would not have interrupted your journey by having you come here for it."

Robert nodded. He skimmed over the papers quickly, then sat down to read them in earnest. Caroline, after a quick glance to assure herself it was not bad news, settled down to ask Eliza for news of London.

The clatter of a horse outside, however, brought their brief conversation to an end. Mr Darcy, going to the window, announced that it was only Mr Bass.

"I thought he had business in town," said Eliza. "I am sure Mrs Reynolds told me so when we arrived."

"It seems he has returned."

Their speculations drew to an end as the door opened and the butler announced the clergyman, who entered quickly. He was beaming.

"I had just arrived in Kympton when I was informed that you were now once more in Pemberley. It would have been very remiss of me to fail to welcome you back. And, now that I see Mr and Mrs Robert Darcy are here, I am able to offer them my congratulations as well. For to enter the holy state of matrimony is to take a serious step which cannot be undertaken lightly. What God has joined together let no man put asunder."

Robert, busy with his letter, was forced to put the letter down. He accepted the clergyman's congratulations graciously.

"Thank you," added Caroline, hoping he did not plan to give them a sermon, and wondering if there was a way to distract him.

Eliza, with a significant look at Caroline, rose to ring for refreshments. Robert returned to reading his letter, and Darcy sat at the escritoire and began to write.

"Duty requires that I return to the parsonage. However, I would not be so uncivil as to turn down refreshments when they are offered. Even though I have always followed Aristotle's injunction, thou shouldst eat to live; not live to eat."

Mr Bass stayed just long enough to eat two slices of cake, which he praised highly, two lemon tarts, which he pronounced delicious, three biscuits, which he declared his favourites, and one profiterole, which he judged superior to any he had eaten before. These he washed down with three cups of tea, and then stood, apologizing for his discourtesy in leaving so soon.

Eliza watched the door shut behind him. "How I wish, Fitzwilliam, that Wickham had accepted the living you offered him at Kympton. How different things would have been! Though poor Wickham had no interest in writing sermons, I cannot help but think he would have been a better man for the job. At least we would not have had most of the parishioners asleep during the service."

"Had Wickham lived long enough," said Mr Darcy, "who knows what might have happened? But now we will never know. I always worried he might come to a bad end, but I would not have wished this upon him. To die so young, before he even had the chance to discover the folly of his actions!" Mr Darcy appeared perfectly composed, but Caroline was now familiar enough with him to know he was deeply troubled.

Robert, who had been too absorbed in his reading to hear the exchange, put down his letter. Caroline tried to ascertain whether his news was good or bad, but failed. She could not wait an instant longer.

"Oh, pray tell me what has happened? Is it bad news? Has the business foundered?"

Robert gave a wry smile. "No, no, not at all. In fact, the news is excellent. My brother has managed very well. He has succeeded in negotiating an agreement that will not only save the business, but improve it as well."

"That is excellent news!" exclaimed Caroline, at a loss to determine his mood, for he did not seem overjoyed. "At least you need not worry about returning to Boston immediately."

"Yes," said Robert. "This is precisely what these papers are about. They have been drawn up by a solicitor to turn over the business to my brother. Which is the wisest course to take, since none of us knows how long the war between Britain and the United States will last. But I cannot help but mourn the loss of something that I worked very hard to build. Perhaps I am only being selfish, but handing over everything to my brother cuts my ties with my past. I no longer know what my role would be, if I were to return."

Caroline wished they were in private, so she could console him. "If the business had foundered," said Caroline, "then your whole family would have suffered the consequences. So you *must* rejoice that your brother succeeded so well."

Robert nodded and gave her a quick smile. "I am melancholy over nothing," he said, putting the letters aside and coming to sit next to her on the sofa.

Darcy cleared his throat. "I had hoped the letter would report some good news, and I am glad to see that it has," he said. "Because I am afraid I have some possibly unpleasant news to impart."

"Oh, my dear, you must not present it that way," said Eliza. "They will surely not think it *such* bad news!"

"The news will impinge upon their future," said Darcy, thoughtfully. "And they may not receive it well. But I will leave it to you to communicate it."

Caroline exchanged a glance with Robert. They waited, tensely, wandering what could possibly make such a difference to them.

Eliza tried to look earnest, but fell short, as a wide smile illuminated her face. "I am really sorry. I know *you* might be disappointed, but *I* am not. I am increasing," said Eliza, her eyes glowing. "I am carrying a child."

All eyes turned towards Robert. But Robert, without the smallest hesitation, came quickly to his feet, his joy evident on his face. He took up Eliza's hand and kissed it. "I am so very happy for you, Cousin Eliza, and for you, of course, Fitz."

"Are you certain you are not upset, Robert?" said Mr Darcy.

"Why would you expect that of me? You know I wish you and Mrs Darcy well," said Robert, frowning.

"I have led you to believe that you will be my heir."

"Only in the event of there being no boys. And do you honestly think I care for such a thing? By God! I have enough property to manage as it is."

"Caroline might not be quite so happy about it," said Eliza.

Caroline, who had held back to assure herself of Robert's reaction, protested strongly. "Elizabeth," she said, severely, "I have never heard anything so monstrous in my life!" Then she, too, rose, and went to embrace Eliza, to express concerns about her health, and to wish her well.

They emerged from the house as the last rays of sunlight sank down into the earth and dusk began to fall. The lake shivered as the sun touched it, sparkling with joy.

"I could get used to living here," said Robert. "But when the war is over, I want you to come to Boston, to meet my family." There was something wistful in his voice. "I think you will like it there. Although Boston society can be stifling, much as it is here, I cannot but feel that things are freer." He looked far into the distance, as though if he looked hard enough he could see across the land and ocean to the coast where he had grown up. Caroline made a slight movement, and it brought him to the present. He grimaced. "By the time the war ends, we will probably have a whole brood of children around us," he said wryly, "and we will be little inclined to embark on a long journey and take them with us."

"You do not think the war will last that long, do you?"

"Who knows?"

Robert, who was standing beside her, took her hand in his. "You will have to help me settle into English society, at least for now. I am counting on you. In fact, you have before you an impossible task. You will need to help me become a proper gentleman." She was so intent on what he was saying, it took her a moment to realize that he was teasing her.

"I am afraid that is not possible," she said, with mock serious-ness. "It is far too late for you to lay claim to such a thing."

"In that case, I am free to indulge in completely ungentlemanly behaviour, and kiss my wife in full view of the whole household."

He pulled her towards him. She laughed, but then, as she came so close she could see the tiny specks of silver in his azure eyes, eyes that were velvet with love, the laughter died. She closed her eyes, because she wanted nothing to interfere as she leaned her lips towards his.

When she opened them again, the windows of Pemberley glinted down at them, and it seemed to Caroline that they winked at her.

The lake, wide and open to the sky, drew her eye, and the world came into focus. "You know," she said, her voice wobbling like a top that was too slow to stay in balance, "From this angle, the lake does not look so very lop-sided. I suppose it all depends on one's perspective."

He considered the lake that had lain there for countless years, indifferent to the artistic needs of people. "You are right," he said. "One has to view it from the correct angle. We cannot know where the eye of God lies, but if we stood where He stands, it would be absolutely perfect."

"Robert," said Caroline, glancing uneasily about her, "are you sure you are not being blasphemous?"

Robert laughed. "I am very glad that after almost a month of being married, I still have the power to shock you. I have not lost my touch then."

Caroline threw him a saucy glance. "I can assure you," she said, without even a hint of bashfulness, "that your touch is quite what it should be."

"Mrs Darcy! You must guard your tongue! Such lack of delicacy is very unsuitable for a well-bred lady like you."

For a moment, Mrs Drakehill's face rose before her, speaking those very words, and Caroline wondered if she was still teaching in that exclusive academy, subjecting a whole new group of young ladies to her strictures. She shuddered, and Robert, not knowing her reason, drew her closer.

"Come, come, my love, I have not upset you, have I?"

His earnest visage replaced that of Mrs Drakehill, and Caroline quietly dispatched her school-mistress to a dark corner in the attic of her mind, leaving her to lie there and moulder away, to be slowly covered with cobwebs and dust.

She turned once more to stare over the lake, watching the ripples of the blue water as they rose to lick the sides of the shore.

"No, I am just thinking how much smaller my world would have been if I had not fallen apart and cried at your feet that first day," she said, laughter bubbling up inside her.

He took her hand and tugged it, turning in the direction of the house.

"It is time for us to move on. We have spent enough time in Pemberley. If you are sure you can tear yourself from Mr Darcy," he teased, "I would like to take you home."

"I could never tear myself away from Mr Darcy," said Caroline, her eyes brimming with amusement. "For there is only one Mr Darcy, and he is standing next to me."

The End

About the Author

As a literature professor, **Monica Fairview** enjoyed teaching students to love reading. But after years of postponing the urge, she finally realized what she really wanted was to write books herself. She lived in Illinois, Los Angeles, Seattle, Texas, Colorado, Oregon, and Boston as a student and professor, and now lives in London.

Mr. Darcy's Diary
AMANDA GRANGE

"A gift to a new generation of Darcy fans and a treat for existing fans as well." —AUSTENBLOG

The only place Darcy could share his innermost feelings...

...was in the private pages of his diary. Torn between his sense of duty to his family name and his growing passion for Elizabeth Bennet, all he can do is struggle not to fall in love. A skillful and graceful imagining of the hero's point of view in one of the most beloved and enduring love stories of all time.

What readers are saying:

"A delicious treat for all Austen addicts."

"Amanda Grange knows her subject...I ended up reading the entire book in one sitting."

"Brilliant, you could almost hear Darcy's voice...I was so sad when it came to an end. I loved the visions she gave us of their married life."

"Amanda Grange has perfectly captured all of Jane Austen's clever wit and social observations to make *Mr. Darcy's Diary* a must read for any fan."

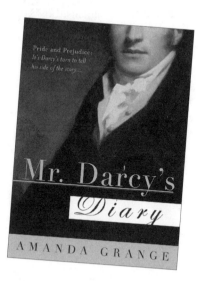

978-1-4022-0876-8 • $14.95 US/ $19.95 CAN/ £7.99 UK

Mr. and Mrs. Fitzwilliam Darcy: Two Shall Become One

SHARON LATHAN

"Highly entertaining... I felt fully immersed in the time period. Well done!" —*Romance Reader at Heart*

A fascinating portrait of a timeless, consuming love

It's Darcy and Elizabeth's wedding day, and the journey is just beginning as Jane Austen's beloved *Pride and Prejudice* characters embark on the greatest adventure of all: marriage and a life together filled with surprising passion, tender self-discovery, and the simple joys of every day.

As their love story unfolds in this most romantic of Jane Austen sequels, Darcy and Elizabeth each reveal to the other how their relationship blossomed from misunderstanding to perfect understanding and harmony, and a marriage filled with romance, sensuality and the beauty of a deep, abiding love.

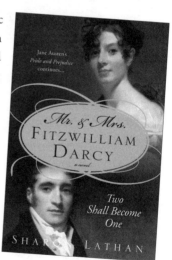

What readers are saying:

"This journey is truly amazing."

"What a wonderful beginning to this truly beautiful marriage."

"Could not stop reading."

"So beautifully written...making me feel as though I was in the room with Lizzy and Darcy...and sharing in all of the touching moments between."

978-1-4022-1523-0 • $14.99 US/ $15.99 CAN/ £7.99 UK

Loving Mr. Darcy: Journeys Beyond Pemberley
SHARON LATHAN

"A romance that transcends time." —*The Romance Studio*

Darcy and Elizabeth embark on the journey of a lifetime

Six months into his marriage to Elizabeth Bennet, Darcy is still head over heels in love, and each day offers more opportunities to surprise and delight his beloved bride. Elizabeth has adapted to being the Mistress of Pemberley, charming everyone she meets and handling her duties with grace and poise. Just when it seems life can't get any better, Elizabeth gets the most wonderful news. The lovers leave the serenity of Pemberley, traveling through the sumptuous landscape of Regency England, experiencing the lavish sights, sounds, and tastes around them. With each day come new discoveries as they become further entwined, body and soul.

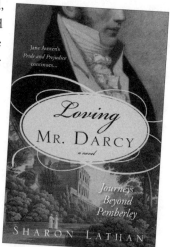

What readers are saying:

"Darcy's passion for love and life with Lizzy is brought to the forefront and captured beautifully."

"Sharon Lathan is a wonderful writer... I believe that Jane Austen herself would love this story as much as I did."

"The historical backdrop of the book is unbelievable—I actually felt like I could see all the places where the Darcys traveled."

"Truly captures the heart of Darcy & Elizabeth! Very well written and totally hot!"

978-1-4022-1741-8 • $14.99 US/ $18.99 CAN/ £7.99 UK

Mr. Darcy Takes a Wife

Linda Berdoll

The #1 best-selling Pride and Prejudice sequel

"Wild, bawdy, and utterly enjoyable." —*Booklist*

Hold on to your bonnets!

Every woman wants to be Elizabeth Bennet Darcy—beautiful, gracious, universally admired, strong, daring and outspoken—a thoroughly modern woman in crinolines. And every woman will fall madly in love with Mr. Darcy—tall, dark and handsome, a nobleman and a heartthrob whose virility is matched only by his utter devotion to his wife. Their passion is consuming and idyllic—essentially, they can't keep their hands off each other—through a sweeping tale of adventure and misadventure, human folly and numerous mysteries of parentage. This sexy, epic, hilarious, poignant and romantic sequel to *Pride and Prejudice* goes far beyond Jane Austen.

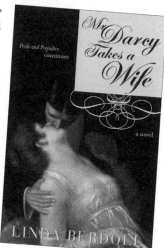

What readers are saying:

"I couldn't put it down."

"I didn't want it to end!"

"Berdoll does Jane Austen proud! ...A thoroughly delightful and engaging book."

"Delicious fun...I thoroughly enjoyed this book."

"My favorite *Pride and Prejudice* sequel so far."

978-1-4022-0273-5 • $16.95 US/ $19.99 CAN/ £9.99 UK

Eliza's Daughter

A Sequel to Jane Austen's Sense *and* Sensibility

JOAN AIKEN

"Others may try, but nobody comes close to Aiken in writing sequels to Jane Austen." —*Publishers Weekly*

A young woman longing for adventure and an artistic life...

Because she's an illegitimate child, Eliza is raised in the rural backwater with very little supervision. An intelligent, creative, and free-spirited heroine, unfettered by the strictures of her time, she makes friends with poets William Wordsworth and Samuel Coleridge, finds her way to London, and eventually travels the world, all the while seeking to solve the mystery of her parentage. With fierce determination and irrepressible spirits, Eliza carves out a life full of adventure and artistic endeavor.

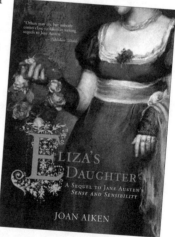

"Aiken's story is rich with humor, and her language is compelling. Readers captivated with Elinor and Marianne Dashwood in *Sense and Sensibility* will thoroughly enjoy Aiken's crystal gazing, but so will those unacquainted with Austen." —*Booklist*

"...innovative storyteller Aiken again pays tribute to Jane Austen in a cheerful spinoff of *Sense and Sensibility.*" —*Kirkus Reviews*

978-1-4022-1288-8 • $14.95 US/ $15.99 CAN

The Pemberley Chronicles

A Companion Volume to Jane Austen's Pride and Prejudice
The Pemberley Chronicles: Book 1
REBECCA ANN COLLINS

"A lovely complementary novel to Jane Austen's *Pride and Prejudice*.
Austen would surely give her smile of approval."
—BEVERLY WONG, AUTHOR OF *Pride & Prejudice Prudence*

The weddings are over, the saga begins

The guests (including millions of readers and viewers) wish the two happy couples health and happiness. As the music swells and the credits roll, two things are certain: Jane and Bingley will want for nothing, while Elizabeth and Darcy are to be the happiest couple in the world!

Elizabeth and Darcy's personal stories of love, marriage, money, and children are woven together with the threads of social and political history of England in the nineteenth century. As changes in industry and agriculture affect the people of Pemberley and the surrounding countryside, the Darcys strive to be progressive and forward-looking while upholding beloved traditions.

"Those with a taste for the balance and humour of Austen will find a worthy companion volume."
—*Book News*

978-1-4022-1153-9 • $14.96 US/ $17.95 CAN/ £7.99 UK

The Darcys Give a Ball
ELIZABETH NEWARK

"A tour de force." —MARILYN SACHS, AUTHOR OF *First Impressions*

Whatever will Mr. Darcy say...

...with his son falling in love, his daughter almost lured into an elopement, and his niece the new target of Miss Caroline Bingley's meddling, Mr. Darcy has his hands full keeping the next generation away from scandal.

Sons and daughters share the physical and personality traits of their parents, but of course have minds of their own—and as Mrs. Darcy says to her beloved sister Jane Bingley: "The romantic attachments of one's children are a constant distraction."

Amidst all this distraction and excitement, Jane and Elizabeth plan a lavish ball at Pemberley, where all the young people come together for a surprising and altogether satisfying ending.

What readers are saying:

"A light-hearted visit to Austen country."

"A wonderful look into what could have happened!"

"The characters ring true, the situation is perfect, the conclusion is everything you hope for."

"A wonder of character and action...an unmixed pleasure!"

978-1-4022-1131-7 • $12.95 US/ $15.50 CAN/ £6.99 UK

Mrs. Darcy's Dilemma
DIANA BIRCHALL

"Fascinating, and such wonderful use of language."
—JOAN AUSTEN-LEIGH

It seemed a harmless invitation, after all...

When Mrs. Darcy invited her sister Lydia's daughters to come for a visit, she felt it was a small kindness she could do for her poor nieces. Little did she imagine the upheaval that would ensue. But with her elder son, the Darcys' heir, in danger of losing his heart, a theatrical scandal threatening to engulf them all, and daughter Jane on the verge of her come-out, the Mistress of Pemberley must make some difficult decisions...

"Birchall's witty, elegant visit to the middle-aged Darcys is a delight." —PROFESSOR JANET TODD, UNIVERSITY OF GLASGOW

"A refreshing and entertaining look at the Darcys some years after *Pride and Prejudice* from a most accomplished author." —JENNY SCOTT, AUTHOR OF *After Jane*

978-1-4022-1156-0 • $14.95

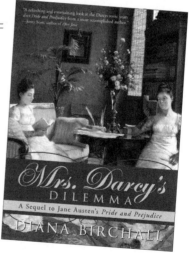